THE MONSOON KILLED THE TIGER

Also by Jack Lyndon Thomas

Whirling Fire (Poetry on the Vietnam War)

Coyote Jack/Drawing Meaning from Life and Vietnam: A Memoir

Training Runs: The Regenerative Power of Motorcycling Back Roads (eBook)

Lights on the Water/Impressions in the Sand: A Motorcycling Odyssey (eBook)

THE MONSOON KILLED THE TIGER

by

JACK LYNDON THOMAS

lyndonjacks publications
www.JackLyndonThomas.com
lyndonjacks@att.net

ISBN 978-1-7340993-0-0 (paperback)
ISBN 978-1-7340993-1-7 (eBook)
Library of Congress Control Number:2019915194

Thomas, Jack Lyndon, 1944-
The Monsoon Killed the Tiger by Jack Lyndon Thomas
First edition 2013
Second edition 2019

lyndonjacks publications
1681 River Rd #3110
Boerne, Texas 78006

Acknowledgments

Many thanks go to members of my writing critique group whose sharp, unbiased readings, suggestions, and comments have improved this work—Rick Nelson, Charlotte Jones, Chuck Brownman, John Oehler, Marcia Gerhardt, and Marty Braniff. Your dedication to excellence is greatly appreciated. Any screwups or omissions are mine.

Chris Rogers, a wonderful teacher, a talented writer, and an eclectic artist, contributed significantly. Special thanks also go to JP Goggin for the book cover design. Finally, I want to recognize James C. Smith and my fellow team members serving on Advisory Team 43, Duc Hue District, Hau Nghia Province—1969 to 1970.

Dedicated To

Steve, Harry, Richard, & Jim
Summer & Allison
Mason & Ava

The Awakening

One

Kannon Ballard rounded a tight bend and saw a fallen tree blocking his route. He squeezed the front brake lever while simultaneously pressing the rear brake pedal. His motorcycle skidded to a stop on the rutted, rocky road. To his right rose a gradual slope filled with golden, quaking aspen. According to his topo map, on his left but obscured from sight lay a narrow canyon with a two-hundred-foot vertical drop.

May as well shoot a few photos before clearing a path, he decided. Without much room to work, Kannon dismounted, unloaded his camera equipment, and walked through the brush to the edge of the cliff.

Kannon's chest tingled as he stared at the canyon floor. It'd be damn easy to slip on the wet rocks and tumble into the chasm. He listened to the quiet, caught the faint sound of a chortling stream, tracked it, and found that the stream spit from a cavern of ice-encrusted snow.

Kannon wished he could excise his demons as thoroughly as the earth disgorged its streams. The unsettling letter had reached him at his Texas hill country home three days ago. Postmarked 25 June 2002, Hồ Chí Minh City, Việt Nam, it read:

> *Dear Trung-Úy Ballard,*
> *Must see you. We have unfinished*
> *business.*
> *Chấn, the Deer Walker.*

Now it was Thursday, 26 September, and the last thing he wanted was to revisit a war he desperately wanted to forget. He'd assumed his interpreter was killed when the communists overran Sài Gòn. To hear from Chấn after all this time resurrected memories filled with the stench of human waste burning in diesel fuel, and Kannon had no desire ever to return to the war-torn country he'd helped break in two and which had broken him in two.

After wallowing in indecision, he'd taken off, and it was here, encapsulated by the San Juan Mountains in southwestern Colorado, he sought to exorcise his rekindled demons.

Turning from the rugged granite cliff, Kannon faced the mountain slope. The San Juan wind swirled and rustled the aspen trees. Positioning his tripod, Kannon peered through the camera's viewfinder and waited. In a moment, the gust died, and the forest settled. He focused the lens on an array of orange and red teardrop-shaped leaves, their veins protruding like shining tendrils. Satisfied, he set his medium format rig for bracketed exposures and then stepped away from the camera.

Kannon fired the remote, cycling a five-round burst. The metallic-sounding shutter clicks reminded him of the distinct pops of distant AK47 rounds. What the hell was Chấn referring to . . . this *unfinished business*?

On the journey from Texas, he'd ridden recklessly, covering the straightaways exceeding one hundred miles an hour and the sweeping curves at over seventy-five. The problem was when he stopped, the memories didn't.

Photography wasn't masking it either. He considered cutting short the wilderness trip and hightail it to Silverton, surprise Meghan. She, with her auburn hair and creamy skin, was holding a room for him in her rustic hotel. They had met a year ago last summer and connected. Full of depth and grace, Meghan was great to talk with, although she tended to probe beyond his comfort level.

Kannon smiled whenever he recalled the first time they'd made love. The sex eased his discomfort. Afterward, Meghan presented him with a long, thoughtful look.

"What's the matter?" Kannon had asked. What he'd worried about was whether his lovemaking had been *adequate*.

"I'm wondering if I should give you a room discount."

They had shared a laugh over that comment. It helped seal their connection. Yet, shit happened, like Chấn's letter. Would he be able to enjoy Meghan's company, or she, his?

The letter also soured Kannon's dreams of a blemish-free retirement. With his career as a chief financial officer over, the cash from exercised stock options invested, and custom-made suits donated to charity, he was primed for a fresh start in life.

Kannon frowned. Self-deception didn't work as well as it used to. Everything was tainted. In his gut, he'd done what had seemed right that night, but Major Farber concluded otherwise. Even though the threatened court-martial never materialized, it persisted as an overhanging indictment. The worst part was the death of his men. That carried a perpetual stink.

Ironically, after his mother and father died, he and his brother Roger had elected to sublet the family home. If they'd sold it to a developer, there wouldn't have been a tenant to forward Chấn's letter. Like breaching a tripwire, the note triggered his combat fears: fear of being maimed, fear of being killed, fear of being captured, but his greatest fear was of screwing up.

The last thing Farber had done was to spit a wad of chewing tobacco on Kannon's boots. The South Vietnamese regional forces who witnessed Farber's verbal castration had bowed their heads, embarrassed at the degradation. His boots were stained, more from the blood than spit. After giving him two weeks in the Long Bình Stockade, the U.S. Army shipped Kannon out of Việt Nam. After completing his military service as a backroom administrator at Fort Polk, Louisiana, he'd been granted an honorable discharge.

For years afterward, he'd shaved using an electric razor and handheld mirror, and then he'd grown a beard to avoid a full look at a face responsible for the death of his men. "What are you hiding from?" his wife often asked. After an ugly divorce, the question never came up. The only communication between the two of them had concerned their son.

Kannon returned to the camera position and removed the remote cable release from its housing. After detaching the Mamiya 645 from its tripod, he placed the camera in the trunk pannier, then collapsed the tripod and secured it on the passenger seat with bungee cords.

He knelt, studied the fallen tree. No big deal. About a foot in diameter, the displaced fir rested on a sizable rock, which he could use as a pivot point to swivel the tree clear.

Done.

The crisp, pungent fragrance from moist pine trees wafted

past. Kannon swung his leg across the saddle and started his BMW R1150GS. While he chugged along the spiraling forest road, impending dusk silhouetted the western ridgeline, and golden aspen leaves lost luster in the fading sun.

He approached a fork. One branch splintered south, the other north. The latter one looked as if a maintenance crew hadn't touched it in years. Kannon steered north. Fifty yards later, he came to a weathered sign.

Restricted Access
No Vehicles Allowed

You've got to be kidding.

Opting for the unknown, Kannon rode two miles before spotting a clearing. An alpine meadow slanted westward, affording a distant view of Redcloud Peak. Except for the constricted opening, thick brush and a dense stand of fir trees rendered the horseshoe-shaped meadow impenetrable.

He downshifted and slipped into the deep emerald cavity, where he killed the engine and dismounted. A fetid smell penetrated his raised faceshield. Removing his helmet, he followed his nose until spotting animal scat soiling the mountain grasses.

The wind moaned, and conifers swayed above the quaking aspen. Tree branches rasped in a guttural symphony. As Kannon watched the thickening clouds color the jungle-green landscape to charcoal, his desire to photograph faded. He turned toward the motorcycle, started to mount—and froze.

Not five yards away, a bear the size of a battle tank blocked his escape, chucking her head from side to side. The hair on her massive shoulders bristled, the silver-tipped fur barely distinguishable from the sharp-needled fir trees.

She rose on her hind legs, opened her great mouth, and roared from the abyss of hell, her lacerating teeth lining its portal. Her foul breath, smelling like decayed garbage, blew past as an angry wind.

Remaining motionless, Kannon fought to control his bowels. The hair on his neck bristled. An unseen weight dropped on his shoulders, forcing him to kneel beside the motorcycle. The bear came to ground. Measuring him at eye level, she edged forward, sniffed, and growled. She was close enough he could have reached out and touched her. Bowing his head, Kannon prayed for forgiveness from all those he'd harmed and for a quick end to himself.

With a swipe quicker than a boxer's jab, the bear struck Kannon's shoulder. He fell against his cycle and curled in a fetal position. The bear didn't move. Neither did Kannon. He just waited for jagged jaws to clamp on his neck. But it didn't happen. The she-bear must have accepted his submission, for she turned and stamped away.

Shaking, he sat up and allowed himself to breathe, shallow at first, then longer, deeper. He rubbed his shoulder. It was slightly bruised, nothing more. He thanked God the bear hadn't ripped into his flesh. Yet, Kannon couldn't stop trembling. He scooped up clumps of earth and sifted the dirt between his fingers. He repeated the process, action eroding fear until a sense of control returned.

Kannon ran his grimy hands through his hair, then stood and withdrew his satellite phone from a side pannier. The sat battery was low. He rummaged for the charger that plugged into the accessory outlet on his motorcycle. Where the hell was the damn thing? He couldn't find it. In his haste to pack, post-Chấn's letter, he must've forgotten to include the charger.

Christ! He was out of sync. A quick call to Meghan, that's all he wanted to do now. She answered on the third ring.

"How's the photography going?" she asked.

"Pretty well, but I'm considering cutting this outing short and heading into Silverton. Is that all right?" He'd never told anyone about his fuckup in 'Nam, and he wasn't going to mention the bear incident either. No one would believe him, anyway. But Kannon was clear about one thing. He was getting the hell out of the San Juans come daybreak.

"That would be super. I'll set up a room. When do you plan to arrive?"

"Early afternoon. The battery for my satphone is running low. I need to sign off."

"Before you go . . ."

Crap. Well, at least he'd gotten a call through, but Kannon wondered what she had been going to say.

Thoughts of Meghan and Silverton replenished Kannon somewhat. He'd loved the old mining town ever since he and his brother Roger had visited as kids, courtesy of their parents. What had sealed his love for the place was that ride on the black and belching, steam-driven, narrow-gauge train. Perhaps he and Meghan could make a run. That made him smile.

Kannon remounted his motorcycle and eased back onto the rutted forest road. The sun bore through a narrow aperture in the clouds, bathing softball-sized rocks in a fuzzy glow, like miniature moons viewed through a soft-focus lens. Hazy shadows distorted his perception. It reminded him of the lull between dusk and darkness, the period of deceptive calm before establishing an ambush position.

As he approached a ridge, the switchbacks tightened, cresting in the center. Thunderheads blackened the sky, and light rain peppered the timbered mountains, making the way slick like the crown of a muddy rice paddy dike.

The rain intensified, assaulting his body as it had the night of his last patrol. Lightning struck a nearby tree, followed by a frightening clap of thunder. Kannon looked over his shoulder, expecting to see Major Farber, then glanced over his other shoulder, expecting to see the bear.

Distracted, he steered off the trail in the middle of a sharp, left turn. His front wheel glanced off a rock. Kannon twisted the throttle and struggled to maintain traction. With rpms revving, the motorcycle wobbled, and the rear tire spun—finally, it bit. The rig straightened and thrust forward over the edge of an embankment. Heading downslope, Kannon squeezed the brakes, but the cycle slid on wet grass, then struck a jagged chunk of granite. It came to rest amid a pile of rocks, the twin-cylinder engine still chuffing.

His right leg was pinned beneath the gas tank. When he tried to move, a sharp pain shot through him.

"Son of a bitch!"

Good fucking move, Kannon. What are you going to do for an encore?

More lightning flashed, illuminating a slick film of oil or fuel in the pooling rainwater. The risk of fire was minimal, but Kannon hoped the oil pan or gas tank hadn't been punctured. He groped for the handlebar-mounted kill switch. It lay out of reach. Again, he tried freeing his leg. Rooted, he couldn't budge it.

Kannon drew his left knee up to his chest, placed his foot against the side of the tank, and slowly extended his leg until he pried enough clearance to extract his injured leg. He tried standing, but when he put pressure on his ankle, it hurt like hell.

Lungs burning, he sank to the ground. After catching his breath, he crawled to the kill switch and snuffed it. What had started as a beautiful fall day had rapidly deteriorated into a *Dante* nightmare.

"Shit! Shit! Shit!"

The motorcycle lay on its side against a berm. Kannon pulled himself up by the handlebars and balanced on his good leg. Extracting a flashlight from the tankbag, he played the beam over the oil pan and gas tank. No punctures.

Opening the exposed pannier, he groped for the satphone, but it and his laptop were in the other side case, which was wedged into the mud. He hoped the batteries retained a smidgeon of power by the time he dug out of this crap.

If only the damn rain would stop. It was like someone dropping ice cubes down his back. Shivering, he leaned on a boulder. As oppressive darkness settled in, Kannon's losses closed around him: the war, the failed marriage, his estranged son, this crash . . . signs of imperfection, which in his father's eyes, as well as his own, equated to failure.

Kannon could blame his crappy state on his dad, or the war, or on Farber, even on Chẩn's letter. He could blame it on his ex-wife—Shelly—who wouldn't accept that depression couldn't be cured by anything other than making the right choices. The mask of *normalcy* he'd used during the progression of his work life failed to carry over to his home life. Shelly's final words at the divorce hearing three years ago rang clear.

"Genetic! Trauma! Medication! Kannon, you're making excuses for your behavior. Our marriage is dead."

Propped against the boulder, Kannon glared at the foreboding sky. Stars shone in a thin band between the horizon and the thunderheads.

He slumped to the ground. Less than a foot away, fir saplings, only inches tall, clustered like a small family. He twanged one, like shooting a marble with his index finger, and the fledgling forest stalwart snapped back.

Resiliency. If a scrawny, twiggy tree bounced back, so could he. It was his responsibility, no one else's.

Unfinished business.

Might he dare interpret the letter as an offer of hope? Chấn, the Deer Walker, had excelled in combat, in reading his people, and in navigating the land, invaluable traits that earned him his nickname. If Chấn hadn't been wounded during a previous mission, he would have accompanied the regional force patrol that night. Perhaps with his presence, they could've avoided the ambush.

Most importantly, does the Deer Walker possess information I don't?

The wind whipped the clouds in a frenzy as they scudded across the sky, blotting out the remaining stars. The moisture-laden cold penetrated Kannon's leathers and worked beneath his skin.

Crawling to the motorcycle, he retrieved his pistol and a down sleeping bag. After unrolling the mummy-shaped bag, he slapped it across the wet, rocky surface, and then slipped inside. His ankle throbbed like someone had whacked it with a sledgehammer. He wouldn't be jogging or riding anytime soon.

Marooned in the San Juans, Kannon closed his eyes for what figured to be a restless night. Beneath the low-hanging clouds, the winds quieted, but an alien sound disturbed the stillness. Kannon listened intently. Somewhere upslope, the bear chuffed. Maybe she would shuffle by with a saddle and a harness so he could ride her out. Yeah, right.

He fingered the semiautomatic.

Empty a Sig Sauer .40-caliber magazine into seven hundred pounds of raging jaws and claws, then scream in agony as the bear tore his body apart. Better to put the muzzle end against his right eye and pull the trigger. It'd be over. Or would it? Would his soul face demons for eternity, a reincarnation of his hell on earth?

Without leaving the sleeping bag, he retracted the Sig's slide, chambered a round, and then, hopeful of chasing away the bear, squeezed off a shot. The pistol's report exploded like the crack of a ruptured ice floe. The muzzle blazed with fire.

Silence and darkness reclaimed their hold. Once again came the night of 5 October 1970.

5 October 1970, 2100 Hours

First Lieutenant Kannon Ballard sat on his cot in the command bunker, two hundred square feet of sandbagged rural bliss with an earthen floor and skittering rats. Writing beneath a flashlight bulb wired to a battery and hung inside an inverted plastic cup, Kannon finished the letter to his brother Roger and sealed the all-in-one stationery provided by the U.S. Army. On the face of the envelope, he wrote: *Five Months in the Crapper, Seven to Go*, before placing the letter in a pouch for the resupply chopper.

Kannon tossed aside the canvas strip covering the bunker opening and walked outside. Thanks to South Vietnam's monsoon season, the night was cool. No moon or stars shone. He expected rain at any moment.

Hearing muffled voices, Kannon turned toward the western perimeter line. His NCO, Sergeant Clifford Malcolm, was jawing with two soldiers of the South Vietnamese 895 Regional Force Company. Kannon liked Malcolm. He was experienced, calm under fire, and diligent.

For the past four months, his five-man mobile advisory team had been short three men: an officer, a senior noncommissioned officer, and a medic. Every time Kannon requisitioned the province senior advisor for replacements, Major Farber's answer had been the same.

"I'm doing what I can, Lieutenant," the major said in a dismissive tone. "End-of-duty rotations . . . the fucking new guys are being assigned to traditional units. It's tough to get replacements."

The U.S. Army Way.

At least they had Võ Chấn, their interpreter, who must be rooting around in his own bunker.

The square-jawed Malcolm approached. No matter how tired the sergeant might be, his shoulders never slumped.

"How's it going, Sarge?"

"The soldiers are edgy."

"How do you read it?" The concern etched in Malcolm's face heightened Kannon's senses. The last time he'd seen that look spelled trouble.

Malcolm dug in his heels, frowned. Six feet tall, he stood a couple of inches shorter than Kannon, but he was broad and thick. The sergeant's tour of duty ended in six weeks, and he was anxious to get home to his wife and their two teenagers. But Kannon didn't worry about short-timer's attitude affecting Malcolm. He was a pro.

"A cousin of a friend's friend has spread the word the VC are moving tonight, Lieutenant."

In the field, underground intel tended to be more accurate than the Army's official reports. "I've called in preset defensive targets," Kannon said, thankful for fire support from the 25th Infantry Division, "so we're set there. Everyone stocked on ammo?"

"They're ready, sir." The sergeant resumed checking the perimeter.

He and Malcolm had been through a lot together. The most jarring attack on the outpost occurred a month after Kannon's arrival. The two of them rallied the 895 Company and repulsed the Việt Cộng. From his haven at headquarters, Major Farber had radioed Kannon and ordered him to pursue the retreating guerilas.

While shadowing the VC, Kannon's team had been surprised by an illumination flare popping overhead. As they dove for cover, he'd seen the glint of an AK barrel protruding beneath a low-hanging palm.

"VC at nine o'clock!" Kannon opened up. So did the others. He, Malcolm, Chấn, and a platoon of RFs routed the enemy unit, thwarting the ambush. Their actions earned him and the sergeant the Silver Star. Chấn received a Bronze.

Kannon never discovered who or what had triggered the flare. The illumination saved their lives, but it just as easily could have gotten them killed.

Weeks later, Farber pinned the medal on Kannon's chest, yet scolded him at the same time. "Lieutenant, I know you're a rookie, but next time, I expect you to react instantly when I give an order."

Kannon hoped there wouldn't be another time. He wanted to go home alive, not in a box.

Now, looking skyward, Kannon didn't see any breaks in the low-hanging clouds. He walked to the well, lowered the rope-tethered bucket, and hauled up some water. After splashing his face, he poured the rest of it over his head. Pure or not, the water felt damn good.

He returned to the command bunker, rummaged in the ammo can where he kept his personals and grabbed the pipe and a package of stale tobacco. Back outside, he searched for Lieutenant Đinh, his counterpart. Kannon wanted to get his take on the underground intel. He strode toward the crew in the mortar pit.

"Where's—"

Whoosh!

An explosion followed the split-second sound.

"B40 rockets," Malcolm yelled.

The range of that weapon is two hundred meters. The Việt Cộng are close.

More rockets slammed into the trees and bunkers, blasted Malcolm to the ground. Kannon vaulted a water trench and slogged across the mud to his sergeant.

"We're in for it, Lieutenant." Sarge scrambled to his feet and wiped the sludge off his face.

"You okay?"

Malcolm nodded.

"Find Đinh," Kannon ordered.

"On my way." Sergeant Malcolm bolted for their counterpart's bunker.

Enemy mortar rounds pummeled their position, gouging holes in the ground. Shrapnel whistled overhead.

"Chấn, bring the radio," Kannon said, his ears ringing from the explosions.

Crouched beside the bunker, his interpreter ducked inside, then emerged, lugging the PRC-25.

"Here, sir."

Kannon grabbed the handset. "Purple Onion, this is Tiger Seven Four. Over."

Heavy rain began pelting An Dinh, a half-acre-sized outpost composed of thirty sandbag bunkers wedged between irregularly spaced palm and bamboo trees. Bordered by rice paddies, the triangular-shaped garrison hung at the northeastern tip of Đức Huệ

District in Hậu Nghĩa Province, sixty kilometers west of Sài Gòn. Except for modern weapons, the living conditions reminded Kannon of images he held about Native American camps in the 1860s.

"Tiger Seven Four, this is Purple Onion. Over."

"Onion, we're taking heavy incoming mortar and B40. Coordinate with Fire Direction Center for defensive targets three and four. Do you copy? Over."

"Roger, Seven Four."

The regional force soldiers fired their M-16s, grenade launchers, and machine guns, trying to provoke return fire to determine the size and direction of the attacking ground force.

Within two minutes, U.S. Army artillery shells streaked through the sky and struck pre-plotted targets. Finally, Kannon's legs stopped shaking.

Malcolm returned.

"Where in hell's Đinh?" Kannon asked.

"Couldn't find him, Lieutenant."

Christ!

"Chấn, have the mortar squad pop a flare."

"Yes, sir."

The flare blew out of the tube and ignited. As if bristled by the intrusion, the monsoon winds howled and rendered the artificial light ineffective. "Adjust direction. Fire upwind—"

Kablam! Kablam! Kablam!

Kannon flinched.

Malcolm's expression turned rock hard. "Bangalore torpedoes."

Another flare thumped. This one illuminated the area.

Abruptly, AK47s, with their distinctive, popping retorts, filled the night.

Chấn leaped on top of the command bunker, steadied himself, and scanned the perimeter. "Sappers in the wire! Sappers in the wire!"

"Azimuth?" Kannon flicked his M-16 off safety.

"Two hundred eighty degrees." Chấn hopped down.

An agitated regional force soldier spoke in Vietnamese.

"What'd he say?"

14

"*Trung-Úy*," Chấn said to Ballard, using the Vietnamese word for lieutenant. "They got Đinh and Lộc. Rifle grenades."

Kannon's chest palpitated as if a beehive round had exploded nearby. His counterpart, Đinh, and Sergeant Lộc, Đinh's most effective platoon leader, were down. To hell with the advisory role, it was time for Mobile Advisory Team III-56 to take charge.

"Chấn, tell the sergeants I'm—Malcolm, look out!" Fear lodged in Kannon's throat. Enemy sappers, seasoned guerrillas who'd breached the defensive wires, charged toward them, lobbing hand grenades at the mortar pit and command bunker.

"Motherfuck!" Malcolm yelled as he hit the ground.

Kannon raised his M-16 and squeezed off five rounds. Chấn braced himself and fired a rapid burst. Between them, they felled five enemy soldiers. As in earlier combat, Kannon experienced a detached, surreal sense of elation.

Then, amid the rain and odor of gunpowder, he raced to his sergeant. "Malcolm, where are you hit?"

"My leg!"

"How bad is it?"

Malcolm rose, unbuttoned his fatigue pants, and let them fall to his ankles. An ugly, jagged piece of shrapnel protruded from his left thigh. He stared at it, then slowly withdrew the metal fragment. "It's not deep. Just a flesh wound. Sorry I yelled."

"No problem." Kannon understood. The shock from being hit often overrode the seriousness of the injury, even for a tough sergeant. "I'll hit up Farber again for a medic," Kannon added, disgusted with the lack of support from his commanding officer.

"Good luck with that," Malcolm said. He wrapped a field dressing around his thigh and then hitched up his pants. He stared at Kannon. "Lieutenant, I'll manage. Do what you need to do."

Chấn approached, his eyes wide with alarm.

"Our mortar tube is destroyed," his interpreter said.

Shit.

"Take over the radio," Kannon commanded Malcolm. "Call Purple Onion. Demand gunships."

"Roger."

"Follow me," Kannon said to Chấn. Fueled with adrenaline,

15

he sprinted to the northwest corner of the breached bunker line, his interpreter close behind.

"Look!"

As if launched by catapults, shadowy figures sprang from the rice fields and assaulted with small arms and grenades. Kannon fired into the malignant maelstrom, dropping one, who collapsed in a twisted heap as if his bones had turned to marrow. Darting with the agility of a deer, the wiry, slender Chấn killed another three with his vintage carbine. Another regional force soldier wiped out two more VC.

Shrapnel whizzed by Kannon's ear. He turned. Two guerrillas were closing fast, Chicom pistols at the ready. He shoved Chấn aside, leveled the attackers, then released the empty, banana-shaped magazine and switched to a full one.

"Good show, *Trung-Úy* Ballard. Good show." Chấn sprang to his feet. A big mistake because another guerrilla took his interpreter down with an AK round.

Kannon spun and faced the sapper who now aimed his AK at him. Before the guerrilla could squeeze the trigger, Kannon fired a burst from the hip, then ran to his interpreter's side. "Where'd they get you?"

"My ankle," he said, grimacing.

Chấn's pants legs were bloused into his boots, and Kannon didn't want to risk aggravating the wound. He withdrew his knife and sliced away the bloodstained fabric. Bone was shattered, but the round didn't appear to have severed an artery.

"*Lại đây.*" (Come here.) Kannon directed a regional force soldier to administer first aid.

Afterward, the regional force unit regrouped and discharged controlled, interlocking fire at the sappers assaulting the perimeter. Thirty minutes later, the small-arms assault ended.

"Cease fire! Cease fire!" Kannon commanded the RFs.

Chấn, helped to his feet by two of his comrades, repeated the command in Vietnamese. As the word spread, the regional force soldiers obeyed.

While there seemed to be no live enemy soldiers remaining inside the perimeter, incoming mortar rounds still hammered the outpost. U.S. artillery continued its supporting barrage. Kannon, dodging the fallen VC, hustled to Malcolm, who supported his wounded leg by leaning against the bunker.

"Our interpreter took a hit, too," Kannon said, examining the sergeant's wound. Heaviness set in. He needed to get Malcolm, Chẩn, and any other wounded medical attention. "Radio for a medevac."

Malcolm made the call, then turned to Kannon. "Not a bad performance . . . for a twenty-three-year-old lieutenant," his sergeant said with a wicked grin.

"Yeah?" Based on his Dutch-German ancestry, which imbued discipline, sacrifice, and hard work, it's what Kannon expected of himself. "Wipe that smile off your face, Sarge. I oughta make you drink nước mắm sauce."

Malcolm managed a weak laugh. It was their private joke.

"Where are the damn gunships?" Kannon wanted Cobras on station before the VC disappeared into their tunnels.

A radio transmission crackled through. Malcolm held up his hand for silence. When he did, Kannon realized the incoming was tapering off like a spent thunderstorm.

"Cobras on the way. ETA one zero. Call sign's Green Phantom." Malcolm brandished the radio handset for emphasis. "Flare ship, too."

"Ten minutes? Why so long?" Kannon's mouth turned dry. He took a drink from his canteen. "Have artillery fire two more salvos, then abort."

Malcolm nodded and pressed the handset against his ear. "Done, sir." Five seconds lapsed. "Major Farber's on the command net."

"What does he want?"

"Casualty assessment. You gonna inflate the body count?"

"You know I don't believe in that shit."

Chẩn hobbled to their position on a makeshift crutch. Kannon smiled at his interpreter friend. "Glad you're still with us. I need a casualty count."

"Thirteen enemy KIA inside the compound," Chẩn rasped. "Platoon leaders report seven RFs KIA. Three wounded. One bad."

Too damn many.

The South Vietnamese political action sergeant trotted over and whispered to the interpreter.

Chấn nodded. "We have two POWs."

"Great. We need to get them to S-2 before our RFs chew 'em up. Malcolm, you copy?"

"Roger."

"Any word on the medevac?" Kannon asked.

"Not yet."

Crap. These guys could bleed to death.

"Sir, our RFs need to get on the bird," Malcolm said, "but I'm not leaving you guys."

The sergeant's grit impressed Kannon.

"I will not go either," Chấn said.

"Yes, you will."

Chấn shook his head.

Malcolm lowered the handset. "Farber says the medevac chopper has been rerouted. And he orders you to lead a reaction force in the direction of attack."

Kannon's blood charged as another surge of adrenaline hit. "Does he want to get us killed?"

Two

Staring at the Chinese wall calendar hanging next to a threadbare tapestry, Lan understood, even accepted, that 2002 would be the last year of Võ Chấn's life. She held her brother's pain as if she, too, were dying.

Lan walked to the window and opened the shutters to draw in the afternoon sun. From the second floor of their home on Sài Gòn's Bùi Viện Street, she looked upon an atmosphere as clogged as her brother's mucus-filled lungs. Low-hanging clouds trapped the foul stench from the exhaust emitted by diesel-fueled buses and trucks. Bicycle bells and Lambretta horns and the whiney, high-pitched, two-cycle engine squeals invaded the Võ family home like hysterical parrots.

"Sister."

She padded to his bedside. "Your furrowed brow looks like a plowed field. What bothers you?"

"Did I receive a letter today?"

She set down her fried vegetables. "You know I will tell you if one arrives. What makes you think Mr. Ballard will write, much less return?"

"He will come." Chấn kneaded the damp coversheet. "He must."

"I do not want to destroy your hope. But it was long ago. What if he no longer lives?"

Chấn did not answer. What more could she tell her brother? She had failed to find an Internet address or email listing for a Kannon Ballard. The address they used belonged to Kannon's mother and father, and that was thirty-two years old. She knew her brother's fragile hold on life depended on his belief, however desperate, of seeing this American he once fought beside.

After her brother's return from the reeducation camp, he had spoken little of the war. She had reintroduced him to Sài Gòn society, but soon he became disconsolate.

"The city's infrastructure has deteriorated," he had said.

He held menial jobs until she found him a position at a private school teaching Vietnamese to Cubans. Still, he brooded. And then his skin turned the dreaded yellow.

"Hepatitis B virus," the doctor told them last summer. "The disease is chronic. Nothing can be done. It is amazing he has lived this long. His liver is no longer able to process the poisonous waste that swims through his body."

"What of the drug interferon?" she had asked.

The doctor replied it was impossible to obtain. After the diagnosis, Chấn began to speak of his ordeal. "Lan, those camps were like living in a shithouse. All prisoners suffered deprivation. And they inoculated us with contaminated needles."

Lan shuddered when remembering his words. She did not understand why her people inflicted pain on their brothers and sisters. She would have turned the camps into hospitals and schools. But now, it was too late for her brother, for toxicity overwhelmed his body's defenses.

Chấn struggled to recline against the headboard. "If *Trung-Úy* Ballard does not come, I am doomed. And so is he." His raspy tone reminded her of croaking frogs.

"Your talk scares me. Why are you doomed?"

"I failed Buddha. I am doomed. *Trung-Úy* Ballard—"

A pneumonic spasm cut short his words. His eyes expressed best his depleted state. Each day the irises lost more gleam. Each day the sclera lost more whiteness. He closed them now and fell asleep.

"I will miss you, brother," she whispered.

* * *

When he awoke, Chấn put his hand to his heart to reassure himself it still pulsed. Sometimes his heart pounded so fast he feared it would pop out of his chest. Other times, like now, it beat wobbly and slow, like a rickety old man walking with a cane.

Outside his window, the morning din assaulted his ears like screaming guards in reeducation camps and reminded him of the communist takeover—dishonorable, disruptive, and inept. And it was because of them he was dying.

"Another day welcomes you," Lan said.

Turning his head to the open doorway, he found his sister's radiant smile. Even her disheveled áo dài could not mask the sense of strength and love she conveyed. He extended his right palm and motioned her forward. She set a glass of water and a pitcher of warm tea on the table beside his bed.

How many more days will there be? he wondered.

Lan wiped his brow with a damp cloth, then kissed the purified spot. "Are your feelings on a pleasant journey this morning?"

"No. It's—" Chấn coughed. His guttural utterances disgusted him. "I think about what I hate. The communists."

"I know you hate them, brother. I do as well, but at least we are free of war."

"Free of war, yes, but we have no freedom." As Chấn leaned forward to spit, he caught his odor. He smelled like a butchered pig.

"Please do not get upset. You only worsen yourself."

"To die under oppression destroys all I have lived for." His sister's naiveté irritated him. He recalled the thrill at being called upon to help unite Việt Nam, but the glory faded. After the North Vietnamese Army overran Sài Gòn, the Việt Cộng who sacrificed and fought for the glorious liberation day became communist marionettes. The guerrillas may as well have immolated themselves like the monks.

"I see little difference in governments." She propped the pillow behind his neck. "President Diệm's government was a sham democracy. A dictatorship."

"True, sister." And it was not a benevolent dictatorship. Diệm gave no voice to those who protested his oppression. Chấn thought of the disaffected Buddhists, teachers, lawyers, doctors, peasants, and farmers who joined the guerrilla movement.

"You frown, brother. Is it the noise? I will shutter the window."

"No, leave it open. The noise is bothersome, but to hear is to live."

What his country had become saddened him. He hated to admit it, but after Diệm's assassination, South Việt Nam worsened, with four different leaders in four years. And Thiệu, the last

21

American puppet, even though he ruled eight years, proved ineffectual.

He managed a chuckle. *"Trung-Úy* Ballard used to say, 'Hồ Chí Minh, Presidents Diệm and Thiệu, and Presidents Kennedy and Johnson created this war, and now you and I are slogging through their shit.'"

"You have never said why you need to see this Kannon Ballard."

Chấn regarded his sister's concern and pressed his hand into hers. "To right a wrong."

She let go of his hand, pulled a chair close, and sat down. Lowering her head, she folded her arms across her chest and curled within the chair. It was as if she drew into herself, letting her wrinkled garment reflect the burden he imposed. After a moment, she raised her head and spoke. "You conducted an immoral act? Do you mean war?"

Both questions racked his being as typhoons ravaged ships on the sea. Immoral? War? She would think this way, simple and pure. "I must hold my answer for the American."

Disappointment flooded his sister's face. He knew the wound he had just inflicted lingered in her breast. "Come, let us talk of something else."

"Then speak of our father's life when you were a boy."

Ah, she has rallied her spirit.

Chấn sipped tea from his cup. He could not remember when his father began instructing him. To Chấn, it seemed he awoke one day and there sat his father, Thu, as if he had been sitting there since his son's birth.

"Politics and faith fascinated him. Father used to say, 'Chấn, government is like religion. Failure to execute does not invalidate the concept. It is people who fail.'"

"Not his serious side." She released a tender laugh. "I want to know what he was like. Did he play?"

Chấn too wished Thu could have laughed. "Father did not play. He only prepared for war."

"Oh." As if desiring a different path, Lan squeezed shut her eyes, but at last, opened them and sighed. "All right, then, please go on."

"Father said, '*Con trai*. (Son.) The path to enlightenment, nirvana, centers on absorbing the Four Noble Truths. Life is full of suffering. It takes root from wanting too many of the wrong things. Suffering can be diminished and possibly eliminated by not pursuing the wrong things. You must walk the middle path.'"

"Did not his teachings get boring?"

"He made it interesting. On the Tết holiday, during the fifth year of my life, Father took me to visit his friend, Ngọc Hội, who lived in Tân An. Ngọc Hội cultivated bonsai trees, some over one hundred and fifty years old."

"I wish Father had shared such things with me. I have few memories of him."

Her sorrow entered his heart and made it sag.

"Remember, sister, war disrupted life."

Her eyelids fluttered, and her lips opened, a tired smile of resignation, acceptance. Chấn continued. "'*Con trai*,' Father would say, 'you must nurture your religion as carefully as Ngọc Hội nurtures his bonsai trees. The middle path, the Eightfold Path, is the most difficult to follow.'"

Lan nodded. "Mother taught me the eight steps were similar to the Ten Commandments for Christians and Jews and centered on emphasizing right actions."

"Yes," he said, knowing his mother would have stressed the commonality of man. Thu's approach was different. Chấn remembered copying down his father's mantras until he committed them to memory and needed only keywords to recall the sacred sayings.

"If only the world lived as our mother and father and the monks taught."

"Good words. But a mere dream." He gripped the edge of the bed and rolled to his side. "I must rest now."

Yes, he was tired, too tired to tell Lan he had been demonized by teachings embedded during childhood. Too tired to tell his sister that their father did not follow what he preached.

"Following the Eightfold Path is the way to become free of this world, so you return not as a rat or a snake but as a good thing until finally, you need not return at all. The better you live each time, the less you suffer when you return."

Chấn failed his religion and his religion failed him. The Mahayana Buddhists, elitists of the Greater Wheel School, believed not in a God but one truth, *Tathata*, and in *Sunya*—all things are temporal. If true, and nothing on earth was real, why was he terrified to die?

He knew he could not get free of this world, but he hoped he could do better than coming back in the lowest form imaginable. To avoid it, he needed to make something right—to speak to *Trung-Úy* Ballard. He also dreaded facing his Vietnamese brothers in the afterworld. He wondered if those brothers whose deaths he had caused now invaded his body as the killer hepatitis and pneumonia.

Chấn thought that 2002—a Year of the Horse—might not be a bad year to die. He might make it to 2003—the Year of the Goat. Besides, it would be nice to hear the fireworks from another Tết. But he worried about his sister. He did not want to return as a rat or a snake and bite her.

Three

The mother bear lumbered downslope, tossing her massive head from side to side, sniffing out potential threats to her environment.

Funny looking horse, she thought. Tough hide. Her teeth just slid off it. She pawed something round. It spun. Softer . . . but still too hard to bite. What's that on the ground?

She ambled toward the object, reared on her stout hind-legs, and looked down with contempt upon the pathetic figure curled in a fetal position. "Your flimsy cocoon won't protect you," she roared. "You'll have to get out."

"No," Kannon shouted. "My God. You can't order me into that fusillade. Incoming is falling like molten lava. B40 rockets are ripping through here like flechette rounds. The AK fire is thicker than hornets."

A shrouded figure snarled, "Go."

The bear looked at the still figure and dropped her front paws. She dug furiously into the ground and sprayed dirt behind her, then thundered away into the tree line.

* * *

Kannon awoke to a gunmetal dawn. A light dusting of snow blanketed exposed tree branches, rocks, and grasses. Bare aspen stood like ivory sentries, surrounding mountains the prison walls—he and the fallen motorcycle, vanquished.

"Get moving," he told himself.

His legs felt shackled, numb. Then he realized the bottom half of the sleeping bag was covered with dirt. Shaking free, he unzipped the bag and crawled into the chill.

Kannon noticed a freshly dug hole, delineated by claw marks. Large, five-pronged impressions trailed up the ridgeline. The bear dream slashed through his mind. If he was in her feeding area, no need to stalk, she could maul him anytime.

He tried to stand, but his right ankle crumpled, so he hopped. Kannon studied the position of the motorcycle against the berm. The right cylinder and pannier absorbed the brunt of the impact. He looked for stout deadfall to use as a crowbar, but none that he could handle lay nearby.

What else might work? If he turned the handlebars to the right and slid the rear of the motorcycle clockwise, he could scoop out some rocks, forming a pocket to brace himself. Kannon hopped to the front of the motorcycle and turned the steering column. Returning to the right rear, he planted his left leg against the berm, his back against the cycle, and lifted. The GS moved. Then, after unearthing and discarding several rocks, he created the necessary depression. The last step before attempting to raise the motorcycle was to position a large, flat rock on the other side to support the side stand.

Next, he took off his belt and wrapped it around the engine guard, making a loop like a slipknot. Sitting down in the earthen bucket seat, he grabbed the improvised belt safety loop, positioned his contracted left leg against the bottom of the tank, and pushed. Slowly, the motorcycle rose. He kept extending his leg until the center of gravity shifted, then, holding onto the belt, let the momentum pull him upright. The side stand landed on the stone and held fast.

Gulping for breath, Kannon inspected the guts of the motorcycle. The damage was cosmetic. No vital fluids leaked. Best of all, he could access the rest of his gear. Had his satellite phone retained a modicum of power? After removing it, Kannon keyed the on button. The sat didn't activate. Damn! He wished he'd invested in a solar-powered battery charger.

A gust of wind scattered fallen leaves and rattled aspen branches. The San Juans encompassed a lot of territory. Meghan couldn't very well send out a rescue party because he hadn't given her a grid coordinate.

He needed mobility.

Make a crutch.

Kannon stuffed his survival knife and some duct tape in his pockets, then lay on his stomach, crossing his bad ankle over the good one, and pulled himself forward. He skittered some twenty yards across the rock-strewn ground. Several times he stopped to catch his breath. Finally reaching the aspen grove, he grabbed onto a limb and hauled himself to a standing position.

Using the serrated blade of his knife, he sawed off a five-foot-long, two-inch-thick branch with a forked end. He lopped off the suckers and then wrapped the fork in duct tape to cushion the fit under his armpit.

Could he ride?

If unable to put pressure on his right foot, how could he handle the rear brake pedal? Kannon didn't relish tackling the treacherous mountain roads using only the front brake. He considered hobbling to the T-junction and leaving a distress note.

Or, he could camp.

Hunger gnawed his gut, but he wanted to ice down his ankle. He paused, leaned on the makeshift crutch, and looked around for snowdrifts.

Kannon saw her sitting on a knoll upslope, beneath a charred, chopped-off aspen that looked like a lamppost. He scuffed toward the GS, watching the bear watch him.

The morning wind shifted to the east, carrying with it a soft clattering sound, like falling leaves or a gurgling stream. If a stream, he could soak the ankle in it. Kannon returned to the motorcycle. The she-bear maintained her position.

After emptying the tankbag of everything except duct tape, a canteen, a small towel, and a dry pair of socks, he followed the sound. Supported by the makeshift crutch, Kannon dragged his right leg forward, stepped with his left, and limped ahead. The bear paralleled his course on the ridgeline above.

Kannon groped through an increasing number of trees and intertwined branches. Sweat poured off his brow and stung his eyes. Finally, the aspen and spruce opened into a corridor, which acted as a conduit and amplified the clattering sound. Five minutes later, he came to a narrow stream and sat down on its nearest bank. He unzipped his right boot and took it off, then removed his sock and plunged foot and ankle into the water.

"Christ!"

His ankle went numb within two minutes. He expected to see miniature ice floes sailing downstream. Kannon grappled with the bitter irony of being here. After he'd graduated from college, the draft board struck as fast as a West Texas rattler. Test scores qualified him for Infantry Officer Candidate School, and ten months later, at twenty-two years old, he was commissioned a second lieutenant. Cannon fodder.

Like a lot of young soldiers, he'd been full of piss and vinegar, eager to display his newly acquired knowledge of tactics and leadership. After a year's stateside assignment, he received orders for special warfare school. There, he learned about the Vietnamese religion, culture, and language. The army assigned him as an advisor to a South Vietnamese regional force company and farmed him out to Indian country west of Sài Gòn, not far from the Cambodian border.

A rustling sound and a blur in the brush jolted him back to the present. Just the wind, he hoped. Kannon checked his watch . . . ten minutes since immersion. He scooted away from the stream and dried his ankle. After putting on the dry sock, he wrapped his injury with duct tape, slipped on the boot, and managed to zip it partway.

He refilled his canteen and popped in a couple of purifying tablets, which tainted the flavor almost as much as the iodine tablets he'd used in the army. One day he'd get a backpacking filter, one with a charcoal core.

Utilizing his crutch, Kannon scrambled to his feet and trekked back to the GS, his progress a little smoother. He looked upslope. No bear, just his ex-wife with a book sitting in an easy chair, derisively scanning over her half-moon glasses the scene unfolding below. Shelly, with the flaming red hair and love of life, owner of an antique shop, who said, "Kannon, you have no right to be depressed." She had no use for the past—Việt Nam in particular—which depressed him even more. Which he then marinated with alcohol and unfaithfulness and garnished with impossible expectations for son Stefan.

Kannon shook off the images and erected the tent, which practically sprang up by itself. After mixing freeze-dried noodles with water, he warmed them over his camp stove. The concoction tasted bland, like wet cardboard, but at least it provided nourishment.

Later, concerned the bear might ransack the camp, he secured his mess kit, freeze-dried pebbles, and granola bars in a detached pannier. Then he dragged the carrier and placed it in the crook of a tree several yards distant.

Light snow began to fall. Soft, wet flakes floated lazily to the ground like inebriated parachutists. He grabbed his Meerschaum, opened the tobacco pouch, and packed his pipe with a Mark Twain blend. Shielding against the wind, he struck a match, drew breath, and lit the tobacco—aromatic smoke released into the wild.

Should he attempt to hike back to the main road? He'd ridden two miles to the clearing, where he first encountered the bear, and another two miles before crashing. Four miles, sixteen laps around a quarter-mile track, but in bad weather and rough terrain, just to leave a note that might never be read. He didn't think so. Meghan would worry, though, and that bothered him.

* * *

For three days, the snow fell and for three days, he soaked his ankle every four hours in the frigid stream. After each soaking, the ankle seemed stronger and more stable.

Each morning, when Kannon left to soak his ankle, the bear occupied her accustomed throne. She tracked his trail from above until he lost sight of her in the tree line. It was a fragile bivouac, a peaceful but uneasy coexistence. That the bear was master, Kannon didn't challenge. In one sense, it seemed the bear allowed him to transgress through her domain, while she stood watch to ensure he didn't desecrate it. In another sense, it was as if she were his protector.

At night, he read under candle lantern. And it was there, smoking his pipe, he penned two letters to Chấn, undecided which one to send.

On the fourth day, the sun shined, illuminating golden aspens and dark evergreens sporting thin mantles of snow. Tired of eating mush, Kannon decided to fish for something more substantive. He cut off a length of fishing line from the spool he carried and fastened it to a small, willowy aspen branch. Then he tied on a small spinner lure and hook.

Discarding the crutch and limping slightly, he followed the

meandering creek downstream and searched for pools complaisant to rainbow and brook trout. After a quarter mile, the stream converged with a larger one, and two hundred yards farther, he found his pocket beneath an overhanging tree trunk.

A west wind whistled softly through the evergreens and fluttered the aspen leaves. He shed his jacket and hunkered down with his back against a twisted pine, one so knurled it suggested a Bristlecone. The rippling waters quieted in the diminutive pool. Dark shadows darted beneath the mid-day sun. He unleashed the improvised fishing rig and dropped the hook and lure into the water. Five minutes later, a foot-long rainbow nibbled and took the lure. Kannon tugged lightly to set the hook, then hand over hand reeled the fish in. An hour later, he caught another of similar size.

Satisfied, Kannon wound the line, put it in his coat pocket, and hiked back to camp. He hastened to the tree securing the pannier and retrieved his cooking gear. As always, he looked upslope, and, as always by late afternoon, the bear's throne remained vacant. On impulse, he marched to the throne and set at its base the larger of the two fish.

After leaving his offering, he walked back to his cooking area and kindled a fire. He filleted the trout, quartered the halves, and slapped the pieces in a small frying pan. Lighting his Meerschaum, he smoked for an hour and tended the coals, then set the frying pan on a makeshift rock grill.

In a few minutes, the popping, crackling sound of natural juices filled his ears, and the aroma, broiling trout tinged with wood smoke, filtered through his nostrils. He ate with zest, the hot trout melting in his mouth, and he washed it down with fresh spring water. Kannon watched the afterglow roll up the mountain and settle underneath the cumulus clouds, saturating them in tangerine, violet red, and deep magenta.

He thought of another fish dinner, also outdoors, only those fish weren't trout but a species unknown to him.

* * *

It was his first night in the outpost, and he walked by as Sergeant Chấn and Sergeant Malcolm, his seasoned noncommissioned officer, were preparing to eat. All were squatting on the ground in what became for Kannon an extremely uncomfortable position.

"*Trung-Úy? Ăn cơm chưa?*" Chấn asked. (Lieutenant? Have you eaten yet?)

"*Không, Trung sĩ,*" he replied in his crude Vietnamese. (No, Sergeant.)

Chấn, understanding the young American lieutenant possessed a less than full grasp of the Vietnamese language, switched to English. "Come, *trung-úy*, join us."

"*Cám ơn,*" Kannon answered. (Thank you.)

He squatted on the ground next to Chấn, who gave him a bowl and chopsticks. He grappled with them but fumbled his chopsticks while trying to pinch bite-sized morsels of fish and rice. It was like trying to pick up Mexican jumping beans. His new comrades made no attempt to muffle their chuckles. When he accidentally flipped a piece of fish into Chấn's bowl, the chuckles erupted into laughter. Unfortunately, that was not the end of it. Malcolm handed him a smaller bowl containing the most foul-smelling liquid he had ever encountered, worse than Limburger cheese.

"What am I supposed to do with this?" he asked Malcolm.

"Drink it like wine, Lieutenant."

He drank, and then, in a futile effort to hide his contorted face, bowed his head to keep from offending his new hosts. But his bowels tightened like taut bowstrings, and he fled for the single-digit commode behind the tree line, hearing guffaws and Sergeant Malcolm's resonant voice, "Welcome to Việt Nam."

Later that night, Kannon took Sergeant Malcolm aside. "Hey, Sarge, what was that stuff?"

Malcolm turned his wizened face to Kannon and lit up with a mischievous grin. "That's their fish sauce, Lieutenant. They marinate it in the ground. Throw all kinds of crap in there. No hard feelings?"

"No hard feelings." They shook hands. "Why are there footprints on the commode seat?"

Again, Malcolm doubled over in laughter. "They shit squattin', not sittin', Lieutenant Ballard."

31

"Let's secure our shitter."

* * *

The fish dinner amused him now. The disaster six months later, along with Sergeant Malcolm's last words, "Goddamn, Lieutenant. You walked us right into it," haunted him still.

Kannon stared into the dying fire. He took the two letters from his inside jacket pocket. The first, he crumpled and tossed onto the embers. The paper smoldered, then burst into flames. The second letter he retained, hopeful it would lead to redemption, fearful it might, instead, be the siren song—a shrouded dream enticing him into a specious realm.

6 October 1970, 0100 Hours

Kannon snatched the handset from his sergeant.

"Major Farber, Trung-Úy Đinh and several key regional force soldiers are dead. Our interpreter's out of action. Malcolm's wounded, and so are—"

"No excuses. You're a goddamned infantry officer. Get your ass moving!"

"Yes, sir." Kannon let out a deep breath as he slung his M-16. Farber did say he'd see what could be done about a medevac.

A static radio transmission broke the tension. "Tiger Seven Four, this is Green Phantom. Show strobe. Over."

"Strobe's lit." Rain stinging his eyes, Kannon watched for the twin Cobra gunships. He heard the rotors before the ships dipped beneath the clouds.

"See your strobe," Phantom said. "Advise situation. Over."

"This is Seven Four. Incoming ceased five minutes ago. Mortars came from the northwest, estimated range fifteen hundred meters. Ground assault consisted of sappers with B40 rockets, AK47s, and satchel charges. The enemy force has withdrawn. Suggest you sweep west to north. Over."

"Roger. Will stay in touch," said Green Phantom. "Be advised flare ship is right behind. Call sign, Swivel Hips."

"Roger that, Phantom." Kannon turned to Malcolm. "Can you hold on? I need to assemble the patrol."

"Yeah, I'm okay." He grimaced and tightened the bandage. "Bad tactics, though, bad tactics. It's too dangerous to go without Đinh and Chấn. Let the choppers handle it."

"I'm going."

Malcolm narrowed his eyes. "Make it a short patrol."

"Chấn, which platoon leader speaks some English?"

"Dương."

Kannon slung his rifle. "Assemble the third platoon. We're going to pay those boys a visit."

"Okay, Trung-Úy." Maintaining his disarming smile, Chấn repositioned his crutch and shuffled away.

"Malcolm, call Green Phantom. Tell them to stay fifteen hundred meters north of the OP. We'll go no farther than a klick."

Kannon strapped the other twenty-three-pound radio on his back, then called the flare ship. "Swivel Hips, Seven Four. Taking out a pursuit element. May need you to light 'em up. Over."

"Roger, Seven Four. We'll have our eyes and ears open."

Chẩn returned. Malcolm placed his radio on the ground, then looped three bandoliers of M-16 magazines around his chest. "Man the radio," he said to their interpreter, who nodded.

Kannon gaped at Malcolm. "What do you think you're doing?"

"What the hell's it look like?"

"You're not going out with a leg wound."

"My leg's fine."

Kannon regarded Sargent Malcom with admiration and pride, even love, if love was possible in war. They grinned at each other, then assessed Dương and his makeshift platoon. Altogether, fourteen RF soldiers.

Malcolm shook his head. "Hardly more than a reinforced squad."

"I know." Kannon looked at his watch. It was 0100 hours. "Ready?"

"Let's go," Malcolm said.

Walking point, Dương led the platoon single file on a serpentine route through the mangled, protective wire. What the sappers didn't destroy with their satchel charges the RFs did with the claymore mines. Kannon deployed them in a wedge formation, then radioed Chẩn to have a squad conduct a perimeter sweep for more enemy KIAs.

As the patrol sloshed over the mushy ground, the rains intensified with a vengeance. The odor from buffalo dung stung Kannon's nasal passages. It was like wading through sewage.

After five hundred meters, he brought the reaction force to a halt and whispered into the handset. "Green Phantom. This is Tiger Seven Four. See any movement? Over."

"Seven Four. Phantom. Negative. You clear of us?"

"Roger, Phantom."

"Seven Four. Phantom. We'll be sure they know we're here. Wait one."

The twin gunships unleashed rockets and strafed the ground with miniguns, marching the rain of fire south.

"Phantom. Seven Four. Impressive." Kannon paused a second. "Continuing forward movement. Over."

With Dương still on point, the force moved out. Three hundred meters farther, Dương halted the column. "*Trung-Úy*, I see something. There."

Through streaks of lightning, Kannon observed enemy troops seventy-five meters ahead.

"Swivel Hips," he whispered into the mouthpiece, "this is Seven Four. Drop a flare two hundred meters southeast of Green Phantom. Over."

"Roger, Seven Four. Will do."

The reaction force got on line and propped themselves behind a rice paddy berm. As Kannon knelt, his knee immediately sank into the muck.

Wishing Chấn were here, Kannon peered into the darkness and waited. The flare popped and drifted into position, illuminating wind-blown palm and bamboo. Flooded rice paddies shimmered in iridescent pools. In the eerie light, thirty to forty enemy soldiers froze, then dropped to the ground alongside a ragged tree line.

"Malcolm, how do you read it?"

"Their rear element is loaded down with something." He rubbed his eyes. "Looks like bodies."

"Dương, as soon as the flare dies, we'll crawl to the next rice paddy dike," Kannon said. "I'll radio Swivel Hips to drop another flare. Catch them by surprise. They'll be expecting the Cobras but not us."

Five minutes later, the second flare popped. There they were. Enemy in the open. The reaction force fired their M-16s in all their fury, felling several Việt Cộng with controlled automatic bursts. Receiving sporadic return fire, Kannon lowered his M-16 and hunkered behind the berm. He pressed the push-to-talk switch on the radio handset. "Green Phantom. Tiger Seven Four. Direct your miniguns into that hedgerow where the green tracers are coming from."

"Roger, Seven Four," the pilot said. The Cobras erupted.

Soon, it was over. Relieved, Kannon sucked in a deep breath. "Let's get the hell out of here."

"Agreed," Malcolm said.

Another radio transmission crackled through.

"Tiger Seven Four. This is Green Phantom. Be advised we've been rerouted. An element of the 25th Infantry Division reports heavy contact."

"Phantom. Seven Four. No problem. Situation's clean. We're returning to the outpost. Thanks for your help. Over."

"Dương, put your men in a staggered column," Malcolm said. "Stay alert."

The air, laced with the odor of gunpowder, hung thick as they plodded toward the OP. Kannon's legs felt as heavy as if he were wearing leaded boots. He turned to the bedraggled Malcolm, who dragged his wounded leg. "Gonna make it?"

"Yeah, but I'm worried about our troops. They've lost discipline."

Kannon noticed it too and became alarmed. All sixteen men were bunched together, a classic violation of sound tactics.

"Spread out your men!" Kannon commanded Dương.

"Dangerous. Must not separate, *Trung-Úy*."

"At least position point and flank security."

Dương stopped, shook his head. Then all hell broke loose.

Four

Another week passed with no letter. Chấn worried *Trung-Úy* Ballard would not respond in time.

"Lan, we must talk." He sipped canh rau, the tangy vegetable soup she made to clear him out. "I want to tell you more about our father."

She lit three incense sticks and placed them in the burner. A sandalwood scent mingled with steaming spices. "Our father was born in Sài Gòn. He became a teacher. His—"

"Stop." Chấn raised his hand. In his weakness, the action was like trying to lift a Lambretta. "Father wanted to protect you and never told the complete truth."

His sister took a deep breath as if to prepare for revelation. "What is the truth, brother?"

Before answering, Chấn wondered for the thousandth time, because of his father's deceit and duplicity, what form his rebirth might have taken. Regardless, Chấn decided to reveal to Lan their father's dual life and inconsistencies.

"The Võ family came from the north, near the Red River Delta, not far from Hà Nội."

She refilled his bowl with canh rau.

"Father Thu mastered his studies in Hà Nội. Then he became interested in politics. When Nguyễn Tất Thành adopted the name Hồ Chí Minh and formed the Việt Minh, predecessors to the Việt Cộng, Thu became obsessed with the movement."

When Lan lifted her eyes, Chấn understood she pondered his words.

"But our father was no communist," she said.

"He became one," Chấn said. Convulsive coughing shook his body.

She cradled his head and dabbed his cracked lips with a wet cloth. Then she helped him sip water. "It does not matter."

"Yes, it does." He did not like seeing his sister agitated, but he must prepare her before she heard it from another source. "Hồ

Chí Minh modeled Việt Nam's Declaration of Independence after America's. Our father wanted what Uncle Ho preached, a unified Việt Nam. When the war with the French escalated, Thu jumped at the chance to come south and join the guerrilla movement."

"Father walked the Hồ Chí Minh Trail?" Her tone and the lines in her face reflected irritation and bewilderment.

"Yes," Chấn said, "before the trail got its name. The path was difficult, cut through mountains and jungles."

She wrung her hands. "I cannot believe Mother never spoke of this."

Chấn shook his head. "Mother knew little. She believed what comforted her." He wondered what she must have thought whenever her husband left home in the middle of the night.

"Lan, why do you think our father taught math and science as well as Vietnamese and French to the children of French aristocrats and elite Vietnamese?"

"Brother, you must stop this talk. Father was honorable. He sought to teach young minds."

"Oh, he taught them all right. Father sought to gain the trust of both ruling classes."

Chấn envisioned Hồ Chí Minh shaping his father's idealism. Minh used his father's appearance—his unusual height and slender build, his thick, wavy dark hair, and the wire-rimmed glasses—to belie his foremost role as a guerrilla.

She folded her arms. "What does this have to do with you?"

"Duplicity is the family legacy. After we defeated the French, and the country split in two, Father saw new President Diệm for what he was, a corrupt dictator unable to hold the south together." If Diệm had not been killed in a coup, though, things might have turned out differently.

Tears formed in Lan's eyes.

"Chấn, I am ashamed. Untruths blacken our family."

"You have done nothing to blacken the family name. Neither did your mother and sister when they were alive. You were the honorable ones."

Chấn paused to clear his throat. "Conditions worsened. In 1961, the year of your birth, America started sending advisors.

Father said the Americans would replace the French and fail also, but not before many lives were lost."

"If Father loved us, why did he desert his country? How could he leave you, the one to carry on the family name?"

"Father worried whichever side won, the other would kill him." Father had not said it would kill his son too. "You were seven when I got drafted, which ended my advanced studies. I did not want to fight, but if I did not serve Thiệu's South Việt Nam, I would have been incarcerated."

"Ridiculous. The communists imprisoned you anyway."

He nodded. "Since I spoke three languages, the government thought I would make a good interpreter. They assigned me to work with the Americans in Đức Huệ District of Hậu Nghĩa Province."

Thunder reverberated, portending the daily monsoon. The ceiling fan cooled the air, which soothed his dry skin, a better feeling than his shame from believing destiny decreed a democratic Việt Nam.

His assignment had placed him in a strategic position, providing access to regional force plans, American intelligence, and villagers' mouths. He participated in a simple, covert communication system—using signs, landmarks, and lanterns to inform the NVA and Việt Cộng about troop movements and ambush positions of the U.S. Army and the Army of the Republic of South Việt Nam. Believing he was helping his brothers stay alive, his actions resulted in more deaths than lives saved.

"Brother, return to me."

"My mind strays," Chấn said, shifting position. "When the NVA overran our outpost, they found my regional force uniform. They said since I worked with Americans, I was contaminated and must be cleansed." He retched and regurgitated an ugly blotch of phlegm.

"Father and I had code names and pre-assigned points of contact with contingency backups. If one of us failed to show at three successive sites at the appropriate times, the other was to assume his death. We agreed not to look back.

"I know it was Hai, a wicked man, who ordered me to the camps. Hai lied to my father, told him I was dead."

In a bitter, guttural chuckle, Chấn relived his supreme irony. Only a reeducation camp could purge him of impurities. But he did not lose his impurities: he acquired more. What he lost was his idealism.

"Brother, I listen to your dreams. You speak Hai's name often. Can you not forget?"

His wretched stomach churned whenever he thought of the man who had played him like a mandolin. Hai, a man Chấn once took pity on, because, in his fanatical dedication to the Việt Cộng, Hai had accepted castration, and then watched as his handler burned the *student's* testicles in a fire. Without the ability to reproduce, the theory was, a rebel leader would better perform his mission. Losing the procreative use of his member, however, did not eliminate Hai's emotional desire. As a result, a brutal sadist was born.

"No, Lan. I cannot forget. Hai lives."

Chấn wished he had known the identity of *Chiến sĩ vô Danh* (the Unknown Warrior), and whether he still lived, for he was the only man capable of eliminating Hai. But he never would tell his sister about this.

* * *

"Who is Đăng Đạo?" Lan asked.

She watched his face unmask, perhaps to reveal another secret.

"How do you know this name, sister?"

"You speak of him in your dreams. Not with fear, but with love."

"Đăng Đạo is . . ." Chấn choked. "He is . . ."

"A soldier? A comrade?"

"A younger fellow."

"How young?"

"Two, when last I saw him."

"How well did you know him?"

Chấn's mouth twitched. His eyes implored her to stop.

"Did you know him as a father knows a son?"

She watched tears flood his eyes and roll down his cheeks as he gave birth to her nephew after all these years.

"Your son." Lan balled her delicate fists against her breast.

"I did not say anything because nothing could be done. Hai took Đăng Đạo when they sent me to the camps. Do you forgive me for not telling you?"

"I forgive you." She caressed his cheek. "It is, well, Đăng Đạo is family, and I am frustrated in not knowing him."

"I understand."

She ached for the emotional pain she caused her brother, but she hoped his talking would purge his poison and better prepare him for the afterlife. "Did you have a wife?"

He smiled. "She lived in a hamlet close to Hiệp Hòa village. We planned to marry. She was young and beautiful."

"What happened to her?"

"She was killed when the NVA tanks stormed the district." He sobbed. "You would have liked her."

"Oh, I would have." She tried to visualize the woman her brother had loved. "Do you have a photograph?"

"No."

"Do you know what Hai did with your son?"

"Years later, in the camps . . . I heard the rumor . . . to America."

"Is that why you wish to see Mr. Ballard? To find your son?"

He shook his head. "It is useless."

"Whatever it takes, I will find him."

"Sister." Chấn gripped the sheets. "No more talk of Đăng Đạo. Even if you could leave Việt Nam, you would never find him. America is too big. He is lost forever."

She brushed the hair from her brow. "I will find Mr. Hai. I will ask him where—"

"No." Chấn gasped and spat out phlegm. "You must never engage this man."

"I do not fear the one you call wicked."

"Lan, listen to me. Hai is a sadist. A torturer."

Stepping away from her brother's bed, she leaned against the wall to collect herself. It was fruitless to question him further about Đăng Đạo. Tiring, Chấn worried her. Yet, the realization lodged in her heart that she might have a living nephew. She would try later to obtain more information, after rest and nourishment.

41

"Are you hungry?" she asked.

"No." His lips opened in a weak smile. "Lan, your thoughtfulness and beauty transcend this world's ugliness. It is your love that has kept me alive this long. It is wasted on me now."

"Love is never wasted."

"Ah, you are as sweet as the flower of your birth. You carry your faith as powerful as when the phoenix rises. Are you sorry you never married, that you chose to care for me?"

"I am not, dear brother. I have chosen to be with you." A fleeting image of a long-ago love filled her vision, a Vietnamese scholar working on his doctorate who succumbed to pancreatic cancer. She washed away the image. "When I wrote the letter to Mr. Ballard, you had me sign it, Deer Walker. Why?"

"*Trung-Úy* Ballard gave me the name. He said the Vietnamese reminded him of Native Americans due to the similarity in our body structure and facial features. I should have this name because I moved as silently and gracefully as a deer. He chose Deer Walker."

"Tell me about this American."

Another ragged smile spread across his wan face. Lan knew he struggled to put his feelings into words.

"A good man, for an American. He learned to like our people and our ways, except," Chấn gasped in a pneumonic chuckle, "he could never stomach our nước mắm sauce."

"It warms my heart to see you smile."

Chấn pointed to his cabinet. "In the top left drawer, there is a leather bag."

Walking to the cabinet, she opened the drawer and retrieved a musty bundle. "No, the other one." She replaced the first one, grasped a blue buffalo hide bag and handed it to Chấn, then watched as he withdrew a cracked, leather-bound book.

"Your memories?"

"It is a meditation book *Trung-Úy* Ballard gave me. I want to show you something."

She watched him struggle to turn the pages. Finally, he pulled out an old black-and-white photograph. "Here is his picture."

Lan took it, stared at the image, and chuckled.

"What do you find amusing, sister?"

"His hair looks like goose down."

Chấn laughed. "It was blond like the newborn deer."

"His mustache looks like a sour new moon."

"It turned sweet when he smiled, sister. Made him handsome."

"I have never found Americans attractive." She lingered over the picture. "What happened between you?"

"I liked him, even though the American government raped our country. We accompanied many combat patrols. At first, he listened to his experienced sergeant and to his counterpart, *Trung-Úy* Đinh. *Trung-Úy* Ballard was naïve, but he learned fast.

"As the interpreter, I saw through the eyes of the Americans, but they failed to understand our conversations. That gave . . ." he stopped and cleared the phlegm blocking his passageway. His eyes glazed in resignation and pain as he stared at the ceiling. Lan handed him a cup of tea. "That gave us a great advantage. Often, we told the Americans what they wanted to hear."

"What good was Mr. Ballard?"

"He coordinated artillery and helicopter gunship support when my brothers the NVA and Việt Cộng attacked our outpost, with me in it, even though I had provided intelligence. Some gratitude."

She began to understand what her brother was telling her. "Vietnamese attacking Vietnamese does not make sense."

"No, it does not. Anyway, *Trung-Úy* Ballard wanted the unit to become more aggressive in search and destroy missions, particularly night ambushes."

"I do not like to talk of war."

"I know. But I must show you one more thing," he rasped.

Annoyed, she willed herself to indulge her brother. She watched as he turned the pages of his meditation book. He pulled out a medallion—a star hanging from a faded ribbon—and offered it to her.

She took the star from his feverish, sweating palm and held it to the light. "A medal?"

"Yes. The Silver Star Kannon Ballard earned. He gave it to

me. Said I deserved one as well since they had awarded me only a Bronze." Tears misted in his eyes.

Lan remained silent but embraced her brother.

Chấn regained his composure. "*Trung-Úy* Đinh resented Ballard's brashness. Before Đinh was killed in combat, he often complained to the District Chief and the senior American advisor that *Trung-Úy* Ballard was dangerous."

"How was he dangerous?"

Chấn rolled his vacant eyes. "They put a price on his head."

"A price. What do you mean, a price?"

"They thought Ballard was getting too close."

"Who were *they*?" Lan asked.

Just as she wanted to hear more, her brother collapsed in a stupor. What else was to come?

Lan took the meditation book. When she started to put it into the buffalo hide bag, another photograph slipped out, a two-inch by two-inch portrait. She smoothed its creases and stared at the image. A bright-eyed, bubble-faced baby boy with thick, dark curls stared back.

Five

The bear maintained her observation post on the morning of Kannon's departure. He hoped she enjoyed the fish, for he considered her his ally. With the she-bear's spirit, they would blow through the hedgerows and face down the water buffalo.

It was Tuesday, 1 October. Clumps of evergreens and aspen basked beneath a sapphire sky as Kannon rode down a natural sluice to regain the forest road. The tires crunched through the snow-laden ground. His leathers crackled with each movement. He turned right at the T-junction and soon crested the summit where the Cinnamon Pass sign, withered from age and splintered from shotgun blasts, stood like an abandoned waif. He stopped the motorcycle, dismounted, and walked to the sign. He stroked the weathered wood, thinking how quickly people and places deteriorated without care.

At mid-afternoon, Kannon reached a highway junction and rode north into Silverton. Reminiscences of the past—gravel roads, barn-wood structures, a narrow-gauge steam engine belching out black cinders and smoke—belied outward appearances, because personal computers and cellular phones percolated away in the crevices of historic buildings.

Kannon turned off the main thoroughfare, rode past the Railroad Depot, and then alongside the chalky Animas River, where he and Meghan had first joined their troubled souls. He then cycled to the Post Office and dropped off the letter to Chấn, sealing his commitment to his former interpreter.

Reentering Greene Street, he approached Meghan's pride, the three-story Hotel Victoria that overlooked the wide main street between 11th and 12th. At the bogus hitching post, he snuffed out the shuffling boxer twin, removed his helmet, and lifted his gaze toward one of the modern pioneers. Meghan was one of the few who stayed in Silverton year-round. Standing on the slightly elevated boardwalk, she wore a pastel sundress, which bared her shoulders and suggested openness. Perhaps a tad more filled out since their last visit, her body emanated sensuality, even as she wielded a broom.

"Good Lord. It looks like you rode through a coal mine," Meghan O'Brien said.

"Mud and snow."

"I've been worried." Meghan propped her broom against the wall and descended the steps.

"I ran into a little difficulty." Kannon wanted to hug her, but he was filthy. He gave her a light kiss instead.

"Are you all right?" she asked.

"Yes."

"When you didn't show, I thought about calling the Ranger Station, but I didn't know what to say. I didn't know if you'd had an accident or just changed your mind about coming."

My bad.

"And you didn't have a location."

"No." Meghan brushed some dirt off his jacket. "What happened?"

"I'll tell you about it," Kannon said, "after a hot shower."

Together they climbed the steps to the portico. She sat on the bench, crossed her legs, and patted the space beside her. "Sit for a moment."

"Okay." He smiled inwardly. The probing had begun. That was all right. It was worth it, sitting next to the first woman he'd become interested in since his divorce.

"I heard the tension in your voice when we spoke," she said. "Now I see it in your face. What's going on?"

The wind feathered her auburn hair against his cheek. She carried the scent of lavender. He was sure he carried body odor.

"I crashed during a rainstorm and injured my ankle. It hurt so bad I couldn't ride. I ended up camping in the snow."

"That's what I was going to tell you, the snow forecast for the mountains. But you cut out."

"My battery died." He really needed to shower.

Meghan uncrossed her legs and scooted to the edge of the bench. She faced Kannon, boring down on him with eyes cut from smoky quartz. "The phone call . . . was it before or after the accident?"

46

"Before." She was digging for the source of his tension, Kannon thought.

Meghan leaned back. "I'm waiting."

There wasn't any reason to tell her about the bear. It wasn't relevant to the main issue.

"I received this in the mail." He took the letter from his inside jacket pocket and handed it over.

Meghan unfolded it. The rough-textured paper flapped in the wind and sounded like bicycle spokes trashing a playing card.

"Mysterious. Who is this guy?"

"Chấn, the Deer Walker, was my interpreter in 'Nam. We also became friends."

She pursed her lips as if holding herself in suspension. "You know what this is about?"

Kannon stared at a man's hat being blown down the street. "No."

"What does Deer Walker stand for?"

"I gave him the name." He told her how Chấn glided over the rice paddy muck, moved through the thick brush, stealthy.

"But you don't know what this man's referring to?"

Uncomfortably close to divulging the ambush, his disgrace, and the bear dream, Kannon shook his head. He wanted to tell Meghan things, like how the nightmare reminded him of his fear when first under mortar attack at An Định, or that he was responsible for the death of fifteen men and that he'd been threatened with a court-martial?

"Something awful happened. That's all I'm going to say."

Meghan rubbed her palms over her thighs. "Afraid I'll judge you?"

She hit him with a high, inside fastball. What would she think?

"I wrote two letters on the mountain, both to Chấn. One, saying I wasn't coming, and the second, saying I was. I threw the first one in the fire."

"You think this guy holds the answer to this dreadful event?" Meghan asked, frowning.

"I hope so."

"It was so long ago, Kannon." She paused. "Do you trust Chẩn?"

He hesitated, but, "Yes."

Meghan sighed. "Well, I think you destroyed the wrong letter. You're retired. Let the war go. Enjoy life."

Doubt raised its ugly specter. He squashed the intrusive thought. "I have to, Meghan."

Kannon looked for the hat sailing down the main street. It was out of sight.

"After my husband died, I grieved. When I began to heal, I told him," Meghan touched Kannon's arm and then pointed skyward, "'I'll always love you. And I know you'll understand that I'm ready to move on.'"

The love word jolted him. All she'd said before was that she was widowed. She had revealed another side of her now.

"I'm confiding in you as a friend," he said. "I'd . . . I'd like your support."

"I'm glad you're sharing this." Meghan blew a wisp of hair away from her forehead. "And I respect your decision. That doesn't mean I agree."

"I don't expect to be gone long," he said, standing.

She rose, placed her hands on her hips. "I understand that, Kannon. It's just that, well, I want people in my life who are going forward, not backward."

"No argument." Kannon figured she might not offer a room discount this time. "Once I settle this, one way or the other, I'm done. Forward motion after that. Okay?"

Shaking her head, Meghan grabbed her broom and gave him a playful swat. "Go sign the register. You're in 2G."

* * *

Meghan watched Kannon enter the hotel. Despite his living in the past, she felt a warm flush toward him. His intellect and self-deprecating humor, when he showed it, entertained her. No, entertainment wasn't the right word, it—

"He's the guy you told me about."

Meghan turned as Elizabeth, owner of The Silver Gallop, a specialty shop sporting high end, handmade turquoise jewelry, approached. The two of them shared losses, only her friend had lost her husband through a divorce, not in an automobile accident.

"Been watching from across the street, my dear? Yep, he's the guy." Meghan wondered if Kannon might've lost friends in that war. She'd heard stories, read about POWs. Maybe his distress had something to do with it.

"You didn't tell me he rode a motorcycle," Elizabeth said, her saucer-shaped eyes sparkling like those of a high-school tease.

"I didn't tell you much at all."

"He's kind of cute. Think he'd like to dive into a chubby little bowl of jelly like me?"

"Don't be crude, Elizabeth. He's just here for a day or two. No big deal."

"Nice denial, lady. What's the real deal?" Elizabeth asked.

"Oh, sit. If I tell you, will you stop pestering me?"

The bench creaked as Elizabeth positioned herself.

"He's the first. You know how it is, after being with one man for years."

"I'm into seconds and thirds," Elizabeth said.

Meghan laughed.

"You still miss Jake?" Elizabeth asked.

"In some ways, I'll always miss Jake. I was mad at him for a long time."

"For getting himself killed?"

"My husband had to finish his article for *Out There* magazine." Meghan thought back four years, the freak snowstorm near Blackhawk, the delivery truck that hit a patch of ice, sliding into the opposite lane, and Jake's barreling around the turn.

"Jake's car flipped into the creek, and he drowned, just like that." Meghan snapped her fingers. "One life and a twenty-year marriage scraped off the register."

"Wow. And I thought I had a bad time of it." Elizabeth put her arm around Meghan and hugged her.

"It's okay now," Meghan said, squeezing her friend's hand.

"And this guy, Kannon, he shows promise?"

"I'm not sure. He either showed up at the right time or the wrong time." Meghan cast a measured look at Elizabeth. "His sadness bothers me."

"Forget that. How is he in bed?"

"I'm still not answering that question." Meghan couldn't help but smile.

"I bet he's good. I've heard tell motorcycle riders get a hard-on from the vibration."

"You're terrible." Meghan feigned disdain.

"I can help him unpack, or help him bathe," Elizabeth said, giggling.

"No, he needs help in learning how to live."

Six

Kannon lugged the saddlebags to the second floor and unpacked, then indulged himself beneath a stream of hot water. Afterward, he slipped on a pair of jeans, then connected the laptop to the phone line, dialed in, and went online.

The Embassy of Việt Nam's website flared on screen. He clicked his way through well-formulated cyber options. Requirements for a one-month tourist visa seemed clear, and the application straightforward. Nevertheless, he wanted to see if other options were available and, therefore, he called the Consular Section. For two hundred dollars, a six-month multiple-entry tourist visa was available, and the Vietnamese sponsor requirement could be waived or dropped. Normal processing took ten days, but it could be expedited.

Experience taught him the benefit of due diligence. He would pursue a six-month visa. If his initial visit bore fruit, then perhaps he could entice his son to accompany him on another trip, where he could say, "Stefan, this is where—"

Thunder shook the hotel. He walked to the window, raised it, and poked out his head. The fresh cold washed his face, and the pungent ozone stung his nostrils like smelling salts.

From the west, ominous, dark underbellies of roiling cumulonimbus clouds, their bulbous, leading thunderheads a deceptive white, advanced on Silverton like an artillery barrage. Jagged lightning ripped the sky, overwhelming the waning sunrays that darted like lasers between the clouds.

Glad not to be riding in the storm, Kannon lowered the window and finished dressing. He clunked downstairs in his motorcycle boots, the sound echoing along the worn pine steps. When he entered the lobby, Meghan lowered her teacup and stared at him as if he were a sphinx. "Find the key and release my turmoil," he wanted to say. Instead, he mumbled, "Interested in dinner?"

"I could eat a bite, but I need to close first. Oh, phooey! No one's going to bother this place. Let's go."

"You look nice." He touched her arm as they exited.

"And you look like a ruffian," she said, returning his touch.

They ordered dinner at the Renegade Depot. The bar and restaurant cohabited a room warmed by a massive potbellied wood-burning stove.

"Is there a love in your life?" Meghan sipped on her Cabernet Sauvignon.

An unexpected question, since theirs was a non-exclusive relationship. Yet, it was a fair one and didn't bother him. "Motorcycles and photography. And you?"

"A man in Durango I see on occasion. Nothing serious." She poured more wine.

The bartender stoked the fire with another log. Sparks flew within the metal cylinder. "I apologize for the disturbance, folks. How's the grilled salmon, Ms. O'Brien?"

"Perfect. Tell Louis he still has the touch."

Kannon chewed a bite of grilled chicken and chased it with a swig of Heineken. He told her about applying for a visa.

"Still think you're making a big mistake."

"I know."

"You're chasing ghosts. What do you expect to find? How do you know this Deer Walker isn't using a ruse to lure you back—for God knows what? It's crazy."

Kannon bristled. "I've got nothing to lose. I'm looking for the life I lost over there." He recognized her look—the look a professor gives a recalcitrant student.

"You haven't lost your life. It's inside. You're looking in the wrong places. Only you and God can heal yourself, and that's through forgiveness, a mutual pact."

"I'm going, Meghan. Maybe God dispenses a veteran's forgiveness through a Vietnamese substation. I need to be there to access it."

"I don't think so," Meghan exclaimed. "Let's take a walk. I want to show you something."

"What's that?"

"You'll see."

Kannon paid the bill. They walked out of the restaurant. She led him down the street, turned left, and walked three more blocks. They halted at the Christ of the Mines Shrine.

"Why did you bring me here? I've been saved."

"I love this shrine. We don't have a Loretto Chapel with its magical staircase like Santa Fe does, or even a chapel like the one near Angel Fire that a father built in honor of his son killed in the war. I never told you this, but my husband was a veteran."

"I didn't know." He fought off a stab of jealousy. "But . . . your point is?"

"Faith, Kannon, faith. Trust and let go."

Thunderclaps reverberated among the mountains that enclosed Silverton valley. Even when expected, the sharp retorts rattled him. The skies above Silverton burst and torrents of water began pelting the town.

As he turned to dash for cover, one knee up in the air, Meghan grabbed him by the collar. "Don't run. Life's too short."

Just as he had all the years before, he resisted, pushing away anyone who tried to care. Therapy helped him understand but didn't bring forgiveness. He wondered if the born-again Christian ritual was another sham because what it bestowed upon him seemed only a partial salve. Engulfing waves of shame caused him to lose sight of the Savior. Could he ever forgive himself?

"I appreciate what you're trying to do," he said, acquiescing to her demand to slow down. "But for me, going back is my faith."

"Some people are slow learners. You're tempting fate, not testing faith."

Good words but irrelevant.

"I've already begun arrangements—leave the motorcycle in Durango, fly to Denver, then Austin." And ask his brother Roger to pick him up and drive him to his hill country cloister.

Meghan raised a finger to her chin, as if in thought. "I hope you find it healing."

Silence ensued as they sloshed along the sidewalk. He put his arm around her. She responded in turn, her touch affirming, warming his heart.

"It's nice to be touched," he said.

"I have a surprise," she shouted above the unseasonable

wintry blast.

"Now what?"

"I've added a hot tub out back."

"Super." He shivered as if he were back on the mountain. "Except, I don't have a bathing suit."

"Improvise," she said as they reentered the hotel.

He waited until she disappeared into her bedroom, then took the stairs three at a time. Once inside his room, he cut to mid-thigh a pair of silk liners he wore beneath his leathers and pulled them on. He descended the stairs and exited the back door where a partially submerged Meghan awaited him. A multi-level redwood deck wrapped around the hot tub. A stiff canvas awning shielded the tub from direct rain, which drummed onto the earth. He plunged.

"Ahh!" Kannon said. The hot water offset the chill.

"Here." She handed him a glass of wine.

They soaked. Sipped wine. Whispered tenderness, after which they went to her room. Meghan offered herself to Kannon, mutual pain and loneliness once more the bridge of connection, encrusted souls each hoped to soften with the touch of a body. They kissed softly. Her mouth—warm and moist—invited exploration.

Gently, he caressed her smooth, firm thighs, enjoying her wetness as he worked his way up and stroked her clitoris. She ran her fingertips over his chest, his legs, then stroked his penis. He kissed his way up her body and entered her. It was like immersing his body in a hot spring. He thrust with her as if trying to drive away his demons, and for a few blissful seconds, as the life poured out of him, memories of Việt Nam vaporized from his consciousness.

They lay together. Meghan fell into a peaceful sleep, her breasts gently pulsating from steady breathing. As he lay in her arms, the peaceful sleep he longed for eluded him.

He slipped off her body and went to the window. Lightning flickered to the east. Thunder trailed behind, the muffled rumbling still portentous. The rainstorm that claimed this dusty town had moved on. He walked to a chair opposite Meghan's four-poster bed. He sat down, wrapped a comforter around his body, and waited for his own storm to inundate him.

Five minutes later, Kannon rose from the chair, left her

room, and climbed the stairs to 2G. He flipped on the light switch, and his eyes locked on the reflection in the window—a taut face with wild, tired eyes and creased forehead. He snapped off the light to dispel the image. Only this time, Chấn peered back, waving the letter, imploring Kannon to respond to his call.

6 October 1970, 0300 Hours

AK rounds from the front and right flank ripped into their column. The area seemed to be on fire as muzzle flashes and green tracers poured from the hedgerows. Blood spattered as Dương, and several in his platoon went down without firing a single shot. An AK round slammed into Kannon's M-16, shattering the bolt and magazine well, just missing his hand. A regional force soldier was cut in half by an AK burst. An RPG round blew another soldier's head apart. Still, the remaining regional force troops kept returning fire.

Tossing his useless weapon aside, Kannon grabbed a fallen soldier's rifle. Where the hell was Malcolm?

Kannon emptied a magazine as he sprinted to an opposite hedgerow. A grenade exploded. Shrapnel slammed into his radio and sent him flailing headfirst into the muck. Lying in a depression, Kannon tried to reach Green Phantom and bring the gunships back, but the handset was dead.

Hugging the ground, Kannon slipped in another magazine. When he pulled the trigger, the muzzle ruptured like a peeled banana. The barrel was jammed with mud.

Then, silence. Were all his men dead? Had the enemy withdrawn? He rose to one knee and took stock.

Malcolm's crumpled figure lay against the base of a palm tree. Kannon hustled to his side and checked his pulse. It was weak. Turning him over, Kannon saw nothing but frothy bubbles across his chest. It was a sucking chest wound. Malcolm must've taken the full brunt from a hand grenade.

In their haste to depart, neither of them carried a first aid kit. Even if they had, the plastic from the field dressing was too small to create an airtight seal on the number of holes in Malcolm's chest.

Malcolm opened his eyes. "Goddamn, Lieutenant. You walked us right into it," he growled. Malcolm's head slumped back, eyes wide open, never to see again.

Shrill whistle blasts pierced the sound of rain and thunder. VC in black pajamas and NVA wearing pith helmets peeled from concealment and maneuvered between waving rice stalks. That answered his question about the location of the enemy.

They swarmed the area and raked the bodies with automatic weapons fire. Crawling deeper into the brush, Kannon figured his life was over. But the whistle blared again, and the enemy vanished into the night.

Kannon lay still for thirty minutes. Nothing stirred. He sat up, removed the worthless radio from his back, and leaned against a tree. Twisting off the top of his canteen, he lifted the spout to his mouth and swallowed hard.

Standing now, Kannon scanned the battle scene. His eyes again fell on Malcolm, who appeared to be napping. But he wasn't napping. It wasn't even Malcolm.

Exhausted, Kannon tried to sleep, as if slumber would erase this living nightmare. The sleep didn't come. Instead, fifteen dead men trampled across his brain. He shouldn't have gone out. Should've defied Farber's orders. But he recalled his father's words, words to die by, good words for a pawn. "Follow your field officer's orders, son."

Dawn broke. A crimson sun burned like a fever through an acrid haze thick with moisture. Kannon pulled himself erect and double-timed to Malcolm's body. He knelt, lifted his former mentor on his shoulders, and began the trudge back to the outpost. Progress was slow because he kept slipping off the crowned rice paddy dikes.

He tried slogging through the muddied paddies instead. With his added weight, each step sank further into the muck. Feeling suffocated within the war's grasp, Kannon had difficulty breathing. The stench from Malcolm's body made him gag. He plodded on, stopping every few minutes to rest. Finally, he reached a familiar trail. There wasn't a soul on it.

Why hadn't Chấn sent out a recon? But then, why would he? No radio contact. No way for him to know what was happening. Even if Chấn had tried, he wouldn't have been able to obtain chopper support. Without American advisors on the ground, U.S. regular forces, fearing a trap, seldom responded to South Vietnamese calls for aid. Especially at night.

Yapping dogs told him he was close. Kannon peered through

the fiery haze and saw a pair of Cobra gunships escorting two Huey helicopters—one emblazoned with a bold Red Cross. The gunships hovered while the two Hueys touched down at the OP. Regional force soldiers hollered when they saw Kannon. Two came to his aid and relieved him of Malcolm's body. With the physical weight lifted, the emotional enormity of loss settled in.

Kannon weaved his way through the protective wire and collapsed against a bunker wall. Among the regional forces, Chấn was nowhere to be seen.

Major Farber, followed by Captain Jeffrey, his second-in-command, disembarked from the command Huey. Following them was Lieutenant Lucas Stairn, a gopher.

Farber, his jaw jutting solid like a bulwark, walked toward Kannon. Jeffrey, lean at five feet ten, resembled a laborer or farmer. His narrow, gray eyes contrasted dully with sallow skin, while his military crew cut accentuated the protrusion of oversized ears. A beak-like nose completed a predatory appearance.

These were the last two men Kannon wanted to face. One of the South Vietnamese guys must have radioed in after all.

Farber approached. The major's strut reminded Kannon of the disjointed gait of a mountain goat. He clambered to his feet, standing eye level with the six-foot two-inch major. Kannon managed a weak salute.

Hands on his hips, Farber ignored it. "What the hell were you doing?"

"Sir, we were in a firefight—"

"Lock your heels when I'm talking to you."

"Yes, sir." Coming to attention, Kannon almost fainted but composed himself. "A VC element must have doubled back and laid a classic L-shaped ambush."

Farber leaned forward, his nose touching Kannon's. "You dishonor the officer corps."

Kannon took a deep breath but held his tongue.

Farber turned to Jeffrey. "We don't need an officer like this, do we, Captain?"

"Not in this man's army." Jeffrey's voice sounded as strident as a screech owl's.

"How would you know, Captain Jeffrey!" Kannon kicked the ground in disgust. "You've never seen combat."

"Kill the insubordination, Lieutenant." Farber scanned the outpost, then fixed his stare on Malcolm's corpse as it was being stuffed into a body bag. "Where the hell are the rest of your men?"

He drew a deep breath. "All dead, sir."

The major executed a one-eighty and again got in Kannon's face. Farber jabbed a finger in his chest. "You incompetent bastard. I'm gonna court-martial your ass."

Seven

Agitated, Kannon pulled on a pair of jeans and moccasins, a flannel shirt and a light jacket, and went outside to calm himself. The night was cool and crisp, the fragrances of the land, released by the slashing rain, wafted sweet and poignant. It should always be like this, he thought. After working up a chill, he returned to the hotel and checked on Meghan. Sleeping on her back, her hair splayed over the pillow, she seemed content.

The next morning, he descended the stairs carrying his panniers. Head bowed, she stood at the front desk rifling through some paperwork.

"Good morning," he said.

No answer. What's with the silent treatment?

Outside, a dust devil swirled along the dusty street. The early sun burned crimson, illuminating the washed buildings in a fiery glow. It was as if the town itself had undergone a religious conversion.

After attaching the panniers to the GS, he returned to the lobby. Meghan still ignored him. "Anything wrong?"

She lifted her eyes and blew at a puff of hair dangling over one eye. "I'm miffed."

"Why?"

"Do you always get dressed after making love?"

"I couldn't sleep."

"Bullshit. You're afraid of intimacy. You can't stay in one place, and you can't stay with one woman."

Startled, Kannon looked at her, tempted to proffer another feckless explanation, but instead, said, "I'm not sure what I'll find or what I won't find in Việt Nam. But I've got to go."

She slapped the hotel registry shut, sending loose papers flying to the floor. "You use all those things—Việt Nam, photography, motorcycling—as a crutch. Did nothing I say last night mean anything to you?"

"It means a lot," he said. "But why is it I must be the one to hear and not be heard myself?"

"I hear you. You choose to go to Việt Nam instead of being with me." She walked from behind the counter and put her hands on her hips. "I'm not just a piece of ass, mister."

"I'm not just interested in sex."

"Seems like it. Hit and run. Get lathered up and carry into battle the life I poured into you. You use women to prop yourself up."

"That's not fair," he said. "It takes two to make something work. I like talking to you and being with you. But for now, you're right. I am consumed with Việt Nam."

"Then tell me why. Help me understand."

He scuffed the floor with his boot. "How's this?" he said through clenched teeth. "I was accused of willfully disobeying orders. I was accused of leading my men to their deaths."

She held up her hands, palms outward as if imploring him to stop.

"Major Farber threatened me with a court-martial. And I believe it wasn't my fault. I was set up." He pounded his fist into an open palm. "Could you live with those accusations, Meghan? Because I can't any longer. Chấn is my last hope. I must return."

Meghan's shoulders slumped in resignation. Her eyes turned misty.

"I'm sure that was hard for you to say. I pray you find what you're looking for."

"So do I." He strode out the door.

Eight

Kannon walked through Austin-Bergstrom International and exited to passenger pickup.

"Welcome back to Texas, brother." Roger extended his hand, and Kannon gripped it. "How was the flight?"

"Abrupt." A puff of wind carried the smell of jet fuel.

"I understand," Roger said. "Riding allows you time to decompress. Where did you leave the motorcycle?"

"Durango. For service and storage." As they approached the car, Kannon realized Roger had shaved his mustache and added a few pounds, because his belly strained against his faded tweed trousers and a blue turtleneck. "How's academia?"

"All right. Revising an advanced accounting text. Plan to dump it on the unsuspecting seniors next year."

"Things easier since you got tenure?"

"Worse, actually. There's more pressure to publish."

Kannon nodded. "What's Karen up to?" he asked, feigning interest.

"She's at home. Watching *The Gods Must Be Crazy*. Must've seen it a hundred times." Roger opened the door for Kannon, then walked around the car and squeezed his six-foot five-inch frame into the driver's seat. "What's with the return trip to 'Nam? Little old to reenlist, aren't you?"

Nice jab, Roger. As far as Kannon knew, his older brother suffered no emotional cancer that caused him to hang his head. Kannon sucked in a deep breath and started to retaliate but decided against it. "See you got a new rig," he said, looking at his brother's retro vehicle, a silver Volkswagen beetle.

"Yep. Snazzy, huh? Good mileage, too, especially helpful with the high price of oil."

As they exited the airport, Kannon scanned the runways and bled nostalgic for the B-52 bombers now relegated to another terminus. Wary of attempting substantive conversation, he was content to let his brother ramble over the merits of his new beetle during the thirty-minute drive to his house off Spicewood Springs Road.

Karen, Roger's wife for thirty-five years, greeted them at the door. Standing a foot shorter than Roger, she also had added a few pounds and cut short her red-dyed hair. What hadn't changed were the piercing green eyes.

"Hi, Karen," Kannon said as he entered.

"Hello, Kannon." She saved the smile for her husband. To Karen, her brother-in-law drank too much, squandered away the love of a good woman, and earned every ounce of disrespect from his son. To him, she belonged in the musty basement of a long-forgotten county library.

"Okay, guys, I'm going to bed," she said. "You know where the drinks are."

"Chivas on the rocks?" Roger said.

"Glenlivet," Kannon answered, peering at the portraits of two grown children hanging on the wall. He remained standing as Roger mixed the drinks.

"Here, grab a seat."

"Thanks." Kannon sat on the edge of the mauve sofa while Roger settled into his recliner. "I'm not reenlisting. I'm seeking a clean exit visa."

"I'm not with you," Roger said.

Kannon twirled his ice with a finger. "If you thought you were unjustly accused of something . . . say, child molestation or murder, wouldn't you want to clear your name? Or would you let it ride?"

His brother shifted uneasily. "Heavy question. Depends—"

"On what? Whether it happened to you or somebody else?"

"Pardna, what are you trying to tell me?"

Rising from the sofa, Kannon paced the room. "I received a letter." He told Roger about Chấn, the decision to return to Việt Nam to resolve unfinished business, but not ready to trust his brother's reaction to his shame, omitted reference to the ambush.

"Phew, bro. That's crazy. What do you expect to find after all these years?"

"Peace of mind."

Roger lifted his eyes skyward as if searching for the right words. "You're a decorated soldier for God's sake. What's the big deal? The war is over. Get on with it."

"The big deal is there's more to the story, and it's rotten." Kannon stopped when Roger held up his hand.

"This trouble you've been carrying—you know what the Bible says. Take Christ's yoke, and your burden will be lighter, easier."

Easily said by a man who's never killed, Kannon thought, or lost men in combat. "God has not been accused. I have."

Roger stood and walked to the wet bar. His frame filled the mirror above the sink. After refreshing his drink, he turned back to Kannon. "You searching for a Vietnamese angel to set you free? Care to disclose details?"

The condescension was gone from Roger's tone. "I can't. Not yet."

Both reclaimed their seats.

"Getting information out of you is like reading ambiguous footnotes in a company's annual report. How do you expect people to understand when all you do is shut them out?" The angle of light sharpened tight lines in Roger's face, accentuating the gray strands in his thinning hair.

Kannon lowered his gaze. "You're right. I've been inaccessible. But I have a chance . . . a chance I never thought I'd have, to wipe the slate clean."

"And if you don't?"

"Write a book."

A smile spread across Roger's face. "You'll need an editor."

Kannon gazed through French doors onto a tight cedar deck. Flood lamps illuminated thick cottonwoods cordoning off the rear property line. "There's another possibility."

"Which is?"

"Chấn may want to leave the country."

"We'll sponsor him. I've got connections," Roger said.

Surprised, Kannon almost dropped his Scotch. "I appreciate the offer."

"Besides, I know you're going. You never listen to me,

anyway. I hope the trip helps." Roger removed his pie-shaped lensed glasses and rubbed his eyes, "If you wait till spring break, I could go with you." A lump clogged Kannon's throat like a baseball lodged in a drainpipe. "I need to go as soon as possible."

Roger leaned forward as if to honor the confidence between them. "Your son aware of this decision?"

He wished Roger hadn't mentioned Stefan. "No. I called him last month before I received Chẩn's letter. Invited him to go skiing to celebrate his twenty-seventh birthday."

"How'd he respond to the slopes offer?"

"'Ask someone who cares.'"

Kannon wished the phrase "Who cares?" be stricken from the language. Yet, he couldn't blame Stefan for rejecting the twisted messages he systematically drilled into his son's head. Hell, he'd done the same thing to Stefan his father did to him.

Achieve perfection and I'll love you.

"How do you expect him to be interested in you when you show no interest in him?" Roger said. "You oughta spend time salvaging your relationship."

Kannon brushed back the graying hair cupping his ears. "I'll call him before I leave."

The next morning, after a hearty breakfast, Roger drove him west for an hour before reaching the house Kannon had built on fifteen acres purchased through the veteran's land program.

"See you got rid of the cactus and scrub cedar," Roger said.

"Yep, the place is shaping up. Nobody bothers me. Maintenance is easy, no lawn to manicure, just natural flora the local fauna nibbles on."

"Good luck, sport. Call me if you need anything." Roger reached in his pocket. "Here's a gadget to take with you."

"A pager?"

"Video camera, with a wide-angle lens, disguised as a pager. Comes with a monitor."

"Thanks." Kannon accepted the camera and accompanying instruction booklet. The gift touched him. His brother was more supportive than he'd realized. "Could come in handy."

"Stay out of the tunnels and away from booby traps, like

local women."

"Tell you what," Kannon said over a lingering handshake, "when I get back, we'll have a barbeque, and I'll dump the whole story."

Kannon waved goodbye, then opened his garage—half again as large as the house. Alongside the red Jeep Cherokee and ten-year-old Alfa Spider stood three motorcycles like sculpted warhorses, each connected to a battery charger, waiting for ignition and begging to be ridden.

He entered the house and went straight to his study to prepare for the return to Việt Nam. Afterward, he tested his ankle on a five-mile run.

* * *

Two weeks later, visa in hand, inoculations complete, Kannon called his son's office in Dallas.

"Stefan Ballard."

"Stefan, this is Dad."

"What do you want?"

Jesus Christ! He didn't know ice could flow through a phone line. "Just calling to see how you're doing. Got any interesting cases in progress?" He detected a sigh on the other end, a sigh of exasperation.

"I'm prosecuting two Laotian immigrants indicted for murdering a Cambodian over fishing rights. It happened on Lake Meredith in the Panhandle. It seems they have difficulty sharing. I think the case roots go beyond fishing, though."

His mind drifted as his son spoke about the case. All Stefan had needed to do was use his gifted intelligence and physical attributes to make A's and land an athletic scholarship to The University of Texas. Along the way, Kannon would have supplied the money, the drive, and the car.

The problem was, Stefan scorned the game plan, choosing offensive activities like chess and drama. Kannon recalled his ex-wife's sharp rebuke. "Your son lives in pain because you don't accept who he is." Only now could he admit his envy regarding Stefan's courage to follow his heart.

He should tell him—

"Hey, Dad, you listening?"

"Yeah, I was just thinking . . . I'm proud of you for graduating from Columbia and then finishing in the top ten percent of your law school class." He heard a sharp intake of breath.

"Well, that's a surprise. Better late than never, I guess."

"Should have told you sooner. I've had some things on my mind."

"For twenty-seven years! Shit, Dad. You've always had things on your mind . . . except for Mom and me."

Nice barb, son.

"Stefan, look, I called for a specific reason."

"What?"

"I'm returning to Việt Nam to see an old friend."

"Việt Nam, huh?"

"Yes, I—"

"Bring me a father."

The line clicked dead. Kannon stared at the receiver in his hand. Yes, he would return as a father. If he made it back.

The Orchid

Nine

Five minutes. Five minutes standing in the customs line at Tân Sơn Nhất and the familiar blobs of perspiration, exacerbated by his body's excreting the insidious effect of metabolized scotch, soiled his shirt. What Kannon couldn't metabolize, however, were his son's parting words. "Bring me a father."

"Purpose of your trip, sir?"

"Tourism."

The customs agent stamped Kannon's visa: Monday, 21 October. He was once again in-country.

The Việt Nam Airlines flight from Hong Kong provoked a bewildering array of images, like looking through a kaleidoscope. Except for a few Caucasians from central Europe and Scandinavia, the passengers were Asian, and the majority of them were Vietnamese.

After clearing customs, he peered around the airport. Through the maze, he spotted a Vietnamese man holding a sign with his name.

"I'm Kannon Ballard."

"Hello, sir. I am Mr. Ngọc. Welcome to Hồ Chí Minh City."

That name would take getting used to. Sài Gòn would always be Sài Gòn to him.

"Mr. Ngọc . . . to the Moon over Sài Gòn Hotel," he said, following the man to his car.

A flickering lightning trail trailed away in the west, prescient of the monsoon season's drawing to a close. Raindrops smacked the ground in sporadic, thick splotches. The porous pavement soaked up the miscreant driblets like a blotter.

Riding to the hotel, Kannon observed this new Sài Gòn through a stained windshield. New construction was evident. TV antennas flared above rooftops like stick-figure art. The slick streets played host to all kinds of vehicles jockeying for position. Horns blared incessantly. Diesel trucks emanated their sickly sweet odor. How in the hell did anyone navigate this maze?

At the front desk, Kannon bought bottled water and a detailed Vietnamese/English city map and retired to his room. The furnishings were unspectacular and, other than a low, firm bed, the furniture was modern in its simplicity and could have been placed almost anywhere.

After putting away his clothes and camera equipment, he placed his new English-Vietnamese dictionary on the small desk. Then he spread out the map, highlighting familiar landmarks. He located Bùi Viện Street—Chấn's residence—the repository of Kannon's salvation.

The next morning, Kannon stepped from the hotel and was immediately accosted by enterprising guides overwhelming him with offers.

"Hey, you, I show you Sài Gòn."

He selected a cyclo—a three-wheeled, modified bicycle contraption where the passenger sat in a coal bucket for a front seat while the operator sat behind and pedaled.

Kannon pulled out his map. "*Đấy,*" he said while pointing to Bùi Viện Street.

"Yes, suh. I take you. You Americun, huh? Pay Americun dolla?"

American currency was illegal, yet street merchants flashed U.S. dollars, labeling themselves as qualified players in the black market. The driver gobbled them up like a child consuming Christmas candy.

Sài Gòn throbbed with life, pulsing to its own heartbeat, a quivering mass of machine mobility and street flesh. Việt Nam's population had swollen to almost eighty million, twice that at the end of the war, and it seemed half of the country must be in Sài Gòn.

The cyclo driver dropped Kannon off at the eastern end of Bùi Viện Street. Bristling activity greeted him: hawkers stalking victims, vendors displaying fresh produce, and enterprising chefs roasting chickens over small wood fires. The odor of nước mắm, Việt Nam's piquant fish sauce, added a mystic poignancy to the whole scene.

Kannon pulled the letter from his pocket and read the address for the hundredth time. As he strolled farther along the street, activity subsided. He came to a modest, nondescript two-story house. A weather-worn, faded, slate tile roof angled down sharply from its crown, extending a couple of feet over terra-cotta walls. A tiny, secluded courtyard, cordoned off by an ancient, drooping bamboo tree, extended to the right. Opposite the bamboo stood a cultivated banyan tree. Potted plants dotted the trim courtyard.

Kannon knocked.

When the door cracked open, a stunning face greeted him, the hint of a questioning smile rendered funereal by something beyond his ken, like a whiff of expensive perfume on an elusive woman. You knew you couldn't reach her, couldn't grasp her aura, only knew you'd been transformed—haunted if it were—and you never forgot that you didn't understand.

"*Dạ?*" she asked in Vietnamese. (Yes, well?)

"My name is Kannon Ballard. I've come to call on Võ Chấn."

A puzzled look spread across her face, adding to the allure. Maybe this was the wrong house, or perhaps she didn't understand what he said.

"*Chào ông, tên tôi là* Võ Thị Lan." (Hello, sir. My name is Miss Lan.)

"Do you speak English?"

She compressed her lips in a self-effacing smile. "I speak English well. I am Chấn's sister. We hoped you would come, but this is a surprise."

"You didn't receive my letter?"

"No, we did not."

Confiscated? he wondered.

"How disappointing. I mailed it three weeks ago."

"No matter. What is important is that you are here. Please come in." She gestured as gracefully as a ballerina.

"I'd . . . I'd forgotten Chấn had a sister."

Mesmerized, he locked his eyes on her. Thick, auburn hair, which she wore swept back from her forehead, purled down in smooth layers like a travertine waterfall. Her oval face held the color of peach, the complexion of her arms rich sienna.

Hmm. The color auburn. French ancestry? He'd never

noticed it in her brother.

She had a full sensuous mouth that opened into a tired smile when she spoke. He estimated her height to be five feet three, and she wore traditional white pants, covered by a short-sleeve Vietnamese tunic—its color luminescent teal—the áo dài, a long flowing garment slit high up her thighs and molded to the contours of her body. Deep-set, dark eyes pierced his being with a furious intensity as they probed him from head to toe.

Good lord, what's behind those eyes?

"Cô Lan," Kannon said, remembering to use the prefix, Cô, when addressing a Vietnamese woman, "thank you for seeing me. I am pleased to be here and excited to see your brother again."

Her image brought back the lust he'd felt for these women during the war. It poured over him like a country stream flowing over a low-water bridge crossing. He smiled when remembering what Chấn used to say, "The áo dài covers everything but hides nothing."

"I recall his showing me a black-and-white photograph of his family standing near, where was it, some pagoda?"

"Oh yes, the Xá Lợi Pagoda," Lan said. "Please, take a seat." She indicated a straight-backed chair.

The home was spartan but clean. A Buddha icon sat on a small mantel. Incense smoldered in its belly, releasing through its mouth a thin plume of tinted smoke, scented in Asian mystique.

The main room contained three sturdy chairs and a deeply carved teak coffee table inscribed with a mythical story of Vietnamese culture. A small television set sat in one corner. Off to the left, linen scrims shielded a bamboo bed. An armoire stood against the opposite wall. An open doorway directly in front of him led into a small kitchen. The high-pitched, wailing sound of traditional Vietnamese music played in the background.

He shook off the image of Lan behind the linen scrims.

"Is your brother here? We have much to talk about."

Lan's quick smile contorted into a painful frown.

"Mr. Ballard . . . this is hard," she said. Kannon flinched at the quivering mouth. "My brother Chấn is dying from hepatitis. It is his will to live until he talks to you."

Kannon's heart collapsed like a punctured balloon. The sudden somber mood rendered him silent. He hadn't realized how much he hoped—no, prayed—for an epiphany from seeing Chấn again. His efforts at an easy answer seemed attached to a falling star. His naiveté lived within him still.

"Come," she said.

He followed her up a narrow, winding staircase that moaned under his weight. She led him into a small bedroom where a near-death stench hovered like a malignant cloud.

She motioned Kannon to the bedside. He hardly recognized Chấn, whose body looked as rumpled as the tangled sheet cast aside. He'd aged, aged terribly, looking nothing like the virile young man he remembered. The hair was gone. So was the smile.

"Brother," Lan whispered delicately, "Mr. Ballard has come to see you. Are you awake?"

Chấn's eyelids fluttered. Then his eyes sparkled in recognition. Kannon offered a hand. Chấn took it in both of his hot and clammy hands.

"*Trung-Úy* Ballard. It has been too long." These words exhausted him, and he took a moment to gather strength. "I have much to say," he rattled, "but little time."

"Speak slowly," Kannon said, trying to hide his angst. "It makes me sad to see you ill."

"I must tell you . . . about that night." His breath came torturously short and raspy.

"The night of the ambush."

"Yes. What they did. You see, they . . . they thought you knew. That's why—"

"Knew what, Chấn? Who were *they*?" Kannon fought to suppress his excitement.

But Chấn's eyes faded to black. He lapsed into a deep sleep. It was useless to question him further. Kannon stood helpless and looked to Lan for an explanation.

"This occurs more often," she said.

Not a good sign.

"Has he said much else?"

"In the past few days, he has spoken of our family

73

background, issues I was not aware of. Regarding your situation, I believe he has been holding those words only for you because he fears I will be ashamed of him."

Ashamed. A familiar word. If shame was the issue for Chấn, Kannon damn sure wanted to know the reason. He turned back to Lan.

"This morning, I saw in my brother's eyes the need to release himself from his burden."

She spoke as if she were a poet writing verse, and he stifled the urge to speak as she did. "And?"

Lan shook her head, then gave him a sympathetic look. "He drifted into sleep. Each time I fear he will not wake up."

This is like an endless merry-go-round, Kannon thought, forever chasing the elusive brass ring. His hope wilted like the dry potted hibiscus positioned on the windowsill.

Leading Kannon downstairs, she asked, "Would you like some tea?"

"I would."

Lan motioned him to take a seat in the small courtyard. The mid-morning sun bore down furiously, drawing beads of fire on his forehead. She brought out a carafe of tea and poured him a cup, warm to the touch. She sat down opposite him.

As he drank the tepid liquid, he wanted to shout his frustration. He needed to probe, to push deeper into her family's psyche, to disgorge the vital information that would release him from the devil's hold.

Tempering his impatience, he opened conventionally. "Have you lived here long?"

"This is our family home," Lan said. "Our mother and father settled here in 1949, a year after they married. My father's name was Thu, and my mother's name was Nguyễn Loan. Loan means Phoenix, like the bird, to rise again."

"Pretty name." And a powerful philosophy.

It dawned on him Lan used the past tense when referring to her parents. He refrained from being invasive, choosing not to ask if they still lived. If relevant, she'd reveal it in due time. And then he remembered there had been two girls in the Võ family photograph by the pagoda.

"Lan also is a lovely name. What does it mean?"

"Orchid. Do you think . . . the name beautiful?"

"Oh, yes." Kannon blurted, dribbling tea down his chin. Embarrassed, he dabbed at it with a napkin while she put a hand over her mouth.

An orchid would have to be an exotic hybrid to do her justice. The color of her hair, the shape of her mouth . . . Must be part French, he thought, but he didn't recall Chẩn's ever mentioning a French heritage.

A slight breeze brushed the leaves of the banyan and bamboo trees. "Cô Lan, I know this is difficult," he said, "but please tell me anything you think might be helpful."

She remained silent and motionless for a moment, then pierced him with a resolute stare. She reached in her pocket and withdrew a slip of paper.

"My brother handed this to me this morning."

Kannon reached for the paper, his fingers brushing hers. A light gust whipped the paper from his grasp, and it fluttered to the ground.

He retrieved and unfolded the paper—it handled like crisp parchment—and he stared incomprehensibly at three series of numbers.

457144
447144
44251436

Kannon massaged his forehead. "Cô Lan, do you know what these numbers mean?"

"No, Mr. Ballard. I hoped you would."

"Has he ever mentioned the names Farber and Jeffrey?"

"No."

"What about An Định?"

She shook her head. "We are Buddhists. All my brother said is that he needs to make something right with you . . . so he can die in peace." She hesitated, then added, "And come back as a higher being."

"I'm sure he will."

Teardrops clouded her eyes. "You have helped him already. I saw it in his face."

He anticipated the response to his next question. "Do you know what Chấn meant by, 'They thought you knew'?"

"No." She refilled his teacup.

"Seeing your brother brings back many memories."

The lump in his throat—thoughts of his lost men—nearly strangled him. He averted her startled look. When he faced her again, light danced in her eyes like reflections from a stream.

"How did he become ill?"

"After the war, the communists accused Chấn of being a traitor and confined him to reeducation camps. They tortured him, deprived him of food and medical care. When he came home, I just wanted to take care of him."

Kannon's shame soared. He doubted whether he could ever devote his life to another. "It's tragic and unfair Chấn was treated this way. He was my best Vietnamese friend."

She brushed a wisp of hair away from her cheek. "My brother has suffered terribly. I chose to make his last years as comfortable as possible . . . I am sorry, I am not supposed to cry."

Touched by Cô Lan's tears, he patted her arm.

She smiled. "I feel the respect and affection my brother has for you."

"Thanks. That means a lot." It would mean a lot more if Chấn could explain the message in his letter. "May I look in on him again?"

"Certainly, please use the backdoor," she said. "I will wait here."

Pushing on the armrests, he rose, entered the house, and went up the stairs and into the bedroom. His former interpreter still slept on his back. Kannon leaned over him.

"Chấn. Chấn the Deer Walker," he whispered. Not an eyelid flickered.

The room swam in psychedelic heat, and a ceiling fan revolved in futility. If only he'd come sooner.

On the opposite wall, he noticed a chest. He was tempted to tiptoe across the room, pull the drawers open, and examine the contents. But he couldn't invade . . . wouldn't breach her trust.

She looked up expectantly when he returned to the patio. He shook his head. The light left her eyes.

"Well, I guess it's time to go," he said. "It's been a pleasure visiting you."

"I would ask you to stay, but he may sleep for hours."

"I understand. Do you have a phone?"

"Yes."

"I plan to remain in Sài Gòn as long as necessary . . . or until they run me off. Please call if he can talk again."

"I will."

He scribbled his hotel room and phone number on a piece of paper and handed it to her. She gave him hers as well.

"*Chào*, Mr. Ballard."

"*Chào*." He touched her shoulder, hoping to draw her into an embrace. She stiffened and pulled away. He'd misread the situation and took this as a rejection. As for the long-sought answers from Chấn, they seemed lost.

* * *

Lan watched the American walk down the street, sorrowful for the dejection in his slumped shoulders. The camp walk, her brother told her, when hope diminished.

She flung the remaining tea over the splayed roots of the bamboo tree. Why was she not happy and relieved Mr. Ballard had come?

Somehow, however, Lan worried she had done wrong, unsure if she had told Mr. Ballard too much or too little.

Talking about her family's history confused and embarrassed her. How could she disclose to the strange American that both her father and brother had been double agents? But she could not imagine her brother betraying anyone, even an American like Mr. Ballard.

Besides, what her brother said, "They thought you knew," implied others were the cause of Mr. Ballard's distress and not her brother. Yet, Chấn kept saying he was the one who did wrong.

She gathered the teapot and cups and carried them to the kitchen. Placing the dishes in the sink, she ran the water, turned off the spigot, and walked into her bedroom. A framed photograph of her mother and father hung over the armoire. Now she wondered if she ever knew them.

Trời ơi! Flustered and frustrated, she feared for her sanity. How much longer could she withstand the strain? Her life and the Võ family narrative had been ripped apart, and she did not know how to put it back together.

Lan trudged up the stairs. Chấn slept, but his breathing was erratic, like that of a newborn puppy.

"Brother Chấn, what have you done, and why have you not told me what to do?"

Yet her brother slept on.

Ten

As Nguyễn Hai strode along Nam Kỳ Khởi Nghĩa Street toward his business, The Grand Plantation, the sultry weather reminded him of the unseasonably warm day he commenced his trek down the Hồ Chí Minh Trail. From an early age, he had determined to make a name for himself. He began by experimenting with dogs and cats—muffling them, skinning them alive, soaking their raw bodies in gasoline, then igniting them. A school principal recommended him to a North Vietnamese Army Intelligence Officer.

"Comrade Hai, would you like to assist the Việt Cộng in their glorious struggle to liberate the south and unite Việt Nam?" the intelligence officer had asked. "You can perfect your techniques and extract valuable information from the enemy."

The idea of working with Việt Cộng assassination and interrogation squads and helping to unite his country held a strong appeal. When he had left behind his home in Hòa Bình, southwest of Hà Nội, he suffered no qualms from resettling. Since then, he had come a long way.

Reaching the street entrance to his business, Hai input his security code, opened the door, and entered his world decorated with jade-encrusted marble dragons, fanciful silk tapestries, and in the center, a six-foot-long bronze tiger. The internal electronic security system already had been deactivated, which meant either Ling, Đăng Đạo, or both, were already there.

Hai locked the front door and rode the elevator to his second-floor office. He walked across the room and sat behind his desk, then turned to face Ling, his ethnic Chinese Director of Operations seated on an austere wooden chair.

"Who is he?"

"A round eye. I do not know specifically," Ling said.

Hai cast a side-glance at Đăng Đạo, whose five-foot five-inch frame filled the vintage chaise lounge he stretched upon. Returning the look, his son sat up and combed his hands through long, jet-black hair. With an amused look, he licked his lips and observed Ling.

"You do not know!" Hai pushed away from his elegant Louis XV rosewood desk. He rose and moved toward the Chinaman. "Did you follow him?"

"Yes, sir, but I lost him."

Hai backhanded Ling's cheek and catapulted him to the floor. Ling wiped the blood trickling from his mouth with a handkerchief, then stood, righted the chair, and retook his seat.

"Mr. Hai," Ling said, "I cannot get close without compromising our position."

"You impudent minion. How dare you question my command, yes?"

"I mean no disrespect, sir. Chinese reticence."

"Chinese reticence. Ridiculous. No wonder you primitive Asians have never won a war."

"May I?" Ling pointed to a pitcher of water.

Hai nodded.

Ling tipped the pitcher and filled a glass. He raised the glass to his mouth and swallowed hard. "The round eye might be a Russian doctor the woman brought in."

"No, no doctor, I think." Hai paced around the room and then returned to his desk. "Chấn is close to death. No doctor can help him. Show me the photograph."

Ling handed it over. Hai studied the print but did not recognize the man. "Đăng Đạo, look at this. Familiar?"

Đăng Đạo rose from the chaise lounge. The sharp creases in his American-bought clothes crinkled as he approached the desk and sat on a corner to study the image.

"No, Father. Might be Russian . . . or Scandinavian."

Was he recruited from the other side of the border to disrupt his trafficking of goods? Hai wondered. Or could this be an American? More of them were entering his country now.

Hai turned to Ling. "Do you believe he has told his sister anything?"

"No, sir," Ling replied. "Chấn will take the secret to his grave. He knows you would kill Cô Lan."

Hai returned to his desk and wrote two names on his letterhead. "Ling, see if either of these men has registered a business in Sài Gòn. As for this other round eye," he held the photograph aloft, "get the surveillance tapes and passenger lists from airport security."

"Great Buddha. That is impossible."

Đăng Đạo's firm jaw lines hardened as this time he popped Ling. "You lazy Chinaman! Get off your ass and get to work."

Hai was not finished. "Check the major hotels beginning three days before you spotted him. Compare round eye names and faces. Report tomorrow at 1700."

Ling bowed and left. Đăng Đạo waited until the door closed before speaking. "I am curious, Father, why you have never spoken about this man Võ Chấn?"

"He betrayed me during the war."

"How?"

"Assisted the Americans."

"Then why did you not kill him?"

"Because once we were like brothers. And he has been useful. We will speak of it no more." Hai collected the photographs and slipped them inside an envelope. "When do you return to America?"

"In two days," Đăng Đạo replied.

Hai walked to the window. He looked down at the masses swarming down Nam Kỳ Khởi Nghĩa Street, its tree-lined sidewalks courtesy remnants from the French. It saddened him to witness the decline of much of the old colonial architecture.

On the other side of the coin, the country was rebuilding. When Hai had started The Grand Plantation, his legitimate business front, all he brokered were inexpensive garments and shoes, a little coffee, and tea. Slowly, he expanded to include rubber products and rice. Imports had grown to include cotton and small pieces of machinery and equipment. He wanted to add steel to supply the myriad joint venture construction companies setting up shop in Việt Nam. His firm traded with Singapore and Hong Kong, Taiwan, South Korea, Thailand, and now America.

Rice was the staple export. He liked its packaging potential.

Amazing what you could stash inside large bags of rice. Which brought him back to Đăng Đạo.

"Let's have your report," Hai said.

"As instructed, we have increased the number of distributors to five-member cells in each of the twenty largest population centers."

"Does your core group consist of only Vietnamese?"

"One exception."

Hai cast a reproachful glance. "Explain."

"He is of mixed race—Italian and Hispanic. He was abused as a child but talented."

"Son. It is dangerous to mix cultures. Be careful."

Đăng Đạo's lower lip twitched. "Yes, sir."

"Largest expense item?"

"After the cost of the product . . . personnel. Retaining qualified distributors continues to be a major problem. Everyone wants a bigger piece of the pie."

"Do many of them try to establish their own network?"

Đăng Đạo nodded.

Hai stared at the ceiling, then at his son. "How do you handle that?"

"With discipline," Đăng Đạo said.

Hai decided not to pry.

"Good."

Hai massaged his temples while Đăng Đạo reported stable sources of supply from Columbia and the Far East, with Mexico being the primary conveyance route. His son concluded by summarizing the cash positions held in offshore Isle of Man and Cayman Islands' accounts.

"Concentrate no more than fifteen percent of funds in one bank." Hai noticed a look of humility, or was it defiance, in his adopted son's eyes. "I want to see the computer reports."

Đăng Đạo flipped open his laptop and entered two security passwords, then sat down.

Hai keyed in the third password, clicked, and clicked again. A tabular report scrolled onto the screen. Hai studied, by region, the revenues, gross trading margins, and net earnings—percentages as well as dollar fluctuations. After asking a few questions, he went to the summary notes.

"Ecstasy's profit margin percentages continue to be the highest. Local manufacture?" Hai asked.

"Yes, sir," Đăng Đạo said, "but we buy direct. Too complicated to become involved in manufacturing operations."

"Correct answer," Hai said. "Heroin revenues are down in Regions Three and Five. Why?"

"The product mix is changing. There is a shift to more free-based coke. If you look—"

"Yes, yes, I see. Concentrate on our staple."

"Yes, sir," Đăng Đạo said.

"Overall, good work, son." Hai allowed himself an inward smile as he glimpsed at his son's college diplomas from the states— honors graduate with a double major in linguistics and computer science, then an MBA. "I have an additional assignment for you."

Đăng Đạo waited while Hai scribbled on a pad.

"These are the names I gave Ling. Christian Farber and a Mr. Jeffrey. I do not know the last man's first name. I worked with these Americans during the war," Hai said, handing Đăng Đạo the note. "If Ling fails, find out if they live, and if so, where, and what they do."

"Do you think there is a connection between these men and the new round eye calling on Cô Lan?"

"It is possible. Men like Farber and Jeffrey might seek revenge, but they will instigate others to do their dirty work."

"You will keep me apprised of Ling's success or failure?" Đăng Đạo asked.

"Of course."

Eleven

Kannon plodded through the stifling heat and humidity back to the Moon over Sài Gòn, his frustration and dejection paramount. He'd come halfway around the world only to find his link to the past embraced in the clutch of death.

Chấn's cryptic messages hung over him like Huey Cobra Gunships hovering above their prey, only the Cobras could act, executing decisive maneuvers rendering conclusive judgments. It seemed to Kannon every time he tried to clean up the toxic waste dump that was his Việt Nam, another contaminant popped up.

"They thought you knew," reverberated through his brain like someone pounding on an anvil.

Numbers. He'd worked with numbers all his life—explaining to analysts and laymen the meaning of financial statements and footnotes. But now, three simple number sets mocked him: a cipher or some sort of code, but what? They might be from the shackle code system used to disguise radio frequencies, patrol objectives, and other secure information. Yet, he couldn't remember if those codes contained alpha, numeric, or alphanumeric characters. Even so, he had no book, no clue to decipher them.

Feeling lost amid the swelling mass of humanity, Kannon walked. Street vendors jostled him, their clammy touch making his skin crawl. A legless beggar vaulted by swinging his arms like a chimpanzee—definitive, on a mission.

Overwhelming loneliness washed over Kannon like a monsoon, and he ached for Meghan's kisses in the rain.

* * *

Before he went to bed, he called Lan. When he woke up the next morning, he called Lan. The answer was the same. "No, Mr. Ballard. I will call you when appropriate."

When appropriate! As in, he'd been inappropriate.

He moped, then ordered breakfast. The steamy aroma of fried eggs and bacon grew stale as he probed his memory, trying to tap into dormant brain cells to reveal the key to "they" and "who" and "knew" and random sets of numbers.

The clock radio displayed 1:27 p.m. when the phone rang.

"Mr. Ballard. He is awake and asking for you."

He raced out the hotel door and into a waiting taxi. Seven minutes later, he stood on the Võ family doorstep. She met him there, a look of anguish on her face.

Oh no, Chấn's dead!

"I fed him canh, a vegetable broth. He seemed alert. But right after I called, he fell asleep again."

Kannon sighed in relief. "Did he say anything?"

She shook her head.

* * *

Later in the day, they went upstairs.

"I will try again to wake him." She laid a hand on Chấn's chest as one would a baby. "Brother, Mr. Ballard is here."

"*Trung-Úy* Ballard, I want my joss sticks," Chấn said, never opening his eyes.

Kannon shrugged in bewilderment.

"Buddhists believe burning incense is a way of connecting with the afterlife," she said. "These are special ones. I will get them."

He waited until she went downstairs, then moved closer to the bed. "Chấn," he whispered, "who thought I knew . . . what?"

No response.

"The numbers, Chấn, what do they mean?"

No response.

Hearing Lan's footsteps on the staircase, Kannon stepped back and sighed in exasperation. She entered the room, tears in her eyes.

"What's the matter?" Kannon asked.

"They are all gone," she said. "I wish we had more."

"Can you get them?" he asked.

"In Chợ Lớn," she said.

"Then go," he said. "I'll wait here."

"No. I will not leave him."

"Okay. I'll get the joss sticks."

* * *

The taxi driver read the address Lan had written down and handed the notepaper back to Kannon.

"Hokay," the driver said. "You pay American dolla?"

Kannon nodded.

"Good," the driver said. "We see Chinese pagoda."

They wove southwest through the city center and turned off Nguyễn Trãi Street. Thirty minutes passed before the driver brought the cab to a halt alongside a narrow alleyway.

Kannon hopped out.

"Chờ," he said, telling the driver to wait.

"Hokay," the driver said.

Kannon stared in the direction of the driver's outstretched hand. Entering Chợ Lớn was like dropping through a hole and landing in another dimension—a city within a city, a culture within a culture—the ethnic Chinese market commanded a sizable percentage of Sài Gòn's commerce. In this tight confine, Chinese swarmed like ants.

He scrambled down the sidewalk, his hustle fitting into the Chợ Lớn maelstrom, where legal and illegal tender exchanged hands twenty-four hours a day. Toothless old men on the sidewalk clicked Mahjong tiles. Cackling voices fractured his concentration like shattered glass.

Shortly, a pungent odor seared his nostrils. He stopped in mid-stride, pivoted to his left, and entered the pagoda. Thick smoke swirled about the room as if it were on fire. Repeating Lan's words, he asked for Ông Sư, the presiding monk. Presently, a man wrapped in saffron robes, who looked to be a hundred years old, shuffled forward. His silvery beard flowed like silken threads down to his chest. He bowed before Kannon.

Kannon returned the gesture before handing him the written note. The monk padded away while Kannon waited anxiously. The monk returned with a package of foot-long joss sticks, wrapped in waxed brown paper. Kannon thanked him, took possession of the parcel, and paid in the local currency, dong. Holding the parcel like a football, he emerged from the pagoda and threaded his way toward the cab. Just before he turned into the alley, he glanced across the street and found himself the subject of a telephoto lens.

Round-eyes are still a novelty, he guessed. The man lowered the camera and smiled. It wasn't a friendly smile but a knowing, invasive one.

Disquiet swept through Kannon.

* * *

"I trailed the man at a discreet distance back to the Võ home," Ling said. "After Lan let him in, I drove here."

Annoyed, Hai studied the photographs and notations. Kannon Ballard was an American, and from Texas. He drummed his pencil on his desk. Who was Kannon Ballard, and what was he doing with Chấn?

"Another thing, sir. The Ministry of Interior and the Ministry for Foreign Affairs both report a Farber & Jeffrey, Inc. application for an import and export license. No executed contracts or negotiated office space are shown as yet. It appears their interest lies in brokering."

They must be the same Farber and Jeffrey, Hai thought. And perhaps this Ballard walked point to gather intelligence from Chấn for the purpose of destroying his network.

It is possible. I must discourage their presence.

"Ling, track the progress of the license. Keep me informed. Now, I will send a message to Mr. Ballard."

* * *

When Chấn didn't awaken at the burning of the joss sticks, Kannon returned to the hotel. Exhausted, he helped himself to a Beer 33 from the minibar. He sat down on the bed and fluffed the pillows.

After finishing the beer, he stripped, walked to the bathroom door, and opened it.

A rancid stench like a clogged-up commode assailed him. Irregular drops spattered the shower floor, resonating in the stall as if it were an echo chamber. He flicked on the light switch. A purplish fluorescence bathed the closet-sized room. He yanked the shower curtains apart. Bright red globules, iridescent in the artificial light, swam down the drain. His eyes traveled up the dripping stream. He reeled back, stunned.

The severed head of a tiger cub hung from the showerhead,

its eyes pointing directly at him.

Twelve

They poured out of the spider holes like angry rats fleeing a flooding cistern. Whooping and hollering, tomahawks flailing and arrows flying, they chased him down a sinuous trail cut through an intricate maze of palm and bamboo. He looked for the cave. Seeing an opening, he lunged for it and smacked his face against an earthen wall.

Groggy, he got up. Ran. A splayed root from a massive bamboo tree grabbed his ankle and flung him headlong into rice paddy muck. He struggled to get up, but his sodden legs turned rubbery and betrayed him. He thrashed his arms, tried to swim through an eddy thick as molasses. Then they were about him, swarming above his body like killer bees and jabbing him with dung impregnated punji stakes. They brought him before the face, a tiger face. And . . . a bell rang.

The phone jarred him awake. Disoriented, soaked from perspiration, he needed a moment to adjust to his new room. He looked at the clock. The LCD display read 3:17 a.m.

He answered gruffly, "Ballard."

"Mr. Ballard, it is time," Lan said.

"I'm coming." He scrambled out of bed and yanked on his clothes.

"Incredible," Kannon muttered as he exited the hotel and stepped out into the fetid air. "There's still a glob of traffic."

A wall of pollution corralled the city's light and bounced it back like a gigantic photoflood reflector. A three-quarter moon hung diffused above the noxious curtain. He hailed a motorcycle taxi. Several minutes later, he disembarked in front of the Võ residence.

Within the garden enclave, an odd shape hung from a limb of the knurled banyan tree, catching Kannon's eye. He took a closer look. Strange! Why would anyone hang an animal carcass . . . ? A cold shiver rippled through him as though he'd been packed in ice. The animal was the headless torso of the tiger cub. Disgusted, he cut it down and hurled it onto the street.

The house lay quiet. Kannon's mood vacillated between solemnity, fear, and anger as he approached the heavy wooden door and knocked. Lan opened it with the touch of an angel.

"Come in, Mr. Ballard. I apologize for calling you in the middle of the night."

"It was necessary," he said.

The joss sticks emitted lazy, pencil-thin columns of smoke, a sickly sweet aroma. Small, flickering candles cast shivering darts of light on eerily blank walls. Buddha seemed to peer down from his perch in melancholy.

He walked upstairs and tiptoed to the bedside. A stench lay suspended like a low, menacing storm cloud, waiting for the cry from the afterworld before dropping its veil and embracing the Võ household. He revolted at the smell in the room, fought to suppress the bile threatening to choke him.

Chấn lay motionless, his breathing steady but labored, his eyes translucent, as though tendering a clear passageway to the next life. Kannon gingerly grasped his hand. Chấn sat up with a start, his face aglow. It transformed a death look into one of ephemeral exultance, yet his eyes seared through Kannon's and burned into the wall beyond.

"You must find . . . *pha . . . hang. Pha . . . hang.*"

"Chấn. What? What?"

"The monsoon . . . killed the tiger."

Chấn coughed horribly, gasping for the air blocked from his lungs. He was choking to death on his own mucus. Lan rushed forward and shoved Kannon aside. She turned Chấn's head to the side, poked her finger down his throat, and tried to clear his passageway.

Kannon grabbed Chấn from behind and pulled him upright. He wrapped his arms around Chấn's waist, made a fist, and placed his other hand over the fist and thrust. It didn't do any good. He lay his former interpreter's frail body back down and massaged his chest, but it was too late. Chấn suffered his death rattle, a frightening cacophony of guttural cries, and then, a final sigh.

Kannon's hope departed along with Chấn's soul. Nevertheless, he touched Lan's elbow and said, "I'm sorry."

"I want to be alone with him."

"I understand."

This was not the time to tell her about the tiger. He descended the stairs and left the house.

* * *

After Kannon left the room, Lan folded a piece of paper containing the Võ family's mantra, *Follow the Middle Path,* and wrapped it in a blue cloth. Then she wove a string through the amulet and placed it around her brother's neck.

She stepped back from the bed to watch his soul depart his wracked shell and join the mystic smoldering on its journey to the afterworld. Surely, she thought, brother Chấn had suffered enough and sought truth sufficient to justify his coming back as a higher being.

Despite the heat, she shuttered the windows to muffle the outside din. She opened her armoire and set the somber yellow áo dài on her bed. Then the tears came. For a solid hour, they poured from her eyes and down her cheeks until there were no more. Only then could she call and arrange for her brother's body to be wrapped in layers of cloth, soaked in oil, and cremated.

It was time to cleanse herself. She took off her clothes, stepped into her bathroom, and bathed until she washed the death away.

Feeling restored, she walked upstairs and opened the cabinet drawer that contained her brother's blue cloth bag and meditation book. She prayed he would understand why she must read his work now.

Lan sat down and leafed through the book. Poems. She didn't know Chấn had written poetry. The name Thủy-Châu repeatedly filled the title line. She must have been Đăng Đạo's mother. Lan envisioned the young peasant girl who had opened Chấn's heart. What did she look like? What was her nature?

Would she and I have liked each other?

She read on—about pain and separation, and love and togetherness and longing and fulfillment.

Lan read one passage aloud.

91

A lovefire starts slowly
flickering flames, kindle, touch,
then ignite, embrace, and entangle.
Lovefire is born,
passionate, provocative, powerful,
feeding off its own core.

She turned the page. A piece of folded paper fell out. She picked it up. It handled stiffly and crinkly, like parchment. She unfolded it, gently smoothing out the edges. It looked like a child's drawing, with squares and triangles and water ponds and squiggly lines. Could her nephew Đăng Đạo have done it? she wondered. She refolded the paper and slipped it between blank pages of the book, then read herself to sleep.

* * *

Back at the hotel, Kannon collapsed into bed with his clothes on, nightmarish images disturbing his subconscious.

Hours later, the macabre display of the tiger cub and enigma of Chấn's messages jolted him awake—death and random words with three sets of numbers swimming in turmoil. Was the man behind the camera connected to the tiger? Whoever carved the carcass put Kannon and Chấn together. Or was Lan the connection?

He picked up the phone and started to dial. He needed to warn her, but of what?

Couldn't do it, he'd interrupt her grieving. Frustrated, he slammed the receiver onto its cradle.

Instead of calling, he searched for an answer to his puzzle, but there were too few pieces and no shape. Chấn's words, *pha* and *hang*, stumped him. The words burrowed under his skin like hill country ticks, and Kannon wasn't sure if they had been spoken in Vietnamese or English.

Sitting at the desk, he clipped a Cohiba and opened his English-Vietnamese dictionary. The Vietnamese language befuddled him. The same letters formed words of many meanings, depending on the enunciated tone and inflection of each syllable when spoken, or placement of distinguishing diacritics when written.

Pha had several meanings in Vietnamese. Among them were

to mix, to joke, and, if used with a diacritic—as in *phá*—to destroy or demolish. When used in conjunction with other words, forget it, the alternatives seemed endless.

He tried phonetically sounding out *pha* in English—fai, fedra, fan—no relevance. He tried a different angle—far—as in Farber? It was a stretch, but possible, although he couldn't put it into context because *hang* brought forth no recollection at all. He'd never served with anyone whose name sounded remotely like *hang*.

Other than being a mixed metaphor or parable or whatever the hell it was, who or what was the monsoon, and what was the connection with the tiger? And Chấn said he, Kannon, was supposed to have known something.

Damn it. Nothing made any sense.

Kannon rose from the table and walked to the window. The sun hung hot and high over the horizon. He chewed on the cigar and stroked his mustache while gazing at the street scene below.

He'd feel better if he ordered something to eat. Kannon called room service. The manager himself brought his order: steamed rice, chicken, and bamboo shoots.

"I hope everything is alright, sir."

"About the tiger cub . . ."

"Yes, sir?"

"What action have you taken?"

"Internal security is working on it, sir."

Internal security, whoever it was, hadn't spoken to him. Kannon stared hard at the young man, trying to extract the truth from his inscrutable face. Resolute, the young man stared back.

The more Kannon considered it, he didn't need internal security, the police, or anyone else interfering. He preferred to remain anonymous. "On second thought, you and I can handle this ourselves." Kannon pulled a twenty-dollar bill from his wallet and held it in front of him.

The expression on the manager's face conveyed that he was not unhappy with the suggestion and took the bill. "Thank you, sir. I will provide excellent service."

"I'm sure you will."

Kannon sat down to eat but couldn't find his appetite. The

butchered tiger cub haunted him. A symbolic murder? Was he or Lan next? His chest reverberated as if he were sitting front row at a quarter-mile drag race when he placed the next call.

"*Chào*," she spoke into the receiver.

"Lan. I know this is a bad time to call," he said.

"What is it?" she said, sounding annoyed.

"Something ugly has happened. I need to see you."

"Oh, not now."

"I must," he said, his voice unsteady. "You may be in danger."

Thirteen

Waiting next evening at the Lemongrass Restaurant on 4 Nguyễn Thiệp Street, recommended by the now deferential hotel manager, Kannon was chewing on the same unlit Cohiba when Lan arrived. A cultivated mandarin tree with burnished, reddish-orange fruit sequestered the table from other diners. A purple orchid, its petals trembling from the downdraft of a ceiling fan, floated in a bowl of water.

Despite the solemnity, he couldn't take his eyes off her. She wore a flowering pink áo dài, its delicate, silken texture a stark contrast to her dark features swathed in grief.

He pulled out a chair for her, then reclaimed his own. "Are you all right?" Kannon placed the cigar in his shirt pocket.

"Yes. I was prepared for my brother's death. But my life is empty now."

"Is there anything I can do?"

"No, thank you." She uncrossed her legs and leaned forward, elbows on the table. "What is it I have to fear, Mr. Ballard?"

"Please, call me Kannon."

"All right."

A waiter approached. They ordered a fruit dish of mango, mandarin orange, cucumber, and papaya. Kannon waited until the waiter walked out of hearing range.

"Your brother's words, 'The monsoon killed the tiger.'"

"I do not understand."

Kannon told her about the mutilated tiger cub, the severed head hanging from his shower stall, the bottom half suspended from the banyan tree.

"Oh. How hideous!"

Her lips quivered as if disbelief suspended her reality. He wanted to hold her, comfort her, and soothe himself in return.

"At first, I regarded the monsoon as a parable for the war," Kannon said. "Now I'm not so sure. Monsoon could refer to a person or a rogue Việt Cộng cell."

95

Lan hunched her shoulders.

"I have hurt no one. Why would anyone want to harm me?" She sounded tired, overwhelmed.

"I don't know," he answered, "unless someone thinks you have damaging information."

"Nothing." She looked up as if appealing to Buddha for help. "Oh, except, often in his sleep the last few weeks, Chấn mentioned the names Đăng Đạo and Hai. I asked him about them. Do you know the names, Kannon?"

He raised his eyebrows. He remembered the names all right. Each gouged his memory, polarizing the sweet and the rancid.

"They mean something to you," she said. "What is it?"

Unlike the probes and challenges from Meghan and Roger, Lan's simplicity disarmed him. It opened a spillway, a soft corridor in which to travel, but he didn't want to enter just yet.

"What did your brother tell you?" Kannon asked.

"Đăng Đạo is his son, my nephew."

"I take it you never met Đăng Đạo."

"No."

"Do you know if he survived the war?"

"I believe so, but Chấn told me to forget him."

"Why?"

The waiter came and placed before them bowls of fresh fruit and glasses of blended pineapple/papaya juice.

"Chấn said Hai sent Đăng Đạo to America."

Sending Chấn's son to America didn't seem to fit with Hai's reputation. Did Lan know more than just a fringe about Hai's character?

"I never encountered Hai. I knew of him as a Việt Cộng leader," Kannon said. Local Vietnamese called him the butcher. "Did your brother say anything else?"

"He is a wicked man," she said.

"You said, is. You mean—"

"Yes, he is alive."

He wondered why Chấn would tell Lan about Hai, unless Chấn believed Hai represented an overhanging threat to his sister. He slapped an oval-shaped mango around his plate like a hockey puck as a muddled, improbable picture of Hai, Chấn, Farber, and Jeffrey formed. Farber, the nightmarish major who ended Kannon's dream of becoming a general officer, fit the puzzle.

Yet, he couldn't fathom Chấn's setting him up for an ambush. Or why! Unless, Hai had threatened to kill Lan and other family members if Chấn didn't cooperate. In war, fear-induced duplicity created strange partnerships. Squashing doubt was like trying to stuff vapor in a bottle.

"Hai may be behind the butchered tiger cub," Kannon said.

"What would he want with us?"

Kannon cornered the mango and snipped off a bite.

"I think, Lan, that's one thing your brother wanted to tell me."

"If only he could have said more." She looked sad, defeated.

She wished for it? Kannon wished it more. Chấn—the Deer Walker—the man he hoped would reveal the answer to his perennial nightmare, would divulge nothing further. Yet, there was his Texas home for him to return to, and family. As for Lan, it seemed as though little was left of her world, not to mention the potential danger facing her.

"I'm concerned about your safety," he said.

"Safety?" She brushed her hair back as if dismissing his alarm. "I can take care of myself, but I will remain alert." Lan made direct eye contact. "What I really want is to find out about my nephew."

Kannon understood this.

"Did you ever see him?" she asked.

"Yes." Kannon rolled back in time. "I saw him. He was about two. A handsome little fellow. He looked just like your brother."

She raised her glass and rolled it between her fingers. "Chấn and Thủy-Châu must have held high hopes for the baby when they named him."

Kannon watched her pull an envelope from her purse. She opened it and removed a photograph. "Does this look like the boy?"

Kannon took the photograph and examined it. "That's the boy," he said, grinning. "I took this photograph."

Lan smiled in return, seemingly grateful for the connection. She set her glass down and leaned back. Her nipples nuzzled against the silk.

"Will you help me find him?"

"Huh?" Embarrassed, he looked up.

She wanted him to find a baby grown into a man. Nigh impossible.

"It'll be difficult . . . But I'll try, Lan. If I can have a copy of the picture, I can circulate it within the larger Vietnamese communities."

"Can you make the picture grow old? Display both?"

"You mean age the photograph?"

"Yes."

Surprised by the suggestion, he realized he had no idea whether she had a profession. "Where'd you get the idea?"

"From the Internet. I have read you can do such things using the proper software."

Christ, he should've thought of that. He was the photographer. "Is that your work, computers?"

"I teach. But I have been absent so much my job is, how do you say, at risk."

"I understand."

He twirled the purple orchid with his index finger. Ripples flowed to the outer edge of the bowl. "I'll look into finding your nephew."

"Thank you."

"We need to talk about the monsoon and the tiger," he said.

Her smile died. Obviously, this was not a situation she cared to discuss. Regardless, he continued. "Even if you don't know anything, someone thinks you do."

She gripped the table and lifted her chin, the veins in her neck protruding so vividly it looked as though she might explode. "My brother is dead. An American I do not know comes halfway around the world and tells me I am in danger. What do you expect from me?"

"You shouldn't be alone. Is there a friend, someone to stay with you?"

"Not now." She looked away as she answered. A bittersweet expression clouded her face as if in remembrance of a past lover.

He wrestled up the courage to offer himself as a protector. "I'd like to help."

She compressed her lips, then said, "Thank you . . . but no."

Deflated, he felt as though she had squeezed his heart.

"There may be a place I can go," she added.

"Oh?"

"Chấn's letters mention a family, the Minhs, living in Đức Huệ District. Distant cousins. This would be an opportunity to meet them."

"Great idea," he said, as he signed off on the credit card receipt. "I have a couple more questions about your brother. Do you mind?"

"No. I know that is why you are here."

She dipped her head, a gesture he interpreted as a disappointment that his interest pertained only to Chấn. Or was that only his fantasy?

"Did you find anything like a codebook, something to explain the three sets of numbers?"

"No . . ."

It seemed like she wanted to say something else. Come on, out with it. Forget the Asian reticence.

"I went through my brother's belongings . . . photographs, his meditation journal."

A journal, Kannon mulled. Boy, he'd like to see that.

"Have you read it?"

"Yes. Poetry fills the volume."

"I'd like to see a translation," he said.

"Someday, perhaps."

Someday, perhaps. A hopeful sign?

He pulled at his mustache. "You know, if you are related to the Minhs, perhaps they possess information about Đăng Đạo."

"They might."

"Can you tell me anything else?"

"I think not."

He screwed up his courage again. "Lan. I want to return to

my operating area. Since the Minhs live in Đức Huệ, what if we . . . well, went together?"

He didn't have to wait long for a reaction. Creases ran across her brow like ruts in a road. She started to speak but stopped with her mouth half-open as if sensitive to the impact her chosen but necessary words would have.

Had he blown it?

"Day after tomorrow, we will go."

Her words sounded like a song pitched in velvet.

Fourteen

Two days later, at 0745 hours on Sunday, 27 October, Kannon, dressed in blue jeans, low-quarter hiking boots, and a jungle-green, long-sleeved cotton pullover, brought a rented 150cc Honda motorcycle to a halt outside Lan's home. He breathed a sigh of relief when he spotted her in the courtyard. She'd refused his offer to relocate to a separate hotel room, insisting that she was in no danger. She wanted two days alone in her own home.

"Hey," he called out. Lan was bowed at the waist as if paying tribute to a fallen icon.

She rose and smiled, then resumed pouring water from a rusted pail. "I am trying to bring this hibiscus back to life."

She placed the pail on the ground and motioned for him to follow her inside. In contrast to the ghoulish scene three days ago, a serene aura emanated from the Võ family residence. Open windows drew in the morning sun, its diffused rays spattering dappled beams on the whitewashed walls. It was as if a new life had burst forth after Chấn's death. Even Buddha seemed to have a smile on his face.

Lan retrieved her bag, hips swaying beneath billowy white cotton pants. A wine-colored tunic and traditional cone-shaped straw hat completed her dress. He packed her gear on the motorcycle.

"Ready? Let's mount," he said.

Her thigh brushed against his hip. Clutching the day bag in her left hand, she settled her right hand like a feather on his shoulder as she positioned herself English saddle style. Her touch kindled a flame.

Kannon reminded himself he was there to gather information. He didn't need to lose his head over a Vietnamese fantasy, particularly since Meghan was in the picture. He'd been preoccupied and hadn't even called her. He made a mental note to do so, but Meghan's image vanished when the engine pulsed to life.

They threaded their way out of Sài Gòn. Clumps of humanity dispersed. Housing clusters fragmented. Water buffalo pulling carts plodded along Highway 1. Sampans and Chinese junks with painted tiger faces sailed along canals.

Tiger faces . . . as if he desired a reminder of the dead tiger cub.

Within the hour, they passed through Củ Chi village and turned left on Route 8A toward Bào Trai. Every ten minutes, he activated the belted pager video and captured two-minute segments of modern Việt Nam.

A sultry breeze gathered pungent rural scents and whisked *trigger* fragrances through his nostrils. The heavy air settled in his lungs like stale cigarette smoke. His lungs burned, burned like they did when incoming rounds sucked oxygen from the air.

Clouds rumbled in from the west, casting deep shadows. Swampland gave way to ripened rice fields, the same fields that haunted a recurring dream.

Just released from the Long Bình Stockade, his record clear, First Lieutenant Kannon Ballard was returning to his advisory outpost, full of optimism and hope. But every time he reached the rice paddies, he found himself cast adrift on a raft floating wildly among the waving grains.

"Idiot," he told himself, "the war is over. We lost. Remember?" But his war wasn't over. And his record wasn't clear. Farber had stamped bad time on his brain.

Bào Trai loomed ahead. Lan tapped his shoulder, indicating for him to pull over. He stopped beside the marketplace of the former province capital.

Laughing, she gingerly brushed the ever-widening bald spot on the back of his head as they dismounted. "You need a hat, Mr. Kannon Ballard."

A rush of blood flushed his cheeks. Vietnamese held a sacred view of the head, which involved one's soul escaping through another's hand. He didn't hold that superstition and ran his fingers over his scalp to capture her touch.

"I will buy you one," she said.

Amused, he watched her select one with rainbow colors. While he waited, he surveyed the country market. A roadside café sat close by. It might be a good place to ask questions, Kannon thought.

"You have a faraway expression," she said, after rejoining him.

"Memories."

"That was Chẩn's look when he did not want to talk."

No, he didn't want to talk. He wanted to listen. "I'm thirsty," he said. "How about a beer?"

"I'll have tea," she said.

They sat at a corner table near a squalor-glutted side street that emptied onto the main road. A wrinkled, leathery woman hobbled over and took their order. Kannon waited until she returned to the counter.

"Do you know what Chẩn meant by *pha* and *hang*?" Kannon asked.

Lan bowed her head as if contemplating what her brother might have meant. "I was standing near the window when he spoke, so I did not hear clearly. As his health declined, he often fell between Vietnamese and English. He was difficult to understand."

The wrinkled woman smiled through rotted teeth as she mistakenly brought them two bottles, a Beer 33 for him and a Tiger Beer for Lan. How appropriate, another Tiger.

"You wanted tea, didn't you?"

"Beer is all right," she said.

Kannon continued. He related his findings on Vietnamese variations of the word, *pha*, and the possibility of Chẩn's referring to Major Farber. "But *hang* doesn't remind me of anybody I served with. What Vietnamese definitions apply to those words?"

"You are correct about the Vietnamese words, *pha* or *phá*." Lan jotted the words on a stenographic-styled notebook she carried. "*Hàng*, too, has several meanings in Vietnamese. It could mean to surrender or fall in line. *Hàng* could also refer to a den, cave, or trading house. It depends on the accent. We must know the other words he wanted to . . ." She choked and could not finish the sentence.

Now he'd done it, pushed her too far. Nervously, he peeled the label off his Beer 33 and slapped it on the plastic table cover. "Are you all right?"

Lan released a deep breath as if to collect herself. Then she drank from the beer and shuddered, perhaps unaccustomed to the taste. "I am fine. Do you know Buddhism, Kannon?"

"Your brother and I discussed religion."

"Our family is Mahayana Buddhists—of the Greater Wheel School. Originally, it was elitist, but not so much now."

Shrill horns blared outside the restaurant. A Vietnamese man unceremoniously dropped his motor scooter along the side of the road and stomped into the café. Kannon glanced in the man's direction, wondering what the problem was. Lan frowned at the intrusion and paused until the commotion stopped.

"We call the teachings of Buddha the *dharma*," she said, "the Four Noble Truths. Do you know these?"

He scavenged the recesses of his mind. "I believe the truths pertain to suffering or avoiding suffering."

"*Dharma* offers a soothing way to live." She explained how suffering was part of life, that one must accept it as reality. "When we understand our discontent lies within us and learn to stop wanting so much, we can better walk the middle path."

"Christians talk about letting go, turning things over to God," he said. "It sounds similar."

"Somewhat."

"Will you explain in more detail about the middle path?"

Thwock!

Distracted by the loud sound, Kannon turned toward it. The man who had just entered the café pounded the countertop with his beer.

"Hey!" the guy said, apparently to the wall since no one else was there. He continued jabbering. Hostile currents rode the scorching draft that swept through the open café and settled on Kannon. He hoped it didn't show on his face.

"Most of us are not rude," she said.

Apparently, it did. Shake it off, Kannon.

"The middle path?" he asked.

"Yes. It is also called the Fourth Truth or the Eightfold Path. Each path concentrates on *samma*, the right way of doing things."

"As in right versus wrong?"

"No. We search for the most appropriate in each path."

"And the paths are?"

"I will write them down." She opened her pad to a clean page.

While she wrote, he observed the obnoxious Vietnamese man. The man spoke on a cellular phone but shifted his gaze and glared at him. No need to react to the man's darts, Kannon determined, as Lan tore a page from the notebook and slipped it in front of him. He read the words.

Pursue the right way of seeing things, with the right intention, speech, and action. Work the right way, with the right effort, and think and meditate as if your soul depends on it.

"Thanks, I'll study the message." But what did any of this have to do with Chấn's unfinished business with him? He folded the paper and put it in his pocket.

"My brother spoke of his guilt because he did not follow Buddha's teachings," she said, apparently reading the puzzled expression on his face.

"What did Chấn say specifically about his guilt?"

"He yielded to self-destructive temptations of the Ten Fetters," she said.

Jesus Christ, another lesson. "The Ten Fetters?"

"Yielding to the Ten Fetters interferes with the path to Nirvana—enlightenment. Doubt is one of the fetters. My brother doubted Việt Nam would ever become united."

"Well," Kannon said, "the country's united under one flag now." Although it's the wrong one, he mused.

"In our hearts, we are not one. The communists lie to us. They oppress us. Chấn said they treated the Việt Cộng badly."

Kannon pulled at his mustache. Lan's mentioning his former enemy raked the scabs off his wounds. "Did Chấn say anything else about the Việt Cộng?"

"Most Việt Cộng were good, southern Vietnamese who turned to the communists for support," she said. "Diệm's government gave them no recognition."

"I understand," he said. "Americans generally equate the Việt Cộng with the communists." Both were the enemy, he reminded himself.

This time Lan sipped her Tiger Beer without making a face. "Conceit, self-delusion, ignorance, sensual lust, and greed, among others, are also fetters."

Like the seven deadly sins, Kannon realized.

"Chấn was conceited and self-delusional," she said. "He thought his job as interpreter granted him special status."

Kannon scraped the dirt floor with his boots. Despite himself, he couldn't help but take another glance at the ornery man he now considered an interloper. The man caught his gaze and displayed his middle finger crossed over the forefinger—the Vietnamese version of America's obscene gesture.

Same to you, asshole.

"Did he describe the special status, Lan?"

"Chấn said our father had been a guerrilla."

"Guerrilla." Instinct told him to probe. Self-preservation told him to hold pat, fearful of what she'd disclose. He rubbed his temples.

She didn't respond to his comment.

"Chấn also lusted for material things. Greed shackled his path to enlightenment. This caused him to dishonor two of the Ten Perfections—truthfulness and morality. And this led to his relentless worry, one of the Five Hindrances."

Việt Cộng . . . Guerrilla . . . Father . . . Chấn . . . the Deer Walker. Betrayal? Hai and Farber, yes. But Chấn? No? Yes? The rest of her words failed to penetrate because the ones he tripped over coagulated in his mind like the last image in a jammed kaleidoscope.

"What is the matter?"

Sabotaged again by the Việt Cộng, Kannon gulped down a big slug of his beer.

The man in the corner got up and walked to their table.

"Hey, you Americun piece ah shit. We number one country now. You want boom boom, number one fuck fuck? Not with our wimen. Get ta hell outta here."

The last thing he wanted was to draw attention. Lan's face

turned beet-red.

"Aw, mate, I'm no American. I'm an Aussie. Here on holiday. Don't care for Americans myself. Fucked up your country, they did."

"Aussie, eh? Bull sheeit."

Lan scooted back her chair, stood up, and faced the man. She spoke Vietnamese in a low, controlled voice. The man backed away.

"What'd you tell him?"

"You are on a mission to see about opening a children's clinic."

"Nice answer. You think fast on your feet."

The Vietnamese man returned. Kannon stood up and dwarfed his challenger. His unctuousness reminded Kannon of a grease pit. Suddenly, he grabbed Kannon's arm and spoke menacingly. "You must pay to enter this district."

Piqued at the young man's audacity, Kannon wanted to throttle the weasel but restrained himself. This was not the time to fight and get arrested.

"How much, mate?"

Fifteen

Mid-afternoon found them puttering into Hiệp Hòa. Kannon, still aggravated by the confrontation in Bào Trai, took little pleasure in the information uncovered so far. It was vague, circumstantial, and provided no direct link to Farber, his predetermined adversary. Worse, the more substantial chain of accountability led to Chấn, the man he least suspected. And Lan divulged information about as fast as a tortoise wobbling to sea.

The village appeared much the same—ragged central market, rusting corrugated tin roofs, and bleached wood exteriors. He noticed one freshly painted structure crowned with a pagoda-like, bright red tile roof. Yet, new construction was minimal and stuck out like a ripe banana in a basket of rotten apples. Regardless, the market hummed, and children ran freely without the threat of war.

When he reduced speed, passersby cast curious glances at the pair of round eyes peering from beneath his conical-shaped hat. Kannon's pale face and blond mustache confirmed he was not one of them.

They stopped. Lan dismounted and smoothed her áo dài. Kannon swung his leg over the saddle and stood once again on Hiệp Hòa soil. Piquant odors from the marketplace drifted through. Street traffic consisted of scooters, bicycles, pedestrians, and livestock.

"Why are you shaking your head?" she asked.

"I don't believe it. A Papa-san is talking on a cellphone while driving his water buffalo."

Lan giggled, but it was short-lived. She pointed to the police station, an old French-constructed villa, capped with a swirling communist flag blatantly exuding declaration of control. Tall, French-colonial doors framed by terra-cotta facing marked the entryway.

"Come with me while I inquire about the Minh family," she said.

"All right." But it wasn't all right. He expected to be accosted by a policeman, arrested as a murderer of their people, and incarcerated in a reeducation camp.

Inside, sandstone-colored stucco flaked off dreary walls and cluttered the faded mosaic tile floor. Policemen and villagers huddled in the center of the room in what appeared to Kannon as thinly controlled mayhem. A U-shaped array of desks backed up against the rear wall. An officer in crisp, gray khakis sat behind the middle desk, his face lined in exasperation. When he saw Kannon and Lan approach, the officer brightened.

"Tôi tên Võ Thị Lan." After announcing herself, she introduced Kannon as a family friend and said they were there to locate her cousins.

The officer treated Kannon courteously if not deferentially. Still, it was nigh impossible for him to read Vietnamese feelings. Lan and the officer rattled briefly in their native tongue. Then the officer took pen to paper and mapped out a route to the Minhs.

Ten minutes later, they rode away. They backtracked four kilometers northeast on pockmarked Route 7A, part of the labyrinth of dilapidated laterite roads that spider-webbed the area. Kannon steered left onto a small trail, which quickly turned scabrous, and he had to stand on the footpegs to maintain balance.

Mired among shadows, he lost track of time and space. Telephone pole-sized rattan and palm walled them in like a box canyon. A peasant bicycled from the opposite direction. Kannon stopped and glanced back at Lan. She sat serene and poised, but her features were intent, and only then did he realize this trip might be as important to her as it was to him.

She flagged down and questioned the cyclist.

Kannon took out his handkerchief and wiped his brow. "Much farther?"

"No sweat, we are close," she said.

No sweat. How often had Kannon heard his counterparts use the American colloquialism? He half expected her to address him as *Trung-Úy* Ballard. But he caught her tone. She was getting anxious, alone with a stranger, with the sun descending below the ragged, enshrouding hedgerows.

They rounded a bend in the trail, and, lo-and-behold, the Vietnamese version of "Ma and Pa Kettle's Farm" unfolded. Pigs, chickens, ducks, weird-looking dogs—always the weird-looking dogs, with pointed ears and catlike bodies—ran helter-skelter around the dirt yard.

The fresh, thick scent of tilled earth drew his attention to the fields. An old man trailed in gaited rhythm behind his water buffalo and hitched plow. Kannon skidded to a stop on the dry ground. A withered, frail-looking woman emerged from the house. He remained on the motorcycle while Lan dismounted and made introductions.

The mama-san, her teeth blackened from chewing beetlenut, emitted a high-pitched wail. The papa-san trotted over, a spring in his step. The three of them formed a circle and chatted like teens celebrating rescinded curfew. When they turned to look at him, the old couple cackled.

Kannon blushed. "A friendly greeting, I hope."

"It is. This is the Minh family." Her lips parted in a wide smile. "They welcome us."

"I'm honored," Kannon said. He smiled at the couple as he swung his leg across the saddle. "Tell them I am grateful to be accepted into their home."

The Minhs motioned them inside. The woman padded to a bamboo curtain and threaded her way between the strands, leaving them clattering like skeleton bones. Peering through the curtain, Kannon noticed her bending over a wood-burning fire in a clay oven. Vapor hissed from a simmering teapot.

A rough-hewn table and chairs made from teakwood occupied one corner of the main room. A large tapestry hung from a rafter, brushing the top of an armoire nestled against the wall. Sepia-toned photographs, arrayed in military precision, framed an unsheathed sword. In another corner, an empty hammock strung between supporting timbers swung loosely near an open window. An omniscient Buddha seated on a wall-mounted pedestal watched over the wooden slat bed. Oil lanterns illuminated the dim dwelling.

"They would like us to sit," Lan said.

She spurned the chair and assumed the lotus position on a well-swept dirt floor. Kannon followed her lead, except he crossed his legs at the ankles instead of the thighs. The mama-san brought cups of tea on a worn bamboo platter, then squatted on the floor beside her husband. Gestures and animated language infused the home with life.

"They have a son who works for a contracting company in Sài Gòn." Lan leaped between Vietnamese and English and sips of tea. "I will locate him upon our return."

"What's his name?"

"Thanh." Her eyes reflected the orange glow of lantern-like pools mirroring the setting sun.

Kannon, his legs already numb, shifted position. It was hard not to feel like an intruder.

Lan patted his knee. "My father and Papa-san Minh are first cousins. They came down the Hồ Chí Minh Trail together in the late forties. I am a first cousin once removed in my relation to him. Do you know these relationships?"

"I get confused." An aunt charted the circuit for him, but he still couldn't remember.

She addressed the papa-san, who then rose from his squatting position, tottered over, and grasped Kannon's hand with both of his.

"What did you say?"

"I told him you and Chấn were friends, that you worked with each other in the war. They want us to stay."

"Great."

But her smile faded as if listening to a mournful song. "I will tell them about my family."

As Kannon watched the Minhs' expressions droop, his mind drifted, wondering who else Chấn visited other than his village girlfriend. And would he hear the rest of Lan's tale?

While Lan and the papa-san talked, mama-san prepared steamed rice, boiled vegetables, and fish over an open pit fire. The ubiquitous nước mắm sauce spread its aroma like garlic and Limburger cheese. Papa-san brought out bottles of warm beer to wash it all down. For the first time, Kannon was glad he'd come. Setting his shame aside, and despite the terrible destruction rained on their country, he wanted to believe flourishing seeds of democracy had been planted. Only time would tell.

Kannon whispered to Lan, "Have you asked about Chấn's son?"

"No. I will do so now."

The flickering oil lantern threw dancing light. Kannon watched facial expressions for indications of how the conversation was going. They hung their heads and spoke in hushed tones.

"Aieeee!" the papa-san wailed.

"Jesus Christ!" Kannon jumped to his feet. "What's he screaming about?"

"It is worse than my brother said. They say the wicked one killed Đăng Đạo's mother."

Papa-san Minh rose, walked to a dangling tapestry, and reached behind it. He palmed a small tin canister and shuffled back. He opened the canister, withdrew a stiff piece of paper, and slapped it on the table like a playing card.

Kannon picked it up: a full-length, sepia-toned photograph of a Vietnamese man. He judged the subject to be of average size for a Vietnamese, about five foot four inches tall and a hundred and thirty pounds. An ugly scar, jagged like lightning, branded his right cheek. His aquiline nose pointed to a thin, cruel mouth, and his eyes, a beastly black, blazoned a corridor to hell.

He showed Lan the photograph. "You ever see this man?"

She shook her head.

"Ask Papa-san Minh if this is Hai, the wicked one?"

She did. The papa-san grimaced as if he had been stabbed, then nodded.

Kannon studied the photograph again. Not someone he cared to meet.

The evening ended as sour as the fish sauce, Hai's image the spoiler. The Minhs declared Lan would sleep indoors with them, while Kannon would sleep outside. He strung a hammock between two trees and gathered himself in. He rocked lightly, but his thoughts ran wild. Amid the stagnant barnyard odor, all of Việt Nam converged—the war, the opaque clues, Chấn's death, and the beautiful but now saddened Lan.

As the night chill crept beneath his skin, he resisted lumping Chấn with the Việt Cộng and men like Hai and Farber. Every time he bundled them together, the package exploded like a fragmentation grenade.

Sixteen

Unable to sleep, Kannon rolled off the hammock and strolled around the hedgerow. The pull from his old outpost called stronger and stronger. During the war, the wild, unkempt hedgerows represented to him a dichotomy, either shielding family intimacy or harboring fortified positions and underground weapons caches. Whenever he went on patrol, he wondered which circumstance each thicket enclosed. He put the memory to rest and stopped at the edge of a clearing. A waxing moon shone, bathing the fields in a pale glow. Harvest time. The rice stalks, robust and virile, swayed rhythmically in the gentle breeze. The quiet overwhelmed his senses, and it seemed incongruous to make war anytime, anywhere.

He turned back toward the house. Light from an oil lamp as if filtered through a sieve fingered its way across the packed earth. The dwelling's irregular shape, silhouetted against the moonlit night, appeared like the mouth of a cave. An apparition materialized from the groping shadows. Lan glided to the well, set down a rope and bucket, then strode to stand beside Kannon.

"In case you want to wash," she said.

"Thank you."

Butterflies flitted within his chest. He wanted to pull Lan to him, to touch her skin and lose himself in her. Instead, to still his churning, Kannon ambled to the well, grabbed the rope, and lowered the bucket to the water table. After filling it, he hoisted the bucket, doused his handkerchief in the water, and swabbed his face and neck.

Then he faced her. "Are you having trouble sleeping?"

"The wicked one speaks to me," she said. "He has a strong voice."

"I hope it gets quieter."

Her lips opened in a thin smile but closed in a frown. "My brother. The memories." She lowered herself to the ground and hugged her knees against her breast. "Men like Mr. Hai make a beautiful world ugly. Why?"

"I believe God gives us a choice."

"I understand choice," she snapped. "I do not understand why men make destructive ones."

He didn't either. Then he recalled his drinking binges.

"Papa-san should destroy Mr. Hai's photograph," Lan said, digging her heels into the dirt.

"Perhaps he keeps it to remind himself not to do evil."

"I believe tearing up a portrait rips apart the person as well."

Kannon knelt in front of her. "It's an attempt to sever an attachment, but it doesn't harm the other person."

Appearing stung by his words, Lan stared at him. "I see we disagree," she said, rising to her feet. "It is all right. But the time is late, and the day has been long. I must go in now."

Way to go, Kannon.

She seemed to sense his disappointment and touched his shoulder. "Is there anything else you need?"

"I'm fine." But his heart didn't want this to end. He stood as she turned to walk away. "Please, wait. I'd like to know about your family."

After taking a few steps forward, Lan stopped and bowed her head, as if deciding whether to respond. Diffused moonlight glimmered off her auburn hair while she remained in that position. Finally, she straightened and turned around.

"Father, mother, and sister drowned, trying to escape the communists. I pleaded with them not to go and wait for Chấn. But Father said he was dead. I refused to believe it."

"Your brother must have been grateful you stayed."

"Yes. But he was angry at our father."

Kannon didn't know what to say.

She wrung her hands as if reliving her frustration and loss. "Father worried about the weather more than gunboat patrols. He had arranged for a small sampan to be moored where the Rạch Bến Nghê canal meets the Kinh Tẻ. From there, they sailed the Sài Gòn River until they reached the South China Sea, where a Chinese freighter waited to pick them up. They never made it. Strong monsoon winds capsized them. I knew in my heart and soul the moment of their loss. When they launched their journey into the next Buddhist world, a veil dropped, and I lost sight of them."

"Were their deaths confirmed?"

"Yes. A man who captained a much larger sampan attempted to rescue my family, but he was only able to retrieve the Võ family bag. After returning to the mainland, he sought me out and returned it."

Her story seemed overwhelming. It was hard to know how to respond. "I lost my family through divorce," Kannon said, thinking he too was dead as far as Shelly and Stefan were concerned. "It's a different kind of death."

"I understand such pain," she said.

"What will you do now, with your brother gone?"

"Find my cousin Thanh in Sài Gòn. Resume teaching. I think, when you leave, it will be safe for me in Việt Nam."

When he left. As if he carried the plague.

"Have you considered leaving the country?"

"I would love to go to France." She smiled, the kind of smile that traveled a path far different from any he was on. "I want to study classic literature, fine arts, and music. I dream of owning a piano."

France. She not only shut the door but locked it. "I hope you realize your dream," he said.

"Why are you here, Kannon Ballard? What did you hope to learn from my brother?"

As if impelled by a spirited force among the verdant rice fields, Kannon decided to pour out his soul. It seemed safe, halfway across the world, to surrender his feelings to a woman he'd never see again, to unload a burden never shared with anyone. Pseudo intimacy allowed confidential disclosures for him.

"When I came to Việt Nam, I believed we had a just cause— to stamp out communism in the name of democracy. People needed to die so others could live better."

"Do you believe it still?"

"No longer," he said, thinking about incompetent politicians and jaded military commanders manipulating young soldiers. He opened the last beer—another beer to loosen an already loosened tongue. "Life began to matter. It seemed crazy to be helping

Vietnamese kill Vietnamese. Religion, economics, and politics complicated it more. It reminded me of America's Civil War."

"I do not know this war."

The wind kicked up and rustled the palm branches. Somber shadows flitted across her face. She leaned against the large palm tree as if to support herself against the verbal onslaught while he told her about Americans butchering Americans.

Lan nodded, apparently agreeing with the similarity. Then she centered her intense, dark eyes on his. "I must hear the cause of your suffering."

She was granting him permission, a liberty he'd never granted to himself, and so he began. "Our five-man advisory team was down to two and assigned to an outpost within a kilometer from here. Your brother served as interpreter."

"What was your role?"

"You name it. Provide training, teach tactics, aid logistics. Gather intelligence. Liaison with U.S. forces. Support the pacification effort."

"From the little Chấn told me, you performed well."

He took a sip of beer. "To a point." And then he told her why his team had been below strength, because of casualties and transfers with no replacements, and about the 5 October 1970 attack.

"Families lived nearby. You threw fire on them?"

"Not intentionally. But sometimes it was unavoidable," Kannon said, remembering how the Việt Cộng knew the no-fire zones and for that reason often delivered their mortar barrages from those same villages.

"Such a waste of life," she said.

"Yes, it was."

She shuddered. "I believe I will have some of your beer."

He handed it to her. As she tipped the bottle, the curve of her neck, exposed and vulnerable, drew taut. Unable to take his eyes off her, Kannon stopped speaking. He wanted to drop the war talk, drop it forever, and take her in his arms. He moved forward a half step. She held up the palm of her hand.

Embarrassed, he couldn't acknowledge the rejection in words, just stepped back to let her know he received the message.

After an uncomfortable silence, he retreated to his story, how he was ordered to pursue, which resulted in a firefight. And ultimately, the ambush. And death.

"Did my brother accompany you on pursuit?"

"No."

Lan stiffened. "Why not?"

"He had been wounded in the attack. Shot in the ankle. He couldn't have gone. Chấn never told you about this?"

She shook her head. "It explains his limp, though. Still, it does not seem smart for you to have gone without your interpreter," she said.

Again, her directness startled him.

"No," he agreed, "it wasn't smart, but I followed orders."

"How many soldiers died?"

"Fifteen."

"Fathers and brothers denied a future," she said, "children never born." She shook her head as if condemning all the evil in the world. "You were not wounded?"

"No. An AK round shattered the magazine well of my M-16 and spun me around. Then a grenade burst and slammed into the radio, knocking me to the ground."

"Your God has kept you alive for a reason."

Kannon paused, then speculated and tossed out a baited hook. "I assume, Lan, Chấn's guilt had something to do with his having to remain in the outpost. If he'd accompanied the patrol, he might've detected the ambush."

"I do not know. Chấn never said how he thought he had wronged you. But, no wonder my brother . . ."

Kannon opened his mouth but choked on the words he wanted to release, "Damn it. Was I set up or not?" It was like he was outside of his body and talking to himself. "No wonder your brother what, Lan?"

"It is just . . . well, if my brother had accompanied your patrol, he also might have been killed. And I never would have gotten to know him."

Her response was quick but unsatisfactory. "I'm glad Chấn lived," was all Kannon could say.

"What happened next?" she asked, her eyes glistening.

"The worst part was lying among the bodies all night." And Sergeant Malcolm's cursing him with his last breath. "I waited until morning to return to the outpost. Farber and Jeffrey were already there."

"How did they know?"

"Chẩn radioed through Vietnamese channels the patrol failed to return. Farber said I disgraced the officer corps and would be court-martialed. He called me a coward and that I should have been killed, not the others."

"I do not understand this . . . court-martial."

Kannon explained. He wondered if she now detested him.

"If you were following orders, why did he want to court-martial you?"

"He claimed I disobeyed his command to stay in the outpost . . . all I wanted was glory, another medal. I never received the order." He scuffed the ground in disgust. "They put me in the Long Bình Stockade for two weeks. But since no formal charges were filed, they released a directive for me to leave the country."

Lan gazed around the farm compound, then fixed her eyes on Kannon. "The consequences of war spill over."

"Like a tsunami."

"Yours is a sad story." She hesitated a moment. "I have one other thing to reveal."

"Yes?"

"Chẩn said you were getting too close. They put a price on your head."

Palm fronds bobbed in the breeze while stars twinkled caution. The night no longer felt cool as beads of perspiration bubbled on his forehead like oil simmering on heated steel.

"Too close to what? Who put a price on my head?"

"He never said."

"Is there nothing else you can tell me?"

She brushed her forehead to untangle wisps of hair, as if they impeded clarity, then took a step forward.

"No." She placed her hand on his cheek. "Let it go. Embrace the peace you brought my brother."

"I would if I could . . . that's why I came, hoping your brother would say something to clear my mind."

"My brother told you enough." She paused. "Remember the Four Noble Truths."

Lan said softly and then walked away, toward the house.

Clouds scurried overhead as if running with a herd of antelope. Kannon grasped at her meaning, tenuously embraced it, but the image dissolved into a fog as he watched her make her way inside. She snuffed out the oil lantern, and his world turned black.

The Wall

Seventeen

"Silverton's cold. Frosted. Beautiful," Meghan said, tapping the channel button for a clearer signal. "When did you get home?"

Outside the Hotel Victoria's front window, an early November snow dusted Greene Street in cylindrical swirls. The wind shrieked through the narrow alleyway. The adjacent wall moaned in protest.

"Last Friday."

Halloween. How appropriate, she thought. Hopefully, Kannon had buried his demons and was ready to embrace life. She sat on her rose-patterned sofa and listened while he summarized his findings from Chấn and his sister Lan. "You mean he was a Việt Cộng."

"Chấn told Lan their father had been a guerrilla," he said. "Which means Chấn may also have been one."

The front door burst open. Crystal-white flakes whipped into the lobby as her friend Elizabeth scuttled inside. Meghan stood and muffled the mouthpiece. "He's back in Texas," she said.

Elizabeth stomped the snow off her boots and shed her parka. "The searcher. Is your smile for him or me?"

Meghan swiped at her with the back of her hand. Elizabeth stuck out her tongue and pirouetted with the grace of a sack of potatoes.

"What's the commotion? Sounds like a storm brewing," Kannon said.

"Yeah, my pesky friend," Meghan said, retaking her seat. "Go ahead."

"Chấn died without telling me much more."

Meghan held out her cup for Elizabeth to refill, then sipped the hot cider. The liquid soothed her throat, spread its warmth. "It's a shame he died," she said. "But . . . if he was a Việt Cộng, doesn't that prove you were set up?"

"Not necessarily," he said. "I've been speculating."

"You would."

"Maybe Chấn learned something the night he was ill," he said.

"Wouldn't he have told you in 1970?"

"I never saw him after the ambush."

Meghan looked at Elizabeth sitting across from her and sighed. Again, she put her hand over the mouthpiece, then mouthed, "Says I don't understand the dynamics. Even if Chấn had been a Việt Cộng, he wouldn't have betrayed him. They fought together."

Elizabeth whispered in return. "Tell him to forget Việt Nam and instead fulfill your bodily desires."

"I can't tell him that." She realized Kannon had spoken and removed her hand from the mouthpiece. "What did you say?"

"I said I think Chấn's comments just scratched the surface."

She chose her next words with care. "Maybe Chấn sold you out to stay alive."

"I need something more definite."

Suddenly, the cider tasted bitter. Meghan placed the cup on the table. "I don't see how you're going to find it."

Elizabeth mimicked decapitation with the slice of her hand. Meghan squeezed a lap pillow as if to squelch the attitude flowing from the other end of the line.

"Kannon, this is depressing. I can't live my life waiting for you to decide when enough is enough."

"Meghan, I'm telling you what happened."

"Here's what I think. You need to talk with Major . . . what's his name, Faberge."

"Farber."

"Whatever."

"I plan to. First, I must locate him," Kannon said.

"Then do it."

"You don't have to get testy."

Meghan bit her tongue. "I'm moving forward with my life. I hope you will do the same."

"I am. Killing a ghost is part of it."

"Your ghost needs to die quickly," Meghan said, "or we will."

She ended the conversation on that frosty tone.

"Is he coming up?"

Meghan frowned. "We didn't get that far."

"You said your deceased husband was self-absorbed, too," Elizabeth said, "and you supported him like a hernia harness. Are you doing it again?"

Elizabeth's seriousness surprised her. "Maybe. I worry about his ability to give."

"I'm not sure *give* resides in the male vocabulary."

"Neither am I." But something else troubled her. It was the tone in Kannon's voice when he spoke of Lan.

* * *

Kannon slammed down the receiver. Despite her companionship and sensuality, Meghan frustrated him. She didn't understand. He swiveled his desk chair from the antique, roll-top desk to face his computer. One mouse click, then another. No response from Lan. Apparently, she didn't visit an Internet Café as often as she said. Or—he fretted, flailing away at a nagging doubt— she didn't want to answer him.

Two women, one from each country, instead of piecing his separate halves back together, pried him farther apart. Each, in her way, had offered disparate versions of salvation. Turn it over to Christ. Follow the Four Noble Truths. Nice theology, but in his view, neither addressed the consequences of war as he knew it.

* * *

November drudged past like a river of sludge and bled into mid-December. Outside the study window, a frigid, dismal rain dropped from a coal-black sky. Kannon stepped onto the deck and listened to the rain pattering the oaks, thumping the cactus.

The cold, damp wind whipped his body and drove him inside. He studied the vibrant photographic landscapes blanketing three mahogany-paneled walls, thinking it ironic they depicted harmony. On the fourth wall, brushed limestone framed a massive wood-burning fireplace. He lit a fire, then clipped an Avo Uvezian Pyramid cigar, a favorite from the Dominican Republic, and poured himself a Drambuie.

Retirement sucked. His days drifted by in nothingness as if there were no purpose to exist. He exhaled a plume of smoke and watched it curl into the fireplace.

"Depression—wasted time—does that to a person," his therapist had said.

The rain turned to sleet, then hail. Frozen pellets clattered on the deck like AK47s on full automatic. Often, Kannon wondered whether a court-martial might have exonerated him, or if not, cleansed him of guilt through incarceration. Instead, he held mock trials in his head, which invariably culminated in a conviction.

Time failed to deliver clarity. The random pieces of his puzzle remained incomprehensible. And Chấn? Kannon found it difficult to reconcile who he thought his former interpreter was compared to what he now appeared to have been. He refueled with another Drambuie, then, for the first time in a month, extracted his notes from a thin file.

1) Three number sets, two sets of six and one of eight.
2) They thought you knew.
3) *Pha . . . hang*, or *phá* and *hàng*.
4) The Monsoon Killed the Tiger.

A reservoir of hope kept him from severing these slender threads. The contents lodged in his mind like a cedar tree overgrowing strands of a barbed-wire fence. The fire crackled. In marked contrast to the plummeting temperature, a subtle glow charged through him, as if the narcotic effect of the liqueur and a cigar dislodged frozen brain cells.

Damn cigars work better than anti-depressants.

His eyes roamed the bookcase. Victor Frankl's *Man's Search for Meaning* caught his attention. He plucked the thin volume off the shelf and sprawled on the tooled leather divan. He thumbed through marked passages about the concentration camps: "Everything can be taken from a man but one thing: the last of human's freedoms—to choose one's attitude in any given set of circumstances, to choose one's own way. Whoever was still alive had reason for hope."

The doorbell rang.

Kannon walked to the front and looked out the window. A UPS delivery truck was parked in the driveway. He opened the door, signed for the delivery, and looked at the postmark: Việt Nam, 13 December 2002—two weeks ago. His fingers trembled as he opened the small parcel and read the note.

> Dear Kannon, I apologize for taking so long, not thinking of this sooner. I found this drawing inside Chấn's meditation book after his death. At first, I assumed the sketch to be child's work, but after examining it again, I wondered whether it might be a map. I hope this helps. I know this is the holiday season in your country and pray yours is a bright one.
> Lan.

His spirit soared like a hot-air balloon. "Hearing from you helps. It helps a lot," he muttered aloud.

Indeed, it was a hand-drawn map. No grid lines, but the crude drawing included a string of penciled-in military symbols. The bottom right-hand corner contained a faint legend he couldn't decipher.

As a stand-alone document, the map meant nothing to him. Nevertheless, whoever compiled it understood military symbols and topography. Another piece of the puzzle? Maybe he could piece them together after all.

Kannon dialed his son, the prosecutor.

"Stefan Ballard."

"Hey, this is Dad. Gotta minute?"

"At most," Stefan said.

The ice hadn't thawed. "I need a favor."

"To repay all you've done for me," Stefan said.

Christ! Let it rest.

"Stefan, I understand. Someday I'd like to talk to you about it."

"Yeah, sure. What do you want?"

"I have a photograph of a two-year-old Vietnamese boy," he said, holding the picture of Đăng Đạo in his hand. "Can you guys age an image thirty years?"

"Yeah, we do it all the time, either using a sketch artist or computer," Stefan said. "Just shoot a digital image over."

"Appreciate it."

"Is he part of the story?"

"Yep, part of the story."

Kannon weathered an uncomfortable pause.

"Is he yours, Dad?"

For the first time he could remember, his son's voice held an edge of tenderness. Kannon wondered if his voice had ever sounded tender to Stefan.

"No, Stefan, he's not mine. He's the son of a Vietnamese friend who died recently. The young man may be in the States. I'm trying to locate him."

After they terminated the call, Kannon stood up and gazed onto the patio. Now, sleet popped the hailstones and sent them scattering like marbles, similar to what he'd done with special people in his life. How much time remained before Stefan gave up on him altogether? He wanted to tell him about his Việt Nam War. And while he feared his son wouldn't be interested, he worried more Stefan would be ashamed of him.

Kannon returned to his desk and searched the Internet for information on various veterans' groups. Several mouse clicks later, he found Counterparts, an organization serving former advisors. A good website with email addresses, it also provided an online application form. Finally, he found a phone number, called, and was referenced to another.

"This is Kannon Ballard. I'm looking for some guys I served with in 'Nam?"

"You a member of our group?" a gruff voice sounded.

"Just filled out the application. Who is this?"

"Rock."

He sounded like one. "Okay. Now, will you answer some questions?"

"Maybe. You MACV?" Rock inquired.

"Military Assistance Command, Vietnam. Yes." Kannon recounted the same documentation he'd provided for the on-line application.

"Sounds real enough. Drop the hard stuff in the mail. What

can I do for ya?"

"I'm trying to find a Farber, Jeffrey, and Stairn."

"Last names, I assume."

"Yes."

"First names?"

"Don't remember."

"NCOs or officers?"

"Officers," Kannon said.

"Hmm. Just saw your application," Rock said. "You were one of those six-month-wonder lieutenants."

"Yep," Kannon said, choosing to dismiss the unflattering rap.

"Checking our database," Rock said.

As Kannon held the line, he heard Rock humming the "Battle Hymn of the Republic."

"Not listed."

"Any suggestions?" Kannon asked.

"Try the National Archives in DC. Most of the records— intelligence and after-action reports, duty rosters, and general orders—have been declassified. I'll give you a guy's email address. He's a member of our organization as well as an archivist. Look to the military orders for assignments, citations, or leaves for full names and social security numbers."

"Thanks, Rock. Let's have it."

He took the information down and immediately fired off an email to the Archives.

The weekend passed, as did Monday. Daily five-mile runs helped occupy his mind. On Tuesday morning, while drinking coffee, his Westminster chime rang out. He opened the message.

Dear Mr. Ballard: received your inquiry from day previous. Please be advised we need specific assignment dates, unit designation, and geographical data, including province/district information. Let us know your expected arrival, and we will arrange to have information available. Only

takes a day or two.
Daniel, Archivist.

Kannon emailed the required details. Then he turned his thoughts back to Meghan in Silverton and to his GS in Durango. He found it easier to relate to the motorcycle than to Meghan. The motorcycle didn't talk back. But then, a motorcycle didn't give affection or companionship—a hell of a trade.

She answered the second ring.

"I'm going to D.C.," he said.

"What for?"

"To chase my ghosts by researching military records. After my Washington trip, maybe we could get together."

"Call after you're finished. We'll talk about it."

"You bet."

After hanging up, he stepped outside. The harsh front had passed during the night, carrying away the angry sleet and hail. The sky blazed cobalt blue. Swaying oak trees sprinkled last bits of moisture over the saturated earth. A sweet cedar fragrance filled the cold air. Evaporation would soon dry the slick sheen on the back roads.

It was New Year's Eve, time to celebrate. He walked into the garage, unhooked the battery charger from the K1200 RS, and rolled it out on the Tarmac.

The cool air scudded over his helmet as he clipped through the curves, leaning the motorcycle first one way then the next. The afternoon passed as quickly as the miles. Feathery tufts of clouds speckled the western sky as Kannon turned onto a promontory overlooking the Pedernales River. An orange tinge spread beneath the chalky puffs, ripening to magenta as the sun plunged beneath the horizon. The undulating hill country unfurled like a rippling flag, fresh and full of promise. And he made a vow.

He would seize the flitting shadows, mold them into substance, and uncover the truth.

Eighteen

It was Friday morning, 3 January 2003. After two long days in the saddle, Kannon had arrived late the night before at a motel in College Park, Maryland, which was close to the Archives on Adelphi Road. The music of Ferlin Husky and Webb Pierce, along with an electric vest and heated handgrips, helped reduce the boredom and soften the cold, but overall it had been a monotonous motorcycle ride, except when traversing the Blue Ridge. As a testament to nostalgia, meandering split-rail fences marched across snow-bound bowls, setting apart white-powdered evergreens and spidery limbs of deciduous trees standing stark against pallid skies. Any other time he would have stopped and photographed. But as he neared his destination, he grew anxious to begin work.

Kannon rode to the National Archives, parked, and entered the facility. He sought two things: full names and social security numbers of the province senior advisors—Farber in particular—and any information addressing events leading up to and including 5 October 1970, the night of the fatal ambush.

After enduring a mandatory ten-minute orientation, which included filling out a computer form, being photographed, and reading a set of rules, Kannon received his researcher's card. A guard scanned the card, then Kannon entered the researcher's room and obtained his badge before being escorted to Room 2400, home of the archivists.

"I'm here to see Daniel Sellers."

"You're looking at him." A pudgy man about five feet seven, with bulbous eyes and thinning gray hair, extended his hand. The archivist wore old U.S. Army dog tags, and they chinked when he moved. "And you are?"

Kannon introduced himself and reiterated the team records he wanted.

"Hold on a second." Daniel stepped away from the counter with a noticeable limp.

Kannon surveyed the text room. Researchers buried their

heads in the past, the only sounds being rhythmical clacking of laptop keyboards and diligent shuffling of yellowed documents.

The repository surprised him. Instead of an archaic, musty structure with sluggish ceiling fans and groaning wood floors, he found a modern six-storied building, sterile but functional, containing text, cartographic, audio and video, microfilm, and electronic records. Spacious workstations equipped with electrical outlets and fluorescent lighting imparted a scholarly atmosphere.

The archivist returned. "Hậu Nghĩa Province, Đức Huệ District, Advisory Team 77, May '69 through November '69. What's the deal, have a short tour?"

"Yeah, short tour," Kannon shot back.

"The boxed documents have been pulled and are being loaded on a cart."

Kannon sighed. "Okay."

"Any questions on security? No briefcases or folders allowed," Daniel said. "You can purchase a debit card to make copies. No originals are to be taken out."

"I understand."

Kannon signed for the cart and wheeled it over to a vacant workstation. He plugged in his laptop and surveyed the folders containing over eighteen thousand pages. Each folder was about an inch thick, well-indexed, and neatly arranged.

* * *

Kannon plunged into another realm. "Orders and Awards," the tab indicated on the fifth folder he selected. The sheaf of papers contained Letter Order Number 3-31: Headquarters, U.S. Army Advisory Group, III CTZ, Việt Nam—10 October 1970. Inventory of Sergeant Clifford R. Malcolm's Personal Property. Killed in Action on . . .

The words jumped from the page, carried shame as their companion.

He set the October folders aside and skipped back to May. Ease into the fire rather than leap. The folders contained Duty Rosters, Spot Reports, Intelligence Summaries, District and Province Senior Advisor Reports, and After Action Reports chronicling enemy contacts, but none of the latter after September.

What happened to the rest of them?

Lunchtime passed without a break. He combed the earlier folders for another three hours to re-familiarize himself with the tactical situation.

Next, Kannon took up the duty roster folders, which indicated the daily status of each advisor, whether on a field assignment, sick call, or R & R. From these, he extracted another link to his past. Excitedly, he jotted down full names plus their social security numbers:

Major Christian J. Farber

Captain Leonard S. Jeffrey

Lieutenant Lucas R. Stairn

Stairn, he remembered as an administrative puppet. Jeffrey had been obnoxious but feckless. Kannon riffled several more folders and found nothing of consequence. When he looked up, the afternoon had slipped by and it was time to sign off for the evening.

The next morning, Saturday, dawned wet and frigid, a fitting atmosphere for Kannon's first task, visiting the Việt Nam Veterans Memorial at The National Mall. The somber granite wall spilled out of the ground like polished lava and rose to its lengthy summit before tapering off at the other end—a massive, mock graveyard listing more than fifty-eight thousand names. Pictures, medals, bracelets, caps, jackets, dolls, and knives lay strewn throughout the base of the memorial—icons spanning two dimensions.

He walked to the alphabetical index mounted on a pedestal. After finding Malcolm's name, Kannon located the respective wall panels and made tracings, as if trying to bring his soul back to life.

"God, I'm sorry," he whispered. Kannon considered whether he should attempt contacting Malcolm's widow and the two children, now adults. What good would it do? What could he tell them that might ease their pain? It was so long ago. Contacting them may do more harm than good.

An old woman approached the wall, her wobbly steps supported by a walker. Purposefully, looking neither left nor right, she homed in on one name. Someone's mama, he figured. Wonder how many times she's been here? She kissed a name, turned, and shuffled away. Had Malcolm's mother ever come by? Would his own?

Three names left to check. He returned to the index. Neither Farber nor Jeffrey showed up on either the Killed or Missing in Action list. Stairn? KIA 13 October 1970.

Business concluded, Kannon motorcycled back to the Archives on Adelphi Road and resumed his research. He scoured several folders containing intelligence reports and set the more intriguing ones aside for later review.

A folder labeled "Transcripts-Interim" caught his eye. Underneath the cursive label, someone had penciled in "Classified-Destroy." A curious label, not standard military jargon. He opened the folder.

Handwritten After Action Reports, October. Stairn's job, administration, typing reports. Maybe Stairn never saw them. Maybe he had been assigned to the field after Kannon's departure. Hard to type when you're dead.

He flipped pages and there it was, the report detailing the black night, 5 October 1970. His hands trembled as if he were disabling a booby-trapped hand grenade. "Stop stalling," he chided himself. "You're closing on the objective as if you were bracketing artillery fire." He began reading but stumbled over the first sentence.

"Goddamn!" he blurted out loud, loud enough to cause several researchers to raise their heads and look at him disapprovingly.

Dumbfounded, he couldn't believe what he read. Kannon double-checked the dates and sank deep into the chair. He forced himself to read the whole report, then read it again.

Headquarters

Hậu Nghĩa Province—III CTZ

Đức Huệ Sub-Sector/Advisory Team77

6 October 1970: After Action Report

The report read in part:

On the night of 5 October 1970, at 2100 hours, the

133

An Dinh outpost came under heavy mortar, rocket, and ground attack. The 895 Regional Force Company successfully repulsed the enemy . . . After the attack, at 0100 hours, Lieutenant Kannon L. Ballard, First Lieutenant, Infantry, leader of Mobile Advisory Team III-56, acting against direct orders and exhibiting an egregious lack of sound military tactics, discipline, and common sense, exposed his men to a murderous ambush and needless death by sending out a reconnaissance patrol. The 25th Infantry Division S-2 (Intelligence) had reported a large enemy troop concentration, battalion-sized or better, regrouping three kilometers east of the Vàm Cỏ Đông River.

At 0030 hours, I had transmitted this alleged sighting of enemy movement to Lieutenant Ballard and told him to keep all patrols in that night, that he had neither the firepower nor the men available to confront a force of this size. I, Major Farber, plotted defensive fire targets for the artillery and alerted helicopter gunships and "Spooky" to be on maximum alert for a follow-up attack. I informed Lieutenant Ballard and commanded him to coordinate his regional forces to stay on maximum alert.

Lieutenant Ballard intentionally disobeyed this order. In reckless disregard for the safety of his fellow advisor and fourteen South Vietnamese regional forces selected to accompany the recon, he exited the outpost and commenced patrolling. At a point one thousand meters west of the outpost, Lieutenant Ballard's patrol was overcome and obliterated in an ambush by a superior hostile force. All were KIA except for Lieutenant Ballard, who, taking up the rear of the column, survived. Further, at the instance of receiving hostile fire, Lieutenant Ballard failed to return fire, offering no resistance to the enemy.

Lieutenant Ballard's willful misconduct and act of cowardice resulted in the loss of life for fifteen men—one American and fourteen Vietnamese. As a result of this action, Lieutenant Ballard disgraced the uniform of a U.S. Army infantry officer and lost face with the South Vietnamese units he served. He is no longer fit to serve his nation. Lieutenant Kannon L. Ballard is immediately relieved of duty and will be reassigned to the rear, with further disciplinary action pending.

Major Christian J. Farber, Infantry

Senior Advisor, Hậu Nghĩa Province, Military Assistance Command, Vietnam.

Until now, all Kannon had received was the verbal lashing. Reading a written report intensified the indignity and infuriated him.

"That's not what happened, you son of a bitch."

Again, fellow researchers looked up from their work and raised their eyebrows in protest. An attendant approached. "Sir. Please quiet down," she said.

Kannon snapped his pencil in two and eyeballed the stocky woman built like a rugby fullback. "Ma'am, I've just read a lie."

"You're disturbing the other researchers. Talk to an archivist. He can assign you a glass-enclosed office if you need more privacy."

Kannon shook his head. "I'll calm down."

Enraged over Farber's report, Kannon waited until she waddled off and resumed her wall post, where she glared Machiavellian style as if daring him to open his mouth again. He snatched another pencil and studied Farber's report a final time, hoping for a cryptanalysis to materialize between the lines and reveal the truth.

A wave of horror engulfed him. The shame over the death of his men weighed like a cornerstone. What if that was the way it happened? What if he had so deluded himself that he'd concocted a story to protect his haunted psyche? Maybe Farber had radioed for him to stay in that night. Maybe he, Kannon Ballard, through prolonged denial, had fabricated an impenetrable fortress, like a criminal who vehemently refutes his violent crime until he convinces himself he is innocent.

Rapping his pencil over the report in drumbeat cadence, he cycled again through the sequence of events.

The report was false.

Kannon wrapped up the files, put them on the cart, and numbly rolled it back to the archivist. Maintaining silence, he left the Archives and rode to a liquor store, bought a liter of cheap scotch, and backtracked to his motel. He filled a bucket with ice, then fixed his first drink.

* * *

Sappers flew over the wire, screaming like Satan's disciples. Three shrouded faces, amid an incoming barrage of mortar and small arms fire, hovered above his prostrate body. They slashed at him with steel-like fingers, lifted him above the fray.

Fiercely flapping their wings, the three carried him up into the night sky and then flung him into a deep cave, black as midnight in a coal mine. He scrambled desperately, trying to claw and gouge his way out. But scalding mud macerated beneath him, and he slid further and further into the pit.

An unseen, fiery hand reached up and ripped him off the wall. His arms flailed as he tumbled backward, backward into the abyss. Abruptly, he slammed into a huge tube. A hooded shape hideously laughed as he jerked a lever, shooting Kannon out of the cave like a mortar round. He hit the ground with explosive force. Then they came for him, diminutive devils gnashing and gnarling in a spectacle of torment.

Another nightmare.

One after another, terrible dreams had invaded his sleep since the war. Deep down, Kannon realized that all along his subconscious had been driving him to search for the truth.

Nineteen

Kannon rose late Sunday morning, his aging muscles aching from the poisonous scotch, the poisonous dream. A cold shower sharpened his senses. After dressing, he rode to a park and ride, then caught the Metro to Arlington Cemetery. In an attempt to relax his body and mind, he walked across the Memorial Bridge and strode alongside the Potomac.

An opalescent film engulfed the nation's capital. Dormant cherry trees stood stark against gray skies, their spidery limbs clutching clumps of snow like children holding dreams. A blue heron swooped low over the river and scooped up its breakfast. Sitting on a park bench, a lone woman huddled in an overcoat and stuck her head out like a cuckoo bird to draw on a cigarette. She looked lost, like him.

Fifteen minutes later, he again found himself staring at the granite slab sandwiched between two historical icons, the Lincoln Memorial and the Washington Monument, which honored two of the nation's greatest leaders. Three elements in Farber's report churned in his mind: the recited radio transmission he didn't recall, the charge for disobeying orders, and the alleged intelligence sighting by the 25th Infantry Division. If the report was accurate, he should find a corroborative statement in the intelligence summaries.

Since the Archives was closed today, he'd have to wait to find out. He spent the rest of the day touring the Mall, including a visit to the Tomb of the Unknown Soldier. This death, and all the others in that war, he slept with that night.

"Good morning, Daniel. How's my favorite archivist?"

"Colder it gets, the stiffer my leg," Daniel said.

"Sorry to hear it. Came for my cart."

"Sure." Daniel rolled it out.

"Hope your leg loosens up."

Kannon carted the documents across the text room. "Ma'am," he said when passing the rugby-sized attendant, who parted her mouth as if to respond but compressed her lips in silence once she recognized him. He sat down at a vacant workstation and began.

First, the statement from Farber's report: "The 25th Infantry Division S-2 (Intelligence) reported a large enemy troop concentration, battalion-sized or better, regrouping three kilometers east of the Vàm Cỏ Đông River."

Excited, Kannon poured over advisor intelligence summaries for several days before and after 5 October 1970. The majority of the reports referred to sightings made from one- to three-days *before* the written report date, meaning the information was stale by the time it filtered through official channels.

No wonder they never knew what the hell was going on!

None of the reports dated during the week before or the week after 5 October 1970 referred to anything but minor enemy troop movements. The most significant one referred to a sighting of three lanterns ten meters apart—possibly a tax collection squad or curfew-breaking fishermen.

The absence of any intelligence report alluding to a large troop movement struck him as strange. The omission raised three possibilities. He wrote them down.

- An intelligence report citing a main force battalion moving across the river, then regrouping after the 5 October attack, had been written but lost or destroyed. And if destroyed, why?
- A main force battalion was sighted, but no formal report was filed, a violation of standard military protocol.
- Farber's report constituted a complete lie, and no one bothered to corroborate it.

The possibilities he left hanging. Advisor After Action Reports, intelligence summaries, and spot reports consumed the rest of the day. Kannon made photocopies, took notes, and tabbed key reports, including the indictment against him.

Altogether, he'd reviewed two-thirds of the folders when he came to one marked, "Sundry Reports." He opened it and found nothing of consequence until he leafed to the back of the folder.

Analysis of Alleged Black Market Activity

Hậu Nghĩa Province

17 September 1970

As part of the annual review ordered by MACV Headquarters, Tân Sơn Nhất Air Base, I, Captain Leonard S. Jeffrey, Assistant to Major Christian J. Farber, conducted appropriate inquiries and interviews among senior U.S. military advisors in the province and districts, their respective Vietnamese counterparts, including district and village chiefs, as well as random interviews with noncommissioned officers on the district advisory teams.

The report contained considerable boilerplate, just like a law contract, and also indicated the questions asked and to whom. The report concluded:

While numerous reports have filtered up from various districts in Hậu Nghĩa Province concerning rumors of a wholesale black trading market operating, a thorough, intense investigation proved otherwise. No evidence exists to support the contention that there is any organized, illicit trading activity—of drugs, merchandise such as stereo and photographic equipment, weapons, or any other contraband—occurring in the province.

Some isolated incidents were ferreted out, and those U.S. servicemen involved will be disciplined accordingly. Names of alleged Vietnamese perpetrators have been turned over to appropriate Vietnamese officials. An example of such an incident involved trading a small black-and-white TV to a Vietnamese for a ChiCom pistol.

Jeffrey's signature sanctioned it. Hell, Kannon didn't remember any such survey. A cover-your-ass memo if ever he'd read one. He always considered it strange, the three officers from province headquarters seldom visited his outpost and never accompanied him on operations, nor did they invite him to participate in pacification projects in the villages. "Not your job," they'd said. "Your job is to wage war."

Was Jeffrey's report a preemptive strike to ward off the Inspector General's Department? Regardless, the alluded-to small trading wasn't unusual. American servicemen traded all the time. Everyone Kannon knew, including himself, wanted to come home with a Chicom pistol, AK47, or Việt Cộng flag.

Whoa, what's this?

The last page in the folder contained several Vietnamese names written in pencil. Scanning the list, Kannon recognized Chấn, Minh, and Hai. The name Thu also seemed familiar.

Who was Thu? Kannon racked his brain. Oh, yeah. Chấn's father, that's who. Had they been the nucleus of a Việt Cộng Infrastructure cell? If so, Papa-san Minh hadn't been just an innocent farmer. And Chấn. He still didn't want to believe it. Or, were they CIA contacts recruited under the Vietnamese-initiated Phoenix program to identify members of the Việt Cộng's political arm? It didn't seem likely concerning a man with Hai's reputation, but stranger things happened.

Beneath the last name on the list was written the word "unknown." Strange, but it meant nothing to him.

A slim envelope taped to the upper part of the inside back cover caught his attention. Stairn's name was on it. Carefully, he peeled the envelope away from the tape, then pried open the lip and extracted a thin piece of meticulously folded paper. A legend, scaled in both kilometers and meters, appeared at the bottom.

"Holy shit. It's Chấn's map."

"Shhh!" the rugby-sized attendant hissed.

* * *

Evening fell. At the motel, Kannon set to work on his laptop. He removed the media bay module that contained the CD and diskette drives, pried off the cover from his spare battery, then

141

snapped into place the extra cover over the empty bay.

Sleep eluded him. He tried reading. That, too, proved pointless. His mind was supercharged.

First thing next morning, Kannon sought out Daniel.

"Where are the maps kept?"

"Third floor."

Kannon took the elevator up to Cartographic Records.

"Morning, ma'am. How do I obtain specific maps for Việt Nam's operating theater?"

The stern-looking woman behind the counter, dressed in battle gray and sporting a hair bun tight enough to make a spinster proud, lanced him with eyes capable of ferreting out the staunchest of spies.

She eyed his badge with the sternness of a drill instructor. "You a vet?"

"Yeah, I—"

"Lost my man in 'Nam. Stupid war," she said, then added, almost as an afterthought, "Series L-seventy fourteen, a one-to-fifty-thousand legend map for any quadrant in Việt Nam."

Kannon marched to the index, located the Việt Nam series, and selected the appropriate quadrant plus three adjacent ones. A few minutes later, he handed her a completed form.

With a sullen scowl, she trudged behind secured doors, emerging ten minutes later with maps in hand.

"What'd you do in 'Nam?" She spoke in a softer tone.

"Advisor to South Vietnamese regional forces," he said.

"See action?"

"Some."

"Welcome home," she said, touching him on the arm.

"Thanks. Where can I copy these?"

"There." She pointed to a larger copier.

After inserting his debit card, he listened to the high-pitched hum as the copier reproduced images. Afterward, Kannon returned the originals. He took the copies downstairs, laid out the primary quadrant on his workstation, and re-acquainted himself with grid coordinates, villages and hamlets, trail intersections, and major canals intersecting the river. Something rang familiar about the coordinates.

Numbers, numbers, numbers. Wait a minute!

Kannon reached for his wallet, opened it, and took out the notepaper inscribed with Chấn's final words and three number sets. Then he again studied the topographical map.

XT 457-144

XT 447-144

XT 4425-1436

X-Ray Tango. XT. Grid coordinates. Idiot. This should've registered sooner, much sooner.

The number sets were straightforward standard military coordinates. Six-digit numbers identified landmarks, targets, and objectives located within a hundred-meter segment, close enough for artillery and mortars as well as for combat patrols and medevac choppers. They had always used six digits. An eight-digit coordinate fixed a point within a grid to the nearest ten meters. The eight-digit set and the missing alpha prefix on Chấn's note had thrown him—those things and the passage of time.

He plotted the numbers. The first set correlated to his outpost. The second fixed a point on the trail one kilometer west of the outpost. This, he was sure, marked the ambush site.

Finally, Kannon plotted the third coordinate, 4425-1436, another 500 meters west and a hundred meters just south of the trail. Kannon shuddered as he remembered this area. Heavily booby-trapped, the dense hedgerow defied aggressive patrolling. They'd lost at least five South Vietnamese point- and flank-men there.

Chấn's map included five hand-drawn military symbols. Kannon didn't trust his recall regarding their meanings. Most likely, the library carried texts on infantry tactics and common military symbols.

After making copies of Chấn's map, Kannon found what he was looking for on the third floor, a *Combat Leader's Field Guide*, Seventh Edition, published in 1967 by The Stackpole Company. The book had the musty smell of an old warehouse. He copied the appropriate pages and then rode the elevator back to the text room.

The first drawing failed to match anything in the book. The text referenced no icon for a fortification. Regardless, what else could the symbol represent?

Was Chấn's map drawn to scale? He overlaid Chấn's hand-drawn map over the Archives' topographical one, aligning the hexagonal-shaped symbol over the outpost two kilometers from An Định hamlet.

The next symbol represented ordnance, and the third, non-military, appeared as a starburst. Both correlated with the second coordinate, the ambush site.

An oval with Xs meant minefield. The fifth symbol, an inverted blockhouse, meant underground shelter. For whom? The last two symbols tagged the third coordinate. Inscribed next to the symbol were two lines. The first word on the first line was *Kho*, but the second word, barely legible, was *hang*—with a diacritical mark. *Hàng*, one of the words Chấn used. The second line read: *dưới mặt đất*. He speculated that translation would correspond to the meaning of the map symbols.

The map? It could have been compiled after the ambush, part of a follow-up review. If so, why would Farber have fabricated his report? Was he covering his ass in an attempt to deflect his responsibility for sending out the patrol? What was the significance of the third site?

Also, Stairn's name appeared on the envelope containing Chấn's map. Stairn—killed in action eight days after the ambush. Was there any connection? Kannon wondered if there was a report describing the circumstances of Stairn's death.

Kannon sat back and rubbed his chin. He wanted to destroy the original reports, purge all references that degraded his character worse than it already was. Shifting the cart to screen his actions, he removed Farber's ambush report and Jeffrey's black-market whitewash, then started to fold the reports and place them inside his laptop. No one else would ever read them. Like wiping the slate clean with a brushstroke, he'd clear his record if not his mind.

He looked around to see if anyone was watching, but his eyes settled on a closed-circuit camera. *I don't need to be charged with a felony.*

Reluctantly, he inserted the two original reports in their folders, hating they'd be available for others to read and forever carry a distorted, tainted view of who he saw himself to be.

Twenty

Kannon cleared Archive security, then walked outside and inhaled the damp breath of moisture-laden, cold air. He walked to his cycle and mounted. By the time he steered onto the entry ramp, the freeways already showed signs of strangulation, which mirrored his attitude toward leaving the false but condemning reports behind.

Having passed on lunch, he stopped at a Vietnamese restaurant and ordered take out. Once inside the motel room, he removed the validated copies of the reports and Chẩn's map and set them beside his two-way Vietnamese/English dictionary. He opened a notebook and scribbled while nibbling on sesame-encrusted chicken and steamed rice.

Kho hàng meant warehouse, pure and simple. *Dưới* meant under or below. *Mặt* translated to face or surface, among other possibilities. The word *đất* denoted earth, soil, land. *Dưới mặt đất*—under the face of the earth. Underground warehouse. A rough translation, but the words meshed with the fifth symbol, which confirmed his earlier speculation at the Archives.

Nevertheless, he wanted verification. He could call Lan later and confirm the translation, a good reason to hear her voice.

Plugging into the Internet white pages, Kannon searched for Farbers and Jeffreys, using all possible combinations of Christian J., Christian, C. J., and C. Next, he did the same thing with Jeffrey's. No exact full names matched, and the number of first name combinations beginning with "C" or "L" jumped into the hundreds.

A search like this could take forever, particularly since he wanted to maintain anonymity. He tapped away on the keyboard. Ten minutes later, he purchased a sophisticated Internet search service. He supplied names, social security numbers, and the 1970-listed home address for each, the latter obtained from respective orders assigning each to his advisory role in Hậu Nghĩa Province. The question was, how long would it take?

Curious, remembering to reverse the Vietnamese tradition of putting the family name first, he decided to see if a Hai Đăng Đạo or a Võ Đăng Đạo appeared on the white pages.

There were no Đăng Đạo Hais or Đăng Đạo Võs. Nor were there any double "Ds." Ten D Hais and more than one hundred D Võs cropped up. Shit. He'd hire somebody to make the calls. Of course, if what the Minhs said was true, then Đăng Đạo might be in jail . . . or dead. Still, he wanted to help Lan. If phone calls didn't work, once Stefan provided an aged image of Lan's nephew, he'd circulate it among the larger Vietnamese communities and Counterparts.

Midnight.

Farber's and Jeffrey's names rattled like sabers in his mind. A walk outside might quieten the voices.

Already, a thin crust of hoarfrost covered the grassy area, which crunched beneath his feet as he paced. The city carried the cold, damp bearing of a mausoleum. Streetlamps cast filtered light, and the suffocating mist appeared thick enough to brush aside like a portiere.

A simple thought struck.

Jeffrey had appeared to Kannon as one without substance who obtained his identity from another. Like a leach sucking blood, Jeffrey absorbed the more dominant person's being. What if the two still hung together?

He didn't want to wait for the Internet search to come through. A database program might work, but there wasn't a practical way he could think of to download from the Internet. Would the Archives have one? Then he remembered. Some library systems subscribed to databases.

Returning to his room, Kannon opened a map of the D.C./Maryland area. Okay, he was in Prince Georges County, close to Montgomery County. He began searching library websites on the Internet. Prince Georges County listed several on-line databases, but none seemed to contain the information he needed. Montgomery County listed a Reference USA Data Base, both business and residential, but it was not accessible remote. He'd have to be on site to use it.

It was five a.m. The White Oak location was nearby, but it didn't open till ten, the Archives, not until a quarter of nine. He tried to get some sleep. It didn't happen.

At a quarter to nine, Kannon called Daniel at the Archives. He said they didn't subscribe to Reference USA, so Kannon cycled to White Oak and bided time beneath the frosted holly trees framing the front entrance. When the library opened, he went directly to the information desk, familiarized himself with the system, then found a computer.

Again, no direct match materialized. Next, he searched for Farber's and Jeffrey's 1970-listed home addresses. No dice. The families had died or moved on. Tracking last names only, he found registered in the states over thirty-five hundred Farbers and forty-five hundred Jeffreys, but only forty-two C. Farbers and fifty-eight L. Jeffreys. All you had to do was check the box beside the name, and you could download to disk in a spreadsheet-compatible format—ten names at a pop. This he did.

He stuffed the disk into his laptop drive and opened the file, which was profiled in a database format. Merging the last names, Farber and Jeffrey, into one field, he sorted by state and city. Bingo. A 'C. Farber' and an 'L. Jeffrey' popped up as a tandem in Santa Fe, New Mexico. Could it be?

Whipping out his cellphone, he started to key in the Farber number. But he shut it down. He wasn't ready. Kannon considered performing a business search as well, but he wanted to get back to the Archives. Instead, he called his professorial brother.

His secretary at the university said he'd taken the day off and was at home. Kannon keyed the speed dial, got Roger's answering machine, and left a message. "Hey, Roger, this is your road-weary warrior brother. This is important. If you're home, pick up."

A moment later, "This isn't the best time."

"Yeah. What are you doing?"

His brother yawned into the phone, voiced over by Karen's annoyance. "What does he want now?"

Kannon couldn't hear Roger's response to his wife, but he heard the rustle of bedsheets. Now he understood why it wasn't the best time.

"Wait a minute," his brother said. "Let me get to my study."

Kannon chewed on a pencil while waiting.

"Okay, what's up?" Roger asked.

"You've got access to every sophisticated database in the country. Could you, or one of your graduate assistants, pull up every business name in Santa Fe, New Mexico, listing the principals' names?"

"You sound pumped. Desperate search for a woman?"

"Nice broadside." Good old Roger, always a skeptic when it came to his brother, a consistent view at least. Better than Karen's opinion of him, which seemed to degenerate with every encounter. Yet, they had something Kannon didn't, love and togetherness. "No, I'm looking for Christian J. Farber and Leonard S. Jeffrey." He gave Roger the resident addresses and phone numbers. "If something shows up, I want to know what kind of business they're in, revenues, credit history, primary suppliers—everything."

The fact was, his brother had helped him several times over the years. Kannon assisted Roger when Roger needed a practical explanation on implementing one of the myriad, complex tax law changes enacted with frightening frequency—so he could teach his students something of value or add a dose of realism to his published textbooks. And Roger put his assistants to work helping Kannon research case studies and understand the technical nuances of those same tax laws.

"Give me a couple of days," Roger said.

"You got it. I'm leaving D.C. tomorrow. I'll call you."

"You riding?"

"Yeah."

"Be careful."

"Will do."

Back at the National Archives, Kannon entertained another idea. In the field, advisory groups and regular U.S. Army units functioned under separate chains of command. There was a good chance a sizable enemy troop movement would have been reported by the regular U.S. unit's S-2.

Kannon cleared security and walked to the main counter. "Daniel, can you pull the 25th Infantry Division's intelligence reports for this period?" He wrote out the dates.

"Hmm, should be able to. Give me an hour."

While waiting, Kannon studied the advisory files for mention of Stairn's death. After combing all folders for two months succeeding the date of death inscribed on the Việt Nam Memorial, all he came up with was a simple statement:

Lieutenant Lucas R. Stairn. KIA by a hostile force 13 October 1970.

What a message for a family to receive! No circumstances were given. Maybe Stairn hadn't been an administrative gofer after all.

Daniel caught his eye. Kannon walked to the counter. "Got 'em?"

"Locked and loaded. Have fun."

Kannon tackled the inch-thick stack of 25th Infantry Division intelligence reports, bracketing his review at several days before and after 5 October 1970. Surveillance reports before the attack indicated numerous sightings of trails and bunker clusters, including references to a Việt Cộng/NVA battalion moving across the river to establish a base camp. Obviously, the 25th's S-2 had forwarded this information to Farber, who included it in his After Action Report, but conveniently omitted it from advisor intelligence summaries. Worse, neither he nor Malcolm had been informed.

Then a light bulb flashed. Before the attack, Major Farber had ordered Malcolm to switch his radio to an alternate, secure frequency. Even though, in theory, it hampered the Việt Cộng's ability to monitor transmissions, switching to an alternate frequency enabled a unit engaged in enemy contact to avoid interfering traffic on the primary radio net. All support units, the artillery and gunships, had been given the change. Useful and not uncommon, the tactic was taught at the infantry school. But the timing! Why make the change just before they were hit? As opposed to during the attack? It could have been coincidental or anticipatory.

The memory tugged at him. Kannon ran image after image through his mind, like scrolling down a computer screen, and could not remember Farber's using an alternate frequency prior to the ambush date. Curious, he retrieved the advisory team files and scrutinized the province day reports for three days before and after 5 October. The 5 October 1970 day report listed Major Christian J. Farber as being in Sài Gòn.

Something smelled rotten in Đức Huệ District, and it wasn't nước mắm sauce.

Twenty-One

Two days later, Kannon sat on his deck under the fan-shaped oak, welcoming the twenty-seven-degree dry cold. The scent of cedar washed through like a stream, and blue jays jostled among the tree branches, squawking as if to protest the splash of winter.

A steak sizzled on the grill. Charcoal hissed from the dripping fat and released a meaty aroma to stir his hunger.

His gloved hand enveloped the cellphone as he spoke into the receiver to his brother. "What'd you find out, Roger?"

"Seems your men have acquired culture since the war. Dun & Bradstreet lists Christian J. Farber as president and Leonard S. Jeffrey as vice-president of a gallery in Santa Fe called The Farber Collection."

Kannon jotted a note. "Any financial information?"

"No. They've registered as an *S* corporation but, as you might expect, declined to disclose details. Telescan and American Express came up empty too, which means they either have no debt problems or are too small to worry about."

"Tax audits?"

"Come on, Kannon. Let's not go there."

"You've done it before."

"Once."

Yeah, once, Kannon remembered, when a targeted acquiree corporation was perpetrating a tax fraud. He decided to let it go. "What kind of gallery is it?"

"Most of the information's linked to the Santa Fe Website, but we did a little more digging."

Squirrels squabbled and scattered the jays as if they were a covey of quail. "Shut up," he told the scavengers and propped the phone between his ear and shoulder to listen to his brother. "Fire away." His pencil scribbled shorthand as if attached to an EKG. "Got it. Thanks, Roger."

Farber and Jeffrey, together in Santa Fe at The Farber Collection, well, he'd join them. Kannon flipped the steak and popped the top on a Heineken. He took a drink and gazed at the sky. The sun maintained its hold over the land and cast winter shadows. Thin clouds rode the wind like vapor trails, and he thought of his ambivalence toward Meghan O'Brien.

Even though he realized his attraction to her was primarily physical, maybe he could stretch beyond his lust and develop a relationship. As his therapist had said: "Look beyond the body to the heart and mind." He punched in her number.

"Hotel Victoria."

"Meghan?"

"Kannon, hi. I was just thinking about you. How'd it go?"

Her words didn't match the tone. She sounded guarded, the door open just a crack. Kannon decided to reveal the minimum. "I've tracked Farber and Jeffrey to Santa Fe. I'm coming to Durango to pick up the GS and ride there. How about coming along?"

"We need to clear the air first."

The air looked clear to him. "What?"

"Lan."

A sensation of sweeping áo dais and graceful movement swirled in his head at the mention of her name, even if she did want to live in France. Yet, he liked Meghan's directness. No left hook, just a straight jab, but it pinged his conscience and stirred guilt.

"Meghan, Chấn's dead. Lan's important because she's my sole Vietnamese link to the past."

"You're sure?"

"Yes, I've no intention of returning to Việt Nam soil."

"That's the most comforting thing I've heard you say." The line went silent for a moment. "All right. Come ahead. I'll meet you at the airport."

After hanging up, he wondered whether he should've mentioned Lan's request to search for her nephew. It would serve no purpose now, but he might bring it up later. Also, in the back of his mind was a nagging feeling it was wrong to seek comfort in Meghan as a way of softening the impact of facing his demons.

Kannon walked through the house, entered the garage, and stared at his motorcycle gear. The matching helmets with an integrated communication system he'd purchased during his last relationship two years ago sat in unopened boxes.

Twenty-Two

Northeast of Santa Fe, Christian Farber stood on the verandah of his adobe home nestled among the piñon pine, juniper, and sparse sage. The spread commanded a sweeping view of the Sangre de Cristo Mountains. In the fall, it yielded a startling panorama of spruce and fir intermingled with multihued aspen and oak brush. But now, in mid-January, metallic silver prevailed.

Out of the grayness trotted his two Rottweilers, Fang and Snarl. Despite the chill, their black coats with chocolate markings glistened with sweat.

Farber took a swig of beer and pressed a remote control.

"Owlooooooo. Owlooooooo."

"Christian Farber, stop tormenting those dogs," said his wife Jasmine, as she joined him outside.

"Just testing security, babe. You don't want anyone breaking in and spoiling your perfect world, do you?" His breath frosted in the evening air.

A twelve-foot high perimeter wall and wired security system provided protection, which the dogs, controlled by remote-activated electronic collars, augmented with ground patrols.

"My world's not perfect," she said. "Leonard Jeffrey's coming by. What's so important he has to interrupt our Saturday night?"

A good question. Absent from the gallery today, Farber had been investigating a prospective client, a Native American Pueblo jeweler in Taos.

"You know Jeffrey. Gets excited about nothing," he said.

"I wish it were Bertha instead."

"She's ill." Hell, Jeffrey probably hadn't told Bertha he was coming. Farber wouldn't have either. She whined and nagged like a weaning cub.

Jasmine moved toward the doorway, then paused and turned. "Oh, honey, you got a letter today, from the art school. They want to know if you're going to teach Creative Marketing again."

"No, I'm finished teaching."

"Why? You're good at it."

"Fuck it. I'm not interested."

"You know that's how you attract new artists."

"Yeah, that's how I get 'em." He drained his beer and handed the bottle to Jasmine. "Bring me another one."

"All right." She grabbed the empty and went inside.

A low rumble resonated like distant thunder. Farber watched as Jeffrey's headlight swept back and forth like an oscillating searchlight seeking prey.

The barrel-chested dogs growled as the bike drew closer. Jeffrey steered the throbbing twin onto the circular drive, brought the 1996 XL1200S Harley Sportster to a halt, and dismounted.

Fang and Snarl skewered Jeffrey with almond-shaped eyes. Rearing like horses, they placed paws on each of Jeffrey's lean thighs, a sincere warning not to move unless he wanted his balls emasculated.

"Goddamn dogs," Jeffrey muttered. "After all these years, you'd think they'd know me."

Farber prolonged Jeffrey's discomfort before addressing the four-legged sentries. "Fang, Snarl—sit. Hello, Jeffrey. Too bad about Bertha, eh?"

"Said to tell you she couldn't make it. Obligations, you know."

"Yeah, right. She'd interfere with your drooling." Bertha badgered Jeffrey about alleged infidelities, even though Farber had a hard time picturing a woman who'd grant Jeffrey sexual favors.

Jeffrey followed Farber inside.

"Jasmine around?"

"Jazzy, greet the Captain."

She entered the foyer, a slit skirt exposing her tight, trim thighs, and a V-neck sweater displaying firm cleavage.

"Hi, Captain. Welcome."

"For stealing your time," Jeffrey said, pulling a crushed, short-stemmed crimson rose from underneath his jacket.

She considered the offering. "I'll put it in a vase."

Farber watched Jeffrey's eyes trail after Jasmine, a woman

twenty years junior whose body measurements distributed over her five-foot five-inch frame summed up to her hundred-pound weight.

"Drink?" Farber led Jeffrey into the den.

"Bourbon and pineapple juice."

"Jazzy, make the Captain his cocktail. Use the Kentucky Gentleman. And don't forget the crushed ice." He motioned to Jeffrey. "Take a seat, Captain. Tell me what's on your mind."

They sat in overstuffed, leather recliners beside a crackling fire in an adobe-lined hearth. Navaho woven rugs softened the Mexican tile floor.

"I need a drink first." As always, Jeffrey stared at the hunting trophies hung on the wall. "You've got everything working for you."

Farber smiled at the envy in Jeffrey's voice. "Yep, but I miss the military."

"Five years was plenty for me," Jeffrey said.

Fifteen years of service hadn't been enough for Farber. He bemoaned his loss of command. It still pissed him off the Army passed him over for lieutenant colonel, even after two extended tours in Việt Nam. Too heavy-handed. Weak people skills. Would have trouble adjusting to peacetime conditions, they'd said. "Fuck you," he'd said.

"The gallery has been good to us," he said to Jeffrey.

"The estate lawsuit was a pain in the ass, though."

Jeffrey's smirk stretched like a distended balloon.

"I told you never to mention the fucking lawsuit," Farber said. A drawn-out nuisance case, it wasn't his fault the gallery's previous owner had contracted pancreatic cancer. Farber recalled Chellenworth's emaciated body and deteriorating mind, but the man signed on the bottom line and executed a legal contract.

Jasmine brought Jeffrey's cocktail and handed her husband another beer. As she walked away, the scent of gardenia lingered, which heightened Farber's lust to get between his wife's thighs.

"How's the gallery doing this month?" Farber asked, even more irritated at Jeffrey.

"I haven't done the numbers yet," Jeffrey said, scooting forward in the chair.

"Goddamnit, Jeffrey! You know I want mid-month estimates as well as month-end closings. A high school kid could do it."

A sudden wind raked across the back patio. The gust wobbled the outdoor ceiling fan off-kilter. Like Jeffrey, Farber thought, who, when under pressure, often went astray.

"I've been preoccupied," Jeffrey said.

"About what?" Farber's bottle smacked the table. The beer frothed over. "For God's sake, spill it."

"Received this email today." He flapped a folded printout in Farber's face.

He snatched it from Jeffrey's hand and silently read the message addressed to The Farber Collection.

Dear Mr. Christian Farber:

It has come to my attention that you and your partner, Mr. Leonard Jeffrey, have registered an import/export business in Việt Nam. I, too, have an import/export business. For a long time, I have desired to expand my distribution arm in the United States of America. It is my firm conviction we should explore a possible business relationship for mutual profit.

Soon you will receive by mail a catalog detailing available products. If you are interested, perhaps you or your partner can return to Việt Nam for an exploratory visit.

The Grand Plantation

Exotic Arts and Crafts from the Orient.

"So?" Farber said.

"There's more. You read the editorial page in today's paper?"

"Nope." Incredulous, Farber stared him down. "You disrupt my weekend to discuss emails and editorials?"

"One piece addressed the proliferation of minority gangs and suggested a nationwide organization, which included the Vietnamese."

"What the fuck does the editorial have to do with a business solicitation?" Farber asked.

Jeffrey tugged at his collar as if to allow more breathing room. "The editorial reminded me of how Hai operated. You ever wonder if he fled the country?"

"Jesus Christ, Jeffrey. You worry too much."

"You didn't find any trace of Hai when you searched for a partner?"

"No, damnit. I checked the phone book, the Ministry of Trade, the Chamber of Commerce and Industry, and the Foreign Trade Development Center. The communists ground him under when they overran the country. Don't be such a wimp. Live in the present, my boy."

Digesting this rebuke, Jeffrey looked like a kid eating collard greens. It was times like this, when the Captain begged for a bone, Farber's disdain reached the boiling point, almost overriding his appreciation for Jeffrey's obsequiousness and deference.

"Yes, sir." Jeffrey brandished his Kentucky Cocktail. "I reviewed the files. Of potential business partners based in Sài Gòn, you called on several—Sài Gòn Tea, English Channel, the French Legacy, America's Gift, the Vietnamese Consortium, and the Hồ Chí Minh City Connection. But no Grand Plantation. I'm wondering how they reached us."

"I didn't call on Sài Gòn Tea either, just obtained literature. And remember, we're registered for Christ's sake. Maybe The Grand Plantation found us the same way I found its competitors."

"What do you think we should do?"

"Glad you asked. Study the fucking promotional literature and product catalog when they arrive. If we think The Grand Plantation might be a good fit, call on them."

Jeffrey grimaced. "Do we need this?"

"Opportunity." Farber glowered at his subordinate. "The Aussies are already in Việt Nam big time. I expect an influx of capital from both communist and free world countries."

Farber rose and ambled to Jeffrey's chair.

"We get in there now," he said, putting his hand on Jeffrey's shoulder, "we can clean up."

"I don't know about The Grand Plantation," Jeffrey said, "but the other vendor products don't match what we broker."

"Don't worry about it. It's a tax write-off at worst, you numbskull. We'll set it up as a separate business, maybe in a concentrated Vietnamese community in Texas or California. Hire someone to run it."

"I guess." Jeffrey stared at his empty glass.

"Jazzy, refills," Farber hollered.

She sauntered in, plopped down two beers, a bottle of Kentucky Gentleman, a carton of pineapple juice, and a bowl of ice.

"Thank ya, darling. Guess you mix your own," Farber said to Jeffrey as Jasmine stomped out of the room. He decided to lighten Jeffrey's mood. "I ever describe the new brochure I've been thinking about?"

"No."

"The Farber Collection introduces the Developing Artists Wing. We specialize in exhibiting young artists willing to set their idealism aside and sell body and soul to have their work displayed. Integrate your body with mine and receive a commission discount."

"Both male and female?" Jeffrey quipped.

"Both male and female. That's a good one, Captain." Farber slapped him on the back again. This time he caught a whiff of Jeffrey's oiled hair. "There's something else I want you to take care of."

"What is it?" Jeffrey sloshed the contents of his drink over the sides of the glass.

"You know that young Wasp living in Abiquiu, the one making modern jewelry in sterling and turquoise? His work sells well, but Mr. Sanderson is getting a big head. He's threatened to leave us, take his work to another gallery in town that charges half our current commission. Convince him not to do so."

"My leverage?"

"Here's a nice photograph for persuasion."

Farber handed Jeffrey a simple four-inch by six-inch print. It showed a couple engaged in backdoor intercourse.

"I take it the woman's not the man's wife."

"Brilliant, Captain, brilliant," Farber said.

Jeffrey chuckled, but Farber cut him short. "Be sure your passport and visa are in order, in case we need to investigate The Grand Plantation."

Twenty-Three

Light snow dusted northern New Mexico's cropped mesas and bordering sage near the Jicarilla Apache Nation. The sun traveled its mid-winter elliptical orbit and shone dimly as Kannon's motorcycle carved through the scrim-like veil. They'd left Durango mid-morning, four days after his departure from the National Archives, and been riding two hours.

"Dadgummit, I'm freezing back here," Meghan stammered into the headset.

He pulled over. The GS rode high in the back. Maybe she was getting too much wind. "You got the thermostat turned up?"

"Thermostat?" Meghan slipped off the bike and flapped her arms for circulation.

Oops.

"You're not using the thermostat?"

She removed her helmet and set it on the seat, then located the device. "This? It's not working," she said, now jogging in place.

Kannon scuffed the newly fallen snow with his boot. He had purchased for her cold-weather riding gear, including an electric vest, but in his haste failed to mention plugging into the motorcycle's accessory outlet was not enough.

"I assumed you'd know to turn it on. Just flip the switch and rotate the nub there."

"Keep assuming things Kannon Ballard, and you'll have an ice woman behind you, in more ways than one."

Capricious winds raked the powdered snow like whitecaps on gray seas.

"Can't believe you lasted a hundred miles. You're tough."

"Just what I aspire to be. How much farther?"

"Less than a hundred and fifty miles." He pulled out the map. "We'll ride through Dulce and Aztec, then drop south at Chama. It should be an easy ride as long as the weather holds."

They remounted. Kannon activated the intercom system, which so far had behaved sporadically, with considerable conversation lost to static caused by the wet snow. "They own an art gallery. Bought it in nineteen eighty-five, Roger told me. Been together all this time, I guess."

"What?"

He repeated his statement, wishing the intercom featured a better squelch adjustment for wind and noise.

"Sounds legit," she said.

"I can't visualize them in fine arts. I never considered either one creative or sophisticated."

"Fifteen minutes study a day equals an expert over time," she said.

The static faded. "Yeah, yeah."

"Who do they represent?"

"They focus on American west painters—up and comers like Chuck DeHaan and Greg Beecham, but Roger said they've transacted original Remingtons, Russells, and Wyeths. Also, they handle sterling and turquoise jewelry and occasional photographic prints of Cartier-Bresson and Weston."

"Nice. I'm impressed."

"With what I know?"

"No, with what they carry."

"Oh."

"I'm just kidding."

Kannon downshifted into third and rounded a curve. Meghan shifted her weight, one arm a little tighter around his waist. As the road straightened, he inhaled a bucket full of cold air through his partially opened faceshield.

"I think the gallery's a front," he said.

"Oh, God, you would."

Her comment pricked his frustration. Santa Fe would test the relationship all right. He should have had a stereo system installed so they could listen to music.

Finally, by mid-afternoon, they pulled alongside the Hotel St. Francis on Don Gaspar Avenue, one block southwest of the Plaza.

Meghan hopped off the passenger saddle and stretched. "How'd you get a reservation?"

163

"Skier broke his leg."

Kannon surveyed the three-story historic hotel jacketed in sand-hued stucco, which was accented by blue awnings, white window trim, and flower boxes. Ground floor, oval porticos implied openness, while above, waist-high balustrades shielded view windows and suggested privacy. They pinched the bags off the bike and carried them between twin lanterns, across a narrow verandah, then into a high-ceilinged lobby. Embellished by wrought-iron chandeliers, the reception area also included a fireplace.

"You're saved," Meghan said, heading toward the crackling fire. "My fingers don't work." She rubbed her hands together. "And my legs are stiff as boards."

While she warmed herself, Kannon registered, then he and Meghan rode an elevator to the second floor. Inside their room, a king-sized brass bed, an armoire in one corner, and a French writing desk in another greeted them. Green curtains and taupe linens offset burgundy carpeting, and a television and a small refrigerator completed the arrangement.

Kannon plunked down the saddlebags. "How about a liqueur?"

"Sounds good."

He called the Artist's Pub and ordered double shots of Triple Sec. After the drink, a long, hot shower, and a change of clothes, Meghan seemed relaxed. And she smelled sweet, like an almond-scented candle.

"I'm hungry," she said after he finished cleaning up. "Let's eat . . . at a good restaurant."

"Agreed."

Their boots clacked like horseshoes on the red tile floor as they walked across the lobby and past a wood-paneled bar. They exited the hotel and strolled down Don Gaspar to San Francisco Street.

Snowflakes drifted in white tufts but lost color when they hit the ground. Leafless cottonwoods groped into the wintry air. Streetlamps exuded a specious intimacy, like artillery flares bursting under a cloud-laden sky. The shrouded horizon reduced the sun to an orange blip, which wavered like a knuckleball until dusk turned and buried it.

"It's beautiful tonight," she said.

"I'm glad you came."

"Me too."

They walked until reaching the La Fonda Hotel, then entered La Plazuela Restaurant situated in an enclosed courtyard. A young hostess ushered them past tables adorned with bright blue napkins, yellow plates, and daisies, then seated them at a corner table near the east wall.

Meghan ordered the Codorniz, a roasted, stuffed quail, and a fine Cru Beaujolais, while Kannon opted for grilled chicken fajitas and a Corona. Waiting for their order, Kannon's mind drifted to Farber and Jeffrey.

"Your body's here, but your mind's not," she said.

"It's Farber's report and the map."

Her leg brushed his.

"Tell me," Meghan said. "Maybe we can chip away the wall between us."

"You think I can't handle a relationship as long as Farber and Jeffrey are in the picture?"

"It interferes."

"I suppose it does." He placed his palms on the table and leaned forward. "But I have to confront them."

Her eyes widened as if to drill a larger hole in his head to drive home her message. "I don't understand war. I'm trying to understand you and your need to resurrect the dead instead of letting go."

"The issue never died. It lives inside me."

"Maybe I can help you bury it," Meghan said.

That could be nice, Kannon thought, Meghan, the widow, moving past her deceased husband, and he, the veteran, moving beyond his dark cloud.

Still . . .

"I believe Chẩn's use of the word *pha* was an abbreviated reference to Farber. Its usage in Vietnamese could mean to mix, joke, prepare tea, or destroy. None of those fit. He was referring to Farber."

The waiter delivered their dinners. Heat radiated from his fajitas, which teased his appetite. Meghan cut into her quail filled with pistachio stuffing and carved a mouth-sized bite.

"Yum. This is wonderful," she said. "Want some?"

"No, thank you."

Meghan cut her eyes to his. "Your conclusion is convenient, I think. You sure it's not something you need to believe?"

This was not the way to bury it. Maybe this wouldn't be nice after all. "You interested in this or not?"

"Yes, I am. Go ahead."

"I believe *kho hàng* translates to warehouse. And *dưới mặt đất* means underground. Underground warehouse."

"Who translated these?"

"I did."

She raised her eyebrows.

"Lan helped."

He noticed Meghan wince.

"She agreed with the translation?"

"Said it's possible."

"A stretch," she said.

A chill penetrated his soul, caused by Meghan's persistent doubt. "This isn't going anywhere." He swigged the rest of his Corona. "Perhaps it's best I tell you the whole story."

She waved away their waiter. "Finally."

Words tumbled from his mouth like spilled marbles as he repeated what he'd told Lan about the ambush. Her face softened and dropped ten years in the harsh light.

"What a terrible situation. No wonder . . . you never told your brother?"

"No."

"Your ex-wife?"

"No."

"Why did you tell Lan?"

He pulled on his mustache and contemplated his response. "Since the war took place in Việt Nam, that's where my story came out."

She looked up as she rimmed the bottle lip with her

166

forefinger. "You felt safe there."

"Yes. Anyway, I think the third map coordinate identifies a tunnel system or an underground cache of enemy weapons and ammunition. And I believe Farber and Jeffrey knew about it—and maybe Chấn."

"A conspiracy."

"Call it a cabal." He twisted his napkin in knots. "Farber and Jeffrey were entangled up to their eyeballs. If not, why didn't they warn me?"

"What if Farber found out about the cache after the ambush? Didn't you say Chấn's use of the word *pha* could have been in Vietnamese, and if so, wasn't one of the meanings to destroy? What if they meant to destroy the cache? After all, the map was in the files."

"I agree, the map being in the files was no accident." The beer exacerbated the pace and intensified his tone. "But I believe Stairn, who was killed in action eight days later, put it there because he suspected something was going on. And why would Farber fabricate the After Action Report? I think he was covering more than just his ass."

"You're convinced the report was a lie?"

"You don't believe me, do you?"

"It's not that." Her eyes grew round as saucers. "You're accusing two men of . . ."

He tightened his grip on the bottle. "Dereliction of duty. Treason. Murder."

"An American major and captain, why?"

"You still think I'm chasing ghosts?"

"The story's hard to believe, Kannon. I'm concerned you've connected Farber and the underground warehouse because you need to."

"And I need to because?"

"Because losing your men has hurt you terribly and you're trying to do anything, find any reason, to avoid facing your pain."

A current jolted him as if he'd touched a live circuit. "I believe the goddamned ambush wasn't my fault. Oh, Christ . . ."

Tears welled in his eyes, the first time in thirty-two years his emotions had betrayed him. It was like his soul had turned to water, draining the life from him.

She reached across the table and touched his cheek. "I didn't mean to hurt you. But Kannon, you were ambushed, for God's sake. You did what you were told, the best you could. It was a tragedy of war. Why can't you accept it?"

He wiped his eyes with a napkin and gathered himself. "I'd rather die than live with the uncertainty."

"I wish you'd leave it alone."

Meghan shot straight, but Jesus Christ! It seemed she just wanted him to drop the past as opposed to reconciling it.

"I will, once I'm done with Farber and Jeffrey."

They polished off their dinner and departed the café. The earth had spun from beneath the clouds, and stars blanketed the sky like spattered crystal. And somewhere in the Far East, at points in time, monsoons killed tigers.

Twenty-Four

Leonard Jeffrey couldn't help but notice the blond man's emotional leakage. Weak, he thought, to lose control in public. Wait a minute—the man's voice. A distant chord rang familiar.

Bertha stopped chewing and looked up. "What, dear? Did you say something?"

"Nothing."

"Would you ask the waiter to bring another order of tacos?"

Her third, Jeffrey noted. But he couldn't take his eyes off the couple sitting across the room. An attractive, full-figured woman accompanied some guy. He'd never seen either one before. Probably snowbirds.

The face . . . the man's face. No, it couldn't be. "I'll be damned. It's Kannon Ballard."

"Waiter." Bertha's voice pierced the restaurant like a distress signal.

"Do you have to yell? The whole town can hear you."

"Well, someone has to exercise initiative."

Jeffrey ignored her and concentrated on the pair. One trait he carried from his military years, paranoia, normally spawned groundless fears, but on occasion, had served him well. Like the night he dreamed the Việt Cộng stormed The Farber Collection. The next morning, he had concealed himself behind the one-way mirror and scrutinized each visitor as a drill sergeant does recruits. It paid off because he intervened in time to restrain an irate young artist from bludgeoning Farber with a piece of the artist's own craftsmanship, a newly crafted tomahawk made to look old.

"What the hell is he doing here?" Jeffrey mumbled.

"What, dear?"

"I'm not talking to you, damnit. Just thinking out loud."

"Well, pay attention to me," she said.

Please. "Bertha, one of our commission artists just walked past. Farber and I have been trying to contact him, but he's a wandering artist without an address or phone." He scooted his chair from the table. "Why don't you take a cab home?"

Bertha's cheeks puffed like a bellows. "I'll wait, dear."

Jeffrey left the restaurant and tailed the couple to the Hotel St. Francis. As he watched them disappear into the lobby, dormant angst gushed forth like water from a ruptured main. Lieutenant Kannon Ballard, you self-righteous, arrogant son of a bitch. The man he'd always feared might someday surface. Jeffrey did an about-face and returned to the café just as his wife finished ravaging the third order.

"Hi, sweetie. I can't wait to get home tonight. Tacos make me horny."

Oh, God. The water buffalo. Still, if he had to make love with his wife, he now had an indelible impression of Ballard's woman to enhance the experience.

Before retiring for the night, Jeffrey placed a call.

"You're sure?" Farber said.

Jeffrey gritted his teeth. "Yeah."

Twenty-Five

The next morning, when Meghan emerged from the bathroom, she saw Kannon hunched in a chair, facing the opposite direction—still tuning her out. Had she been too prickly the night before? In one sense, she was glad Kannon had opened up. But how could she make him understand she wanted him to let go of it all so they could develop a relationship.

Regardless, she intended to make a conscious effort to be supportive. "What are you doing?"

He turned and faced her. "Just finished watching a video. I shot the footage in Việt Nam with a gadget Roger gave me."

His voice sounded strong, his facial expression, rugged and determined. A whiff of almond stirred her sensually, but Meghan could tell he was preoccupied. "On what? I don't see a VCR."

"This." He held up the pager and an object the size of a Palm Pilot.

"A pager?"

"Appearances deceive. It's a video camera with a wide-angle lens, complete with a thin battery pack."

"How clever. Show me how it works." She massaged her scalp with a rough-textured, peach-scented towel.

A quizzical expression swept across his face as though he doubted her sincerity.

"Really," she said.

"All right." He went over the unit's controls, how to move to capture the optimum image. "It's important to keep the pager straight, upright. Strap it to your belt. It's easy to activate."

She became amused. "You're kidding. What happens if you push the wrong button? Will it explode, or will I have an orgasm?"

"The instructions weren't clear on that point."

"How do you play back the footage?"

"Wireless monitor, complete with a four-inch flip-up screen."

Meghan shook her head in disbelief. "What won't they think

171

of next. You sure you're not a spy?"

"I'm sure."

Ambling to the dresser, she picked up the necklace her husband had given her—a Star of David in roughcast sterling with turquoise near the points—and slipped it on. "I've been thinking about last night. Have you considered suing Farber?"

"Violation of civil rights. Yeah, checked it out, not practical—a statute of limitations, civil law versus criminal law versus military law. Besides, I have no concrete proof. It's my word against his."

Kannon wanted revenge, not a clarification, she figured.

"Where's the gallery?" she asked.

"In the artist district, on Canyon Road."

"I'll go with you if you want."

Her comment appeared to surprise him. He stood, walked to her side, and hugged her. "Thanks, I don't plan to go until tomorrow, so I'll think about your offer. Today I'm going to check with the Chamber of Commerce and BBB. Expect I'll be gone most of the day."

Meghan wondered about the delay, but what could she do? Then it hit her.

"Are you afraid to face them?" she asked.

His cheeks twitched like shaken Jell-O.

"No," he said.

"Kannon."

His eyes trailed far away, perhaps to Việt Nam. "A little."

"I understand." This time she held him close. "I'm sure it's difficult."

"Yes, it is difficult." He stepped away. "Look, why don't you take the day and shop . . . or go skiing. Tonight, we'll talk more."

The sun lifted above a cloud and burned a broad swath through their window. "A nice idea. I might just do it, hit the slopes outside Santa Fe."

"Okay, see you later."

She waited while he pulled on his jacket, then offered a light kiss to her lips. After he left the room, she walked to the bedside table and picked up the pager video. She decided to help, show her support. Go to the gallery and get the layout of the place. See what kind of customers visit. Obtain cards or brochures of the artists they represent. Ask questions tourists ask. They won't know me from Eve.

Meghan faced the mirror and fixed the instrument on her waist belt. She practiced turning it off and on, then grabbed her coat and walked out the door.

* * *

Tired of being Farber's henchman, tired of executing his sordid tricks to keep young artists in line, Jeffrey jerked open The Farber Collection's doors to another day. He understood why Farber kept him around. Like an M-16 without a firing pin, each was ineffective without the other, but it seemed to Jeffrey he was always the one who got squeezed.

He sat down at the computer to work on the month-end financials. Who gives a shit about the bottom line! All Farber wants is a pool of desperate airheads to screw.

Nor did he need the headaches from their fledgling import/export business. They didn't need an Asian wing. Mostly, he damn sure didn't want to return to Việt Nam. Regardless of what Farber said, the specter of Hai haunted Jeffrey. How a man as cruel and ugly as Hai could possess such an inordinate command presence, demanding and extracting unwavering loyalty, had always befuddled him. If he conjured up characteristics defining the cruelest man in the world, Hai fit. At times, Farber took a close second.

Lost in time and memory, Jeffrey almost missed the faint security chirp announcing visitors. He stood and observed through the one-way mirror a raven-haired beauty browsing in the front.

Kannon Ballard's woman.

Jeffrey's agitation turned to lust, even though she was the kind of woman who forever eluded his grasp.

He strolled into the showroom. "May I help you?"

"No, thank you. Just taking a day off from skiing and looking around. Pleasant gallery."

"Thanks." He offered his hand. "Hi, I'm Leonard Jeffrey, the assistant manager. Let me know if I can be of service. Be sure and sign our guest register. We'll put you on our mailing list."

She withdrew her hand and signed the book. Jeffrey allowed an internal smile of satisfaction. Then he excused himself to greet a couple who'd just come into the gallery. After welcoming the new art lovers, he still quivered from the Ballard woman's moist palm.

Mr. Christian J. Farber, swaggering like royalty, entered by the backdoor, distracting Jeffrey from his observations. Jeffrey motioned Farber aside and indicated with a nod to join him in the inner office.

"The woman with Ballard," Jeffrey said, as he closed the door. "Watch. Other than being a knockout, she keeps walking around the gallery, looking at her pager."

"Maybe someone's paging her," Farber quipped. "Hell, Jeffrey, if that was your woman, you'd never let her out of your sight."

Jeffrey savored her moist palm but shifted his interpretation of it from lewdness to nervousness. "She's picked up every brochure and business card in the place. And made notes."

"She has, huh? This is no coincidence. Let's have a chat."

* * *

Holding his unlit Meerschaum, Kannon was reviewing notes when Meghan walked into the room, beaming. "You're back early. You didn't ski?"

"I have something to show you," she said.

He couldn't imagine what enthralled her.

"I think I'm ready for the CIA." She removed her jacket and flung it on the bed.

Meghan unhooked the pager video and then unfastened the harness that secured the battery pack. Eyes gleaming, she handed him the camera.

"What in the world did you do?"

"Connect it to the monitor," she said, grinning.

He did, and they sat on the edge of the bed. He pushed the playback button on the remote. The video was jerky but sufficient for him to watch Farber and Jeffrey come alive.

Both were as he remembered. Farber stood about six feet four. Weight well over 250 pounds, now with a small paunch. Dark hair turned gray. Jeffrey, his face a cross between a vulture and a boar, measured several inches shorter. Still lean and wiry, the balding Jeffrey now wore glasses and appeared to have a tattoo stitched onto his right forearm.

She crossed her legs. "How'd I do?"

Nonplussed, he didn't know how to respond. "Okay . . . I guess."

"I thought you'd be pleased." The excitement and anticipation drained from her body.

"It's their faces . . ."

"You've turned pale," she said.

Kannon leaned against the headboard. Far different sensations packed his mind as compared to the coalesced memories unraveled by thunderclaps, intrusive bad dreams, and the smell of gunpowder. The pain bit, like having a nine-inch incision sewed up without anesthesia. He rewound and watched the tape again, noting the gallery's physical layout, then set the monitor down.

She touched his shoulder. "Do you want to stop?"

"No. What else?"

"Here's the gallery's promotional literature," she said.

"Let's take a look."

Together they leafed through artists' brochures and press releases. They contained little value. But when she handed him a business card, he took a long, deep breath.

"Whoa, fascinating. Roger didn't latch onto this." Along with contact information, the card denoted Farber and Jeffrey as importing and exporting exotic arts and crafts of the Orient. "I didn't see any Asian arts and crafts on the video. Any in the shop?"

"No," she said. "I almost missed the business cards. There were a few in a cardholder on one of the display cabinets. What do you think it means?"

"I don't know. We need to determine what exotic products they trade." He tamped his pipe and struck a match. "The email address could come in handy. Wonder if they have a website."

She pointed to a web address on the bottom right-hand corner of the brochure.

He opened the laptop and hit the power switch. "Here,

connect this to the phone jack, will you?"

Meghan made the connection. "Any luck with the BBB or Chamber of Commerce?"

"Not much. Both gave boilerplate responses."

Kannon waited for the browser to activate. After visiting the BBB and the Chamber of Commerce, he had checked out their residences. Jeffrey lived in a typical middle-class ranchette, easy to observe and penetrate. Farber, in contrast, lived on a sprawling, forested compound, with a probable high-tech security system.

The web browser popped alive. Kannon keyed in the website address, and an Asian art page materialized with the message, "Under construction."

He checked his watch. It read 1600 hours. He pursed his lips and looked Meghan square in the eye. "I'm going."

"Sure you don't want me to go with you?"

"Yes," he said. "We shouldn't be seen together."

She parted her lips as if to question why, but the word lodged in her throat.

"I'm going to lay out everything like a business plan, sequential and chronological."

"Kannon, I understand your chief financial officer approach. But if this man is who you say he is, I don't think he's going to sign a confession."

"I have no idea how he'll react."

What concerned him was Meghan's visit to the gallery, which he considered dangerous for her and for him. Seeing Farber and Jeffrey on video brought to life the evil he attributed to those men. He wondered whether it was a good idea to have brought Meghan to Santa Fe.

Twenty-Six

Kannon clipped to his belt a quick release holster accommodating the bulging Sig Sauer .40-caliber. He pulled on a loose-fitting jacket and slung a camera over his shoulder.

"What?" Meghan wore an exasperated expression. "Is the gun necessary?"

"Hope not."

"You're scaring me."

"I intend to scare them."

He walked out the door, downstairs and through the lobby onto the street, mounted and started the cycle.

The sun wore its late-afternoon shadow. The air smelled damp and cool like a river flowing beneath a wooden bridge. As he rode, his engine hummed with the steady cadence of a hand-beat drum. Riding to the corner of Paseo De Peralta and Canyon Road, he found a narrow alley and stashed the motorcycle. For twenty minutes, he reconnoitered the area, observing major galleries and street intersections. These he committed to memory. Then, concentrating on The Farber Collection, he noted its exterior appeared like a miniature Pueblo dwelling, only in mock adobe, with protruding circular timbers to support its flat roof. He glanced inside. One couple browsed in the first showroom, another in the northwest wing.

Kannon crossed the street to a coffee house catty-corner to the gallery. He ordered a cappuccino and retired to the front patio, spreading a newspaper before him. To him, the publication spouted gibberish, until dusk crept in and obscured the written word.

He waited. Gallery lights splayed onto the street like celestial lanterns. Leafless trees stood as burnished skeletons. As shops emptied, he visualized storekeepers closing the day's work.

He imagined how Farber and Jeffrey would react to seeing him after thirty-two years.

Remember me—you sons of bitches? Lieutenant Kannon Ballard. The one you shafted. Your legacy. He leveled the business end of the .40-caliber at Jeffrey's head and pulled the trigger. Blood spurted from the slimy weasel's forehead. And now you, you arrogant traitor. Farber trembled, started to speak, and hit the floor begging.

Thirty minutes later, Kannon rose, strode across the street, and entered the well-lighted gallery. A bell chimed, and cameras tracked his movement, but no one greeted him. As depicted on Meghan's video, the shop contained two exhibition rooms, which he estimated to total fifteen hundred square feet, with an open door in the rear he assumed led to an office. Western paintings and prints hung on ivory-colored walls, and sterling/turquoise jewelry shined inside five glass display tables.

No one occupied the immaculate, hardwood reception desk, so Kannon walked through the gallery to the office. Farber was seated at his desk, Jeffrey looking over his shoulder.

"Captain Jeffrey. We have a visitor," Farber said, eyes glaring over half-moon glasses. "We wondered when you'd show up."

Their lack of surprise threw him off guard.

"Hello, Major Farber, Captain Jeffrey."

"What do you want?" Jeffrey said, his smirk apparently a permanent fixture.

"How's the import/export business, fellows? Didn't realize the Vietnamese were into Old West realism, or that they fashioned turquoise and silver jewelry."

Farber swiveled aside the computer monitor. "We believe in expansion."

"Expansion from what . . . smuggling weapons and drugs?" Kannon scoffed.

"You piece of shit," Jeffrey said.

"Now Jeffrey, let's be courteous to our guest. Remember, our boy here may be suffering from *mental deficiencies*. We don't want to set him off."

"Perhaps I should call the police," Jeffrey smacked his lips as if kissing a horse's ass, "in case he loses control."

"Oh, I don't think that'll be necessary. We can handle Lieutenant Ballard."

"Cut the bullshit, Farber." Kannon unzipped his jacket and put his hands on his hips.

"Say your piece, Ballard."

"I've come to collect a debt."

"And what might that debt be?" Farber asked.

"The retraction of a lie."

"What lie?"

"The lie you concocted to ruin my life."

Farber shook his head and chuckled. "You're still trying to blame someone for leading your men into an ambush."

Jeffrey stepped back and leaned against the wall, stuffing his hands in his pockets and crossing one foot over the other. Kannon knew they were enjoying themselves and couldn't tell if he was coming close to denting their armor. "The mistake I made was to follow your orders."

"I distinctly remember ordering you to stay in the outpost," Farber said. "You wanted to be a Hot Dog."

"You murdered fifteen people, one American and fourteen Vietnamese, murdered them just as if you'd pulled the trigger yourself. And I, of course, was also to have been killed. And Stairn. Did you have him killed him too?"

"You think anyone gives a shit about the loss of those men?"

"Yeah, I do. And their families."

"Casualties of your incompetence," Farber said.

Jeffrey pushed away from the wall and faced Kannon. "You're the murderer."

"Don't crowd me, asshole."

Jeffrey sniffled, then backpedaled.

Farber raked his chair away from the desk and stood. "Lieutenant Ballard, my boy, if you're concerned about it, why don't you explain yourself to the dead sergeant's parents. I'm sure they'd love to hear how your lust for glory and disregard for human life led to their son's death."

"Might be a little harder with the Vietnamese families," Jeffrey said, laughing.

Steamed, Kannon refrained from clobbering Jeffrey. "For years, I've lived with this guilt. What were you assholes covering up?"

"This has gone far enough. I'm calling—"

"Hold on, Jeffrey. What term do psychologists use? Transference? Our boy's trying to transfer his guilt and incompetence to us."

Artillery fire bracketed—fire for effect. "You like words. I'll give you words," Kannon said. "I've been to the National Archives. Found your fabricated After Action Report on the ambush. Night of five October."

"I wrote a lot of After Action Reports. Accurately. I was a professional."

"You wrote that the 25th Infantry Division intelligence reported a large enemy troop concentration moving across the river to establish a base camp. You never told me."

Farber shrugged.

"You wrote that you ordered us to stay in the outpost after the attack."

"That I do remember. You disobeyed an order."

"No, you commanded me to lead a patrol and pursue."

"It's a lie. And you can't prove otherwise."

"The lies are yours. The duty roster listed you as being in Sài Gòn. Where were you—with Hai at the Việt Cộng command post?"

"Jeffrey, isn't this a nice yarn he's concocted, but we've no more time for fairy tales. It's closing time. I'm going home."

Farber, in that disjointed gait Kannon remembered, moved toward him. He held his ground. "There's more."

"Oh, I'm sure there is," Farber said.

"Remember Chẩn, my interpreter? He's now a US citizen, prepared to testify against you in a heartbeat. He told me everything. The map coordinates. The underground stash."

"You're a poor poker player," Farber said. "Get out before we have you arrested for trespassing."

"I'm not finished."

"You're finished." Farber tried to elbow his way past, but Kannon blocked the doorway.

"Delusional bastard." Jeffrey reached for the phone and started punching the keypad.

Kannon placed his right hand on the pistol butt but thought better of it. He stepped aside, turned, and faced Farber. "I'll be seeing you again."

Twenty-Seven

Kannon wiped the condensation from their hotel room window and pasted his face against the cold glass. Dawn broke clear. Down the street, a sign flashed a twenty-eight-degree temperature reading. In contrast, the memory of yesterday's encounter with Farber and Jeffrey burned like acid.

Meghan threw back the covers and scrambled out of bed. "What are you going to do now?"

"Leave it alone, I guess. I've done what's reasonable. A return visit to Việt Nam. Confronted Farber and Jeffrey." What were his options? Kidnap and torture them into a confession. Would they retaliate? He searched for answers. None came. Given his uncertainty, he resolved to wait and see. "Don't know if I could accomplish anything else."

"I watched the weather forecast while you were showering." She winked at him while pulling on a sweater. "Roads are clear. Fresh powder at Taos. Would you like to go skiing?"

Kannon stroked his mustache. Hell, he was as clean as he was ever going to be. Nothing could erase the tragedy of war. Enjoy life while possible.

"Nice idea. Let's do it." He gave her a light squeeze.

They finished dressing, went downstairs, and crossed the lobby to reach the street. He lowered the bike's tire pressure for better cold-weather traction, then mounted and pushed the starter button.

"Not many folks motorcycle to ski runs. Hop on."

Meghan stabilized herself by holding onto the rear luggage rack. He let out the clutch and slipped into first gear, easing into traffic. The roads were clear. Shifting into second, then third, Kannon proceeded south on Don Gaspar and navigated west along Paseo De Peralta to reach the highway leading to Taos. The crisp air whistled through his open faceshield. The cold blast energized him.

He head-checked over his left shoulder, signaled, and moved into the left lane. A black Jeep Wrangler did the same, then accelerated. Kannon retained visual contact using the motorcycle's rearview mirrors. The Jeep continued quick, aggressive maneuvers.

"Meghan, we have a tailgater. I'm goosing the throttle," he said over the intercom while shifting into fourth. "Hang on."

The Jeep closed the distance between them. Probably a wannabe taking a closer look at the motorcycle. It happened often. Once alongside, the driver gave a thumb-up and moved past.

"Kannon, the engine sounds like it's right behind me."

Again, he looked. The black bruiser filled the mirror. "We have a bad apple."

He countersteered into the right lane.

"It's right beside me," she screamed.

Head-check left. The Jeep kept pace. Kannon downshifted from fourth to third, maintaining a steady throttle while positioning the motorcycle for a quick thrust of torque.

"Can you see who's driving?" He kept his line in the left portion of the right lane.

"No, the windows are tinted."

Kannon increased his speed to sixty-five. The Jeep pulled alongside, then veered sharply into their lane. Kannon executed an evasive maneuver by pushing on the right bar. The centrifugal force caused the GS's front wheel to track right as the Wrangler swept by.

"Asshole," Kannon muttered. "I reckon that to be the end of the show."

The anonymous driver made his point: His beast was king.

The Jeep occupied the right lane, turn signal flashing, indicating a right turn at the Guadalupe intersection. Kannon stayed a comfortable distance behind.

"See there, we're rid of him now," he said.

"Thank God. What a jerk."

Kannon twisted the throttle to sweep around the Jeep just before Paseo De Peralta narrowed into one lane each way. But as he pulled the motorcycle alongside the offending Jeep, the driver swerved left, causing Kannon to execute another abrupt countersteer in the same direction.

"Son of a bitch! Hold tight, Meghan."

The motorcycle rocketed across the opposing lane of traffic.

To avoid getting broadsided, he had no choice but to plow off the road across railroad tracks. He stood on the footpegs and lifted on the bars to help loft the motorcycle.

The front wheel skimmed the top of the tracks, and the rear wheel struck with force, pitching the tail end in the air. When the rear wheel made contact, he applied both brakes, skidding and skimming alongside the railroad tracks. Miraculously the GS remained upright.

Passersby gawked but offered no assistance, only judgmental, condemning stares. Furious, Kannon killed the engine and lowered the side stand. He reached for Meghan but scooped a handful of air.

"I'm behind you."

He turned around and saw her standing between the rails. Kannon raced over and hugged her. She quivered like a wobbling top.

"Are you all right?" he asked.

"Yes, but the jolt launched me straight off the seat." Her words quavered as if she were hypothermic. "I landed like a skydiver, knees bent, and on the balls of my feet."

"The SOB tried to kill us."

"Why?"

"I don't know. Maybe the bastard harbors a grudge against motorcyclists." Or else the encounter with Farber and Jeffrey bore fruit already. Either way, he had no right to place Meghan in danger.

Her breathing steadied. "Did you get the license number?"

"Tried," he said. "It was blacked out."

Tough lady, this Meghan O'Brien. They collected themselves and remounted, re-entered the traffic flow, and continued on Paseo De Peralta.

"There he is again," she said.

Like a tiger lying in wait for its prey, the Jeep pounced from a side street and once more took up pursuit. A stalled car loomed ahead. Vehicles cluttered both lanes, congealing in a snarling pace—an ideal condition.

Kannon split the lanes and goosed the GS to seventy-five miles an hour, which took all of two seconds, then weaved between the crawling vehicles, leaving behind one frustrated, would-be assassin. Disoriented, Kannon steered through the streets until he came to a deserted park where he pulled over and dismounted.

"I need to calm down."

"You need to calm down," she said. "What about me?"

"You ever see the Jeep before?"

"No, why? Think it belongs to Farber?"

"Maybe." He chambered a round into the Sig Sauer.

Meghan gave him a measured look. "I think you're a dangerous man."

Her comment invaded his mind but failed to register.

"Oh, my God." She gripped his shoulder like a vise.

He followed her gaze. "Mount up."

As Kannon started the GS, the Jeep, maneuvering like a Cobra chopper hovering for a kill, turned toward them with its engine racing. Kannon guided the motorcycle up a ramp for the disabled, left the sidewalk, and took off across the park's soft turf.

A cluster of trees stood thirty feet away, a natural barrier. But the tires spun.

"Meghan, get off and push."

She jumped off and tried. "It's too heavy."

"Shit. Get behind the picnic table."

His adrenaline pumping, Kannon got off and rocked the motorcycle back and forth. Then he remounted and inched the cycle forward in first gear. Traction. He made a sliding right as the Jeep roared past, its huge rear tires spattering mud.

Meghan climbed on. The Jeep made a one-eighty and headed straight for them. The motorcycle, now on a thin slab of concrete beside the table, sat broadside to the on-rushing Jeep.

"This is it."

Waiting until the Jeep was a few feet away, Kannon gunned the engine, raising the front end and speeding off just before the Jeep's extended grill cracked into the picnic bench. When the GS's front wheel slammed to earth, Kannon steered the motorcycle amid the trees where the Wrangler couldn't possibly follow. He slapped down the kickstand, drew his weapon, and tore off on foot after the Jeep.

The driver shifted into reverse and tried to run him down. Leaping aside, Kannon raised his handgun and fired two rounds before he hit the ground. The driver ground into gear and sped out of the park, tires squealing once they hit the pavement.

Meghan left the copse of trees and approached Kannon. "Forget skiing," she said. "It would be anticlimactic."

* * *

When they returned to the hotel, Meghan entered the Artist's Pub to order a drink. Kannon, still bristling from the encounter, yet relieved both had escaped injury, went to the room and checked his emails. Before signing off, another message beeped in. He read it. Then read it again. He stared into the computer screen as if to burrow inside and emerge from the other end with answers. None came.

Meghan appeared behind him, drink in hand.

"What are you gawking at?" she asked.

"Another piece of the puzzle arrived." Kannon shuffled to the refrigerator and grabbed a beer.

"So, you're not finished," she said.

"I can't ignore this message."

"You're just interested in completing your precious puzzle, not in this relationship."

Kannon's muscles constricted. She was putting him on the defensive. "I am involved with you, Meghan."

"Bullshit! Who's the message from?"

"Lan."

She smacked her drink down on the table. "I can't believe you. We faced a near-death experience, and you're thinking of her."

"Look, you're upset about the motorcycle—"

"Upset. You miss the point. I don't mean squat to you."

"Meghan, you're not being fair."

"Not fair? I'm tired of your obsession."

"I'm not obsessed."

She moved toward him. "Get out of the way."

He stepped away from the laptop.

Monsoon struck. Hai assailed me on the street. He

186

asked if I liked the year 1950—the Year of the Tiger,

the year of Chấn's birth. And then he said, 'Too bad

you miss Tết in the Year of the Goat. Yes?'
Lan.

Meghan finished reading aloud. "What does she mean?"

The anguish in her tone conveyed a different concern. "Chấn was the tiger—or one of them. And a monsoon killed him. A monsoon named Hai." *Who would kill again!*

"You're not thinking of returning to Việt Nam a second time?" She stared into his eyes. "Oh, God, you are."

"I have to. For Chấn." For Lan. And to explore the third site, the one he suspected contained the cache.

"Lan is Chấn's sister. Chấn was murdered just as if he'd been killed in the ambush. Lan presumed she'd be safe once I left the country. She's not. She's in danger."

"To hell with Lan." She seized a wet towel and threw it at him.

He dodged, knocking over a beer, which spilled onto the keyboard.

"Goddamnit, Meghan." He retrieved the towel and wiped the laptop.

"This is too much." She gripped her suitcase. "This is not about Chấn, or the ambush, or Farber and Jeffrey. It's about you, Kannon Ballard."

"No, it's not."

"It's only about you. And Lan. I don't appreciate your not being straight. I feel used."

"Meghan, please understand. There is nothing between Lan and me except her brother."

"Enough," she said. "I'm returning to Silverton."

He felt as if he were standing on one cliff while she stood on another, a raging river and a thousand-foot drop between them.

He looked across the abyss and saw a face full of anguish and pain, but what could he say.

"This relationship's over," she said.

"Yes, I suppose it is."

"Chasing Lan and clearing your rattled conscience are more important to you."

"This thing has snowballed—"

"Stop it. You're its center." Tears formed in her eyes.

"I'll rent a car. Drive you to Albuquerque."

"No way. I'll take care of myself." She threw the suitcase on the bed and stuffed in her clothes. She stormed out, leaving behind her familiar scent of lavender.

Kannon sat on the bed to collect himself. Another curtain drawn shut.

Something chinked against the wall outside the room.

"Meghan?" He rose and opened the door. The spare motorcycle key lay on the floor.

He picked it up, went inside, and tossed the key beside her helmet, then resumed cleaning the keyboard. At least the computer keys didn't stick, but Meghan's words did. She was right about Lan. He clicked onto favorites and brought up the Lunar Calendar. This year, 2003, was the Year of the Goat. Tết began the first of February. He must act fast. Lan might live another two weeks . . . or just another day.

Twenty-Eight

Jeffrey sat in a booth with a chipped Formica tabletop at a run-down burger shack in Taos, waiting for Hippo, their hired gun. Outside, the wind, howling as if protesting the fading light, worked its way between chinks in the crumbling logs and nipped at his ankles. In the far corner, a broadcast of the Lakers-Suns game blared from an outdated television sporting a snow-marred screen. He stared glumly, recalling his basketball scholarship to Bowling Green, where his coach had demoralized him the second year.

"Son, your quickness is okay, but you're just not big or strong enough to compete against opposing guards in our league. And your crossover dribble—"

"Coach, I can play," Jeffrey had insisted.

"No, son. Not for me."

Relegated to the bench, he quit the team and joined the college's ROTC program. He liked the rigidity—

"Beer?"

"Huh?"

"You want a beer?"

Jeffrey looked up, undressed the waitress, Mabel, shapely at fifty, her skirt as tight as he imagined her snatch.

Mabel stared above his head as if he were a nuisance.

"Two longnecks."

She sauntered away without looking at him. Her indifference feathered the slow burn of injustice that had begun on his parent's farm. His father had belittled and worked him twelve-hour days six days a week during summers while his older brother basked at camp, and his feckless mother languished inside the cramped farmhouse.

"Junior, you'll never amount to a hill of beans," his father used to say. Then he'd grab Leonard's ears. "Learn to flap these, though, and you could get a job in the circus."

He should have buried his old man instead of fence posts.

Mabel strolled from the bar back to his table. She held out

189

her left hand while sheltering the beers behind her back. "Pay as you go."

"Anyplace else would run a tab." He slapped a ten in her palm.

His anger festered, bubbled forth like an underground stream, made worse by waiting for the scum of the earth to make an appearance. The second hand on his watch approached six-thirty. As Jeffrey swirled a half-empty bottle, Hippo ambled through the front door and waddled to the booth.

"About time you got here." Jeffrey thwacked the table.

Hippo squeezed onto the opposite bench, his protruding belly sloshing like a water truck with no baffles. He carried the odor of rotting eggs.

Jeffrey slid a beer across the Formica. "Report."

The burly Hippo raised his bottle and swallowed deep. Budweiser trickled down his black beard. "Scared the hell out of 'em. They won't bother you no more."

"How do you know?" Jeffrey blanched from the hired hand's rancid breath.

Hippo's lips curled. "Last I saw 'em they were hightailing it south to Albuquerque. I followed a short while. Was gonna give another run but couldn't catch 'em."

Jeffrey didn't know whether to believe him or not. "Anyone interfere?"

"Nah. Hell, you ride a Sportster. You know people don't care about bikers. Coulda run 'em over and no one notice. Be a shame to disfigure the sweet honey on the back, though. Bet you'd like to poke her, huh?"

"Mind your own business, fat ass."

Hippo reached across the table and grabbed Jeffrey's collar. "Don't talk to me like that."

"I'll talk to you any way I want. We pay you to do your fucking job."

Jeffrey's hired gun released his hold. "Which reminds me. You owe me expenses."

"For what?"

"Rammed a park bench and damaged my grill."

"Submit a claim."

"I'll do that." Hippo finished his beer and belched. "The envelope, please."

Jeffrey made the exchange under the table. Hippo thumbed the money, then slipped the envelope inside his greasy shirt.

"I want a pay raise before the next mission," the hired hand said. "Twenty percent."

"You know Farber won't go for twenty percent." Jeffrey waited for a reaction, but there was none. "You heading to the mountains?"

Hippo nodded.

"Keep your cellphone charged."

Jeffrey slouched in the corner of the booth and watched Hippo saunter out the door. Farber wanted Ballard eliminated, but Jeffrey didn't relish being an accessory to manslaughter. There was enough weight on his conscience as it was. Farber could go to hell. He'd just tell his boss that Ballard outmaneuvered Hippo.

"Mabel, another beer."

Jeffrey didn't consider himself a bad man, but making bad choices under bad circumstances resulted in horrible consequences. Farber had introduced him to the sacred world of delicious Asian sex and drugs. It made him feel powerful, but Jeffrey had become inextricably linked to the boss man who fed him. Could the price he paid be measured in currency?

Finishing his last beer, Jeffrey scooted from the booth and walked outside to mount his Sportster. The engine rumbled to life but failed to overpower his dread of being castigated by Farber.

* * *

Farber slapped the Saturday morning paper on his office desk. Jeffrey and Hippo couldn't do anything right.

"Goddamnit, Jeffrey. How could the fat-ass Hippo have missed them? It's not hard to hit a motorcycle for Christ's sake."

Jeffrey's ears, whenever he was being admonished, seemed to protrude like twin monoliths, as if his masochistic nature impelled him to catch every word. Despite his anger, Farber found it difficult not to laugh.

"Hippo ran them off the road," Jeffrey said. "They just didn't crash."

"Did Ballard see Hippo?"

"Course not. His car windows are tinted, almost black."

Farber walked to the wet bar. He grabbed two glasses, looked at Jeffrey, then put one back. He poured himself a Jack Daniels. "You realize Ballard's not done with us."

"He might be. Hippo scared them . . . toward Albuquerque." Jeffrey shuffled his feet. Farber interpreted both words and actions as a placating effort to avoid wrath.

"Bullshit. What'd you discover about Ballard?"

"Nothing. Everything's unlisted—address, phone number, email."

Farber swung his drink hand toward Jeffrey and sloshed some Jack on his spineless assistant.

"The O'Brien broad signed our guest register. Go to Colorado." He paused, stringing out the command for emphasis. "Find out what makes her tick, her relationship with the son of a bitch."

"What good's that gonna do?"

Incredulous, Farber's blood reached a boiling point. "She's a link, you idiot. The more you know about your enemy, the less vulnerable you are."

"I can't be in Colorado and Việt Nam at the same time."

"It's a five-hour drive to Silverton. Spend a day. Discover what you can."

"What if Ballard's there? You want me to kill him?"

"No! Just report your findings. I'll handle the rest."

"And then go to 'Nam." Jeffrey shifted his weight and stuffed his hands in his pockets. "This is ridiculous. I'm finished playing your game."

Farber filled his lungs and exploded. "And lose everything we've worked for? Besides, you're in this as deep as I am."

Jeffrey gaped, then shook his head and started for the office door.

Farber tapped his foot on the floor-mounted release button. The door sprung shut. "Look," he said, mollifying his tone, "I need you. We eliminate Ballard, we're home free."

"We'll never be free," Jeffrey said, turning around.

"Got a better idea?"

"No." Jeffrey hesitated, then pulled pen and paper from his pocket. He scratched a note and palmed it. "You think Ballard was telling the truth . . . about Chấn?"

"Doubtful. But to ignore his threat invites risk."

Jeffrey nodded, but scratched his scalp as if puzzled. "I was shocked when you put him in for a Silver Star."

Farber smacked his lips and smiled. He knew Jeffrey would have died for a medal. "Bargaining power, Jeffrey, bargaining power. Build a man up before you tear him down."

"Understood."

"Get moving. You've work to do."

"I can handle Colorado and Việt Nam but not our artist friend," Jeffrey said, handing Farber the piece of paper.

He unfolded the paper and read one word. "Yeah, you'll receive a bonus. And I'll take care of Mr. Sanderson." Farber visualized the incriminating picture of their man engaged in a lewd sex act.

As Farber watched Jeffrey slink out of his office, he poured another drink and entered the password to bring up his personal finances on the PC. Proud of his money management, Farber had parlayed the $100,000 he'd saved in Việt Nam into a decent nest egg, building interest over thirty years, which now summed $4.8 million plus change.

With what he'd inherited after his mother's untimely death—an unexpected windfall, God rest her soul—he never needed to tap into his Việt Nam war chest. Not bad for an only child whose father deserted at birth.

Things were going well with his properties and with Jasmine. Yet, the incident with Ballard disturbed him. An incomplete mission equated to failure.

Twenty-Nine

Meghan, suppressing tears of anger and frustration, was grateful for the near-empty flight to Durango.

"Are you all right, Ms. O'Brien?" A flight attendant lowered her clipboard, which held the passenger manifest.

"I'm fine. Just told someone goodbye."

The flight attendant touched Meghan's shoulder and smiled. "I've been there."

Meghan waited until the attendant left, then pulled Kannon's picture from her purse. She ripped it to shreds and stuffed the remnants in a barf bag. What had begun as a sense of romance and adventure had degenerated into a failed relationship and a harrowing, close encounter with death.

"Here." The flight attendant handed her a plastic water glass filled with ice. "A bourbon, courtesy of the flight crew."

Meghan reached for the palm-sized bottle. "Thanks."

She untwisted the cap and poured. Amber-colored whiskey permeated the chipped ice and made it crackle. She tipped the glass to her lips and drank. The drink tasted bitter, which mirrored her mood. She had hoped Kannon possessed a depth she could tap into. Despite his sorrow, she found his physical presence and sensitivity appealing, and he showed signs of the tenderness she desired. Even though his lovemaking had been coarse, she believed he'd improve in time. Yet, he seldom displayed humor, a trait she valued. Most importantly, she'd invested a year in the relationship and lost. She should have honored her intuition.

She pinched herself, raising a welt on her arm, another battle scar to remember.

Meghan spent Friday night in Durango. Early the next morning, she breakfasted on toasted bagels slathered with apple butter. Then she left the valley and steered her four-runner through the silver-gray forest that delineated the polished mountains and preserved pristine meadows.

The sun lit the Needle Mountains like candles and then

crested to bathe white-capped granite peaks in the west. Her heart grew warmer as the red-banded dawn faded through pink to powder blue. The air carried the fresh, crisp scent of pine and fired energy into her spirit.

She massaged her self-inflicted wound. Who needs Kannon Ballard!

As she crossed Molas Pass, a fog bank rolled over the mystic white, dimming its luster, and her heart faded with the mountain light. A pang of emptiness swept clean her thoughts of Kannon, Leonard Jeffrey's slime, and the land's bare essence, leaving a tortured longing for her dead husband's presence.

Once in Silverton, Meghan drove straight to Hotel Victoria. When she entered the lobby, Charlene, the English woman who'd maintained the hotel in her absence, stirred embers in the stone fireplace.

"Didn't expect you this soon, my lady."

Meghan shed her jacket and gloves and walked to the hearth. She placed her hands on the warm marble mantel. "Never should have left. How'd it go?"

Charlene's eyes held questions. Meghan's look told her not to ask them.

"Let three of the five rooms," Charlene said in her clipped accent. "Total of fifteen nights occupancy out of a possible twenty-five. Not bad, eh?"

"It's good for this time of year." Meghan's spirits lifted along with the unexpected increase in revenue. "Thank goodness for the hardy winter sports nuts."

The next day Meghan sat at her computer using financial software intended for dummies. Her private line rang.

"Meghan, this is Elizabeth. You got a minute?"

"Sure."

"You're not planning to sell your hotel, are you?" she asked in her croaky voice.

"No. Why do you ask?"

"Some weird dude came by this morning. Wanted to know about you and the hotel. Says he's interested in buying it."

"Give his name?"

"No . . . said he's from Ohio."

"Offhand, I don't know anyone from Ohio. Anyway, the property's not for sale," she said, thinking this wasn't unusual. Over the past couple of years, prospective buyers occasionally queried whether she would sell.

"Good." Elizabeth paused. "Guess you're not going to tell me about your trip?"

"Not now, maybe later." No, never. "I'm reviewing my cash position. I plan to invest more money into the place."

"And do what?"

"Replace linens. Fit new bedspreads, pillows, and curtains for the bedrooms. I want to get it done before the narrow gauge resumes its run in May."

"Let me know if I can help."

"I will."

She finished her bookkeeping and opened the spring brochure she'd designed. As the image filled the screen, she gave it a cursory look, inserted tri-fold paper, and printed two copies. She slipped on her parka and stepped onto the porch. A wintry tempest slung snow like a frustrated child threw a tantrum. A lone car plodded by, its windshield washers slapping, its headlights disappearing in the whiteout. She ventured along the sidewalk toward the Chamber of Commerce building. Nature's raw harshness soothed her raw pain.

Sonia greeted her as she entered the Chamber building.

"Hey there, girl. Bet you've come down to tell me all about your new love."

"Oh, God. Are there no secrets around here?"

"Not a one. You're a popular lady."

"What do you mean?"

"A man's been asking about you. Says he's interested in your hotel."

Two inquiries!

"Who?" Meghan asked.

"Ugly dude. Face like a hawk."

"Beak-like nose? Large ears?"

"Why, yes. Describes him well," Sonia said. "And unctuous,

as we'd say back east. Has a Midwestern accent."

"I know who it is," Meghan said, her intuition on full alert. "I need to get back to the Victoria." She turned to leave.

"Wait, Meghan." Sonia bent forward, almost climbed the counter. "Why'd you come?"

"Oh. Look at this and give me your opinion." She dropped a sample brochure on the counter and ran out the door. The snow still fell in sheets. Clutching her coat collar, she hustled to the hotel.

The description fit Jeffrey. She should have never gone to that gallery.

"Come on, come on, answer." Meghan slammed the phone into the cradle. Stupid answering machine. No message, just a beep. Then it hit her. He might've left for Việt Nam already. Tobin. She'd call Tobin. And what would she tell the sheriff?

A man followed her from Santa Fe. She'd only been given a description. Didn't know for sure it was Leonard Jeffrey. Stay calm, girl, stay calm.

She peered through the window. Although the snow flurries had abated, the sky splashed an ashen hue. She locked the hotel doors and walked to The Tinder Box, an eatery.

"Hey there, lady," Elizabeth said. "Help me with this chicken fried."

"I'm not hungry," Meghan said.

"At least take a seat. You look as white as a snowdrift. Anything wrong?"

Meghan plopped in the chair. "Oh, Elizabeth, everything's gone wrong. Santa Fe turned into a disaster. Kannon's a jerk obsessed with Lan and Việt Nam. And I almost got killed."

"Whoa. Slow down."

Meghan sighed. "I don't know what slow means anymore." She ordered drinks, then related her story about the motorcycle chase, Lan's email, and the breakup. Thirty minutes later, each had consumed two margaritas rimmed with salt and emotion.

"You're lucky to be alive," Elizabeth said.

"Luckier to be rid of Kannon." Meghan hooked her heels on the chair support rail and leaned toward her friend. "The man who said he was from Ohio . . . what'd he look like?"

Elizabeth wiped her mouth with her shirtsleeve, then described him.

"Sounds like the same guy Sonia saw," Meghan said.

"I'd be spooked, too. Oh, my God! Looks like your nightmare just walked in the door."

Meghan swiveled her chair and stared at the door just as the man closed it behind him. "It's not who I thought it was." Then her muscles tensed. "Yes, it is. He's added a fake mustache and a toupee. The stupid thing doesn't even fit." She watched him out of the corner of her eye as he sat at the bar and removed his jacket, then ordered a beer. When he looked her way, or rather leered, she averted her eyes.

"Lady," Elizabeth said, slapping an empty margarita glass on the table, "we got to handle this straight on. Follow my lead."

Meghan watched in horror as Elizabeth rose, walked to the ogre dressed in a blue flannel shirt, and invited him to their table.

"Are you nuts?" She drilled daggers at Elizabeth.

"Meghan O'Brien, meet the man who wants to buy your hotel. What did you say your name was?"

"Randall, Randall Simonson." The man cast darting looks about the room. "May I join you for a drink?"

"I'd rather have an enema." Meghan drove her chair back with such force it clattered to the floor. She stood on her tiptoes to get eye level with Jeffrey. "Listen! I know who you are. Get the fuck out of here."

"I've never seen you before," Jeffrey said.

There was no disguising his scratchy, high-pitched voice.

"You mistake me for somebody else," he said.

Disgusted, Meghan mustered her resolve. "The hotel is not for sale. As if that's why you're here."

"Asshole," added Elizabeth.

"Ladies, your comments are uncalled for."

Elizabeth kicked his shin.

"Ow."

"Listen, honey, what in the world does a scrawny man as you want with a hotel?" Elizabeth prodded.

"Yeah, a hotel's out of line with your gallery work, isn't it?"

198

Meghan winked at Elizabeth. She was beginning to enjoy this, a chance to let off steam.

"I'm with a gallery. So what? We buy a hotel, convert the first floor into a gift shop. Lots of local artists here and in Durango." He licked his lips. "As you well know."

Meghan stomped the floor. "You lying son of a bitch. I know you're looking for Kannon Ballard. Well, he's returned to Việt Nam, where he can rot for all I care. Why don't you follow and rot with him?"

"You remember me. I must've made an impression."

Elizabeth scowled. "Honey, who could forget an ugly face like yours? And you need to replace that divot atop your head."

Jeffrey cracked his knuckles and leaned on the back of an empty chair. "Miss," he said directly to Elizabeth, "I'm trying to talk to Ms. O'Brien—"

"I'm not interested in talking to you," Meghan said, joining the offensive. "And if you don't leave, I'm calling the sheriff."

"No need to get belligerent, Ms. O'Brien. Just trying to find an old friend, a man I served with in 'Nam."

"Listen, peckerhead, are you deaf? Kannon's shot his wad and gone to seed. This lady's not interested in him, in you, or in selling her hotel," Elizabeth said. "Take your beak nose and shove off."

"Bitches," they heard him say as he stood to leave.

Elizabeth sat down. "He slunk away like a snake."

"I can't believe you brought him to our table." Meghan tried to sound peeved, but she couldn't suppress her real feelings and burst out laughing. "'Replace that divot atop your head. Take your beak nose and shove off'. Wonderful."

"Still," Elizabeth said, "maybe you're right. Call the sheriff."

"Oh, it's not necessary. He won't bother us anymore." Meghan wanted to kill the memories, not rekindle them. "Anyway, it's a satisfying way to end the day."

"Want to stay with me tonight?"

"No, I'll be all right." Meghan grabbed her coat.

She stepped into a clear, graceful winter night. The stars shimmered like multitudes of lightning bugs. Once more, life was under control. She had stood up to Kannon Ballard. She had stood up to Leonard Jeffrey.

Meghan cupped her arms behind her neck and breathed deeply as she walked down the sidewalk. A dome light inside a vehicle parked across the street shone dimly, silhouetting a lone figure hunched beside an open car door. She suspected it was Jeffrey. But no, it was only Cheezy, a harmless eccentric whose car served as his home. They called him the raccoon because he shuffled about at odd hours of the night. She chuckled to herself and embraced Silverton, just as Silverton, with all its wackiness, embraced her.

Reaching her hotel door, she took off her gloves, reached into her pocket, and withdrew the key set. The cold air stiffened her fingers as she fumbled for the right one. She found it and inserted it into the deadbolt lock.

"Oh, shit!" she screamed before a hand clasped her mouth shut.

"Who do you think you are?" A gravel-pitched voice hissed in her ear.

His other hand gripped her wrist like a vice. She tried to turn and knee him in the groin, but he pinned her body against the door. Then he released his grip on her arm and groped between her thighs. She lowered her body, flexed her knees, and pushed away from the wall using her arms and legs. They lost balance, somersaulted backward across the sidewalk, and landed on the snow-covered street. The man maintained his hold on her mouth. As both scrambled to their feet, a shadowy figure barreled into them like a fullback. She wrenched free.

"Fuck you!" She slashed in the air like a lioness.

"Miss Meghan, I didn't mean nothing wrong. Jus' trying to help."

"Not you, Cheezy, him." She pointed at the lone figure disappearing around the corner.

Cheezy brushed the snow off his jacket. "I been watchin' the fellow. Acting awful strange."

Damnit, Kannon. What have you gotten me into?

Then Meghan remembered she was the one who voluntarily

visited the gallery and signed the guest book. So much for the idea of having regained control over her life.

The Monsoon

Thirty

Lan laid her chopsticks on the table and smiled as she watched her cousin Thanh shovel in another mouthful of rice. She rose and answered her phone.

"*Chào*. Did you have trouble getting into the country?"

"None," said Kannon. "I booked through Mr. Ngọc." During a slight pause, Kannon's breathing sounded heavy, as if he were tired or anxious. "Where do you suggest we meet?"

"The Botanical Gardens," she said, "at three tomorrow afternoon."

"I'll be there."

She replaced the receiver and turned to Thanh, whose wrinkled brow signaled a question. She prayed she had not made a mistake in befriending this American and reminded herself it was her brother's memory she honored.

"Why should I jeopardize myself for this Kannon Ballard?" Thanh asked.

"I want to help him."

"Night vision goggles. Infrared illuminator," Thanh mumbled. "What is he going to use them for?"

"I do not know, cousin. He says they are bulky and did not want to chance bringing a pair into the country."

"It is a risk. Black market item," he said.

Frowning, Lan removed their empty bowls and rinsed them under a slow stream of water.

Thanh repositioned his thick, black-framed spectacles, which set off his moon-shaped face crowned with slick, black hair. In crisp khaki pants and mauve cotton shirt, his appearance befitted his role as comptroller of the state-owned national rubber company. Ever since she had returned from visiting the Minhs and tracked down their son in Sài Gòn, she felt comforted and not so alone. Except, she found Thanh enigmatic. Often, when he spoke, his eyes belied his words and seemed to disappear in a distant sanctuary.

He pulled a briar pipe from his pocket, filled the bowl in

increments, and tamped the tobacco. He struck a match and swirled the flame across the surface. Soon, an acrid aroma filled the room.

"Why do you smoke that awful Russian tobacco?"

"For its potency," he said.

"It smells worse than buffalo dung." She rose from the stiff, straight-backed chair and walked to her armoire. She opened a cabinet door and selected two pencil-thin sticks of hyacinth incense, which she lit and placed in a stand.

"Why do you want to help someone obsessed with digging up the past only to bury it again?"

"Thanh, you did not experience war. How would you know what it is like?"

"Cousin, a mongoose knows when to let go of a cobra," he said.

Lan waved the incense to her nostrils, then faced Thanh. She placed her hands on her hips, splayed her elbows like wings ready to take flight. "And how many cobras have you caught?"

"Irrelevant. You defend this American, I think."

"Assist," she said. "And Kannon Ballard is no cobra."

Thanh flashed his teeth in a wide grin. "It is appropriate you wear the passion color red." He paused to puff on his pipe. "I can get the night glasses through a source with strong ties to Hong Kong."

Her heart lightened. "Thank you, cousin." She held his hand as he headed for the front door and left it ajar to air the room once he departed.

Kannon's return resurrected the turbulence she experienced during her brother's last days—but Chấn's death, while painful, proved cathartic, liberating her from caretaking. The freedom to travel beckoned, to trace the origin of her mother's roots, from whom she inherited the color auburn for her hair. According to Papa-san Minh, the path began in Corse, the rugged mountainous island south of Italy. Lan's father, Thu, fell in love with Loan, a fellow teacher blessed with raven eyes and a gentle manner. Loan had lost her own father, a Frenchman, in *la Guerre d'Indochine*.

Yet, the vision of her nephew ran strong. Đăng Đạo might be alive in America. Friends spoke of relatives who fled Việt Nam years ago and returned to visit. They spoke of glorious American opportunities—how easy it was to move about the country, and how with hard work, a person could begin anew. And America did not have community loudspeakers in towns and villages that force-fed political doctrine or broadcast a doctored version of the news at five-thirty in the morning.

Her anticipation swelled as if with each breath her lungs expanded to allow for this new sensation, for either country promised a new life.

But what was more important, to revisit the past or engage the future?

Thirty-One

Anxious about meeting Lan later today at the Botanical Gardens, Kannon opened the window in his fifth-floor room. A sultry wind riffled the curtains and, even though it was the dry season, brought a damp smell from the Sài Gòn River like unseasonable rain.

His hotel, the Rex, situated on the corner of Nguyễn Huệ and Lê Lợi Boulevards, reflected signs of expansion and renewal, including a fragrant rose garden linking the first-floor lobbies. The hotel had served as a sanctuary for high-ranking officers, journalists, and rear echelon types during the war. The walls held their words. Or had the recent renovation stilled the voices? Regardless, he worried whether his search would unearth anything significant to the new Việt Nam, for his world had irrevocably shifted.

The happenings in Santa Fe reinforced his belief—Farber and Jeffrey did something, knew something, and buried it. Hell, the cache site might be inaccessible, or might no longer exist, the communists having destroyed it years ago.

Determined to resolve the issue, he had brought the tools to do it: a 4.15-megapixel digital camera with extra memory cards. The body design was the same format as his professional 35mm and accepted the same autofocusing zoom lenses and powerful flash. The mélange included a laptop computer, so he could copy and send digital images. The hard drive contained scanned images of the maps and map coordinates. A Global Positioning Device lay beside the laptop. All he needed was for Thanh to provide a night vision device.

Kannon entered the bathroom. As he shaved and trimmed his mustache, he thought again about the split with Meghan, which left him with mixed feelings. The romance belonged to a distant realm. His abrupt disassociation from her once the prevailing environment changed, a dubious skill Meghan had said, protected him but cut him off from intimacy . . . and destroyed others. That was the part he didn't want to admit.

Yet, he agreed with the breakup, wanted it. The emotional support wasn't there. What he felt bad about was misleading her, a tangential effect of misleading himself, upon which he targeted his anger. He hadn't been relegating images of Lan into non-being or even remission but instead used them to fill his greater vision, a relationship with her. However, the likelihood of joining with Lan was questionable because of huge obstacles—

The phone rang. Kannon toweled his face and answered. It was Mr. Ngọc.

"*Chào*, Mr. Ballard. I have a motorcycle for you."

"Describe it."

"Yamaha DT175 with a kick-start, oil-cooled, two-cycle engine. You will like it."

"Color?"

"Black and yellow."

Perfect.

"I'll pick it up tomorrow. Oh, Mr. Ngọc, one other thing, the Rex has an email and Internet service, but I'd rather—"

"Use the Hông Hoa Internet Café," Ngọc said. "It is located not far from you."

"Thanks, talk with you later." Kannon dialed the front desk and was told the Café was on Phạm Ngũ Lão Street, part of the hotel by the same name.

After hanging up, Kannon dressed in a pair of khaki-colored slacks, a burgundy short-sleeved linen shirt, and Hồ Chí Minh sandals. He rode the elevator to the lobby and exited onto the street, then flagged a cyclo taxi to take him to the Internet Café. Asking the driver to wait, he walked inside and found people from diverse ethnic groups, mostly kids, bobbing above keyboards like locusts over prey. After satisfying himself with the range of available services, he established an account.

Next, the cyclo operator navigated the streets like an eel through jagged coral and dropped him off at the intersection of Lê Duẫn and Nguyễn Bĩnh Khiêm Streets, the entrance to Thảo Cầm Viên, Sài Gòn's Botanical Gardens and Zoo near the Sài Gòn River.

"One of my favorite places," Lan had said.

Being early, he strolled around. Sandstone-colored, Buddhastyled walls with ornate cornices and wrought iron fencing, appearing as if corroded by seawater, bordered the zoo and gardens. A stuffy breeze offered no respite from the heat. He checked his watch. Ten minutes had elapsed, an eternity. He returned to the Gardens entrance and fanned himself. What if she didn't show?

Soon, however, a World War II vintage sedan arrived curbside. Lan stepped out and swept toward him, her ivory-colored pants rippling in concert with her hips.

"Lan. You look wonderful," he said. No, she looked better than wonderful, she looked resplendent, decked out in a luminous blue áo dài that appeared iridescent in the suffused afternoon sun. Her rich auburn hair flowed freely, framing her deep-set eyes and full, pouty lips.

"*Chào*." She shook his hand, warmed his blood.

The sedan peeled away. Curious who the male driver was, Kannon remained reticent and didn't ask.

"Shall we go in?" He bowed at the waist, then extended his arm. They entered. Large tropical trees shaded broad walks and a series of greenhouses.

Slowly, like stripping off old layers of paint on an antique chest, their conversation scratched into substance.

"Has Hai threatened you again?" Kannon asked.

"No. Thanh looks after me."

Thanh. The Minhs' son. He must have been the driver, Kannon reasoned.

"I want to see the herbarium." She pointed the way.

Amid the dried plants, Kannon revealed what he'd uncovered at the National Archives, the events that transpired in Santa Fe, and his growing conviction that Farber and Jeffrey had covered up the ambush.

"It's the why I don't understand," he said. "Besides, I can't prove anything. It's all, as we say in America, circumstantial. There's no concrete evidence."

She nodded and led him down a narrow lane to the orchids. "Are they not lovely? My mother cherished them. So much color, deeper than a rainbow."

"Exquisite." As was she, their namesake.

Lan's beauty and the orchids' sweet fragrance, richer than perfume, made it difficult to concentrate. He steered her away from the flowers.

"I think the third site refers to an underground tunnel system or weapons cache. I've got to find out if it exists, and if so, what's in there—"

Lan held up her hand, interrupting. He feared he might have to undergo the same cross-examination Meghan had given him.

"The reason for the night vision goggles?" she said.

"Right. Was Thanh able to get a pair?"

"He has." She clutched Kannon's right arm with her delicate but firm hand. "I worry. Should you get caught, they might send you to prison, or execute you."

He liked the touch on his arm and that she worried. "I know."

After a short pause, she added, "If I had never heard from you again, I would have taken to my grave what I am about to tell you."

His pulse quickened. "I'm listening."

They crossed an ornamental footbridge that spanned a pond and led to a gazebo. She sat on the steps while he leaned against a railing.

"Our Tết holiday begins the first new moon after the sun enters Aquarius. This year, it begins a week from Saturday, the first of February. I visited Papa-san and Mama-san Minh last week to assist with their holiday preparations. Over dying coals from the dinner fire, we drank rice wine and talked until well after the owls claimed the night.

"He told how he and my father had joined the Việt Minh and came south together to support the revolution. After the victory over the French, both Papa-san Minh and my father went underground. They wanted no part of combat but supported one Việt Nam.

"As America deepened its involvement, my father in Sài Gòn and his cousin in the rice fields became part of the political infrastructure resisting foreign intervention."

"You said your father was a guerrilla," Kannon said.

"Việt Cộng infrastructure. It is different."

A tropical fish jumped near the far bank. The ripples fanned out like a peacock spreading his tail.

Not in his mind, it wasn't. "And Chấn?"

"It was no coincidence my brother received the assignment he did."

"A double agent," he said.

"All double agents, even Thanh. Do you understand why?"

"Now, perhaps. I was naïve then."

"Chấn worked with my cousin Minh as part of the network that warned local villagers and farmers of intelligence about U.S. Army combat patrols. They were part of the same cell, and the cell had a code name."

"What was the code name?" But he knew the answer.

"The Monsoon Killed the Tiger."

"Things are falling into place," he said, his sense of betrayal paramount, "at least on the Vietnamese side. And it might explain the ambush, but it doesn't justify Farber's and Jeffrey's actions."

"For your Americans, I have no answer," she said.

"Your cousin Minh was gracious to me when we met." Kannon stroked his chin, wondering, worrying. "Can the papa-san be trusted?"

An empathetic smile spread across Lan's face. "He has no bitterness toward the people who fought the war, only to those in government who ran the war."

"I guess time heals," Kannon muttered.

"No, Kannon, love heals."

Her comment caught him off guard. He tried to lock in the concept, but it was like trying to bottle smoke.

"There is more," she continued. "Mr. Hai was an officer in both the South Vietnamese and the North Vietnamese armies as well as a high-ranking Việt Cộng cadre."

Cadre. The cell's core. "I'm not surprised."

From his pocket, he pulled an Avo Uvezian Pyramid cigar, clipped it, and reached for a match. Her eyes suggested he not do so. He didn't.

"Only the Vàm Cỏ Đông River and a few kilometers separated us from the NVA and Việt Cộng's southern headquarters in Cambodia," he said. "Hai was well-positioned."

She nodded.

An orange tint began spreading across the sky. Clouds billowed as if in defiance of the dry season.

"I believe Hai threatened your brother to keep him quiet." Kannon's eyes narrowed. "With you as leverage."

"Yes, but . . . why keep it going?"

"Either Hai wants the past to stay buried and protect his current position, or something's still going on. Did Papa-san mention the names of other Americans?"

"No."

He fidgeted with the unlit cigar. "I'd like to show him pictures of Farber and Jeffrey." Then he remembered Meghan retained possession of the pager video. He needed her to transmit the tape, or rather still images from the tape. But would she even talk to him?

"Papa-san Minh might recognize them," Lan said.

"Did your cousin ever mention an underground cache—or tunnel system?" Kannon asked.

"He did not say exactly, but . . ."

"But what?"

"Papa-san said you would return."

Kannon raised his eyebrows, alarmed at his predictability. The war bit and never let go.

"Papa-san was right." If Meghan refused to help with the photo idea, Kannon would have to rely on memory to describe the two.

"I will go with you."

The idea thrilled him, but was it a good one? "I'm concerned you or your cousins might get into trouble. It's too dangerous."

"You forget, Mr. Kannon Ballard, my family has plowed a deep furrow in the underground. We are a family of warriors, and I have the family genes."

She had the genes, all right. She was also willful. Or was this part of a master plot to put him underground for good? Regardless, a growing intoxication filled his veins.

"Lan, would you join me for a drink at the Rex?"

She looked at her watch. "I told Thanh . . . oh, I will call and let him know I will be late."

"You're staying with him?"

"Yes. He accompanies me anytime I visit my home. I will be happy when this is settled."

So would he—but settled how and when appeared far away. As they strolled along the garden path toward the exit, he anticipated his first social engagement with Lan and drilled the doubt from his mind.

"Let's grab a taxi," he said.

* * *

Offering a panoramic view, the rooftop bar overlooked the city where lights never slept. Diverse ethnic groups, whose cultures the effulgent Rex Crown statuary anointed with a multi-colored nightglow, occupied the round tables. In celebration, songbirds warbled above bonsai trees and exotic fish tanks.

The maître d' led Kannon and Lan to a vacant table near the rooftop's edge. He seated them. Kannon drank in the aura. What a setting, being here with the woman who captivated and stretched his imagination.

With a whisper-like sound of silk, Lan crossed her legs. "Did you come here during the war?"

Kannon reached into the past. "A couple of times." Before being run out of the country. A waiter, dressed in starched whites, approached in military garb, his hair clipped to match his bearing. Kannon was grateful for the distraction.

"Merlot okay?" he asked Lan.

Her lips parted, and a soft yes came forth like a gentle fawn and vaporized any remaining thoughts about guerrillas and betrayal. While waiting, they stood at the iron railing. The breeze tickled the hair on his arms.

"This is a strange world that has brought us together," she said.

He wanted to say, "I hope we never part." Fortunately, he kept his mouth shut.

The crisp-mannered waiter delivered their drinks. Kannon signed the chit.

She toasted. "May your heart become light with joy."

If only it were possible. They clinked glasses. "Thank you."

Between sips of wine, Lan said she wanted to visit the wine regions of France because of that country's impact on pre-communist cultural Sài Gòn as her mother had described it. But a dream rattling in the back of his mind formed, and he found himself listening half-heartedly. A reference she made to Corse got lost in his fantasy.

"Will you dance with me?" he asked.

Lan flicked her tongue at a drop of wine poised on the rim of her glass, then cut her suddenly mischievous eyes to his. "All right."

Like a high-school kid going to the senior prom, Kannon offered his hand and led her to the second-floor ballroom. A Vietnamese band played their best rendition of World War II big band music, then segued to a string of waltzes.

She followed his lead as they circled and dipped in tempo. For the moment, all distressful thoughts vanished as he lingered with her amid the crowded anonymity. The rhythm slowed. He leaned forward and touched her cheek. She rose on her tiptoes and placed her full lips whisper-close to his, the softness of her breath like lilac. Then, as if linking with each other for what lay ahead, they held tight and firm, her face nestled against his chest.

Part of his fantasy had been made real.

Thirty-Two

Thanh had called for Lan just after midnight. After saying goodbye, Kannon returned to his room, feeling a new purpose in life and spirit.

At 0100 hours local time, 1100 hours the day before in Colorado, he put aside his guilt and dialed the U.S. Country code and Meghan's number. She answered on the third ring.

"Meghan, hey, this is Kannon. Please, don't hang up. I need your help."

"You need my help?" To say her tone was caustic would be an understatement. "I oughta bash your head."

"Why?" As if he didn't know.

"Your friend, Mr. Leonard Jeffrey, followed me here. The son of a bitch threatened me."

Shit.

"I shouldn't have gotten you involved. Did Jeffrey hurt you?"

"No. But I'm mad as hell."

"I can tell. Is he gone?"

"He left the same night."

"Did you notify the sheriff?"

"No, I probably should have. But I didn't."

"This is important. Do you know what he wanted?"

"Where to find you."

"What'd you tell him?"

"I told him you had returned to Việt Nam, and as far as I was concerned, you could rot there. And he could rot with you."

Ouch. Well, he deserved it. But he didn't like Farber's knowing he was in the country again.

"What the hell are you calling for anyway?" Her anger leaped across the Pacific Ocean like an angry missile.

He sucked in his breath.

"You still have the pager video, right?"

"The what?"

214

"The camera."

"Oh, yeah. I'll mail it to your hill country address."

"Would you please do me a favor first?"

"You got to be out of your ever-loving fucking mind."

"Meghan, damnit. I was wrong. I apologize, okay?"

Silence reigned before she spoke. "Tell me what you want."

"I need a graphic artist who can capture still shots of Farber and Jeffrey from the video."

"And?"

"Prepare four digital images, one each of Farber and Jeffrey now, and, using a digital editing program, turn back the clock thirty-two years."

He waited . . . and waited. If Meghan came through, he could retrieve and print the images at the Hông Hoa Internet Café. He thought it possible, should he get Papa-san Minh, hell, even Hai, to recognize and acknowledge that these men aided and abetted the enemy, and then videotape their responses, or even transport Minh and Hai to the United States, then—

"I'm not going to do it. I'm done. Goodbye. Don't call me anymore."

He exhaled a deep breath, but his reservoir of disappointment remained full. She was right, though, he had no business asking anything of her. Guess he'd have to describe Farber and Jeffrey to the papa-san.

Suddenly, as if lanced by a flaming rapier, a sense of horror ripped his conscience. What if something happened to Meghan because of his indulgence? He'd placed her in the line of fire, just like he had done his men. It seemed as though he walked clean through minefields, but those connected to him suffered because of it.

Was it worth it? He pulled the Farber/Jeffrey business card from his wallet and stared at it. Yeah! It was worth it.

Thirty-Three

Later Saturday morning at the Hồng Hoa, Kannon connected to the Internet service and checked his messages, hoping that Meghan might have changed her mind and forwarded images. She hadn't. But there was one curt, abrasive email from Stefan.

You show more interest in this Vietnamese man than you ever did your own son.

It hurt. Would the apparently unbridgeable gap between him and Stefan ever close?

The email, however, contained three attachments. One by one Kannon opened the attached files and watched baby Đăng Đạo age to fifteen years, then thirty. Wow. Did he look like Chấn or what? He printed six wallet-sized images, two from each file, and secured one set in a waterproof envelope, the other set in his wallet.

Afterward, he walked back to the hotel. There, he packed in his backpack the envelope and maps along with the GPS, camera system, and latest generation Nighthawk night vision goggles Thanh had procured the day before. Just before he walked out the door, he remembered to add a change of clothes.

He strapped on the pack, went downstairs, and mounted the Yamaha DT175. When he arrived at Lan's, she was sitting in the courtyard, holding a straw basket with a French bread loaf sticking out. Her hair appeared golden brown in the sun, and the hot breeze wrapped wayward strands around her forehead. She waited until he dismounted, then rose to meet him.

"I've nice thoughts from last night," he said.

She put her finger to his lips and kissed him on the cheek. "As do I. I had not danced in years."

"Ready?"

"I am."

Lan slipped her right arm through the basket's straps, and, since she wore pants, straddled the rear seat. She placed her hands on Kannon's hips and scrunched up against the camera backpack. At

1500 hours, they left Sài Gòn for the Minhs' farm.

Taking the familiar route, Kannon steered the motorcycle over roads ranging from smooth pavement to jagged, unkempt laterite. Short of Hiệp Hòa, they turned onto a sunbaked path, impassable during the rainy season, and motored to the Minhs' farmhouse, arriving just as the sunlight brushed the treetops. Pigs, ducks, and chickens scurried into deep shadows.

"*Chào ông*," said Mama-san Minh. Beetlenut juice sluiced down her cheek.

"*Chào bà*," Kannon said, repeating the greeting.

Lan took Papa-san Minh aside and conversed a moment. She turned to Kannon.

"My cousin says he understands the searcher's soul. Buddha looks favorably upon quests for the truth."

Papa-san Minh spoke again.

"Like my brother, he has come to hate the Communists," she said.

Kannon nodded.

Papa-san motioned them to follow him inside and sit at the table. The wrinkled veteran squatted on the floor and rolled two cigarettes, then stood and offered one to Kannon. He accepted. The old man leaned forward, clasped his visitor's hand, and lit the offering before his own. Kannon inhaled and stifled a cough. Noxious smoke filled his lungs, trailed from his nostrils, and curled toward the ceiling as if eager to get away from itself.

The late afternoon sun streamed through an open window and flung darting patterns of light. Minh padded to the armoire and came away with the same tin canister Kannon had seen on his earlier visit. He took out another faded monochrome photograph. Kannon peered over Lan's shoulder as the papa-san cackled in Vietnamese.

"This is a picture of the Minhs when they were young," she said, "taken in front of their house. It has been rebuilt since the war."

Kannon contemplated the photo. A flash of familiarity stoked his memory. No wonder he hadn't recognized them a few months ago. They looked as if they'd aged a hundred years. Yet, the Minhs didn't recognize him either. Or admit to it. And the old thatched-roof house. At least twice against regulations, he and Chấn had spent the night here.

"I remember." He puffed on the acrid cigarette and exhaled. The smell, too, was familiar. It reminded him of missions past and present, which struck him like a fallen satellite. He turned to Lan. "I have work to do."

"All right."

Kannon excused himself and walked outside. He laid the military grid map and Chấn's hand-drawn map copy on the ground, weighing down the edges with small clumps of clay. Next, he pulled out the GPS. Papa-san and Lan joined him.

"He wants to see what you are doing," she said.

"No problem. You translate," he said to Lan. "This is a Global Positioning System. It reads data from satellites and interprets latitude and longitude to locate a point within a hundred meters. The GPS device incorporates a digital compass and converts latitude and longitude into the Universal Transverse Mercator System/Military Grid Reference System—grid coordinates."

He waited for Lan to translate. She stood there with her hands on her hips. Papa-san Minh looked to the sky as if expecting an explanation from above. "Kannon, I will not translate. There is no way he will understand this," Lan said, an exasperated edge to her voice.

"Okay, okay. Hold on a second." He turned on the GPS, factored in the magnetic deviation from true north, and began taking readings. He jotted down the readings and oriented the map to the terrain.

"These are the grid coordinates from your brother's map," he said, pointing. "The first, XT457144, represents my old outpost near An Định hamlet. The second, XT447144, denotes the ambush site. And the third, XT44251436, I consider to be Site Three, the location of an underground cache."

Papa-san Minh hovered attentively, his facial expression inscrutable.

"Your house is located in this grid square," Kannon said, "XT451122, about two-and-a-half kilometers straight southeast of Site Three."

Papa-san squatted and poured over the maps. He withdrew a stubby pencil and sweat-stained pad of paper from his pocket. Without saying a word, he pointed to Site Three on the map and sketched.

They hunkered down around the drawing like three farmers discussing where to build a barbed-wire fence. "This is the hedgerow," the papa-san said through Lan, as he finished a crude, hexagonal shape. He penciled in foliage. "Here," he added, carving a squiggly line, "is an old trail."

Kannon studied the drawing. Christ! How much did this guy know? The trail entered from the north. If drawn to scale, the trail terminated roughly twenty to thirty meters inside the hedgerow.

Just then, the mama-san emerged from inside the house.

"*Tôi đói lắm,*" she said. (I am hungry.)

Damn, just as he was getting into it. Manners and customs. Customs and manners. Conform and obey.

The three dropped their map study and assisted with dinner preparation. Over a simmering fire, they steamed rice and boiled the ice-packed fresh vegetables and shrimp Lan had brought from Sài Gòn. To this, they added French bread. Kannon contributed a bottle of Merlot from the Médoc wine district in Bordeaux, the same vintage he and Lan had shared at the rooftop bar. The ground served as their table.

After they finished eating, Kannon pulled the waterproof envelope from his backpack and showed the pictures of Đăng Đạo to Lan and the Minhs.

"Oh, you located him." Lan's face glowed as if she had given birth.

"No, no." Kannon's mouth turned south, and he stared down at his feet. He hadn't meant to mislead her. "I followed your suggestion. My son computer-aged the photographs of your nephew. I haven't located him."

She kept her smile. "Đăng Đạo carries his father's appearance."

All were standing now. Lan took hold of the pictures, lightly rubbed her fingers over the images as if trying to conjure into her consciousness memories of the boy's existence. The Minhs appeared perplexed. Lan explained.

The mama-san jigged as if she were keeping time to a fiddle, then reached for her wine glass and held it aloft. The rest did the same.

"Đăng Đạo," they said.

The brief ceremony ended. Mama-san tended to the fire and then disappeared. Kannon returned to his issue at hand.

"Lan, ask papa-san if he knows whether an underground cache existed there during the war."

The papa-san avoided Kannon's questioning eyes while conversing with Lan.

"He said there was a tunnel system but remembers nothing about a cache." Lan's gaze flitted between the two men. "He has not been there since the communists' final offensive."

I wouldn't be surprised if the old man had his own tunnel network.

Embers from the fire died. Lantern light blinked from a window. They walked inside. Lan and Kannon sat on teakwood chairs while papa-san squatted on the floor. Mama-san parted the bamboo strands and emerged with a wooden platter holding four cups of tea. For Kannon, it was like old times, planning an operation under an oil lamp in the dead of night with his Vietnamese counterparts.

Kannon whispered to Lan. "I'm going to describe Farber and Jeffrey best I can. Pass this information along to your cousin. Then ask him if he remembers either one, and if so, did they work with the cell."

"You mean, did the Americans assist their enemy?"

"Yes. Also, were they engaged in weapons or drug trading?"

She interpreted, making shapes with her hands. Papa-san closed his eyes as if trying to recapture people and places. Arched lines cut like incisions around his narrow nose and mouth. Kannon visualized Farber and Jeffrey cloistered in a home such as this, surrounded by Hai, Minh, Thu, and Chấn, discussing their next transaction, perhaps even the ambush.

Outside, chickens squawked. A water buffalo snorted. The wind rattled the hedgerow and brought into the gathering an odor like dried paste. Mama-san ignited sticks of incense to offset the stale scent.

Kannon heard the word, Farber. Minh stood abruptly and spat out the window. "Numba ten."

Mama-san Minh and Lan gasped at this rude display, their mouths cupped open. Kannon edged forward on the chair, amused the papa-san remembered the Vietnamese slang for the worst an American could be, but was tantalized at the possibility of further disclosure.

Kannon set his teacup on the table. "What does he remember about this man?"

She asked. A brooding frown swept the papa-san's face. Minh shrugged, then uttered a few words in his strident tone.

Lan swallowed hard. "Only the name he remembers, nothing else."

He knew more, Kannon figured. He put his hands behind his neck and stretched. The air in the tight room went flat as if a tornado had sucked away the oxygen. "Lan, I've got to enter the hedgerow. It's my only chance to find evidence—"

Papa-san seemed to understand because he spoke immediately.

Kannon waited for Lan to translate.

"The hedgerow may still be mined," she said.

Kannon rocked backward and almost flipped the chair. Still mined after thirty-two years? The possibility hadn't occurred to him. He should pack up and go home. What was he trying to do, get killed? He didn't give 'em enough chance the first time? Yet, to back off now meant an everlasting emotional death—the forfeiture of attaining emotional freedom.

Lan placed her left ankle on the right knee, a gesture Kannon interpreted as intimate. "What are you going to do?"

"Explore Site Three."

She told papa-san this and listened to his response. "Tomorrow, he will take you to the hedgerow. Afterward, his assistance ends."

He studied the papa-san's body language. It was locked in obscurity. "After sunset," was all Kannon could say, preferring darkness to hinder detection.

Lan touched his arm. "This is not a good idea."

* * *

The sappers came for him in the middle of the night. Wrapping him in the hammock, they tied it with a biting, flexible steel cord, then stuffed a gag in his mouth. They tore the hammock loose from the bamboo trees and lugged him away. The sappers laughed the madman's laugh as they lowered him into a deep pit and shoveled foul-smelling muck on his open coffin. Darkness closed the sky. His lungs bursting, he tried to push his way free. The last words he heard were bye, bye Trung-Úy Ballard.

Kannon awoke. Moisture dropped on his forehead from condensation on the broad palms above. Slender bamboo leaves danced in silhouette against the starlight.

Grabbing an overhanging branch, he pulled on it and set the hammock in motion. He reached inside his jacket for his tobacco pouch and Meerschaum.

Suddenly Lan was there, silent as a deer. She laid a mat on the ground beside the hammock and knelt.

"*Lại đây,*" she said. (Come here.)

To this command, he complied. Only when trying to get out of the hammock, he caught his foot on the lip and tumbled onto the mat, cracking his jaw on her knee.

"Ow," they exclaimed in unison.

She put her hand over her mouth to muffle her giggle, a resonant chord that wove into his being.

"Kannon, do you dance the ballet?"

"No," he said. He leaned forward and kissed her cheek.

Lan turned her head and smothered his mouth with kisses. They lingered, tongues searching, hands exploring. She pushed away and stood. She slipped the tunic over her head and stepped out of her pants. Kannon rose to his feet and undressed.

Naked beneath the Vietnamese sky, they threaded their arms around one another. The cool night air feathered their skin, forcing them to press their bodies ever closer, feeding off each other's warmth. She pulled him down and opened her legs. When he entered her, the warmth of her body radiated acceptance, and they rocked in

222

rhythm with the swaying palms.

Thirty-Four

The day passed as if time ran in reverse. Finally, twilight approached.

Papa-san Minh harnessed his water buffalo to the cart. The Minhs, along with Lan, climbed in the front. Kannon sequestered himself in the back under a tarp, his equipment beside him.

The wagon trundled. Wheels creaked. Stiff rope slapped against the harness like the pop of a leather strop. The buffalo huffed, as if disgusted and dreading the drudgery of labor. For fifteen minutes, Kannon sweltered beneath the canvas, thinking of Lan's tenderness the night before, the way she touched him, and the way she guided his hands over her.

"Hyuhh!" Papa-san smacked the pew-like bench with his palm, the signal for Kannon to slither from beneath the tarp and jump to the ground.

The cart's arthritic moans faded as it disappeared down the sinuous trail. Kannon remained motionless, crouched amid dried stubs of a dormant rice field that emptied into a thicket of palm, bamboo, and jackfruit. Dust impregnated with an odor of decayed dung caked his nostrils.

Anxiety tempted him to charge headlong into the hedgerow. But he had come too far for such foolishness.

Star clusters pulsed like legions of fireflies as he slipped on the Nighthawks, which featured a macro range at six inches and a maximum range near two hundred yards. He adjusted his eyes to a green, eerie world. Nothing stirred except the topmost branches among the palm and bamboo.

As if impelled by their motion, he crept forward, his body carrying thirty-two more years and fifteen extra pounds. Five minutes later, he reached the northern perimeter of the hedgerow. His arms and legs ached. Perspiration and dirt stained his clothes like battle paint.

Kannon rolled on his side and swigged some bottled water. Then he adjusted his goggles, bringing the focus to two feet. His eyes swept the 180-degree frontal. No trail. He crawled five meters to the left. Nothing. Reversing course, he crawled another ten meters, again finding no indications of a trail.

Shit.

The tranquility and confidence he'd experienced an hour ago disintegrated. The ludicrousness of crawling through a booby-trapped position, a dimension soaked in evil, threatened his fantasy of redemption. Dismemberment or death seemed more probable.

After fine-tuning the macro focus, he again examined papa-san's rough map. The mouth of the trail should be there. He pulled himself to the spot he'd started from.

Wild growth hindered his vision. Uncertainty retarded his movement. His wrists and ankles might as well be staked to the ground with strips of rawhide.

Hell, he'd call a chopper and be extracted—

Jesus Christ! Stop hallucinating. Get ahold of yourself.

Kannon poked through the thicket and inched ahead. The vegetation thinned. A partial, tree-lined canopy filtered flickering starlight into the hedgerow's interior. Shadows bobbed like darting dragonflies. He surveyed the forbidden zone, made a gut check, and pulled forward another few inches.

Something tugged at his right shoulder. A tree branch or tripwire? Kannon twisted his head around for an awkward look, his neck muscles contorting like knotted ropes. Then he saw it. Just above, a taut wire quivered like a strummed tightrope.

Another few inches and his backpack would have tripped it. He crept backward to track the wire to its source. One end terminated at a low tree branch, the other end led to an M2 fragmentation grenade. It protruded halfway from its cocoon, a hole drilled into the trunk of a bamboo tree.

Utilizing his multi-purpose tool, he clipped the wire and shoved the grenade back into the tree, then took a deep breath.

Close. Close. Close.

The growth continued to dissipate, almost as if someone had gutted the interior and groomed it. Kannon crawled forward, probing with his fingers, a blind man reading Braille.

Clear. He had covered a good three meters, only seventeen to go. Again, he resisted the urge to stand and walk.

Suddenly, the ground buckled beneath him. His body wobbled back and forth like it was on a seesaw. He flicked on the goggle's infrared illuminator.

Goddamn!

The weight of the backpack almost toppled him into a man-made crevasse. Punji stakes, jeering like jagged teeth, jutted from the ground. He clutched the sides of the scaffold and dug his toes into the back end to avoid plunging below.

He'd seen one of his South Vietnamese soldiers impaled on a similar device. It operated like a horizontal revolving door. Once the weight mass tilted the fulcrum point, the platform spun, flipping the victim uncontrollably into a horrible death. If he'd been erect, he'd be flapping on razor-sharp bamboo slivers like a skewered salmon.

Suspended above the pit, Kannon inched his way back along the scaffold. As the weight shifted, he regained a stable plane. The trap had been constructed to accommodate the smaller Vietnamese, so his height worked to his advantage. He anchored his hands on a bush just beyond the pit, then crab-walked past it and stood— trembling, breath laboring in hulking gasps.

After a moment, anger and determination displaced his fear. Kannon knelt, surveyed the immediate frontal area, then advanced.

Three meters. Five. At ground level, a woven web of palm and bamboo stopped him. Kneading through the reeds, he felt a thin current of cool air lick his moist palms.

Could this be the entrance to the suspected cache? Cautiously, Kannon lifted the man-made canopy and peered into a hole.

The deceptive cover concealed another punji-stake trap, almost as chilling as the last. A sharpened bamboo stake spiked from the ground two feet below. Three additional stakes angled down sharply a foot below ground level. If a leg crashed through the false cover, the foot impaled on the bottom stake. When the hapless victim involuntarily yanked his leg upwards, the other three stakes embedded the thigh.

Kannon stood, sucked in the fresh air. He stepped over the hole.

Snap! A branch cracked like a brittle bone.

A grenade rolled between his feet. Instinctively, he swatted the grenade into the hole behind him and dived forward, risking plunging into still one more punji pit. A muffled explosion shook the ground.

Night birds squawked in protest. The wind kicked up and whistled through the hedgerow. He lay still. If anyone heard the explosion, perhaps they would attribute it to a wandering water buffalo setting off an old mine.

* * *

Three kilometers away, Lan lay awake under the stars, fidgeting in Kannon's hammock. He was the first man she had given herself to since abandoning her lover, a poet and university professor, for his infidelity with a student. Even though Quang had promised it was a onetime error, a mistake that would not be repeated, she chose not to give him a second chance.

Could she trust Kannon? She thought so. His loyalty to her brother moved her.

A distant rumble like a wayward clap of thunder nudged Lan, reminding her of firecrackers during Tết. She clutched her chest and closed her eyes.

Chấn's image appeared.

She believed in her brother's remorse, that he had done his best to walk the middle path, but in trying to maintain a delicate balance, had fallen off the beam. Yet, it was her brother who started Kannon down the path to reclaim what had been stolen from him. And to keep Kannon from being stolen from her, she sought refuge not only in Buddha but also in his God.

Lan resumed swinging in the breeze and released a prayer.

Thirty-Five

At 2200 hours, ten minutes after the grenade detonated, Kannon forced himself to move. He traced the rough outline of what appeared to be a door to the underground. He discovered no wires attached to a solid chunk of wood two feet square.

Kannon sought a handhold but found none. He searched the hedgerow's interior for something to wedge into the crack between the cover and the ground. A severed branch lay propped against a palm three feet away. Taking short steps, he reached the tree and retrieved a piece of stout bamboo, then noticed another trail snaking through the underbrush.

Hmm, papa-san hadn't mentioned another trail. It made sense, though, to have an exit route. Was it booby-trapped also? He stepped forward for a closer look and froze. Footprints. And they were recent. The site was active.

The chill of terror assailed him as it had when the sappers breached the perimeter of his former outpost. With the terror came the doubt. Was Lan's lovemaking a ruse? Was this to be a posthumous chapter in Chấn's duplicity, his sister and Papa-san Minh agents of death?

The negative thoughts drained his energy. He realized now how deep ran his rage at the injustice of betrayal. It colored every aspect of his post-Việt Nam life and transformed the rational into the irrational.

Stay on track. Concentrate on Farber.

Kannon took the bamboo branch to the entrance to the underground. He found a slight depression, wedged the shaft in, and pushed down firmly. The cover, which fit like a glove, pivoted easily.

A stench of foul air escaped. The entrance slanted down at an angle. Switching on the infrared illuminator, he peered into the depths of the unknown, revealing a series of steps dug into the ground.

He hesitated. What a cruel irony if he were to spend the last moments of his life underground, his body never to be found.

Kannon descended on hands and knees. The steps, about six inches wide and a foot deep, numbered ten and were firm and dry. The air lay thick and heavy as if the tomb encapsulated the exhalations of all those who'd been there before. He reached the bottom and stood.

A long, narrow passageway emptied into a black abyss. Were venomous snakes suspended from the ceiling? The fear penetrated like an arctic wind. Slogging forward in a crouch, his shoulders brushed against the dirt walls.

Three steps . . . four, five. The aisle widened. The infrared illuminator fed the image intensifier and illumined the empty underground like a macabre dream.

Suddenly he encountered a gaping hole. He flipped up the goggles, grabbed a flashlight from his pack, and flicked it on. Swinging the flash back and forth, he inspected the hole. It appeared to be an exposed booby trap, not a tunnel. Next, he directed the light down the passageway. Darkness swallowed the thin beam.

He switched off the flashlight and waited until his night vision returned before refitting the night goggles. He started to proceed across the gap.

No, wait.

Using the bamboo branch as a probe, he leaned forward and tapped the earthen floor just the other side of the hole.

Whack!

Something ripped the branch from his hand. Shaken, he looked to his right. A machete was wedged into the earthen wall. The spring trap would've cut him in half if its lever hadn't snapped in two.

Cautiously, he stepped beyond the hole and examined the mechanism. The spring-loaded device could be recocked. Should he reset it, in case someone followed? But, what if he needed to make a fast exit? Kannon decided against it.

He crab-walked through the tunnel, which led into another, larger room—a chamber. How much time did he have? Kannon checked his watch. It read 2400 hours, plenty of time before dawn.

Kannon scanned the chamber from left to right. Even in the

marginal light, it didn't take long to absorb what he saw. Unlit oil lamps ten feet apart hung suspended from thick bamboo stakes driven into the earthen walls. A desk and two-drawer file cabinet sat in one corner. Rows of metal shelving, anchored into bamboo studs coupled together for reinforcement, occupied most of the floor space.

The lamps were free of dust and their oil reservoirs were full, which didn't surprise him. He examined the desk, running his fingers lightly around the edges. No wires. He pulled open the single desk drawer, found a box of matches, and lit three of the lanterns.

Ventilation tubes eliminated the oil smoke from the underground. Grabbing a lantern, he paced two legs of the rectangular-shaped cavity and estimated its measure at approximately forty by fifty feet. He judged the ceiling to be ten feet above floor level. Near the entrance, two six-foot-high posts, with metal rings attached near the top and base, rose from the ground. It didn't take much imagination to deduce their purpose—securing a torture victim.

A quick walk up and down the aisles left Kannon with the impression of entering a U.S. Army Post Exchange. Stereo receivers—Sansui, Kenwood, and Pioneer, reel-to-reel tape decks—Teac and Akai, and turntables and speakers filled the lower shelves. Obsolete, but still boxed in original containers, spotless as if just delivered. Unbelievable.

Another row of shelving contained vintage cameras. But it was the neatly labeled crates wrapped in heavyweight, oiled paper that attracted his attention.

Weapons.

God Almighty. Farber, that son of a bitch, knew about this. Hell, he was part of it.

Clipboards, each one securing documents, hung on pegs. He examined one. Crisp and fresh to the touch, the document contained an inventory. Line items were M-16s, M-2 fragmentation grenades, Claymore mines, AK47s, Type 59 Chicom pistols, various explosives, and much more. Harmless, until man unleashed their devastation because of political ineptitude, fear, or hate.

Kannon unwrapped an M-16 and a Kalashnikova, known as

the AK47. The AK, he remembered, fired a deadly 7.62mm round as opposed to the M16's 5.56mm. The weapons looked brand new. The firing pins were in place.

At the rear of this space, opposite where he'd gained entry, two additional entryways branched left and right, forming a T-shaped junction. He entered the one on the left and found a protruding beam to hang the lantern.

The room approximated ten feet by fifteen feet with three rows of shelving containing four shelves each. Belted ammunition—enough to start a small war—occupied one row. Detonation cord, C-4, non-electric blasting caps, time fuses, tape, and fuse igniters filled another. Boxed ammunition and grenades stocked the third. A dismantled tiger cage, the kind used to imprison POWs or discipline intractable soldiers leaned against the far wall.

The room to the right was smaller, eight by eight feet, and contained sealed wooden boxes about two feet square. He retrieved the severed bamboo lever and pried open one box. It was full of wrapped packages. Kannon opened his knife, picked up a brick-sized package, and peeled away the paper, then pricked the substance. He wet his forefinger, touched the texture, which felt similar to hardened modeling clay, and tasted the result—papaver somniferum, the opium poppy, the most precious cargo of all—pure unadulterated opium, the father of morphine and grandfather of heroin.

He'd gotten interested and studied the drug while performing due diligence on biotech and pharmaceutical companies. Kannon knew little history of the opium poppy but knew enough to understand that the harvesting of its pulp was labor-intensive. The pulp not only had to be dried and kneaded, but its impurities must also be boiled out. Finally, the raw narcotic was dried again.

If stored opium aged like wine and cigars in temperate cellars and well-humidified, room-sized humidors, then, he guessed, this stuff should be potent.

Once more, he looked at his watch. 0200 hours. He went back to the desk and slid open the drawer again. It fell to the floor. A pipe and a box of Cuban cigars tumbled out. Cohibas. He scooped out several and pocketed them. Then Kannon smelled the pipe bowl, which instantly induced lightheadedness. It reminded him of what he'd read about Comanches eating mescal buttons. He put the rest of the items back in place, clipped a cigar, and lit it. He no longer cared about leaving a trace.

He wrote a list of questions.

1. Who was involved? Vietnamese? Americans?
2. How were the goods brought in? The money exchanged? Or were drugs bartered for weapons and stereos?
3. Were the weapons and stereos smuggled across the river on sampans into Cambodia—to find their way into Việt Cộng and NVA southern headquarters? Or vice versa?
4. Were the drugs sold to American and Vietnamese soldiers?
5. Had the radio order he received that night from Farber been a valid order in response to an intelligence report about enemy activity in the area?
6. Or, as Chấn said, "They thought you knew." They'd suspected him, wanted to take him out.
7. Were Farber and Jeffrey involved with Hai thirty-two years ago? To what extent and why? And now?

Kannon still had no proof about what he conjectured. He laid out his camera equipment, affixed a 35-70mm zoom lens, attached the flash, then secured the rig on a small but sturdy tripod. He photographed everything in the underground vault, from the stereos to the weapons to the opium, proofing the digital images on the camera's built-in display screen.

Next, he slit open several boxes of stereo equipment, removed the instruction booklets, and slipped them into the backpack's main pocket. He grabbed a Chicom pistol and several eight-round clips of 9mm ammunition, checked its mechanics—a blowback, double-action based on Russia's Makarov—and stashed them in the front pouch. The opium he left alone.

One item left to examine. The file cabinet pivoted on large casters, so Kannon rolled it to the desk under better lighting. Both drawers contained indexed manila folders full of papers written in Vietnamese, and too voluminous to carry.

A notebook lay wedged behind the top drawer. Kannon

removed it and leafed through the pages. Also written in Vietnamese. Nevertheless, he pilfered it as well and started to roll the file cabinet back into its original position when he noticed a canvas tarp.

He tugged at the bottom. The tarp flapped upwards like a window shade. A crawl space yawned beyond the gritty opening. He knelt, switched on the flash, and followed the trail. The light glinted as if reflecting off something metallic.

Rails. Another tunnel.

Kannon lost his concentration and grew spooked. The reality of where he was and what he'd been doing sank in. He stood and repositioned the file cabinet, then walked over to extinguish the oil lamps. In doing so, he stubbed his foot on a tiny mound. He rubbed his foot back and forth. The sound grated differently.

Christ, he could be standing on top of another booby trap.

He directed the flash to his feet and stepped back, expecting a 'Bouncing Betty' to pop up and disembowel him. Instead, what appeared to be a leather handle protruded above the dirt floor. Gingerly, he brushed away loose dirt until an area approximately three feet square lay exposed.

An old leather suitcase, wrapped in clear plastic, lay at his feet. He bent down, lifted the suitcase from its crypt, and set it on the desk. Slipping off the plastic, he forced open the latches and gasped—U.S. currency, stacked and banded in packages of tens, twenties, fifties, and hundreds. A rough count consumed five minutes.

Jesus Christ! There must be at least two hundred thousand dollars.

The money could be helpful. He studied the find, puffed deeply on the rich cigar, and blew acrid smoke into the oil-lit room.

Could Lan make use of the cash? Kannon wondered.

The suitcase also contained a change of clothes. He rummaged through the side pockets—personal effects—he'd stumbled upon the little treasures everyone keeps to capture elements of time: a pocketknife, loose change, a crude, homemade pipe, a calculator and currency converter, batteries, a small flashlight, pencil and paper, and a few photographs.

Please let there be pictures of Farber and Hai.

He riffled the pictures. No such luck. Typical shots of Vietnamese, unrecognizable, except for one—baby Đăng Đạo. It was the same photograph Lan had shown him on his first visit, the one he had taken in 1970. What concerned him was not how the photograph had gotten here, but the why. Kannon doubted Lan's nephew ever made it to America because Đăng Đạo probably died on Vietnamese soil. Lan didn't need to know this.

After pocketing the photographs, he scribbled a note in Vietnamese—*Cám ơn ông* (Thank you)—and put it in the suitcase. Then, withholding the plastic, he placed the valise in the hole and concealed it with dirt.

For a brief moment, he considered leaving his own booby traps or blowing up the cache with hand grenades. He rejected the idea as too dangerous and time-consuming. Instead, he rolled the currency in oiled paper and secured the package with the plastic covering from the suitcase. He snuffed out the oil lamps, then extricated himself from the underground warehouse.

Once on top, he secured the cover, considered the need to obliterate evidence of his intrusion, but abandoned the idea when he remembered the sprung booby traps. Exhausted, he retraced his steps to the trail's mouth. When he emerged, the crescent moon clipped the treetops like a flickering candle. The air was cool and exhilarating.

Not wanting to be seen with two hundred thousand dollars, he decided to bury it. From the trail entrance, he paced off ten steps and hunkered down. With his hands and the severed bamboo lever, he excavated a long, narrow hole, set the cash inside, replaced the soil, and scattered loose brush to camouflage the hole.

Satisfied with the concealment, Kannon pulled out his compass, shot the back azimuth, and began the three-kilometer trek back to the Minh farm. In the eastern sky, an orange glow infringed on the darkness.

He loped into an easy jog.

The subdued light favored his return, but in his giddy state, he almost ran headlong into a couple of bicyclists carrying fishing poles. Flinging himself on the ground, Kannon avoided looking directly at them and waited until they passed.

The Minhs' farmhouse loomed as a silhouette against the rising sun. His success in uncovering the cache, and Lan's lovemaking, fueled hopes long lying dormant—at last, the absence of despair. The victorious warrior revisited.

He strode into the clearing, expecting to breathe in the wood smoke from an early morning breakfast fire. There was no scent. All was quiet about the place. Nothing stirred.

Everyone was asleep, he guessed, even the animals. But there were no animals. He entered the house. Empty. Lan and the Minhs were gone.

Thirty-Six

Wait a minute. Something didn't register to Kannon. Of course, the yellow-jacketed Yamaha motorcycle was missing, and the Minhs' cart wasn't in its usual place. This was the wrong hedgerow. He must have shot an incorrect back azimuth. How could he have been that stupid?

A gleam of light, a reflection, glinted from a metallic surface and caught his attention. He shunted aside scrub bushes and scampered ten meters to the spot. A canvas tarpaulin lay on the ground, the same tarpaulin he'd used the night before. It partially covered his DT175 obtained from Mr. Ngọc. No, he wasn't that stupid after all.

Had they hidden the motorcycle and gone to market, only for the bike to be revealed by a fickle wind? Had they abandoned him? No. That wasn't in their nature.

The chill of isolation swept over him. He returned to the house and searched for clues. The sparse interior revealed nothing, no note, not even a disguised opening for a tunnel, a common element during the war.

Outside, he plodded to his hammock, which hung limply in the morning dew. A small box lay in the webbing, weighing down the middle. He picked up the box and opened it. A faded Silver Star nested inside. His Silver Star. A lump caught in his throat. Who had put it there? Lan?

Bewildered, he scanned the stubbled brown fields surrounding the house. Everything seemed normal except for the deafening silence . . . and the scarecrows. He'd never seen scarecrows in Việt Nam.

Kannon moved toward the stick figures. The stench of slaughtered livestock filled the air. Flies swarmed. The closer he got, the more his legs turned leaden.

"Oh, my God!"

Two decapitated corpses, their bodies tied spread eagle, sagged between flexible bamboo poles. Deep lacerations penetrated their torsos. Fluids coagulated outside the slashing welts. Burn marks penetrated the genital areas.

Kannon circled the sacrificial site, stomped flat by the carnage.

The Minhs' heads, mouths contorted in agony, stared grotesquely from ground level at the bodies from which they'd been severed. Their tongues were grotesquely impaled on sharpened stakes directly opposite the faces. Ridiculously, Kannon conjectured whether the tongues had been cut out before or after decapitation.

His vision swam in psychedelic horror, a bad acid trip. He couldn't imagine Farber and Jeffrey capable of such butchery. It had to be Hai, but then, why hadn't Hai pursued him into the hedgerow? Maybe it was a Khmer Rouge outlaw gang raiding across the border.

Who was he kidding? He'd implicated all of them—the Minhs, Lan, and Thanh. Yet, if they'd talked, Hai would have followed Kannon. Perhaps he had but arrived too late.

The sun rose above the tree line and, like the opening of a blast furnace, released its heat. Insects remained stilled until the passage of dawn awoke their voices, and the sickening, impregnating stink of human death hung as if trapped by a thick cloud.

He slumped to the ground and held his head. It pounded as if a vice full of misery squeezed against his will. Then, like a stunned boxer, he rose and circled the hedgerow in an expanding spiral, trying to find his bearings, trying to find Lan.

Nothing.

Hai took her . . . or she escaped. Please let it be the latter. He'd notify the police and tell them what happened. Yeah, right. Hell, he couldn't go to the police. How would he explain his presence?

Opting to leave the hedgerow, he righted the motorcycle, mounted, then inserted the key to turn on the transmission and kick-started the bike. He estimated the nine-point-five-liter tank to be sixty percent full. Good enough. He damn well preferred to ride through another district in a direction opposite from the villages of Hiệp Hòa and Bào Trai.

The sun and wind scorched his face as he trailed along the

peak of a rice paddy dike, winding through a copse of tight, contiguous hedgerows. Finally, the path converged with a broader cart track. He rounded a bend and came upon two uniformed men on bicycles. One raised a palm and hollered, "*Ngừng lại! Ngừng lại!*" (Halt.)

Christ, those weren't fishermen he'd seen earlier, they were policemen. And those weren't fishing poles they carried but rifles.

Kannon downshifted into second, then, just as he drew abreast of the policemen, goosed the throttle and shifted into third. Startled, they dove out of the way. The motorcycle accelerated down the grooved path, buffeting over the dried mud ridges like waves crashing onto rocks. The whining engine protested the max rpms. Looking over his shoulder, he saw the policemen leveling their AKs.

Rapid-fire reports sounded as 7.62mm rounds pinged into the snarled palm and bamboo overhead. He crouched against the tank and kept riding. In his rear-view mirror, he noticed the pursuers had slung their weapons over their shoulders and were pedaling after him.

The road hooked a sharp right, then arched like a horseshoe. Kannon stood on the footpegs and vaulted over the rugged embankment as if bucked by an earthquake. He almost smacked headlong into a farmer guiding a water buffalo. The man howled and shook his arm in protest.

For twenty minutes, Kannon twisted and shifted west by northwest along worn paths scratched through the fields. Mangroves appeared, announcing the river marshes, and then the land turned hard again. An old cemetery staked claim beside a burned-out pagoda. He pulled behind a latticed row of towering rattan and bamboo that fed into a canal. His chest heaved for oxygen as if it were a collapsed bladder.

There were no signs of his pursuers. Other than the farmer on the road, had anyone else seen him? Would the police patrol the whole area? Enlarge their number? Hopefully, they would think he'd looped in the other direction and try to intercept him on the more direct route to Sài Gòn. If they assumed he was going in that direction.

A larger question loomed. Where was Lan?

His breathing steadied as he struggled for composure. A weathered sampan, wearing neglect like an abandoned house, rocked in the arterial waterway. He hauled it ashore and tested its sturdiness. Satisfied, he wrestled the two-hundred-pound motorcycle into the sampan, cut broad palmetto branches and covered the motorcycle, then shoved the boat in the water and climbed aboard. The sampan tipped but didn't capsize. He poled toward the river and sequestered the rig amid a mangrove thicket.

After consulting his maps and GPS, he remembered that during the war, this had been a Việt Cộng staging area.

If he figured correctly, he had crossed Route 6A east of the Vàm Cỏ Đông River and was only five kilometers from the cache, which lay southeast at 130 degrees. He must have, in part, ridden a circular route. Trảng Bàng lay eight kilometers eastward, at a seventy-five-degree azimuth.

He plotted a route through Trảng Bàng, then north to Tây Ninh, where he'd turn east until running into Route 13, then south to Sài Gòn. He'd have to run it at night.

The sun reached its zenith. Rattan and bamboo branches crackled in the wind. Tropical birds chattered atop the tree canopy, then quieted and settled in their nests. Insects droned a low murmur under the sweltering tyranny.

He took out the Chicom pistol, fingered the intricate Chinese symbols on the grip, then jammed a magazine into the well, pulled back the slide and chambered a round. He placed the pistol in a waterproof bag, sealed it, and shoved the bag in his waistband. The backpack he left in the sampan.

Dull reflections bounced off the canal's cloudy surface. Kannon took off his boots and slipped over the edge of the sampan. The murky water curled around his neck, chilled his body, as he clung to mangrove roots, anchoring himself against the current, anchoring himself against his fear.

Thirty-Seven

The pendulum edged the minute hand forward. Director of Operations Ling glanced at the clock as it chimed six times. It would be one hour before Hai arrived at the office this morning. After all these years, the sacrifices, insults, and denigrations were taking their toll. Never had Ling violated his master's trust, but the brutality in which Hai dispatched the Minhs was more than Ling could tolerate.

He played the first tape again.

"Major Farber and Captain Jeffrey, welcome to the bowels of Việt Nam." Hai's voice sounded as strident then as now.

"Who the hell are you?" It was an American voice.

"Who am I? I am your benefactor. But who I am is not important, yes? It is what I have to show you."

"I suggest you fucking show yourself the way out."

Hai croaked like a rooster, then continued. "We know the district chief, Major Ba, has granted you special favors. If you will kindly study these photographs, yes?"

Ling used the remote to pause the tape then once more studied the photographs he had taken from the envelope. One showed a large American man copulating with a long-legged Vietnamese woman while another woman stood over him with a bamboo switch. The second American, a shorter, slimmer man, favored two young girls, one sitting astride his pelvic area, the other squatting on his face. As far as he was concerned, the Americans were perverts.

Ling resumed the tape.

"Gentlemen," Hai's voice came through on playback, "we have audio tapes proving you have been trading cocaine for sexual favors, an act we do not think you want your commanding officers to know about."

Ling visualized Hai's delight in seeing these Americans squirm.

"Your actions with our women are of no concern to me. I am, however, a consummate capitalist. We will trade."

"You filthy bastard. I won't trade with you," the American voice retorted.

"If you do not, I kill you now. Or, you can live by providing certain necessities, and these tapes and photographs will never find their way into the hands of your superiors."

"Like hell."

"As I swear on Buddha, you will," came Hai's response. "Besides, you make much money. The trading will be harmless, low risk. We want generators, fuel, TVs, and stereo equipment."

"Major Farber, what can we do?"

"Shut the fuck up, Captain."

"These grid squares are never to be shelled." Ling visualized Hai pointing to a military map as the tape played on. "If anything happens to the District Chief or me, copies of the tapes and photographs will be released upon the occurrence—to both the South Vietnamese and your commanding officers."

Scuffling sounds ensued, but Ling could distinguish no words. Then—

"Major Farber and Captain Jeffrey, this is an insurance contract."

"Rot in hell," said the American voice.

Ling listened to the rest. The Americans, with a peculiar aversion to being court-martialed, agreed to make it a practice to protect Hai and the District Chief by reclassifying the area as a no-fire zone. The trading escalated from cocaine to heroin.

Major Farber also ordered weapons in excessive numbers relative to the number of active South Vietnamese soldiers, then withheld large quantities, and traded the matériel to Hai for money, sex, and their lives.

Hai had encapsulated their minds and souls in an emotional booby trap.

Ling wished he had never reported Ballard's second return. What made it worse was Ling had suggested to Hai that Lan and Ballard might have gone to the Minhs. What made it horrible was witnessing the killings.

He rewound the tape and placed it in the safe with the others, then inserted the photographs in the envelope and returned them as well. The Americans he couldn't care less about, but the time was coming for Ling to act.

For now, he gathered the implements and set to work preparing Hai's hookah.

* * *

This morning, the whiff of roasting chickens floated thick as Nguyễn Hai strode along Nam Kỳ Khởi Nghĩa Street toward his office. The smell was the last he remembered, the last he connected to his mother's words. You came out of the womb angry. An ugly boy. She had named him Hai, number two. There was no number one son. What would she think now?

A parrot squawked. It sounded like Mama-san Minh when he had cut her throat. The look of fear in the Minhs' eyes confirmed their duplicity, yet they revealed no information about Chấn's sister or the Texan.

Too old to offer physical resistance, the Minhs died too quick. Hai regretted his impatience and wondered if he was losing his touch.

Even though Papa-san's usefulness to the cell had expired long ago, Hai experienced bittersweet feelings on his demise, because other than himself, no cell member of The Monsoon Killed the Tiger remained. He again wrestled with the identity of *Chiến sĩ vô Danh*, the Unknown Warrior who reportedly had lost his life in the war. He guessed he would never know. But his failure to locate Lan and the Texan frustrated him more.

* * *

Feeling hopeful about throwing off a yoke a water buffalo would be loath to carry, Ling lit the hookah just as Hai opened the office door.

"The Khmer Rouge. They want AKs, yes?" Hai's tone irritated Ling.

"Twenty-five," he said.

"Opium?"

"Two kilos, sir."

"The damn Khmer Rouge will squander it. You know why they failed in Cambodia?" Hai didn't wait for an answer. "Lack of central organization and control. Lack of discipline."

"You do not fail, sir. You eliminated the Minhs with cruel efficiency."

"Shut up," Hai said. "Do not patronize me."

"I speak with respect."

Ling caught Hai's look of disdain. His superior snatched the water pipe and filled his lungs with smoke.

"You have further ideas on the purpose of the Texan, yes?"

Ling did, but he would not express his perception of truth. "I believe the man to be harmless, sir."

"Explain his presence."

"A mystery. How he met Lan, I do not know, but I suspect their association romantic."

"This weekend is Tết, yes?"

Ling nodded. "Why is it necessary to kill Lan? Her brother is dead and can no longer harm you."

"You disgust me, minion. If this continues, you will not remain in my service much longer."

Arrogant beetle. Ling dug his sharp nails into his palm to keep from divulging his growing hatred. I will squash you.

"Lan is a traitor." Hai continued. "She associates with the Texan. This concerns me."

Concern? Ling reasoned Hai wanted Lan dead because he could not have her. The Texan, well—

"Has Major Farber established an office presence in Sài Gòn?"

"No, sir. Only registered." Ling handed Hai a photocopy of the certificate.

"This offers no value." Hai shredded it as he puffed on the pipe. He walked to the wall safe and twirled the combination. The door popped open. He withdrew the envelope containing the pictures Ling had just observed and spread the contents on the desk.

"The Texan does not appear in these photographs." Then, a wicked smile spread across Hai's face. "Great Buddha. I remember who this swine is. He was the lieutenant at the An Định outpost. He survived the ambush."

The revelation did not startle Ling. Even before listening to the tapes, he had pieced together bits of story Hai unfolded over the years. "You know this to be so?"

"Major Farber reported it. My doped-up guerrillas failed to reconnoiter the area after launching the attack. I should have led the ambush myself."

Ling smiled an inner smile. Hai only attacked the defenseless.

"Sir, if you would indulge your humble servant, why would the Americans desire to challenge the cell after thirty-two years?"

"Revenge. Although I cannot imagine Major Farber or Captain Jeffrey setting foot on our land again. They sent the Texan, yes?"

"It is not logical an intended victim would join those who attempted his murder."

Hai inhaled from the pipe and snorted. "Ling, you are an idiot. Farber and Jeffrey never would have told him."

"If you say so, sir."

"I believe Chấn, a piece of buffalo dung, initiated the process, yes?"

Ling considered the possibility. Even though Hai had related how Chấn had proven a suitable double agent, he never exhibited the ruthlessness required from a dedicated combat guerrilla. True, Chấn had killed, but his killing was defensive in nature. Questioning the purpose of the killings, Chấn in his heart overcame his deeds, Ling concluded.

"Why did you not kill Major Farber?"

"They were reassigned, or I would have." Hai spat into the trashcan. "I fear the Texan might attempt to infiltrate the cache. The booby traps are placed as I designed, yes?"

"As you know, no one has infiltrated the hedgerow."

"Inspect the cache anyway. I will make copies of these tapes and photographs and send them to Đăng Đạo. We will teach Major Farber and his fellow Americans to leave us alone."

To conceal his frown, Ling bowed.

As he prepared to leave the office, Ling saw two options. Ransack the cache, steal the money, and vanish. Or, he could make his own copies of the tapes and photographs, release them to the communist authorities, and reveal the cache location. Or both. The communist leaders would not approve of this maverick corrupting their system.

Ling brightened at the prospects. Now, he was happy to comply with Hai's command, because it gave him the chance to find Lan and the Texan first. He could use them, as well his Chinese comrades in Chợ Lớn, who would be pleased.

He had the bastard.

Thirty-Eight

The sun plunged below the horizon, casting the room in a tomb-like gloom. Lan remembered when she had been anesthetized, temporarily put to death in her view, to remove her gall bladder. When she had awakened, she feared she had entered a spirit world and would be forever cursed with blurred vision. Now, that was how she saw her cousin Thanh, draped with a veil of abject subjugation, his silence and impassivity expressing his grief more eloquently than spoken words ever could.

"Did my parents suffer long?" Thanh asked.

This was the question she dreaded. "They died quickly."

He seemed to accept this answer and puffed on his Briar, adding to the stale tobacco smoke that filled the room like a polluted cloud.

"How did you get away?"

The room stopped swirling, and Lan fixed her eyes on the shadowy outline of her cousin, who sat in his burnished mahogany chair, a straight-backed favorite an unknown benefactor had abandoned on his doorstep. "I was relieving myself when they came," she said. "I remained hidden in the trees."

"Then what?"

"I wanted to wait for Kannon, but the horrible one started in my direction." Never had she seen anything so terrible. The mutilation and screams poisoned her soul. It was as if her own nipples were being burned, her own head being severed. These details she could not tell Thanh.

"You are sure the horrible one was Hai?"

"Yes. His was the man's face in the photograph at your parents' farm, the man who threatened me on the street."

"The reason you emailed Kannon Ballard, the reason he came back."

"Yes."

All she wanted to do was to protect and nurture life, yet, in her blind desire to honor Chấn's wishes and support Kannon, Lan

246

sensed it was she who had sentenced the Minhs to death.

"This man Kannon must . . . care for you," he said.

"He does. And I care about him." She choked back any tears. "I did not intend to . . . it just happened."

An acrid gust of wind burst through the open window, threatening to extinguish the lone, flickering candle. It was as if a death draft were trying to annihilate signs of life.

"I have distracted you," he said. "Let us return to your escape."

She looked at the flaming candle, which refused to die. "I was scared and ran. I found the road. Since it was early morning, a Lambretta soon came by, and the driver offered me a ride. Then I caught a bus."

Still sitting in his rigid chair, Thanh rocked his body back and forth as if trying to instill life to an inanimate object. Then he stopped rocking. He stared through bushy eyebrows sagging over compressed eyelids like he was observing her through tiny camouflaged gun ports. "At my parent's farm, you said you heard an explosion when Kannon was exploring the hedgerow but knew in your heart he was all right."

"I did. I remember well because I was lying in his hammock at the time."

"What do you feel now?"

"I fear he may be dead, for I have lost my vision of him."

"As I have lost my parents." Next to Thanh was a teak table embellished with inlaid marble. He slapped the top with his palm. It sounded like a gunshot. "The snake."

His comment gripped her heart, and this time her tears broke through. "Cousin. Is there nothing I can do to soothe your anger and pain?"

Thanh rose from his chair and walked to Lan's side. He put his arm around her. "The reason for your tears?"

Wiping her eyes, she said, "Everything. The death of your parents, losing my brother, Kan—"

"Lan, Hai is the snake, not your American," he said, a grim look on his face.

"You are not angry?"

247

"I am sad," he said. "I hate Hai. I am not angry with you, or at Kannon."

She steadied herself against a Buddha icon. Thanh's wall clock chimed. He reset the chains. Behind his pale-green eyes and asthmatic frame, she now knew resided strength.

"Your mother and father must not have talked," she said, "or else they would be alive."

"No, they would not be alive. Nor would you."

"Perhaps death would have been better."

"Come, cousin. No more shame and sorrow. Besides, there are things you do not know."

How many more secrets? "Our family book is being rewritten," she said.

Lan waited for him to respond. He hesitated as if perched on the bow of a ship, deciding whether to jump.

"I fear to reveal may cause me to lose face," he said.

"You will never lose face in my eyes."

His lips parted in a thin smile. "When I was fourteen, my father approached your father with an idea."

"I want to hear this idea."

He shifted his gaze to the window as though it were a portal for his words to escape, precluding them from landing on her.

"I was a sickly youth, not strong enough to withstand the rigors of war. Your father agreed. They sent me to school in Sài Gòn and arranged for me to avoid being drafted into the military."

"A noble gesture," she said.

"I look at it as neither noble nor dishonorable," he said. "My father gave me a chance to live."

Lan clenched her fists. "I wish governments gave all children the chance to live."

"So do I, but successful revolutionaries often oppress just as badly as their predecessors. Here is the point. Before I left, my father said, 'Con trai, this is a terribly ugly war. One day it will end. Even then, there will be no winners.'"

"I understand your father's words," she said.

"Father also told me he signed an irrevocable pact with the devil."

"The Monsoon Killed the Tiger," she said.

Thanh emptied his spent pipe tobacco in an ashtray. "Members of the same cell."

* * *

By the time Ling arrived at the tunnel complex Tuesday afternoon, he had reconsidered his options concerning Hai. If Hai loved anything or anyone, it was his son, Đăng Đạo, who seemed to respect, if not adore his father. If Ling betrayed Hai, Đăng Đạo would seek revenge, which meant Ling must disappear. Chợ Lớn, China, Taipei, would anyplace be safe?

The burden weighed heavily on him as he approached the rear entrance, an expansion dug out of the earth after the war. To perform the work, Hai had hired a hapless band of Khmer Rouge, which he paid in worthless *đồng* and malfunctioning AKs, the rebels' final stipend a one-way trip to the bottom of the river.

Ling disarmed the spring-loaded, multiple grenade trap, cleared brush, and raised the hatch, which opened into the second underground chamber. He and Hai utilized this staging area for fresh opium ferried across the border from Cambodia and Laos. They immediately transferred the new inventory into the primary chamber using a system of ropes and pulleys to haul modified mining cars along rails. Ling got the idea from watching American western movies.

The new tunnel, with false leads, open punji-staked pits, and effective drainage conduits, connected the two chambers a hundred meters apart. Deception. A false wall that only could be activated from his side shielded the primary chamber. He slipped his five-foot five-inch frame inside a rail car, grabbed the overhead rope, and propelled himself forward.

Ling credited Hai for his cunning. Having grown up smoking raw opium, Hai had developed a tolerance which kept him from succumbing to addiction, an advantage he parlayed into a fortune by enticing his fellow man to temptation.

When they injected, Hai feigned it, injecting saline instead. He smoked with others as an artificial gesture of camaraderie and then became the supplier as their addiction grew, accepting as remuneration either various currencies or bartered goods he could launder into money. His pricing structure worked the opposite of volume discounting—the more one became addicted, the more one paid.

The butcher's haven.

When Ling entered the main chamber, foreign smells filled the subterranean vault. Burned oil residue, cigar smoke, and more . . . the body odor from an American.

Ling scampered throughout the complex like an unchained tiger, examining the inventory and taking note of all disturbances. Noticing the transaction files had been left intact, he added them to the theft. As with the tapes, this information could be useful. In a fit of sardonic self-satisfaction, Ling did a hands-free backflip and laughed.

Mr. Hai, perhaps you have met your match, eh? This American, the Texan, sprang your booby traps, took a weapon, and stole your money.

* * *

"Why should I believe you, Chinaman?" Hai fidgeted behind his desk like a nervous baboon.

"It is true, sir. Here are the Polaroids to prove it."

Ling could hardly conceal his mirth as he watched Hai glare at the photographs: sprung booby traps, rifled suitcase, empty file cabinets, and ransacked merchandise shelves, a touch Ling added for authenticity.

"Yahaaaa . . ." Hai ripped the photographs into shreds. "How do I know you did not do it?"

"Sir, if I had done it, I would not have returned."

"No, you would not, Chinaman. This Kannon Ballard violated the chamber?"

"It appears so."

"It is your fault. You were to stand guard."

"Comrade Hai, I did all I could."

As soon as the words left his mouth, Ling wished to retrieve them. Hai kicked him in the groin. Ling grabbed his balls and fell to the floor, his breath unavailable. He saw the next blows coming but was unable to ward them off as Hai kicked him in the face, smashing his cheekbone.

"Now, we both have no children, yes? And you will not look so pretty."

While he writhed on the floor, Ling watched Hai walk to the wall safe, open it, and withdraw his leather-bound syringe kit. Inserting the syringe into the plunger, he stuck the needle into the creamy brown liquid, then injected himself with a megadose of opium.

Hai had done this three times in the past. On this fourth occasion, Ling huddled in the corner of the room to wait for the demonic eruption.

Hai dropped to all fours and snarled like a mad dog. Spittle ran from his mouth. Then he stood erect and slammed into the solid wooden door, clawing with his fingers and banging his head until his fingertips bloodied and his forehead turned purple.

Then Hai did something different from before. Glaring at Ling, he retrieved the syringe and refilled it. Ling tried to scramble away, but Hai pinned him to the floor with his knees and with an overhand knife hold jabbed Ling in the arm.

* * *

Hai inspected his bloodied face in the mirror. Torn strips of skin hung from his forehead. One eye was swollen shut. A tooth was gone.

He snatched a hot cloth from the sink and swabbed his face.

Again, his anger swelled when thinking of Ling, who had gone into convulsions. Had Ling not recovered, Hai would have taken him to the hospital, not because he cared, but because he needed him. Hai had, however, sent Ling home to pray that Buddha would be gracious and repair his faults. Still, after this matter with Ballard was settled, he might kill Ling and replace him. There was no excuse for his assistant to have been imprudent.

As for Kannon Ballard, Hai determined to inflict on this man the tools of retribution honed to a sharp edge during his tenure as a Việt Cộng cell leader. During the war, Ballard's aggressiveness had become a pain, and Hai wanted him eliminated. It was he who dictated *Trung-Úy* Ballard be sent on the ill-fated mission, to be ambushed and wiped from the earth's face.

Now, Ballard threatened more than his refuge. He had

violated it. The audacity of anyone entering his money pit and disrupting the established Cambodian and Laotian links from Myanmar inflamed his blood.

He would skin the bastard alive. He would beg for death.

Tiredness swept Hai to the floor. Why could not people leave him alone and let him run his business, which, after the war, was all he wanted to do. The Americans had no claim here, never did. It was them he must eliminate.

Time to send another message to Farber and Jeffrey. And now, to find Ballard and Lan.

He surrendered to her image and fingered the wet seeping through his trousers. He had done it again.

Come.

* * *

The waters of the Vàm Cỏ Dông swirled around Kannon's neck. He swatted at the buzzing mosquitoes. Time seemed to have gone into remission. The afternoon sun baked the murderous events into his brain and the river chilled his body and soul. Already he'd goaded Farber and Jeffrey into action but in the process had jeopardized Meghan and also incentivized Hai to expand his circle of evil.

The underground cache added to the suspicions he'd held for thirty-two years, but at what cost, justice? The Minhs' deaths he felt responsible for, just as he did for his fifteen men who died in the ambush. Lan had told him that Chấn's death etched on her heart the family agony. With the Minhs' grisly murder, Kannon had written another chapter.

Would Lan's death be an epilogue? Or had she escaped? Remembering her sweet breath and warm body failed to bring comfort. Nor did thoughts of the police. If they nabbed him, his current worries would be moot.

To free his mind, he immersed his head in the leaden water, a murky baptism in a foreign land. For forty-five seconds, he held his breath, seeking focus, then rose.

And waited.

Twilight crept in with the tide. Kannon pushed away from the tree, swam to the sampan, and clambered aboard. The air, confined by the overhead canopy, hung wet and heavy. Scattered stars sparkled in the east against a somber sky. A veiled moon favored escape and evasion.

Kannon slung aside the palmetto branches, poled the sampan to the riverbank, and hauled the motorcycle to dry ground. Considering it too risky to build a fire, he stripped from his clothing, then massaged his upper body while jogging in place to juice the blood flow. He remembered to check for leeches. He didn't find any. He fished in the backpack for his dry clothes and slipped them on.

Grabbing his wet shirt, he unbuttoned the breast pocket and withdrew the medal. He rubbed his fingers over the tarnished Silver Star as if trying to extract fortitude from its core. Since he had left it with Chấn thirty-two years ago, he never expected to see it again. He doubted whether he had deserved it anyway. Perhaps, somehow, as he slipped it inside his dry shirt pocket, he could earn it now.

Kannon righted the DT175. He stood on the kick-starter with his right leg and thrust downward. The motorcycle sparked and fired, then settled into a low whine. He figured less than three liters of gas remained in the tank, enough to coast into Tây Ninh on fumes.

Thirty-Nine

Feeling life was draining her of all she loved and lived for, Lan stood beside Thanh's car beneath the Sài Gòn sun. The mass of her fellow countrywomen passed her by as if she were not among the living. After losing Chấn, she could not bear another loss. When at the Minhs' farm and making love on the earth-ground with Kannon, their juices flowed together and for her sealed a beginning. For it to end there was almost too cruel to bear.

Thanh exited the hotel.

"Did you learn anything, cousin?"

He shook his head. "The hotel manager said he has not seen or heard from Mr. Ballard."

Her heart grew heavier, as it had when her parents and the sister she hardly knew fled Sài Gòn while she elected to stay. "I have been foolish."

"In what way?"

"I should never have let Kannon go into that hedgerow by himself."

"What could you have done?"

She shrugged. "Shielded him."

"Lan, you could not have protected him from Hai or the booby-trapped hedgerow."

She brought up her hands as if framing a portrait and then dropped them to her sides. "I know."

"The explosion . . . he may have died there."

"He did not die in the hedgerow. Remember my vision."

"I thought you lost your vision."

"I found it again."

"What if your vision is one created just for comfort?"

Lan was getting annoyed and let Thanh know with a critical stare. As if to defend himself, he pulled the pipe from his pocket and tamped the tobacco.

She stamped her foot. "Do not light your smelly pipe, cousin. Because just as I knew my brother survived the war, I know Kannon lives."

"Maybe the police arrested Mr. Ballard."

"I think not."

"Well, what do you suggest we do?" He crammed the pipe in his pocket.

"I want to return to your family home and search."

"Are you serious?"

"Quite serious."

"To return is dangerous. We should wait, at least until the police notify me of their deaths."

"Which may never happen. You know how poor district records are. But I understand if you do not wish to go."

Thanh folded his arms across his chest and looked to the sky. His expression showed resistance and denial, but there was more. Fear?

"When I learned of my family's drowning, I refused for a long time to accept it," she said.

He unfolded his arms and turned to her. His look softened.

Lan touched Thanh's arm. "It hurts to face the pain."

He nodded. Perhaps she was finally reaching him.

"This American, the Texan . . . do you consider him family?" he asked.

"Kannon was loyal to Chấn, as Chấn was in his own way to Kannon. He has come across the sea to reclaim his being, and I have joined with him. Do you understand?"

"I do. But my parents are dead. There is nothing I can do about it, and it is best not to stalk a wounded tiger."

"All right then. I will go alone."

She saw this startled Thanh as again he turned to the sky. A moment later, he locked his eyes on Lan's and placed his hands on her shoulders. "You are right. I must face my parents' death. And I will help you discover what happened to your Kannon Ballard."

* * *

As dawn broke over Kannon's final leg of his night journey, the web of canals came alive with sampans and sailing junks. During the motorcycle ride, he'd encountered no one on the way to Trảng Bàng, and only light traffic on Route 22 to Tây Ninh, where

255

he purchased several liter-sized bottles of gas. The rural road to Route 13, however, had been a different story. An oncoming military Jeep had slowed, and it seemed as if they were going to do a one-eighty and pursue. But, keeping his head down and shoulders hunched, he had maintained his speed and cruised on.

When finally Kannon entered Sài Gòn, the morning sun shimmered above the horizon. Already the heat pulsed in angry waves. Fatigued from his infiltration of the cache, the discovery of the Minhs, and his evasion, he exercised caution in threading through the compact traffic. At last, he turned onto Bùi Viện Street.

Reaching Lan's house, he parked the motorcycle curbside, jumped off, and ran to the front door. He knocked. No one answered. He tried the door handle. It was locked. Then he dashed through the courtyard and tested the backdoor. The knob turned, and he entered the kitchen.

"Lan," he hollered. She wasn't there. A stale, musty odor, like that of an abandoned warehouse, permeated the space. It resurrected the darkness he sensed before Chấn's death.

The reality of her absence bit deep and hurt hard. Up to now, Kannon had clung to a ludicrous hope she would be at her home. He left her house and remounted his motorcycle. Next stop, Thanh's apartment. The same no answer.

Kannon cycled to the Rex, stashed the bike, and entered the ornate lobby, which now struck him like an Egyptian crypt. He stopped at the front desk. "Any messages for Kannon Ballard?" he asked, drumming his fingers on the counter.

His black hair anchored in a slick ponytail, the clerk stared through egg-shaped glasses at Kannon's unshaven face as if reluctant to believe he was a guest at the Rex. "Mr. Ballard . . . let me see."

The clerk tapped on a keyboard and registered a look of surprise. "Ah, yes. One." The young man opened a desk drawer and withdrew a letter-sized envelope.

After taking the envelope, Kannon slit it open. He removed and unfolded a single piece of paper. It fluttered like a flying kite, except no breeze disturbed the lobby. It read:

Wait out the Monsoon.
Lan

She was alive.

Relief surged as though he'd escaped a rampaging arroyo during a West Texas thunderstorm. But how did she escape the hedgerow? And, where was she? He visualized her scrambling amid tangled brush, scraped and battered, running from Evil. Or maybe she hadn't gotten away. What if Hai had found her and forced her to write the message?

"Did a woman give you this?" he asked the clerk.

"I do not know, sir. I was not on duty."

"Forget it," he said to himself. That kind of thinking was destructive. Treat it like a computer file—delete the image.

Kannon then flourished the message toward the clerk and said, "*Cám ơn.*" (Thank you.)

With a lighter step, he returned to his room, opened the door, and switched on the light. His possessions appeared undisturbed. The clothes as he'd left them hung from a rod. The computer occupied the same tablespace. The bed was made, crisp and tight. But a faint sound like tinkling chimes trickled from the bathroom. Oh no, not again. Another tiger? Lan?

He approached the bathroom door and called her name. No response. Kannon twisted the doorknob, but his sweaty palm slipped off. After wiping his hands on his trousers, he turned the knob as if he were opening a combination safe. The tumbler clicked. The door refused to budge. Had anxiety sapped his strength, or was it he didn't want to know what awaited him on the other side? *Fuck this shit.* He kicked the door open.

No Lan. No tiger hung from the showerhead. Instead, water leaked.

He let out a deep breath, and for the first time in thirty-six hours, reckoned he could relax. Changing into his bathing suit, Kannon headed to the swimming pool on the sixth floor, swam a few laps, then lay on a lounge chair and baked in the sun. Afterward, he dressed and went to the Rex Royal Court, where he ordered mango and crab. He picked at his food but lost his appetite when again the grisly sacrifices of the Minhs paraded across his vision.

Sickened, he stalked back to his room, grabbed two Beer 33s from the mini-bar and popped both tops, then sat at the solid, rectangular desk and activated the laptop from stealth mode. To crystalize a tactical idea that began forming after he infiltrated the underground cache, he composed an email.

> To: santafeduo@Farber.JeffreyInc.com
>
> Greetings from Site Three in Việt Nam, or, to put it in more familiar terms, grid coordinate 4425-1436. We greatly valued your business relationship with us thirty-two years ago. And, we are proud to add, we have unfinished business with you.
>
> We hope you will share in our excitement when we tell you that we plan to have a warehouse liquidation sale. All slow-moving merchandise must go. Despite their age, the products we plan to offer remain in pristine condition due to our unique, underground preservation process that ensures proper climate control and protection from the vagaries of inclement weather. We just know you'll want to resume participation as a distributor.
>
> Remember. Volume purchases generate volume discounts. We'll contact you soon. Examine your mail the next few days for forthcoming details. Until then, we remain—
>
> Sincerely yours,
>
> The Consortium

After copying to disk the email and the three digital photos of weapons and drugs in the cache site, he boxed up several instruction booklets he'd pulled from the vintage stereo and camera cartons, then set out for the Hông Hoa. There, he established a temporary email address and transmitted the message and attachments, then removed his disk to ensure no obvious trail remained. He wondered, however, if somehow these messages existed forever in cyberspace.

Next, he humped it to UPS and dispatched the boxed booklets by an international courier. Farber and Jeffrey should receive them the first of the week, he figured, just enough time to let the email sink in, and, hopefully, agitate the hell out of them.

But the giddiness wore off as he walked back to the Rex Hotel. Last night's poisonous doubt assaulted his confidence like sappers charging a bunker line. What if Lan doesn't show up? He collapsed on the bed with the question churning in his mind.

Forty

Wednesday morning, Kannon breakfasted at the fifth floor Apricot Restaurant, then idled in his room to wait for Lan. Hearing nothing by lunchtime, he left the hotel to walk off his anxiety. A man approached from behind and tapped him on the shoulder.

"Mr. Ballard?"

Surprised, he spun around to find a balding and bespectacled Chinese man with an impervious face who, at full height, reached Kannon's chest.

"Yes."

"I am Mr. Ling. We need to talk." A purple discoloration marked the man's right cheek.

"What do you want?" Something about him prodded a memory.

"Exchange of resources."

"I'm listening."

"Please, I do not wish to talk on the street." Ling grabbed Kannon's arm and, as if he were a businessman promoting a radical capital project, marched him along the crowded sidewalk amid the crackling activity in the Chinese market. "In here."

They ducked inside a clamorous bar and took seats. Ceiling fans rotated like whirling tops, circulating a commingled fragrance of nước mắm, body odor, and stale perfume.

Ling signaled a waitress. She brought two Tiger beers.

"I'm impatient, Mr. Ling. Get to the point."

"I have the information you seek."

"Why should you want to help me?"

"I have no interest in your welfare, Mr. Ballard. I am here because we have a mutual enemy."

Kannon squirmed. The Chinese man's demeanor reminded him of a customs agent. Then a light glimmered. It grew brighter.

"You're the guy who photographed me in Chợ Lớn."

Ling smiled as if Kannon had guessed the correct number of rice seeds in a jar.

"And the tiger head? You're behind that too?"

"Most unfortunate. Instigated by Hai," Ling said.

"Intelligent move, selecting this dive. Potential witnesses keep me from killing you. Where's Lan?"

"Safe."

"Don't bullshit me. If you've harmed—"

"No need to worry. She is with her cousin." Ling opened a bottle of pills and popped one in his mouth. "I possess critical information concerning Hai."

"I'm only interested in finding Lan."

"You are not interested in . . . ah, Major Christian Farber and Captain Leonard Jeffrey?"

Kannon's beer traveled down the wrong pipe. Once he stopped coughing, he got nose to nose with Ling. "No more games. What the hell do you know?"

"Everything."

"Why should I trust you?"

Ling folded his hands as if he were about to recite a mantra. "You have a choice. Trust me . . . or spend the rest of your days rotting in a Sài Gòn prison cell."

Kannon worried Ling could put him there. He set his beer on the table. "Spill it."

"There are items to negotiate."

"Such as?"

"Money."

"I have no money."

"Yes, you do. I have inspected the cache. You have Hai's money."

The bar patrons quieted as if to eavesdrop. The statement caught Kannon off guard. Ling must have followed his every move.

"And what do I receive in return?"

Ling smiled, almost fatherly. "Incriminating tapes and photographs of your Farber and Jeffrey taken during the war."

"You have possession of these?"

"I do."

The enticement proved tempting. He wanted to skewer Farber over a fire. If only he could read truthfulness in Ling's face.

"Did you kill the Minhs?"

"I am not a killer, Mr. Ballard. Our mutual friend specializes in such depravity."

Ling's manner, his revealing knowledge of the cache break-in, suggested sincerity. Kannon decided to take the bait and trust the Chinese wasn't a killer. "All right. How much?"

Ling rubbed his chin. "I am a reasonable man. Half."

"Only half? Why so generous?"

"I am also an honorable man."

Honorable enough to twist a knife in the back of his boss man, Kannon thought. "I don't have the money with me."

"Do not trifle with me, Mr. Ballard."

"I can get it," Kannon said, wondering how in hell he could revisit the site undetected and recover the cash. "Okay, we'll deal. Give me the information. Then I'll pay."

Ling leaned back in his chair. "Ah, ha, Mr. Ballard. Together we recover the money, and then I release the information."

Kannon couldn't figure a way to hedge his bet. He didn't care about the damn money, but he should have taken it with him. "You have the leverage, Ling. But I'm afraid it may be difficult to retrieve the cash."

"Why is this?"

"I buried it."

"Not so well you forget where, I think," Ling said.

"I haven't forgotten. It's just that . . . well, the police could be a problem."

"I deduce you hid it near the cache site."

Kannon nodded.

"How do you like our underground cache?"

"It stinks."

"It stinks, yes. It is also our pathway to freedom. I must admit you quite impressed me with your skill and perseverance. But it is all right. I can get us in there."

Kannon twisted his mustache. Ironic, wedged between Vietnamese and Americans, his fate resided in the hands of a Chinese from Chợ Lớn. "Other than the money, what's in it for you."

"Friends of mine do not like the way Hai has treated them."

Kannon sensed reticence in Ling's statement but let it go. "I understand."

Mr. Ling gulped the rest of his beer. "We need to move fast, I am afraid. Hai has always been demented. But, thanks to you, he is worse than ever."

"How?"

"Hai wants revenge on everyone involved," Ling said, "especially you. Shall we return to Đức Huệ District?"

Forty-One

Having swapped his sandals and linen clothes for jungle boots, green khakis, and camouflage shirt, Ling slid in the driver's seat. Kannon, wearing jogging shoes, blue jeans, and a dark shirt, pictured Ling as an Asian model for an army surplus mail-order catalog.

Darkness overcame the light as they departed Sài Gòn. Kannon stared through the passenger window and pictured Lan beside every lantern. The vision intensified as the houses thinned.

"Wait out the monsoon," she'd said.

The problem was, the storm kept growing, and like a recalcitrant child, Kannon felt compelled to follow and leap into the middle of it. The possibility of obtaining information to nail Farber and Jeffrey intoxicated him.

Ling drove into the night, steering his faded-green Citroen over a familiar route. Not many passable roads led to the remote Đức Huệ District.

"You have the stolen pistol, Mr. Ballard?"

"I do."

"You know how to use a PRC Type-59?"

Kannon cut his eyes to Ling, whose maroon beret tilted to one side like a Chinese sailing junk with no ballast. The left side of Ling's face remained hidden in the dark while the right reflected a dim glow from the instrument panel.

"Yep," Kannon said, knowing he could field strip and assemble one in the dark. "But I don't plan to engage communist police in a shootout."

"The police are not all we have to worry about," Ling said. "Anyone could be waiting—police, military, even Hai."

They rode in silence for an hour before encountering rough terrain.

"We called this Indian country," Kannon said, remembering that combat veterans often referred to the bush this way. It was the fear of ambush.

Ling made no reply as he shifted into low gear. The Citroen groaned as it crawled over back roads.

"Not the best time to conduct an operation," Kannon said. "Too easy to be seen."

"Spoken like a true veteran." Ling switched off the car lights even though the moon lay below the horizon.

Two hours after leaving Sài Gòn, Ling pulled into a shadowed hedgerow. "Recognize the area, Mr. Ballard?"

"You know I do." Kannon opened the car door, stepped out, and surveyed the scrambled brush and tall palms. The trees leaned in, adding a suffocating presence. His old outpost. Would he ever get free of this place? "Why here?"

Ling exited the car. "The cache is almost a straight shot, fifteen hundred meters west. I know the trail well."

So did he, once.

Ling opened the trunk and retrieved a U.S. Army entrenching tool. "Bring your backpack, Mr. Ballard, and please present the Chicom pistol and chamber a round."

Kannon complied. Bizarre. Traversing the trail he had covered long ago, a combat patrol of two—his companion a Chinese who might wish to slit his throat at the slightest provocation. Or lead him into a booby trap.

"You take the point, Ling."

Starlight bounced off broad palm leaves as if too feeble to penetrate secrets below. Thin bamboo branches rattled in the wind like thrown dice. A generous earth released an odor of musk, and as they scrambled over the dry trail, Kannon expected Sergeant Malcolm's ghost to rise and admonish him again for poor tactics.

Twenty-five minutes later, Ling paused at the edge of a clearing. He pointed. "There it is. The cache. And now, shall we retrieve our cash?"

Kannon stared in disbelief. Ling was laughing.

"A poor pun, yes, but one sufficient to enrich our lives."

"You know, Ling, I could learn to like you."

"Partners, Mr. Ballard. However, even though I did not rearm the booby traps, I do not care to follow your crawl path into the hedgerow."

"It isn't necessary."

Kannon paced the twenty-five-meter distance with Ling close behind. Hell, the son of a bitch was more nimble than he was. They reached the trail opening into the hedgerow, then Kannon paced off ten steps to the right. He pulled the pistol out of his waist belt and pointed to the ground. "You dig."

Ling shrugged. He unfolded the entrenching tool, fastened the handle, and dipped the spade into a ground softened from Kannon's earlier dig. Ling clucked in Chinese the brief time it took him to uncover the plastic-wrapped package. He dropped it at Kannon's feet.

After retrieving the package, Kannon found Ling holding a snub-nosed Walther PPK. He started to speak, but Ling shook his head and raised his finger to his lips. "Shhh. I hear something."

Kannon knelt to the ground and cocked his ear. He didn't hear a thing.

Suddenly, the staccato crack of an AK broke the stillness. Instinctively, Kannon braced himself for the AK's steady thwack on fully automatic. The rounds tore through the brush and pinged over his head. Tracers cut the darkness like Roman Candles.

Kannon fired five rounds at the direction of the muzzle flash, rolled, then fired three more. He ejected the empty magazine, slapped in another, and released the slide to chamber a round. He rolled again.

Where was his partner? Two pops sounded, and Kannon saw a muzzle flash to his right. Had to be Ling. Three more rounds erupted from that position. The person behind the AK returned fire. Kannon let loose three more. Then a lull took hold.

Light fog descended on the hedgerow like a layer of silt.

A shriek interrupted the quiet, recoiling among the palms as if searching for an escape hatch from a cave. The air filled with the flutter of wings as a hoot owl took flight. Kannon's heart rate skipped into overdrive.

Three minutes passed. Not a sound. Not a word. Silence ruled the misty thicket as if the smoky veil precluded violence.

Kannon held his fire. Who was at the other end of the AK? Why did the shooting stop? Maybe one of his rounds had found its mark. Regardless, he wanted out of there.

"Ling, Ling," he whispered.

No answer.

Crawling through the scattered brush, Kannon found Ling lying on his stomach and jostled his shoulder. "Ling." He didn't move. Ah, shit. A jagged cavity showed where the back of his head used to be.

Kannon turned him over and found a face contorted in its death grimace. He rifled through Ling's pockets, yanked out the keys, and pocketed the Walther PPK. After scattering disturbed brush over the body, he rose to his feet, retrieved the money, and hustled to the outpost site.

The Citroen remained intact. He jumped into the car, inserted the key, ground into first gear, and lurched out of the hedgerow. Kannon's cheeks were coated with sweat. He'd left another ghost behind.

Forty-Two

Kannon checked the rearview mirror. Who'd be looking for a round eye driving a nondescript green Citroen? Armed, with no registration papers, carrying more than two hundred thousand dollars, he steered Ling's widowed sedan over dilapidated Route 10 toward Bào Trai. Despite what Ling had said before the unexpected firefight, Kannon feared an encounter with the police.

Fortunately, the village appeared asleep when he passed through. Proceeding northeast on Route 8A toward Củ Chi, he again glanced at the rearview mirror. Only empty road and swamp marsh filled the expanse, so he slowed, steered to the road's edge, and shut off the motor. He sat. He breathed. As the adrenaline of battle receded, his original purpose surfaced, and he wondered whether Ling had put the promised audiotapes and photographs in the car.

Rummaging through the glove box and beneath the seats, he came up empty-handed. He exited the Citroen. Nothing stirred except the brush and tall grasses rustling in the breeze. A musky scent permeated the marsh like the odor of an unwashed drifter. In the east, a slender orange brushstroke announced the dawn.

This was an area where the Việt Cộng would construct sleeping platforms just above water level beneath the reeds and bed down with the vipers. Kannon examined the cargo trunk and the engine compartment, but his probe revealed no tapes or photographs, which meant no concrete evidence condemning Farber and Jeffrey. Ling must have stashed them elsewhere. If he had ever possessed them. But Kannon would never know because Ling's body hugged the earth in an everlasting embrace.

Frustrated, he slipped behind the wheel and gripped it white-knuckle tight. Then he switched on the ignition, drove through Củ Chi, and turned onto old Route 1 toward Sài Gòn.

On reaching the city outskirts, he spun the wheel to the left and stopped the Citroen alongside a canal. Moored boats rocked gently amid lapping wakes stirred by a single cylinder-powered sampan. The coagulated smell of a thousand scents slapped him in the face as he left the car. He strapped on the backpack, hunched his shoulders to appear smaller, and walked off in search of a taxi, perhaps the richest American on foot in Việt Nam.

* * *

Lan sprang from the chair and ran to his side when Kannon walked through the lobby door. She was dressed in peasant-like black pants and white cotton top, but to him, she looked like Miss Sài Gòn—his world reborn. He opened his arms for an embrace, but she flicked his arms aside.

"I told you to wait out the monsoon," she said.

Her action, her words, surprised him.

"I got caught in the storm. It swooped me away."

Lan gave Kannon a look like a mother admonishing a child. "You tempt Buddha's patience by taking too many chances."

"I can handle myself. It was you I worried about. I was afraid I'd lost you."

"I have been in the land of the wicked."

"I saw it. I thank God and Buddha you escaped." His mouth twitched. He was about to cry, a cry of relief.

The lines in her face softened. She slipped her arms around his waist and pressed her cheek against his shoulder. Her breath washed his chest like a balm and slackened the knots in his body.

"Where have you been? Thanh and I have looked everywhere."

"I returned to the cache site. Ling's been shot," he whispered.

"Who is Ling?"

"I'll tell you about it later. Now, I want to leave central Sài Gòn."

She pulled away and tipped her head toward his. "Thanh's car is outside."

"Christ! He must hate me."

"He does not. Come, I will help you pack."

Ten minutes later, Kannon checked out of the Rex Hotel and encountered again the tank-sized black vehicle shaped like an elongated turtle. Hands on his hips, Lan's cousin stood beside his car. Wearing glasses, a face shaped like a squashed pumpkin, he

269

looked nothing like Chấn and strummed in Kannon an image of a soft bureaucrat, not a man of character and resolve as described by Lan. She introduced them.

"Lan's told me about you," Kannon said.

"And you as well. Please, get in."

Lan sat in front, and Kannon took the back seat, half expecting Humphrey Bogart to be waiting for him. He leaned forward and asked Thanh, "Can you take us to Chợ Lớn?"

Thanh shook his head. "Vũng Tàu," he said.

"Vũng Tàu—the resort city on the coast? Why?"

"A friend has a home there," said Thanh. "We will be safe."

"Your parents. If I'd known . . ."

Thanh shrugged. "An enduring tragedy of war."

Lan scooted sideways and turned to Kannon. Her cheeks fell when she mouthed to him a silent no, a signal he interpreted to mean Thanh's words sheltered his true feelings.

As the sedan threaded through walls of traffic, Kannon and Lan briefed each other on his infiltration of Site Three and her evasion of Hai. When they finished, Kannon remembered the notebook. Removing it from his pack, he leaned forward and brandished it in front of her. "I found this underground. Mind looking at it? Might find something useful."

Without taking his eyes from the road, Thanh intercepted it and riffled the pages. "Inventories. Listings of transactions," he said.

Lan took the notebook from her cousin and read. A few minutes later, she turned to Kannon. "These words may interest you. '*Chiến sĩ vô Danh.*'"

"What does that mean?"

"The Unknown Warrior."

An Unknown Warrior? Ling, Farber, or Jeffrey? he wondered. "Papa-san Minh or Chấn mention this?"

"No," Lan said.

Thanh honked to clear out startled cyclists. "Probably a Việt Cộng long dead and forgotten."

As they departed Sài Gòn's eastern sector, the traffic lessened. Kannon's clothes stuck to the cracked upholstered leather as if plastered by a steam press. He wished he could read

Vietnamese.

"Anything else in the notebook?"

Lan shook her head. "We should give it to the police."

"It is best not to get further involved," Thanh said.

A reasonable conclusion. Besides, Farber remained his target, not Hai. Kannon wiped perspiration from his eyes. "What did you find at the farmhouse?"

"The police already had removed the bodies."

Images of the mutilated Minhs saddened, then angered Kannon. And leaving Ling's body to rot into the soil reawakened his issue of abandonment. He needed to shake these feelings and move forward.

"Were you questioned?" Kannon asked Thanh.

"Yes. I told them we were there to visit my parents. I expressed shock and dismay."

Kannon leaned forward. "Do the police know about the underground cache site?" Thanh's expression in the rear-view mirror reflected irritation.

"We do not know," Lan said.

"But," Thanh said, "two policemen claimed to have seen a round eye on a motorcycle that morning."

"Me," Kannon admitted.

"You," Thanh said. "Except they think you are Russian and working with the Khmer Rouge. They will watch the airport a few days, even though they suspect you have already crossed the border."

"That's to our advantage." Kannon paused, then told them about his brief partnership with Ling and the circumstances of his death.

"The owl's hoot may have saved your life," Lan said.

"My thanks to the owl."

Kannon pulled at his mustache and stared at the backpack. Two hundred thousand dollars plus, and it was all theirs. It was the least he could do. He'd broach it later.

"Thanh, what kind of car is this?"

"A 1946 Packard Clipper."

"It is his joy," Lan chipped in.

The only way to become more conspicuous was to add flashing lights and a siren. The vintage sedan had an "H" gearshift and red hexagonal logo. The musty smell of the half-century-old car reminded him of his granddad's 1939 Chrysler.

"I visited Vũng Tàu once," Kannon said, "on a weekend in-country R and R. It had a French name . . ."

"Cap Saint-Jacques," Thanh said. "We are going to Bãi Dâu, three kilometers northwest of the city. It is more secluded."

An hour later, they entered Vũng Tàu and drove to city central. A tall statue of Jesus sat atop Núi Nhó Mountain. They turned northwest and cruised alongside a crescent-shaped beach lined with coconut trees, restaurants, and kiosks. Mountain-clinging pagodas overlooked anchored freighters and fishing boats that bobbed in harbor swells.

Shortly, Thanh steered between cultivated jackfruit and pineapple trees and pulled into a shale-lined courtyard. Towering palms framed a modest French-colonial, two-story terra-cotta blockhouse with shuttered windows and a red-tiled roof.

They exited the sedan and entered the villa. Inside, the spartan downstairs consisted of a main room furnished with an odd mixture: a cherry wood desk, two rattan chairs, a weathered settee, and a teak dining table with no chairs. The artwork on one wall included a long, story-telling tapestry and two paintings where golden deer watered beneath pearl-and-melon-colored trees on a black background of lacquered wood. A damaged crystal chandelier watched over it all like a wounded sentinel. Opposite the main room stood a closet-sized kitchen and stand-up bath. Between those, an open door led into a bedroom, which Thanh said he would occupy. Upstairs was similar, except there was a dry bar in place of the kitchen. From the second-floor, great room, French doors opened like gull wings onto a verandah. The master bedroom belonged to him and Lan.

* * *

It was the time of day the falling sun fused the sky and ocean. A sultry breeze blew in from the South China Sea. As the three of them sat on the second-floor verandah, an awning flapped like a mainsail out of trim.

Thanh lit a Briar pipe. Lan hacked open a fresh pineapple and carved the flesh into bite-sized portions. With her fingers, she slipped a juicy piece into her mouth and made a face.

Kannon chuckled, then clipped and lit one of the Cohibas he'd pilfered from the cache. Lan whiffed at the noxious smoke fumes as if swatting no-see-ums. He propped his feet on the railing and stared at the gilded trail the sun laid on the broken sea. "Have you considered coming to America?"

Lan and Thanh exchanged looks.

They've thought about it.

"I understand passports and visas are difficult to obtain," she said.

"Perhaps I can help." Kannon unzipped his backpack and withdrew the package wrapped in paper and plastic. He unfolded the wrapping and laid the cash in front of them. Their eyes turned glossy like the inside of oyster shells.

"Are you crazy?" Thanh said. "Where did you get this?"

"Hai's donation to charity."

Thanh tamped his tobacco, then stood at the railing. "My mother and father are dead. Hai's viciousness again has been released like a vengeful hydra." He exhaled a smoke stream and stared at Kannon. "You have disrupted and poisoned my simple world."

"Thanh, you are unfair," Lan said. "Remember, this began as a search for truth."

"And where does the truth end, cousin Lan, with all of us dead? Or arrested, put in prison, and tortured when caught in possession of American dollars?"

"Thanh's right. I have caused destruction, a lot of it. I can't change the past. All I can do is try to improve opportunities for the future."

Thanh relit his pipe. The wind tousled his hair and extinguished the match. Lan rose, poured herself another glass of wine, and topped off Kannon's. He remained seated and puffed on his cigar.

"The money's yours," Kannon said. "To dispose of as you see fit . . . burn, bury, or buy a new life."

Lan touched her cousin's arm. "I want a new life," she said.

Thanh put his hands in his pockets and rattled coins. "This is my country. I know no other." He paused and gazed toward the sea. "It is a tempting proposal, though, because I am not happy with the country's progression under the Communists." Then he freed his hands and riffled a packet of fifty-dollar bills. "With this, we could buy protection . . . and passports."

"Hopefully, with a lot left over," Kannon said. "I know it's difficult to get money out of the country, but—"

"We will manage," Thanh said.

Kannon's initial impression of Lan's cousin was changing.

"And the visas?" Lan snatched an insect out of the air.

"I've done some research. Our Immigration and Naturalization Service can be tough. Typical immigrant categories don't apply. But I've talked with my brother Roger. He can sponsor a visitor visa for business or tourism. The problem is both are short-term."

"Short term?" Her face lost light like the setting sun.

The sweet and bitter scent from Lan's pineapple was ironic and mocking because the sweetness of her presence was tainted by his powerful desire to take down Farber. "I could stay a while, try to work something else out with the visas."

She smiled and spawned her own afterglow. "Are you abandoning the trail of the wicked Americans?"

"No."

"Your world can no longer be black and white but shades of gray," she said. "When you know in your heart what happened, it is enough."

Yes, he knew in his heart. But a big part of him wanted a final confrontation. The plaguing question of "how to accomplish it" was crowded by "why do it at all"? Meanwhile, he wanted to talk to Thanh alone. He grabbed the empty bottle by the neck and twirled it on its concave base. "Lan, would you get more wine?"

She put her hand on his shoulder and smiled. "Yes, I will."

Kannon made sure the French double doors were shut, then turned to Thanh.

"Are you angry with me—about your parents?"

Thanh turned from the sea and propped his back against the railing. "The war never ends. But no, I am not angry. Father understood the risks."

"Still, I'm sorry."

"Thank you."

Kannon looked over his shoulder, through the glass and muslin curtains. Appearing ethereal beneath a pale light, Lan stood in the dry bar wrestling with the opener.

"About the visas . . ."

"I am not worried about visas," Thanh said.

"I understand. But there's an option I need to discuss with you."

"What is it?"

"Our Immigration and Naturalization Service allows a fiancé visa, which permits a foreigner to marry a U.S. citizen. Shorter processing time and permanent."

Thanh remained quiet and solemn, emptied his Briar, refilled it, and placed it in his mouth. Then, with a mischievous grin, he said, "I do not wish to marry you."

Kannon's mouth froze open. Finally, he slapped his knee and burst out laughing. Thanh joined in.

"Seriously," Thanh said, "I do not know if she is ready. You must proceed with caution, like crossing the streets of Sài Gòn. As for me, I may prefer to travel the world rather than emigrate to the United States."

Lan returned, holding another bottle of wine. She poured. "I heard laughter. This is good."

"To the good," they toasted.

Yet, unspoken words must be spoken, the inevitable separation faced. Even with the money, it could take months for them to forge a way out of the country. In the meantime, a simple tourist visa could plug the gap. But the question he hadn't counted on, whether to ask her to marry him, now loomed as a distant galaxy.

Thanh spoke to Lan in Vietnamese. She answered in kind, then took on a serious tone. "In two days, Thanh and I must return to Sài Gòn. Family matters. It is best you stay here."

"What about you two?"

"We will stay in Chợ Lớn," Thanh said.

"But Hai's not just looking for me. He's also threatened Lan." Kannon snuffed the cigar and grabbed his pipe.

Lan moved behind Kannon and cradled his neck. "My cousin will protect me."

Not wanting to lose touch with her, he clamped the Meerschaum between his lips and squeezed her hand. "Please don't go," he wanted to say.

"There is a phone here," Thanh said. "Several hotels have business services, including email connections. I will purchase a cellular and call you with the number. When I think it safe, a helicopter service based in Vũng Tàu can transport you to Sài Gòn."

Kannon watched the surf break and bubble. Not bad, live in a villa on the beach, with sun and sand and shellfish, while deciding which he'd rather pursue—Lan, or a morally bankrupt ex-major, though the choice seemed more obvious all the time. The specter of Hai, however, further tainted and complicated the dilemma. "Okay," he said.

The next two days Kannon and Lan indulged in discovery, sunning on the beach and, when Thanh discreetly disappeared, made love and created their own Tết explosions in the country villa. They dined on fresh pineapple and baguettes, a French legacy consisting of spiced meat and vegetables wrapped in small white bread leaves that Thanh procured from the local market. Lan prepared red snapper from the coast of Phan Thiêt, along with rice cakes and spring rolls dipped in nắm tôm, a shrimp paste. Thanh embellished the gathering with Montrachet from the Côte d'Or region of Burgundy.

When it came time to part, Kannon felt like someone had reached in and gouged his heart, because Thanh was right. This was neither the time nor place to ask for Lan's hand in marriage. Recent events were too raw.

He fished in his pocket and handed Thanh a packet of his specially blended Mark Twain tobacco. "Something to remember me by."

Thanh smiled and took the offering.

"Be careful," he said to Lan, kissing her goodbye.

Kannon watched them drive away.

He entered the villa and walked upstairs into the bedroom. Staring at the hard bed and mosquito netting pinned against the headboard, he fought the undertow that undermined his hope.

The Warriors

Forty-Three

Monday morning for Leonard Jeffrey disintegrated faster than a July hailstorm. By the time he printed the three digital images and laid them alongside the corresponding email, he wanted to slit his wrists.

Business relationship. Warehouse liquidation sale. Underground preservation process. Volume discounts. What the crap? Who represented this consortium?

He walked into the showroom and leaned on one of the display counters. To hell with this. Close the doors to The Farber Collection. Return to skiing in Taos where he'd stalked and scored with a woman whose hourglass-shaped figure more than compensated for her pitted face.

The key was in the front door lock when Farber approached.

"Where are you going?" Farber said.

Oh, Lord. Without a word, Jeffrey slid the key from the lock and reopened the gallery.

"You look like you just lost your pecker," Farber said.

Jeffrey led Farber to the office and clicked the computer screen to life. Farber opened his mouth and then closed it as if all word choices were inadequate. Then his boss rubbed his thumb over the photographs, but the images didn't disappear. "Is this some kind of joke?"

"No joke. Damnit, I knew this shit would catch up with us someday."

"Calm down, Jeffrey."

"You said Hai was dead. You said . . ."

Farber's veins bulged from his forehead like exposed cords on a steel-belted tire. Jeffrey wanted to vanish. Instead, he leaned against the wall.

"Shut up, Jeffrey. Consider what you are saying. If Hai were alive and trying to blackmail us again, he'd use the cell name."

"The Monsoon Killed the Tiger," Jeffrey said.

"Exactly."

"Then the email has to be from Ballard, which means he found the underground cache." Jeffrey thought a moment. "No. If these are current photographs, then the cache site is being used by Hai."

Suddenly, a husky woman in brown shorts and matching pants knocked on the office door.

"Got a package for you fellas," she said. "What are you boys ordering from Việt Nam? Paid a whale of a shipping charge to deliver it this quick."

Farber scratched his chin. "You expecting anything?"

"No," Jeffrey said. He signed for the package and handed it to Farber. He watched as his commander slit it open and withdraw the contents.

"Instruction booklets for vintage stereo equipment," Farber said, his hands trembling. "It's Ballard. The son of a bitch is playing games. We've got to take him out."

Life just got a lot worse. "You can't be serious," Jeffrey said.

"Got any other suggestions? Look at these fucking pictures."

Jeffrey did. Two color displays of M-16s and AK47s and the third, a closeup of a chalky-white substance, threatened his existence. Could the steel hands of retribution crush 'em after thirty-two years? Nausea gripped him as if someone had reached in and wrung his colon.

Another delivery arrived, this one from Federal Express.

"Christ." Farber opened the envelope. "Now what?"

He read aloud.

Dear Mr. Christian Farber:

A pent-up demand exists for merchandise I can supply your firm for distribution. The market potential is unlimited. Frankly, I do not believe you can refuse. As an inducement to entice you to become my partner, I have enclosed incentives. Please review them and respond to me, either by fax or phone, within five working days. If I do not hear from you within that time, copies of the enclosed will be forwarded to The National Inquisitor, your local newspaper, your mayor, the governor, the U.S. Embassy, your wife, and perhaps some prominent, former POWs, just to name a few. Looking forward to hearing from you.

Sincerely,

Mr. Hai, The Grand Plantation.

Farber's mouth contorted. "The Monsoon's alive."

Jeffrey had never seen Farber turn white.

"Look at the rest of this shit," Farber said.

With dread, Jeffrey looked. Pictures of Farber and him engaged in lewd sex acts with Vietnamese women. Pictures of them engaged in conversation with both Việt Cộng and North Vietnamese soldiers.

He shuffled the photos to Farber, who remained quiet, an unusual state. Farber stared at the plush, carpeted floor, as if searching for an answer—if not that, a temporary diversion hidden among the deep piles.

"We could, perhaps, talk our way out of the pictures," Farber said. "They are embarrassing, but what soldier didn't want to fornicate with Vietnamese women."

"You forget the pictures with enemy soldiers," Jeffrey said.

"Yes. Most difficult."

Farber walked to the wet bar and poured himself a Dewar's over ice. "Play the audiotape."

Jeffrey inserted the tape into the gallery's stereo system. They listened.

Recorded conversations of plans to smuggle weapons and opium to soldiers on both sides and across the Cambodian border to COSVN—the Communist Office of South Việt Nam—nailed them. The bastard had even recorded the plans to set up Lieutenant Ballard and his patrol to be ambushed.

Jeffrey switched off the recorder. "Could Ballard and Hai be working together?"

"There's no other explanation."

"I can't believe it. How would they have connected?"

"Remember Ballard's interpreter. I bet he's the connection. Never trusted the little bastard."

"What are we going to do?" Jeffrey wished he could retract the words as soon as they left his mouth.

"All the more reason for you to return to Việt Nam."

Jeffrey's day turned as black as bodies burned by napalm. "Goddamn, Farber. I'm too old for this crap."

"Are you as stupid as you look? Hai's indicated a willingness to negotiate. We'll cut a deal. Anything is for sale at the right price. I'll give you the parameters."

Jeffrey figured this to be a death sentence wrapped in bullshit. But he was in deep and didn't know how to get out. "What about Ballard?"

"We have an ace in the hole," Farber said.

"Meghan O'Brien."

"Meghan O'Brien," Farber repeated. "I'll arrange a temporary change of residence."

Jeffrey shrunk inside himself. "That's a serious action."

"As is being hunted . . . and blackmailed," Farber said. "We entice Ballard into separating from Hai and leaving us alone. Tell him that if he opens his mouth, we'll say he's been involved all along."

"He keeps his mouth shut," Jeffrey said, "and he stays disgraced."

"Right, partner," Farber said, slapping Jeffrey on the back. "Pour yourself a drink. Celebrate your association with a chieftain."

Celebrate? No. Instead, Jeffrey found himself wishing Kannon Ballard had been killed in the ambush because Farber couldn't afford to let Ballard or Meghan O'Brien live, which would make Jeffrey an accessory to murder.

* * *

After Jeffrey left, Farber returned his attention to Kannon Ballard. Efforts to locate him through conventional means had failed—no listed phone number, no street address, and no definitive email address. The message from The Consortium proved untraceable.

Then he remembered Counterparts, an organization that tried to recruit him several years ago. He had declined, but Rock the asshole refused to divulge information on any member unless Farber joined.

Today, he did so.

Rock had faxed the membership roster, and it was there that Farber found Kannon Ballard. Ballard had refused to disclose his address and phone number but had provided an email address. *kannonfire@aol.com*.

Egotistical bastard. Farber had a few favors to call in, at a price, and it was time to lean on one of them, one with whom he'd executed an unwritten contract utilizing a communication system incorporating stock option terms of "puts" and "calls." He keyed a speed dial on his cellphone.

"Yeah."

"Number 4556 here," Farber said. "It's time to consummate a *call*. I want you to take delivery of an item."

"I'm listening," the voice said.

Farber described the nature of the item, its location, and the designated holding area.

"It'll cost ya."

"$100,000—half down, by immediate wire transfer to your offshore Cayman account, with the balance due upon confirmation of package pick up the day after tomorrow."

"Double it."

Prick. But Farber needed this deal. "Okay."

After executing his right to buy services, Farber negotiated terms on which he and the seller would exercise the "put."

If, after fourteen days—the expiration date—from confirmation date, the seller had not received notice to release the item, then the seller was to make a tidy disposal of the property and receive a twenty-five percent bonus, to be held in escrow.

Forty-Four

They glided across the dance floor to the flowing, lamentable, "Tennessee Waltz," secure in the knowledge neither would be spirited away by an unknown lover. She had never experienced unconditional love. Then, as the music died on the last, mournful refrain, her husband's apparition vanished, and she found herself in the middle of an island.

Two men appeared, one from the east and one from the west. The westward vision beckoned, extending his arms and enticing her to come to him. The eastward vision approached, raising his arms to his chest and opening his palms. One seemed beguiling, the other trustworthy, yet she couldn't distinguish between the two.

"Come on, hurry up," the voice said.

Meghan awoke to a nightmare.

"What's going—"

The gag muffled her words, stifled her scream. Wrapped and bound in a sheet, she thought she'd been buried alive. Rough, calloused hands trundled her into the back of a van, which left behind the picture-postcard that was Silverton.

As the van slid over patches of ice, Meghan became disoriented. She knew the highway to be open both north to Ouray and south to Durango, so she had no way of determining in which direction they headed.

The ropes cut through the sheet and bit into her arms and legs, diminishing the normal blood flow. A dispassionate, ruthless cold penetrated the van, exacerbating her growing numbness. She felt lulled into a dreamlike slumber by tires humming on the pavement, and she recalled the long, slow dream interrupted when they collected her.

Cold, bouncing on the floor like a log caught in a flooded stream, Meghan suffered many bruises. She didn't know if thirty minutes had passed or several hours, but she needed to move her bowels. A firewall separated the passenger compartment from its cargo hold. She squirmed like a worm toward the divider, then rolled on her back and pounded with her feet.

The van squealed to a stop, and she heard a metallic click as someone inserted a key into the back-door lock. The door swung open, and someone flashed a powerful beam into her face, robbing her eyesight.

"Well, little lady. Stop the noise," the voice said. "You do as we say, no harm will come to you. Lift your head."

Meghan did as she was told. The light still shone in her face. She jerked her head to the side, trying to peer beyond the beam. She wanted to catch a glimpse of the outdoor world and reassure herself it existed. What she saw instead looked like a silver projector screen. Behind the blinding light, a second silhouetted figure entered the rear of the van and slapped tape over Meghan's eyes.

"Okay, honey, I'm gonna take the gag out. Don't bother screaming, because there ain't no one around for miles. And if you do, here's a taste of what you can expect."

The assailant slapped her twice. Blood trickled from cold, chapped lips. It took Meghan a moment to realize that the hand belonged to a different voice, the voice of a woman, a woman who enjoyed playing rough.

The filthy rag was yanked from Meghan's mouth, leaving an oily taste. She drew several long, deep breaths. "I need to go to the bathroom."

"Afraid you'll have to wait, darling. Roll over." The woman reeked of stale urine.

Meghan held position and unleashed her own salvo. "Who are you? What do you want?"

"None of your business, lady," the gruff, male voice responded. "The less you know, the better. This woman here, we call her Sadie. That's short for sadistic. She's your keeper. That's all the information you need."

"You're kind of cute honey," the woman's voice broke in. "Even if your little old man comes through, I just might keep you for myself."

"Sadie. Keep your damn mouth shut."

Meghan's cheeks stung, but the manipulation that was Kannon Ballard's pierced like a knife. He had to be the cause of this.

There could be no other reason.

"I know about Farber and Jeffrey," Meghan said, "and so does my friend, Elizabeth. Taking me accomplishes nothing."

"Keep talking, honey, and you'll be digging yourself a grave."

A stupid remark, Meghan realized. She might have jeopardized Elizabeth.

"Rollover, I said." Again, Meghan refused, and Sadie flipped her like a flapjack.

Sadie tugged at the ropes and slit a knife through the bindings. Then she grasped the edge of the sheet and yanked upward, spinning Meghan like an errant top that crashed into the van's sides and floor. Once released from the manmade cocoon, she realized that all she had on was a set of flannel pajamas, but her unmitigated anger returned with a vengeance.

"Goddamn bitch!" Meghan said.

Sadie rewarded her with another slap to the face. More blood oozed from Meghan's lips as they dragged her out of the van.

A cold, mountain air bearing the crisp scent of mountain pine and fir greeted her. Not being able to see sharpened her sense of smell, hearing, and touch. A blustery wind rattled pine needles, whistling a mournful tune.

"Put your hands behind your back."

They tied her roughly. Meghan chafed at her impotence.

The man and woman each grabbed an arm and led Meghan from the forgiving turf to a rocky path. Each time she stubbed her bare toes, the cold heightened the intense pain, which shot through her body like a bolt of electricity.

"My feet are killing me," she said.

"For a good reason."

After about ten minutes, they stopped. Meghan heard the creaking sound of a door being opened.

"Here's your new home, little lady," the male voice said. "Listen to Sadie, and you might survive. Don't try to run away. First, there's no escape from this wilderness. Second, with no shoes, your feet would become bloody stumps."

They ushered Meghan across a wooden floor. Sadie unbound

Forty-Five

It was the fourth day after Lan had left. Feeling out of place like the foreigner he was, Kannon grew restless. He'd tried writing but had difficulty concentrating. He stood on the verandah. A chafing wind ruffled the jackfruit and pineapple trees and whistled through open doors. In the distance, beyond the coconut trees and churning surf, the ocean grew vast and lonesome.

Images came to mind of bluebonnet fields, Indian paintbrush, and gaillardia poking through the sandy, rocky loam of the Texas Hill Country. He plotted a timeline in which he visualized showing Lan the deep, oak-covered hills there and then the magnificent desert and mountainous terrain of the Texas Big Bend.

A crashing wave returned him to the present.

Lan's parting words in Vũng Tàu inveigled their way deeper into his vision of what could be. Chấn's death awoke in him a shared and significant trait. Kannon didn't want to die any more unclean than he already was. Chấn had cleared his conscience before he died. Kannon needed to do the same.

Smoke from an Avo Uvezian Magnum wafted toward the patio. Empty bottles of Beer 33 littered the table. Reluctantly, he snuffed out the cigar, the reluctance due partly to the inevitable dispiritedness following the nicotine-induced high, but due more to a prevailing fear of his life being quashed before he lived it.

Thanh had secured a cellphone. From yesterday's conversation with Lan, Kannon learned the two already had visited the Consulate General in Sài Gòn and started the visa application process as well as initiated passport procedures. He and Roger were crafting the sponsor letter.

Might as well hit the town. Kannon chartered a taxi to take him to the Rạng Đông Orange Court to utilize their business service center. Be patient, he reminded himself when thinking of Lan. Things were going well.

At the Rạng Đông, Internet access was slow, but finally, he retrieved his messages. Stefan inquired about the usefulness of the

289

aged photographs. Roger reported a futile search regarding combinations of Võ or Hai with Đăng Đạo. The rest of the emails were clutter, except for one.

It was from santafeduo@Farber.JeffreyInc.com.

Suggest you stop playing games and come to Santa Fe ASAP. Last night we arranged for delivery to a remote facility of a package we believe has a special interest for you. It's a special video recorder, cleverly disguised as a pager. The pager comes with an attachment. Quite a beautiful one, I might add. I'm sure we can arrange for an exchange that will be mutually beneficial. Looking forward to seeing you again.
Sincerely yours

Jesus Christ! Farber had taken Meghan. The time was 0930 hours here, which made it 1930 hours the previous night in Colorado. He placed a panic call.

"Hello?" the voice answered.

"Let me speak to Meghan."

"Who is this?"

"Kannon Ballard. Please, it's important."

"She's disappeared, Mr. Ballard. Someone broke into the hotel. The police want to talk to you."

Christ!

"Are you sure she's not in Durango? She has a friend down there. A graphic artist."

"She's missing, I told you."

Revulsion welled up inside him. My God, what had he caused now?

"Mr. Ballard . . ."

He hung up. The menacing cloud that hovered over him like a suspended wrecking ball released and shattered his dream of tranquility. He'd provoked Farber and Jeffrey into action all right.

Way to go, Kannon.

You've subjected Meghan O'Brien to danger, another casualty exposed to hostile fire because of your clumsy quest for vindication.

Farber didn't answer, home or office. Nothing to do but return to the seaside villa. He paid the Petro House for services and exited into a hot, steamy wind blowing in from the South China Sea. The smell of roasted escargot and crabs and mắm tôm stung his nostrils like noxious fumes.

Forty-Six

It was the Friday after Tết, months before monsoon rains hammered the South again. Hai wished one would blow in and swamp the proletarians plodding the streets below.

The Grand Plantation no longer seemed grand. He'd failed to kill Lan before Tết, hadn't located Kannon Ballard, and his primary assistant was dead. The old network deteriorated as the number of trusted brokers he had cultivated over the years dwindled. Perhaps it was time to bring Đăng Đạo from America and surrender leadership. His son's impetuousness concerned him, but he possessed the talent.

Glimmers of light reflected from the dust on his desk, dust that Ling used to wipe clean every morning. Had Hai not decided himself to verify Kannon Ballard's pillage, he might never have realized his assistant's duplicity.

Just as he exited the cache to reset the minefield, he had heard muffled voices. Firing an AK for the first time in years released adrenaline, a sense of power. The return fire surprised him, but it was the death sign that alarmed him more. The cursed owl and its foreboding wail had sent him ducking into a spider hole to wait out the night.

When he discovered Ling's body the next morning, it proved unsatisfying, not so much for Ling's betrayal but that he died too easily. Yet, one point proved satisfying. After all these years, he figured he'd uncovered the identity of the secret member of The Monsoon Killed the Tiger.

Papa-san Minh, Chấn's father—Võ Thu—or even Chấn himself must have been Ling's sole contact. Clever, he had to admit, recruiting a Chinese into the cell, something an ethnic Vietnamese would not suspect. Traitors all.

The missing money piqued him like a festering wound. The cash must have been stashed in the shallow hole near Ling's body. And the footprints leading away from the battle site were too large to belong to a Vietnamese or Cambodian. Which meant *Trung-Úy* Ballard had been there with Ling and escaped with the money. And he believed Lan and Ballard to be together in country because they could never clear customs with the cash. They might try to launder it in Chợ Lớn.

Damn you, Ling. You are not here to prepare my hookah or watch Lan's house.

Hai finished engineering the water pipe. He lit it, got a good bite, then inhaled the water-cooled smoke. He exhaled. The sweet, pungent aroma permeated the room.

Immediately his mind elevated to an altered state. He reread Farber's email, in which Farber expressed "a willingness to negotiate the particulars of the distribution scheme." Negotiate. The idiot. Hai was not sure he still wanted to negotiate with Farber, much less honor any contractual arrangement.

Jeffrey's pending arrival complicated matters, but confronting this leech, a typical American parasite, would prove satisfying. He took another hit and decided to call Đăng Đạo.

"Yo."

Yo? Ridiculous American colloquialism, Hai realized. "Special team in place?" He had ordered the hit team in case contract negotiations broke down, or if he just decided to have Farber killed.

"Yes, sir."

"Qualifications?"

"Five men, young but experienced, with several kills behind them. All ninjitsu masters, skilled in Tonfa and in throwing the four-point star."

Good choices, Hai thought. If done properly, wielding crushing, spinning batons could break every bone in the body before the victim died. And with expert orchestration, the four-point, four-inch throwing stars inflicted paralyzing nerve damage, yet preserved acute the sufferer's mental faculties. He imagined taunting Farber, whom he loathed because he sold out his own kind, as he twitched to death.

"Headquarters?"

"Taos."

"Where is Taos?"

"Open your New Mexico map," Đăng Đạo said.

Hai opened a desk drawer and removed a packet bound by rubber bands. He slipped off the band and found the necessary map. "Okay. I have it."

"As the eagle flies, the village is located one hundred thirteen kilometers north of Santa Fe. It is in sleepy Native American country. We have a two-room shack on the outskirts, with an outdoor shithouse. Sound familiar?"

Hai smiled as he reflected on America's official spin that these gangs were atypical and not part of general unrest in Vietnamcsc communities. Hai's gangs were well-armed, intelligent, and fiercely dedicated, just as had been their ancestral brothers—the Việt Minh and Việt Cộng. But Đăng Đạo's desire to broaden the team base and management team by recruiting talented, disaffected youth—both educated and uneducated—from other minorities concerned him.

Hai ran his fingers over the map's mountainous terrain above Santa Fe. Kannon Ballard. Was he working with Farber and Jeffrey? If so, the only way Ballard would work with them was to be unaware they had led him into that ambush during the war. Yet, leopards do not change their spots. Farber was devious then, would be so now, and was probably still manipulating Ballard.

Or they had kissed and made up and are out to destroy me? Either option is possible. Neither is acceptable.

"Do you know the name Kannon Ballard?" Hai asked Đăng Đạo.

"No, sir."

"He served with Farber and Jeffrey during the war. It is possible Ballard is working with them to undermine our operation. He has successfully infiltrated our cache here and stolen American currency."

"You must find and kill this man."

The audacity of his son's condescending tone rankled Hai, but he remained patient. "I believe Ballard remains in Việt Nam, but if he escapes, he might reappear with Farber."

"If he surfaces in New Mexico, am I to eliminate him?"

"Not until you discover what he knows and whom he has told. I also want to see how my meeting with Jeffrey progresses. I will keep you informed."

"Understood."

Understood, yes, but compliance was another issue.

After the pause, his son spoke again. "Father, I just remembered. I have heard the Kannon name."

"Source?"

"The underground."

The underground—operative and effective in every country—ordained change. The recollection rekindled dreams of expanding his guerrilla movement worldwide, separate from the Columbian drug lords, Russian mafia, and militant Muslims. He didn't trust them.

"Tell me about this development," Hai said.

"As you commanded, we have been trailing Farber and his associates. I assigned Quán to a man named Hippo, who Farber hired to perform dirty work."

"I would not expect less of our enemy."

"Quán followed Hippo to a bar and overheard him talking with Sanderson, an artist Farber is blackmailing. Hippo told the artist he had been a reconnaissance platoon sergeant in Việt Nam and knew how to extract from uncooperative people information they would rather not divulge. After the artist left, Quán approached Hippo and offered a beer to reward him for his excellent military service in fighting the Việt Cộng. The man drank a lot and bragged about his heroism in the war as well as his current job to protect an important man."

"Đăng Đạo, I am waiting for useful information."

"Hippo mumbled to Quán about a woman they *acquired*."

"And you think the abduction of a woman may be related to Kannon Ballard?"

"Quán said the man told him a guy named Kannon would no longer shoot his wad into the woman. If this is true, it is unlikely Ballard and Farber are working together."

"An interesting possibility," Hai said, "but be careful. A babbling drunkard is often dishonorable."

"We know the general area where she is being held," Đăng Đạo said. "If we locate her—"

"Find her. Concentrate on both the woman and Farber. Everything else will fall into place."

"Yes, sir. Have you a photograph of this man Kannon Ballard?"

"I will email his image."

Hai's second phone line rang. He told his son he would talk with him later and terminated the call.

"*Chào?*"

"I'm calling for Mr. Hai," the caller said.

"Who is speaking?"

"Leonard Jeffrey."

Hai put his hand over his mouth to cover his glee. Things were moving now, fast. He relished the action.

"Why Captain Jeffrey. How nice to hear from you after all these years. You are the only man I ever met who is as ugly as I am. How are you getting your women these days? Still drugging and raping? We have so much in common."

No response.

"Is Farber and Jeffrey, Inc., ready to do business?"

"We're prepared to talk."

"Fine, just fine. I suggest you come to my office tomorrow morning at nine. We will reach a satisfactory arrangement."

Jeffrey said he'd be there.

Hai had something special to show Jeffrey.

* * *

After Jeffrey hung up the phone, his nausea overtook him again. Immediately after he'd left Tân Sơn Nhất airport, he'd become sickened by the stench of diesel fuel and the peculiar Vietnamese body odor. Most people found it pleasing. He never had. And the odor of nước mắm sauce drifting up to his room like rotting garbage exacerbated his nausea. As he sat on the commode, where he'd spent most of his time since arriving at the hotel, he felt as if he were going to die. The oppressive heat with such high humidity seemed intolerable.

He flushed for what he hoped was the last time and sipped from a glass of water, trying to restore precious body fluids he'd been voiding ever since his arrival. He floundered to the bed and fell face forward. Perspiration poured off his body as freely as if he were in a sauna. The bedsheets, saturated from his sweat, were clammy and gelatinous. Suddenly, it dawned. He had a fever. God! Why didn't he just get on the next plane and leave? Deep down, he knew why. The restraint that had plagued him all his life shackled him like handcuffs. Fear.

No one, other than Farber, knew where he was. Jeffrey hadn't even told his wife. Now, he longed to be home, desirous even of being held by his fat Bertha. He tossed and turned throughout the night.

A furious gust of wind blew him off balance. He fell out of the tree and plummeted through space, splashing down in a flooded rice paddy. He opened his eyes. Leeches clung to his body, one clamped on his penis, sucking his life's blood. He flicked his lighter, tried to burn off the offending, bloated worms. A gnarled hand firmly grasped his.

He raised his gaze and met hollow eyes peering from a wrinkled old face, a woman's face. Beetlenut juice sluiced out the corners of her toothless mouth. In one hand, she cradled a pipe. She drew his hand to hers, which held the pipe and ignited the powerful opium. She inhaled deeply, then set the pipe down beside her and began suckling him.

Ugly, evil people stood around, laughing. Someone held a tape recorder. Another, a camera. He tried extracting himself from the rice paddy. But the muck acted like quicksand, drawing him further down into the mire. The woman withdrew, stood up and straddled his legs with hers.

"I am the Year of the Dragon," she said as she metamorphosed before his eyes into a scaly, fire-breathing reptile.

"What do you want with me, Dragon Lady?"

Its eyes blazed. The reptile sprouted arms and lashed wicked claws at his naked body. Hot breath boiled the viscous mud enveloping him. The Dragon Lady shoveled it into his mouth and made him swallow, burning his throat and inflaming his lungs. He closed his eyes in surrender.

Jeffrey bolted upright, waving frantically at the demons. The room lay dark as a tomb.

Gradually, his senses cleared. He sucked in huge, deep breaths, grateful for living through the nightmare. His skin was cooler, the fever gone. He rolled off the bed and strode to the window. Drawing the curtains open, he surveyed the congested streets of Sài Gòn. Traffic flowed like mucus from a bad cold. The stench reminded him of when they used to burn shit.

Fifty-five-gallon drums lay welded to the top of bus cabs, acting as mobile reservoirs for replenishing water lost through faulty cooling systems. Strangely, the water drums reminded him how his father used to tie a radiator-filling water bag to the front bumper of their snout-nosed '51 Studebaker Champion, a family treasure acquired after their best harvest year. He wished he'd never left the reassuring earth of his father's flatland farm.

Forty-Seven

The clamoring rattled Lan as if a gong had been implanted inside her head. She didn't understand why Thanh insisted they stay at a crumbling, rat-infested hovel in Chợ Lớn instead of her home, or even his apartment. The communal toilet reeked like the open sewer it was. The only fresh air she breathed came late at night after she had duck-walked the underground passageway to the Thiên Hậu Pagoda and emerged to stand in its courtyard. Even then, when she looked up to admire the ornate frieze, the blended odor of incense and opium fouled the air.

She walked inside the pagoda and studied the silk paintings, then the icon of Thiên Hậu, the sea goddess. Had her family sequestered here, prayed here, after navigating the labyrinth of central Sài Gòn in their escape efforts? She thought not, for if they had, they would be living in America, and she might soon join them. But then, had they lived, she would not have met Kannon.

Under cover of darkness, her cousin approached from the courtyard. "Were you successful?"

"Shhh," he whispered, raising his finger to his lips. "Come, let us remove ourselves to an outside corner. We can talk there."

The air hung thick with fumes, the stars unseen. While the clanging gongs had subsided, her heart beat as fiercely as a drum. She tried to read Thanh's face, his body language, but no message came forth.

"American dollars speak with a loud voice," he said.

"You have arranged to protect us from the wicked Hai?"

"In two days, we will have security beyond the pagoda. Then it will be safe to return to our homes."

"And the passports and visas?"

"I do not know how long it will take. A trip to Hà Nội may expedite the process. You must remain here until I return."

This news saddened her. "I hope soon."

"We could depart earlier, smuggle our way across the Cambodian border, to Bangkok, and later to Taiwan. But we become like the boat people, refugees, with perhaps no safe landing anywhere, even America."

She clasped her hands behind her neck and stared at the ornamental roof. "You are right. It is best we wait."

Thanh nodded and smiled at her agreement.

"I would like to see Kannon," Lan said

"What makes you think he will come?"

She pinched his ear.

"Ouch." Thanh massaged the tender spot. "I tease you, cousin. Why not call tomorrow! But you must meet at the pagoda."

"All right."

"Kannon mentioned another kind of visa, but he will have to discuss it with you."

She wondered what this could be and why he had not mentioned this in Vũng Tàu at the Bãi Dâu beach when they lay under the stars. "America. A new life awaits."

"Yes, cousin." Thanh hugged her.

"Thank you." A tear washed from her eye and streaked down her face to spill onto her saffron áo dài. "Let us go inside."

They ducked inside the doorway that led to the underground passage. Lan glanced at the nondescript, barefooted Chinese man standing off to one side. He paid them no mind, but as they passed him, she noticed the lethal, black-coated AK47 strapped over his shoulder.

Later that night, as she lay on her back, the wooden-slotted frame bed no longer an uncomfortable consequence, Lan worried about Kannon because, despite their intimacy, words of love had not been spoken.

"It is too soon," she told herself.

Nevertheless, wanting to be clean when again they joined, she considered returning home for a bath and fresh clothes. She could also retrieve Chấn's meditation journal and the golden medallion with inlaid jade left to her by her mother. Would this be wise, she asked herself, to bathe and gather what little defined her life? The answer seemed elusive until she clutched her dream. Besides, the visit would not take long, and Thanh need not know.

* * *

At seven Saturday morning, with thoughts of the flatland farm still in his head, Jeffrey showered, dressed in khakis and a thin poplin shirt, and went down to the hotel's restaurant to order crackers and a coke. At half-past eight, he hailed a cyclo and gave the sullen driver directions to The Grand Plantation. He arrived a few minutes before nine and loitered around the block until time to enter.

The day had already gathered heat, but the air seemed less oppressive and humid than yesterday. A bright sun poked through cumulus clouds, their irregular, fluffy contours a soothing contrast to a lapis-draped sky. This embellished his spirit. Jeffrey studied Hai's building. Its cleanliness and modernity further heightened his outlook.

Maybe this won't be so bad.

Promptly at nine, Jeffrey climbed the steps to The Grand Plantation and knocked on the front door. No one answered. Then he noticed an intercom, punched the button, and announced himself. A moment later, the door opened. He found himself staring into the haunting eyes of Mr. Hai, whose aquiline features had become even more pronounced since the war.

"Come in. So good to see you again, Captain."

Jeffrey winced. Hai's gravel voice grated on him like rusted concertina wire. "It's been a long time." He studied his old nemesis.

Deep lines creased Hai's leathery, impassive face like an errant plow had furrowed diseased troughs through a wasted field. Wiry arms and legs protruded through wrinkled, cotton khakis, and Hai wore, just as he had thirty-two years ago, classic Hồ Chí Minh sandals.

"Enemies no longer," Hai said. "Friends now."

Hai's tone belied his words. "Yes, of course," Jeffrey answered, not knowing what else to say.

"Come with me." Hai led him through the lobby. Jeffrey couldn't help but notice the marble dragons with eyes of jade, but what really spooked him was the carved expression on the bronze tiger face.

"You like my treasures, yes?"

Jeffrey didn't answer. They entered the elevator. Hai

punched button number two, the conveyance lifted, and they rode directly to Hai's office. The interior smelled of thick incense. The décor was French colonial.

Hai walked to a large, wooden desk inlaid with gold and sat on the chair behind it. He didn't offer Jeffrey a seat.

"You have spoken to Farber, yes? You are prepared to do business again, yes?"

Same Hai, Jeffrey thought. Straight to the point, no tact, no foreplay, dig in and destroy the enemy.

Jeffrey wondered what kind of office this was. A computer terminal and keyboard occupied one corner of the massive desk, but nothing present here or in the lobby suggested a business connection he could grasp. It also dawned on him he'd seen no one else in the building. He wanted to execute this transaction and get the hell away.

"We are prepared to act as your stateside distributor," Jeffrey replied, "providing we can negotiate favorable terms."

"Favorable terms?" Hai interrupted caustically. "I see no bargaining ground for you to stand on."

Jeffrey didn't like the results of the first parlay. Good weather be damned.

"Hear me out," Jeffrey said. "We can make it attractive."

Hai stood and kicked a metal trashcan, which sent it careening across the floor. "Speak quickly, or I roast you like a live pig over a searing fire."

As a reflex, Jeffrey shielded his face and scuttled backward. *This must be what hell's like.* "For purchase of product, we'll pay your standard wholesale price, via wire transfer, to numbered accounts in Switzerland, with—"

"Stop. It is not so easy to establish numbered accounts in Switzerland these days, what with all the fuss brought about by the holocaust survivors. The Isle of Man and the Cayman's are still friendly, yes? But we can resolve that. Continue. I find this amusing."

This was like standing on a forty-five-degree muddy slope, losing ground with every exchange, Jeffrey thought.

"Whatever markup we achieve stateside belongs to us."

"First, there is no wholesale price for you and Farber, my friend. You will pay a premium, plus handling, shipping, and insurance."

Jeffrey froze under Hai's black-eyed stare. "Insurance?"

"Yes, we discuss insurance later. You will still make much profit. Cost of product will be my wholesale price plus one hundred percent, with seventy-five percent down, balance due held in escrow until you take possession of the goods. Upon delivery, I receive the remaining twenty-five percent."

"I must talk to Farber," Jeffrey said. "I'm not authorized to negotiate those terms."

"I am feeling generous. You have three days."

"There's one other issue, Hai, that I must speak to you about. It's delicate."

Hai cracked his knuckles. It sounded like snapping a whip. "Speak up, you degenerate."

"We wish to purchase back our principal."

"You Americans, always dancing around the issues and never being straight. No wonder you lost the war. You want the pictures, yes? And the tapes? How much do you propose to offer?"

"A million dollars, U.S.," Jeffrey said. "We'll pay half a million now, with the other half due when you deliver the tapes and photographs."

Hai clucked his tongue and stuffed his hands in his pockets. Then he jumped flat-footed and landed squarely on his rosewood desk, where he squatted. "Five million American dollars is more appropriate."

Jeffrey, stung as much by Hai's feat of agility as the price, muttered, "That's far beyond our means."

"A nice phrase has emerged from America's mergers and acquisitions—the earn-out. You are familiar? Yes? You pay two-and-a-half million now, then ten percent of profits until the five million total is reached."

How does Hai know all this shit? Jeffrey wondered. Then he noticed the Asian edition of the Wall Street Journal on his desk.

"How do we know you'll release the tapes?"

Hai, laughing hysterically, jumped from the desk and further mangled the overturned trashcan. "You do not," he said. "That is my insurance."

Jeffrey stood with his hands in his pockets and a strong need to pee. It was the inquisition again.

"As I said, I must talk with Farber."

"Do so. Afterward, I will take you to see the merchandise. You'll be persuaded the opportunity is limitless."

Hai escorted Jeffrey to the elevator, then out the front door. When Jeffrey exited, he caught the attention of a cyclo driver. Weakened from his bout with dysentery and the encounter with Hai, he could barely muster the energy to clamber aboard.

The cloud cover had dissipated, and the heat bore down like an open-hearth furnace. His underarms were soaked through, and he nearly passed out from dizziness. Horns blared incessantly, and obnoxious fumes hung in the dead air. One thing was clear, there was no way he was going to that infernal underground warehouse.

Forty-Eight

The next morning, the same as he had every day since discovering Ling's body, Hai walked down Bùi Viện in advance of familiar signs that marked the beginning of a Vietnamese day— cooking fires, nước mắm sauce, and tonal communication. Even the demonic traffic flow tapered off.

Effects from his late-night opium indulgence lingered as he turned onto a side street before entering the narrow alleyway that ran between rows of modest terra-cotta dwellings. His rubber-soled sandals alerted no one, while his heart thumped like a 60mm mortar.

The eastern horizon was still dressed in black as he scaled the wall.

* * *

An engine clanked and throttled to a stop outside the home. Hai peered through a crack in the shuttered window and watched Lan exit a faded black Packard Clipper. Her hapless cousin's worthless icon of America's failing imperialism, he reasoned. She looked around as if to see whether anyone was watching, then approached the front door.

She appeared like a wounded waif adrift on the sea, easy prey for the killer storm about to strike. Only he would humiliate and degrade her first. Hai swept aside the gossamer curtains and entered the bedroom, positioning himself out of sight but able to observe using his mirror. The front tumbler clicked, and the knob turned. She opened the door and walked in.

Lan's curved buttocks swayed beneath her silken áo dài when she turned to close the door. It reminded him of a swan taking flight. He visualized sienna-colored thighs scissoring next to her sable honey spot and fought to quiet his heavy breathing while he rubbed his member. But as usual, his accursed penis stayed soft and useless without his testicles, and he felt the familiar rage building toward a volcanic eruption.

Her footsteps padded across the floor and up the stairway. The soft striding stopped, and Hai heard the clattering of drawers. A silence ensued. Then the footsteps resumed, signaling her return downstairs.

Holding a blade between his teeth, he approached from behind and squeezed her forbidden area. The possessions she held tumbled to the floor. She turned, mouth open as if to scream, and he stuffed a rag in her mouth. With the other hand, he pressed the blade to her throat.

"*Chào*, Cô Lan. I am Mr. Hai. Some call me the butcher."

He cuffed her hands and pasted a six-inch strip of duct tape over her mouth, then secured it by coiling additional tape strands around her head. Her guttural utterances he interpreted as orgasmic, and it pleased him.

"I will inform Major Farber of your capture. He will notify your Kannon Ballard, yes?"

She kicked at his groin, but he dodged the blow and threw her to the floor.

"I killed the Minhs. You know this, yes? I think so." He kicked her hands aside and straddled her. "Imagine what I am going to do to you."

He clucked his teeth mirthfully at the look of terror in her eyes. He knelt and pinned her legs with his. Then he grabbed her arm and inserted the needle. Lan attempted to wrench free, but he injected the numbing morphine.

Slowly, he unzipped his fly and lowered his trousers. "You will suck this until it gets hard. Then I am going to carve you alive, in front of *Trung-Úy* Ballard." He watched her pupils dilate.

Hai stood, pulled up his trousers, and jerked the semiconscious Lan upright. She collapsed against his shoulder. He arranged her long auburn hair to shield her face as he led his wobbling trophy through the garden patio into Thanh's Packard. If anyone looked closely, they would have thought of two lovers leaving on holiday.

* * *

Gentle breezes caressed yellow-blossomed tamarind trees and whisked Lan along the garden path. She filled with joy at the sight of the orchids, but as she drew nearer, the blossoms wilted, and the solace she sought escaped her.

"Mother Loan, Phoenix, rise, and speak."

Her mother's spirit failed to answer. Lan feared the death of Loan's physical world portended the passing of her spiritual one.

Then the wind lifted and carried Lan beyond a pond to the bonsai trees, dwarf microcosms of life, which fascinated her with their delicacy and tenacity. As she approached, she shrunk unto a tiny self and saw her family sitting among the branches.

The wind died, and Lan landed beneath gnarled limbs. Offering a smile of joy, she looked to her kin, but a loop dropped around her neck and yanked her off the ground. She struggled to breathe and grasped branches for support, but the limbs turned pliable and transformed into limp ropes.

Lan awoke, coughing on a straw bed inside a dimly lit space. This must be the afterlife. Yet, if it were the afterlife, would her mouth be as dry as rice fields baking in the sun? The air was stale but chilly. Surely the afterlife would provide fresh, warm air.

Using her elbows for leverage, she rose to her knees and tried to stand. A sharp barb pierced her head, injecting clarity. She groped, only to find herself encapsulated by a stout wire cage—a tiger cage—the kind Chấn told her they used during the war.

Slowly, she lolled her head from side to side. An oil lamp, hung from a peg driven into an earthen wall, emitted the faint light. Shelves stocked with stereo boxes and weapons occupied most of the floor space. Lan collapsed in sobs as she realized she lay imprisoned in what must be the underground warehouse—Mr. Hai's den of wickedness.

Revulsion came with the memory of Hai's smell. Her mouth was sore to the touch. Her vagina throbbed with pain. She examined herself, a place only two men in her life had ever entered, and determined she had been bruised but not penetrated by Hai.

"Mr. Hai, you are as impotent as the eunuch." But the earthen walls consumed her outcry.

She sensed a movement, cocked her ears, and heard a scuffling sound to her right. Was someone, or some *thing*, in there with her?

"Ayieeee," she screamed in horror. She jerked her body into the fetal position, raking her naked back against the barbed wire. A

307

large Cobra slithered by, the reptile's fangs having already injected a fatal poison as its unhinged jaws worked at devouring a rat. The raw edge of her nerves and soul were exposed, and all was ugliness.

Where is Buddha?

Forty-Nine

After his meeting with Hai, Jeffrey spent the evening sweating out his poison at a massage and steam bath parlor. He paid for extra services but was too exhausted to perform.

"I want my money back," he said.

"No give back money. You no can do."

The hired bitch blew up a prophylactic, let the air out, and mocked him by waving the limp rubber in his face, then shot him the finger.

And a scalding steam bath failed to bring rest. He left the parlor and hired a taxi to transport him to his hotel, which he reached at 2200 hours. It would be 0800 hours the same day in New Mexico. Farber's voice sounded after the third ring.

"Yeah?"

On the verge of incoherency, Jeffrey managed, through slurred speech and broken sentences, to relay the essence of yesterday's negotiation with Hai.

"He said to take the buy-out offer and shove it up our collective asses."

"You offered him the whole million?" Farber said.

"Yeah. Hai wants five million."

"No way. I can't believe he'd turn down a million for the lousy photographs and tapes."

"He did."

"Hai's absurd," Farber said. "Nevertheless, that settles it."

"Settles what?"

"Eliminate Hai."

As he'd figured, this was Farber's plan all the time.

"You're crazy, Farber. I'm no murderer. Besides, there's no way in hell I could get away with it."

"Must I remind you, you've killed before?"

"That was different."

"Listen and listen good," Farber said. "If we can't get the tapes and pictures, or dispose of the problem, then for the rest of our

309

lives we live under storm clouds."

"I don't care. I'm not doing shit. I'm getting the hell out of here."

"And do what? Disappear?"

Jeffrey held the phone like a knife to plunge into Farber's heart.

"Remember, Jeffrey, Hai doesn't know we have influence with his silent partner."

"I'm not sure Ballard's working with Hai. I've seen no indication."

"Doesn't matter. Our bargaining piece is secure. Ballard will make his appearance."

"What makes you think he'll take the risk?"

"You kiddin'? He's motivated by guilt, and I'm pulling strings."

"Hai may not wait for Ballard."

"Stall," Farber said. "Tell Hai we'll do the deal, but we need five days to get the money together."

After they terminated the call, Jeffrey collapsed on the bed. He couldn't remember the last time he'd slept.

Several hours later, he awoke, unsure of his reality, then drifted back asleep.

Tell Hai we'll do it. How do we get him the money? Don't worry about the money. Stall. Kill Hai. Kill Ballard. Dispose of the bodies. Rot in a Vietnamese prison. What will happen to Bertha?

Jeffrey woke again and rolled off the bed, landing on all fours. He stood, walked to the phone, and called Farber, both at home and at the gallery. Impersonal answering machines amplified Jeffrey's impotence. He stood alone, with nothing between him and Hai except foreboding apprehension.

* * *

Kannon idled away time at the safe house. The cauldron-like night heat agitated his frustration as if he were vapor trapped inside a shaken bottle. Standing on the verandah, he scanned the harbor and fixed on twinkling lights skating unbroken swells.

Why was it he could crawl through booby traps, yet tremble like an abused dog when it came to confronting a despot like

Farber? Whether cloaked behind a woman or the corporate veil, he, Kannon Ballard, former First Lieutenant, Infantry, and Chief Financial Officer in industry, circled around confrontation, fearful of probing core issues.

Kannon returned inside and sat at the desk, where he dialed Farber's office number again. Time—2300 hours in Sài Gòn and 0900 the same day in New Mexico—thirteen hours after his call to Silverton confirmed Meghan's disappearance.

"Yeah?" Farber's voice grated through the line like an anvil dragged on concrete.

"There's a saying in Texas, 'He's lower than a snake's belly in a wagon rut.' Congratulations. You've surpassed it."

"Good to hear from you," Farber said. "How's your Việt Nam tour going?"

"You can't kill me, so you take Meghan. A coward's move."

"Not as bad as your linking with an enemy of the state to extort revenge."

Enemy of the state? Kannon's mind raced over possibilities like turning tumblers in a safe until locking on the combination. The bastard thinks Hai and I are working together, Kannon realized, which he could use as an advantage.

"Then you're aware how much damaging information Hai has on you and Jeffrey," Kannon said. "Information I can use to put you two away."

"Unless I pay, right," Farber said, "but you're asking for too much money."

"The tapes and your confession are worth it, Farber."

"You've overplayed the game, Ballard. First, you're an imbecile to trust Hai, and second, I have your woman."

"Meghan has nothing to do with this. Besides, she's not my woman. We split."

"You're lying. I have something you want. And you and Hai have something I want."

"Let her go."

"No can do." Farber's voice thundered like a gunshot.

"I won't bargain with you."

"If you want Meghan released, you will. All you have to do

is assist Jeffrey."

"Where's your spineless second-in-command?"

"Việt Nam."

"What's he doing here?"

"Ostensibly, to check on our import/export business. In reality, to negotiate." Seconds elapsed. "Jeffrey's in over his head. Help him kill Hai. Destroy the tapes. Hell, I'll award you another Silver Star."

If he'd been standing in front of Farber with a gun, he'd have shot him.

"Suppose I do. Then what do you propose when I return to America? Or do you expect both Jeffrey and me to end our lives here?"

"No, I expect you to succeed."

"What if I told you I have no business relationship with Hai," Kannon said.

"An irrelevant lie."

Kannon pushed away from the teak-paneled desk and stood. A gust of wind ruffled the silken curtains lining the open windows. "And if I refuse?"

"If specific contractual contingencies are not executed to my satisfaction, the other party has instructions to discharge an action, the results of which you'll find displeasing."

Meaning if I don't kill Hai and turn over the incriminating information to Farber, Meghan dies.

"Like I believe you'll release Meghan and expect her not to file charges."

"When you get back," Farber mollified his tone, "we'll make the exchange. You'll be dirty and won't dare risk exposure. Each of us goes our separate ways. We'll each enjoy the fruits of our labor and go down life's road as coconspirators, silent partners if you will. Hell, Ballard. We'll have each won our wars."

Kannon's stomach churned like a cement mixer. There was no way in hell Farber would release Meghan. Should he call the New Mexico state police? That didn't seem like a good option. Except for linking Jeffrey's assault in Silverton, there was probably nothing he could produce to connect Farber with Meghan's disappearance. Meghan's signature on the gallery guest book could be easily destroyed. And Farber might now have the video in his hands.

Disgusted, Kannon said with as much conviction as he could muster, "Let me talk to her. You owe me that much. I need proof. Or no deal."

"No dice. I own your soul."

"Fuck you," Kannon said. He slapped the receiver on the cradle. Throw out the window thoughts of Farber and Hai teaming up again. Still, if nothing else, Farber just indicted and convicted himself by kidnapping Meghan. Proof positive he and Jeffrey had conspired with Hai and his Việt Cộng cell. A lot of good the knowledge did him now.

His world had turned to shit again, and he could kiss Lan goodbye. Walking into the bedroom, he took note of the rumpled sheets where they had lain together.

* * *

After the conversations with Jeffrey and Ballard, Farber locked the front door, then went to the wet bar sandwiched between his and Jeffrey's offices. The bar came in handy for special showings and exhibits, reasons to celebrate. But Farber didn't feel like celebrating now. He needed relief. He plucked a whisky glass off the shelf, plunked in cracked ice, and poured a generous amount of Jack Daniels. He took two quick gulps, then paused to let the bourbon whiskey numb his brain.

He needed to call Jeffrey and tell him Ballard would contact him. His cellphone chirped. Messages waited in a queue, so he checked them first. Scrolling, he ignored the calls from Jasmine and the frantic one from Bertha inquiring about her beloved Jeffrey. It was then he noticed the message light blinking on the desk phone. First, he refreshed his Jack Daniels, then punched the button to retrieve the call.

"Major Farber, through the actions of your incompetent hirelings, you have declared war on the Vietnamese people. We, in turn, have declared war on you." The strident voice, like the histrionic tone of a rooster, leaped through the line with monsoon force and slashed as a serrated blade. "I am no longer interested in

313

negotiating a settlement or returning any sensitive information. You may consider you and your group terminated."

Terminated? What the hell was Hai talking about, hirelings, as in multiple? The little bastard must have concluded Ballard was working with him and Jeffrey. Both were as good as dead. Could the Monsoon reach him in New Mexico? And Meghan O'Brien, had the purpose of her kidnapping been rendered moot?

Things had gotten out of hand. He was half tempted to return to Việt Nam and kill Hai himself. No, Ballard and Jeffrey must kill Hai. And when Ballard returned, he, Major Christian J. Farber, Infantry, would kill Ballard and Meghan.

That's right. Had to. After all, this was war, not murder, simply a continuation of a battle that started long ago and never finished. With his enemies eliminated, the threat of exposure expired, and he would live the rest of his life free from poisonous fangs.

Except . . . what would happen if the tapes and photographs were released? If they found their way into the media, he'd be disgraced at a minimum, or worse, with distorted American values these days, be charged with treason and stripped of life.

He drained the glass, then slammed it on the counter. Grabbing the bottle of Jack Daniels, Farber poured another shot, then sat down on the floor with the bottle between his legs.

* * *

After a fitful sleep, Kannon left the safe house and walked barefooted along the beach to think and sweat out the poisonous, surreal world he'd created. The hot sand burned the soles of his feet. He waded into the surf to cool them off.

Should he or should he not return to Santa Fe to try to find Meghan or negotiate with Farber to release her?

"I'm spinning wheels, wasting time," he told himself.

The longer he delayed, the more he jeopardized her life. Farber would have Meghan killed, dispose of the body, and disappear. Kannon could not, would not, jeopardize or sacrifice her any further. His search for redemption was leading him to commit murder, far different from killing defensively, whether in combat or civilian life.

He remembered lying on the ground in the San Juans and twanging the tiny fir sapling, how it sprang upright. And the bear's admonishing words when visiting his dream: *Your flimsy cocoon won't protect you.*

The answer came clear but stung his conscience, even if a man like Hai was the intended victim. Risk his soul to save someone else's life.

The hardest thing to do was call Lan and tell her what he was about to do and why. It might be the last time they spoke. He returned to the safe house, walked to the phone, and keyed the number. It rang forever. Frustrated, he slapped the cover shut, then decided to try once more.

Something clicked on the other end, but no one spoke.

"Lan?" he said.

"Cô Lan not here," the voice responded.

The voice sounded crackly and high-pitched. It wasn't Thanh. Had he rung the wrong number? He started to hang up and dial again when a voice spoke.

"You are American, yes? Perhaps Mr. Kannon Ballard? I have something you want."

The connection went dead.

Oh, goddamn! Kannon wished he'd been the sixteenth man to die in the ambush.

Fifty

Hai inspected his booby trap network, then mapped a serpentine escape route through his world of rattan and bamboo. He wanted nothing to happen to his prized Lan, who now resided in a tiger cage underground. She had enough water and rice to keep her alive a few days, sufficient time to get word through Farber to Kannon Ballard and entice Mr. Ballard into the open.

A pink hue ringed the eastern horizon as he mounted his bicycle and pedaled five kilometers back to the Citroen hidden near the mangroves. Twenty minutes later, he unhitched the bicycle cart he had used to trundle his fetal-positioned package and placed the bicycle and cart inside the car.

Ling's defection and death made his life more toilsome. Sure, Cambodian mercenaries were on call, but there was no one to run The Grand Plantation, orchestrate operations, or to perform sundry errands like making round trips to the warehouse. But it was nothing compared to the vermin-infested, mud-clogged trek down the Hồ Chí Minh Trail he had undertaken years ago.

Still, he was not a young man anymore, and the physical exertion from bicycling provided time to consider his alternatives. As the sweat oozed from his body, he made up his mind—let Đăng Đạo handle the business with Christian Farber. Once completed, Hai would bring him back to Việt Nam and groom him in earnest to take charge.

* * *

Hai mixed a drink. His package containing a copy of the tapes and photographs and short instruction list pertaining to Christian Farber was on its way by express delivery to Đăng Đạo.

Mr. Jeffrey's voice sounded through the intercom. Hai peered at the monitor and smiled, then went down to the lobby and opened the door.

"Come in, Captain. I hope our time apart has been productive." Hai led him into his office. They stood facing each other, three feet apart.

"Came by earlier. No one was here."

"I value your perseverance. I was taking care of a client. You have talked with Farber, yes?" Hai noted with sadistic satisfaction the degree of Jeffrey's fatigue.

"Farber agrees to terms, but we need time to put the money together."

"Commendable. Unfortunately, the option has expired."

"What, but—"

"Captain Jeffrey, there is no, *but.*"

Bands of sweat formed on Jeffrey's forehead. "Then I've no business here. I'm leaving."

Hai pulled his silenced Walther PPK. "I prefer you to stay."

Jeffrey's mouth dropped open. Hai loved this. Plant a seed of doubt. Watch it spread like poison. Witness the fight as reality conquers disbelief and matures into fear.

"I give you credit for recruiting Ballard. You enlisted Ling also, yes? Exceptional move. But Ling is dead, and I have Ballard's woman. Where is he?"

"I don't know. He's not our partner."

Hai whirled and kicked Jeffrey in the groin.

Jeffrey screamed and curled to the floor, holding his privates, gasping for breath.

"Come now, Jeffrey. Please do not think I am so stupid as to believe Mr. Ballard works alone. And you could not have stolen my money without Ling's help."

"I swear . . . Ballard is not our partner." Jeffrey continued to retch. "I know nothing . . . about stolen money or Ling, much less anything about a woman."

"Get up."

Jeffrey crawled into a chair and sat. Hai raked the rear sight of the PPK across Jeffrey's left cheek. "You lie. Tell me, how did you recruit Mr. Ballard? He must never have discovered you and Farber planned his death."

"We didn't recruit anybody, for God's sake. Leave me alone. We'll get you the goddamn money."

"Speak no more, yes? The money has become secondary." Hai strode behind the chair, placed the muzzled PPK against

317

Jeffrey's neck, and rotated the weapon as if drilling through a wooden plank.

Jeffrey's hair stood on end.

"Put your hands behind you." Hai cuffed them. Then he taped Jeffrey's mouth.

Hai walked behind his desk to the wall safe and spun the combination dial. He withdrew a deep-carved box, with inlaid jade on the sides, opened it, and removed a syringe. "You know what this is?"

Jeffrey shook his head as if to ward off wicked spirits. His eyes widened.

"Morphine." He plunged the needle into an upturned vial and filled the glass piston. With a maniacal scream, Hai jabbed the hypodermic needle deep into Jeffrey's bare arm.

Oomph.

Jeffrey freed himself from the chair and, like a wounded deer racing off in fear, ran headlong into the wall. His body went into spasm, then stopped thrashing. Hai watched Jeffrey's eyes glaze over and waited until the jumbled brain cells turned to mush.

Blood trickled from the puncture wound. The embedded syringe wavered back and forth like a pendulum.

"My Citroen is outside. You will like it. It is old, but it runs. I have added tinted windows and the latest in stereo, tape, and CD changer. Heavy-duty battery. I could not get air conditioning, though. I hope you like Vietnamese music. Are you listening?"

Five minutes later, Hai rolled a wheelbarrow to his interior loading dock and dumped Jeffrey onto the rear floor of the Citroen. He got in the steaming car, started the engine, and punched the remote to raise the warehouse door. He shifted into gear and joined the traffic flow. Evading the blocked arteries, Hai emerged from Sài Gòn rolling north on Highway One, the stereo booming.

* * *

A black night aided Hai's movement into his secondary access site. He connected two rail cars, dumped the semi-conscious Jeffrey in one, and plopped himself in the other. Employing both hands, he propelled the cars a hundred meters by manipulating the overhead pulley while cradling between his legs a jar of buzzing bees.

He reached the main chamber, set the jar aside, and dumped Jeffrey near the desk. Lan's honey pot smelled. "How is my bird? I have brought you company."

She sat in the corner of her cage and spat at him. "The impotent wicked one."

Hai kicked at Lan. "You traitorous whore. I was going to save you until your Kannon Ballard arrived, then do to you both what I am going to do to this man. But maybe this Ballard doesn't come, yes? He has a woman friend in America."

Hai brought out an entrenching tool, extended it, and locked it in place. He wedged the U.S. Army shovel into the ground between wooden posts three feet apart, a foot out from one wall, then greased the shovel's handle. Next, he dragged Jeffrey to the posts, stripped him, and ripped the tape off his mouth.

"I know you will enjoy this part."

He lifted Jeffrey's body and impaled him through the anus by shoving his body down on the shovel's handle.

"Arrrhhhh!"

Jeffrey's face took on a vacant look, the thousand-yard stare the Americans called it, while Hai trussed each arm to a post to stabilize Jeffrey's upper body.

The encapsulated bees, meanwhile, already droning in anger, became further agitated when Hai shook his specially designed jar in Jeffrey's face. He unscrewed the perforated lid and placed a hard rubber funnel over the neck. He punched Jeffrey in the stomach and crammed the funnel's broadened tip inside Jeffrey's open mouth, then drove the bees from the cone-shaped device by pushing the plunger at the bottom of the jar.

When the last bee entered the former advisor's mouth, Hai slipped a tightly woven net around Jeffrey's head and face. "This traps the bees while letting you breathe. Try it. Scream."

* * *

The lantern light flared on the American's emaciated face as if it were on fire.

"*Ông. Ông.* You must chew the bees and swallow them."

Exasperated, Lan drank from the meager portion of water

319

left by Hai. For hours she had tried to reach this man impaled on a stick. She thought if he chewed the bees and swallowed them, he could eliminate the sting of suffering and provide a source of protein for his body. But the only things emitting from the man's mouth were agonizing moans and spittle. She was not sure he possessed the will to live. When she looked again, though, she saw the man's jaws laboring against the net.

Then she resumed her struggle with her own will, made more difficult by Hai's words, "Kannon Ballard has a woman friend in America."

Fifty-One

Kannon was puffing on his Meerschaum when the phone rang. It was Tuesday, 1030 hours, and he hoped it was Thanh calling to say that Lan was with him and that it was safe to return to Sài Gòn.

"I returned from Hà Nội to find her missing."

No! The message received wasn't the one he wanted to hear. He'd been hoping against hope that he had misread the implication from the anonymous phone call. Feeling depleted, he wondered why Thanh had gone to Hà Nội? He should have at least kept Lan close by.

"I know she left Chợ Lớn by free will," Thanh said. He told Kannon how to arrange a chopper flight out of Vũng Tàu, who to look for, and what Vietnamese words to use. "Meet me as soon as possible at the Thiên Hậu Pagoda in Chợ Lớn," Thanh added.

* * *

Skimming over the sparse mountains, waterways, and rice fields brought back the combat rush to Kannon. The chopper's blades swooshed and whoomphed in rhythm during the thirty-minute flight to Sài Gòn.

As agreed, he would pick up the Yamaha DT175 Thanh had moved from the hotel's parking lot to the rear of Lan's house. Dissonant sounds, thick odors, and congested streets attacked his senses as the driver navigated like a shifty running back through the tangled maze to Bùi Viện Street.

Lan's street.

"*Cám ơn, ông.*" Kannon paid the taxi driver, then entered the courtyard laid out like a checkerboard, with alternating red and black clay tiles anchored in hardened clay. A hot breeze softly rippled the banyan and banana leaves, yet a musty odor flooded the place, reflecting its abandoned state.

Chấn's place. Lan's place. A home and a family torn by war now absent its sole survivor, the one whose love he wanted to embrace, the woman he wanted to marry.

The specious image dulled his senses and drained his strength, a soldier's weakness, an opening to vulnerability, the invitation to die in combat. He raked his bare knuckles against the wall to regain his edge.

The motorcycle rested on its side stand near the back door. The two-cycle-engine appeared unmolested. The tires held air, and the bike's hoses and lubricants appeared intact. Kannon seized the DT175 by the handlebars and rolled it out front. He slapped the kick-starter. On the third try, the motorcycle came to life, and again Kannon rode, a hot wind in his face.

Chợ Lớn teemed in its natural, civilized chaos as Kannon parked beside the pagoda and walked inside. A barefooted, gap-toothed man wearing a white overshirt like a hospital gown caught Kannon's wandering eye. He strode to the man's side.

"*Tôi muốn thăm Ông Sư*," Kannon said. (I wish to visit the monk.)

Before long, a youngish-looking monk dressed in Mahayana sect purple robes, head gleaming like a globe, sidled over.

"*Chào ông. Tôi tên*, Kannon Ballard."

"You may speak English," he said, in a thick, broken accent.

"I'm here to see Thanh."

The monk bowed. "Come."

Kannon followed him through the incense-choked pagoda. Pungent lavender, eucalyptus, and sage wafted to his nostrils, made his glands salivate. His stomach rumbled in protest.

They entered the underground and worked their way through a dimly lit tunnel. From the clatter above, Kannon assumed they passed beneath a street. Soon, they outpaced all sound from above.

Fetid concrete passageways blotched with mold fanned out like tentacles of an octopus, burrowing away into darkness and silence. He felt disoriented and claustrophobic. Finally, they climbed a rickety set of stairs that led to a narrow corridor honeycombed with doors as close together as bunks in a barracks. The monk pointed to one on the left, turned, and vanished into the underground mesh.

Kannon knocked.

A metallic click sounding like a forward-sliding rifle bolt

reverberated down the corridor. His muscles tensed, then he heard the word, "*Chào?*"

"Kannon," he said.

The door cracked open, and Kannon let himself in.

"We must hurry," Thanh said.

Thanh's glasses mirrored a bare electric bulb swinging on an exposed electrical cord suspended from the ceiling. A thin ventilation shaft shot through the back wall. The temperature seemed one hundred twenty degrees, and Kannon felt as if his clothes had melted into his body.

"You think she's at the underground site?"

"I do," Thanh said.

Thanh dismantled an AK47 and stuffed it and several loaded magazines into a canvas bag. To that, he added a Chicom pistol, the one Kannon had stolen from Hai's cache, along with several bottles of water. This guy was a comptroller for a rubber company?

"For you." Thanh handed him two objects.

Kannon sat on a stool and examined them—Chấn's meditation journal and a golden medallion with inlaid jade. He held the medallion aloft. "Lan's?"

"Yes. I found them on the floor of her house."

"Thanks." He caressed the medallion as if it were Lan herself, then slipped both items in his backpack.

"The motorcycle is outside?"

Kannon nodded. "Got the night vision goggles?"

"Yes, also food." Thanh zipped his bag. "Leave yours here. It will be safe."

Kannon felt reluctant to leave Lan's treasures and his tools, but he handed the backpack to Thanh, who wrapped it in plastic. Then he stuffed the pack in a pull-down cubby Kannon hadn't noticed.

"We go." Thanh led the way above ground. Kannon kicked the DT175 to life and sped off through the vehicular morass that was Sài Gòn, with Thanh straddling the rear, one hand clutching his canvas bag and the other indicating directions.

Two hours later, sharp shadows stabbed at the road like a volley of arrows. Twilight gave way to dusk, which folded into darkness and swallowed them up. They puttered past the entrance to the outpost on Route 10, turned west on 6A, then went off-road. Fifteen minutes later, Thanh told Kannon to halt in front of a small temple.

Kannon switched off the engine and turned to Thanh. "Why are we stopping here?"

"You know the Cao-Đài religion?"

Kannon stared at the all-seeing eye that adorned the temple face, a protective icon for those who entered its portals. "Somewhat," he said.

"It is a religious synthesis of Theravada Buddhists, Confucians, Taoists, and Catholics designed to bring harmony."

"I remember the main temple in Tây Ninh," Kannon said. "And the mandarin coats."

Thanh hopped off the motorcycle with the agility of a gymnast. "The Cao-Đài maintained their own army until Diệm wiped them out," he said.

An idea that had begun taking shape beneath the Thiên Hậu Pagoda in Chợ Lớn gathered substance.

"Thanh, any of your family connected with that army?"

"Father was. Then he switched allegiance and joined the Việt Cộng."

Did Thanh follow his father? Kannon wondered.

"We are safe here," Thanh said. "The temple is abandoned, but nearby villagers know me."

Kannon put the kickstand down and dismounted. "It's twenty-one hundred hours," he said. "Time to eat, plan, and rest before we go in."

"I agree," Thanh said.

Kannon rolled the motorcycle inside, set the side stand, then pulled from his pocket two maps he carried. He unfolded both, one topographical, with the other being the crude, hand-drawn diagram created by Papa-san Minh.

Thanh gathered wood and busied himself with a cooking fire on the dirt floor. Soon, rice grains coagulated into thick, sticky globules to which he added chunks of pork and chicken. The steamy aroma filled the temple, and the flames threw dancing silhouettes on the walls.

"Think Hai's in there?" Kannon grabbed two bowls and used chopsticks to shovel in a healthy portion of Vietnamese stew.

"A good chance. If not, one or two rogue Khmer Rouge might be standing guard topside."

Thanh's voice, shadowed profile, the way he moved, all reminded him of Chấn.

"They weren't there before," Kannon said.

"That was before you broke in."

"True."

They finished eating, and Thanh snuffed the fire.

"This is the booby-trapped area I negotiated on my second visit. Ling was killed here," Kannon said, pointing to where he'd left the body. "Another trail led in the opposite direction from the underground entrance. I didn't follow it, so I don't know if it's mined or not."

"Count on it," Thanh said.

Kannon stared into the darkness, then turned to his comrade. "Who the hell are you?"

Thanh rose and brushed his hands on his charcoal-colored khakis, then doubled his fists and planted them on his hips. *"Chiến sĩ vô Danh."*

Thanh's revelation and his forceful tone racked Kannon's senses.

The Unknown Warrior.

"Võ Thu, Chấn's father, knew. No one else, not Chấn, Hai, not my father." Thanh brushed a wave of jet-black hair away from his forehead.

"Why?"

"Thu recruited me in Sài Gòn to liaison with COSVN . . . in case something happened to him."

COSVN, Central Office South Việt Nam, headquarters of all communist forces.

"Whose side are you on now?"

"Cousin Lan's."

Did all combat veterans boil down a war that simply? To hell with government-imposed ethics and agenda? The fight was for those whom you loved.

"We do not need maps," Thanh said. "I know the way."

A burden of fear lifted off Kannon. He didn't want to negotiate those booby traps again. "Time to rest," Kannon said.

"Until midnight."

Kannon set the watch alert, then lay on the ground, arms folded next to his ear, and closed his eyes. Familiar voices whispered within the walls: Đinh and Lộc, before they were wiped out, and Malcolm and the others, before they were destroyed three months later. Drinking beer, laughing, carrying on. It was as if their souls wandered the rice fields in search of peace.

Fifty-Two

"*Trung-Úy* Ballard, wake up. It is time."

Thanh woke him just when his watch alert activated. Kannon snuffed the alarm and slogged awake. The fire had died, and the temple-sheltered bivouac held a chill. Or was the chill caused by his dreams about Lan and Meghan, whose delicate images had shattered like splintered glass?

Thanh rustled in his canvas bag and retrieved a pair of silken-textured black pants and a black shirt.

"Put these on."

"How do we bypass the booby traps?" Kannon asked as he changed into the night warrior's armor.

"A secondary entrance exists, one hundred meters west of the first."

"I take it we loop behind Hai's hedgerow," Kannon said.

"Correct. The cache sites are connected by rail, using mining cars, and negotiated by a manual pulley system."

"Noisy."

"Yes," Thanh agreed. "We must crawl through the tunnel."

"Any villagers to worry about?"

"Should not be," Thanh said. "And if we encounter anyone, you must shoot without hesitation."

"Understood. Weapons check."

Thanh tossed the Chicom pistol to Kannon, then handed him two clips. Kannon inserted a magazine into the PRC Type-59, chambered a round, and activated the safety at the rear of the slide. The other magazine he slipped into his breast pocket.

After reassembling the AK at lightning speed, Thanh jammed in a banana-shaped magazine. Next, he attached a sling, aftermarket variety Kannon figured, and taped the buckled ends to silence would-be jingling, then stepped outside the temple.

Kannon joined him and glanced at the sky. Stars appeared, then disappeared, as muddy clouds raced toward another realm.

"Ready?"

"Ready."

They moved out, Thanh on point, Kannon two paces behind, praying for simplicity—that Lan was there, alive, and Hai was absent. No guards.

His brain spewed endorphins. Adrenal glands pumped at full capacity.

* * *

Hai shoved another bowl full of water in Lan's cage, then stood and sauntered in front of Jeffrey. He wished he had brought more becs. Jeffrey's lips distended like a Japanese puffer fish, his cheeks like balloons. Hai splashed water in his face. Then he withdrew his knife and cut away the net covering Jeffrey's mouth.

He cut off Jeffrey's left ear and stuffed it in his mouth.

"Chew that you American son of a bitch."

Hai returned to the cage.

"You cannot hurt me anymore, Mr. Hai. I have made peace with Buddha. I am prepared to die."

Hai poked the cattle prod through the cage and nailed the stinger on the bottom of Lan's barefoot.

"Aieeee!"

"Cannot hurt you? I believe I can, yes? Your Kannon will come? If so, both of you will die deaths worse than Jeffrey."

The ache in his loins gnawed his gut. He wanted this woman. How cruel to be deprived of the use of man's most important tool.

"Like your brother, you are a traitor. You betrayed the revolution. And giving yourself to a filthy American is the ultimate betrayal. Letting his sperm swim inside you is disgusting."

He spat on her.

"Chẩn was the patriot." She spat back. "You would not recognize this, evil one. The afterworld will instruct you."

"The afterworld! How you deceive yourself. There is no Buddha. There is no God. Money and power rule. They always have. They always will."

He jabbed at her with the prod again, but she warded off the blow. "I have broken braver women." He turned to Jeffrey.

"Captain. How is your ear? Next, I cut off your member and put it in your mouth. Then I stick you, American motherfucker. I stick nails in your head. You do not feel so good, I think. You die in this Việt Nam hell pit. You like what I have planned, yes?"

* * *

Beneath palm and bamboo bending in the wind, Thanh and Kannon broke into an easy lope. Thinking of Chấn, the Deer Walker, imbued his spirit. A hundred meters, two hundred meters, three hundred.

"Two kilometers to go," Thanh said.

Five hundred meters farther, Kannon's legs tightened up. Muscles contracting, he went to all fours and hobbled forward like a hog-tied calf. His arms knotted, and he crashed to the ground.

Thanh stopped. "What is wrong?"

"Body's cramping."

"Are you reliving your ambush?" Thanh dabbed water on Kannon's neck. "It took place nearby. The ghosts of the Việt Cộng never depart."

Had his ghosts immobilized him?

Kannon's breath came in ragged clumps. A foggy vision of the disastrous ambush flashed through his mind.

"Maybe . . . or, maybe it's because I'm a tad older now."

"Pinch your lip. Breathe deeply," Thanh said.

Kannon did so. A minute passed, two. He struggled to his feet as if mired in sucking rice paddy muck. If he'd ever needed the Lord's strength, it was now. He prayed for breath to be restored to his lungs and spring to his step.

Kannon dragged his legs forward, stride by stride, moving past his barrier. The wind stilled, and the moon broke free from the clouds to cast a thin glow. With the light came hope, and with hope, freedom. He straightened and ran, ran as Chấn, The Deer Walker.

Seven minutes later, they halted. "Half a kilometer more," Thanh said. He unslung the AK. Kannon heard him click off the safety. They moved forward, slowed the pace to a walk. Thanh stopped again and signaled for the night vision goggles.

"There," he pointed. Thanh's whisper floated the distance like a gentle stream. "Hai's Citroen. The rear entrance is fifty meters away, just inside the oval-shaped hedgerow. He may have posted guards."

Thanh handed Kannon the goggles. He secured the restraining straps around his head and studied the night, locating the edge of the hedgerow, then the Citroen. No sounds. Nothing stirred.

Kannon scanned the field once more. The lenses picked up a glow that swelled as if someone were stoking an ember. He gripped Thanh's arm and pulled him down. Lying on their stomachs, Kannon emulated a man smoking a cigarette, a cardinal sin on guard duty. Luckily, the man had inhaled at the right time.

Was there more than one guard? Yet again, he pierced the mask of night. A few seconds later, he held up one finger and pointed toward the pinhead glow.

Thanh nodded and laid his AK aside. "Wait here." He slipped a blackened knife in his mouth.

Kannon rolled deeper in the shadows, and when he looked up again, Thanh was nowhere in sight.

A sapper if he'd ever seen one.

Five minutes passed. Ten. Twenty. It seemed like forever. Christ, where was Thanh?

He felt the tap on his shoulder at the same instant a hand covered his mouth. Goddamn. He hadn't heard a thing.

"One less Khmer Rouge," Thanh whispered.

They scrambled to their feet. Thanh led him on a crouched run to the cover of the hedgerow. A body lay slumped against a foot-wide stalk of bamboo. The Khmer's head hung grotesquely to one side of his neck.

The cover to the secondary pit lay cast aside. Following Thanh, Kannon found himself entering an underground cavity of undeterminable size. He felt like he was breathing inside an iron lung, except the recirculated malevolent air smelled like a garbage dump.

Mining-shaft cars sat on an auxiliary rail, but to use them would create too much noise. "Five minutes to traverse on hands and knees."

"Let's go."

They crawled forward, Thanh in front with the AK and a red-beamed light attached to his forehead. Utilizing the night vision device to track his partner and keep pace, Kannon followed with the

Chicom pistol shoved in his waistband.

A hot draft poured through the tunnel like the breath from a tubercular-ravaged body. Kannon guided himself by placing his hands on the rails with his knees trailing outside the rims. Five minutes later, his knees felt like raw hamburger meat and the path he crawled, a death corridor to hell.

Fifty-Three

Kannon butted his head against Thanh's hip.

"We are near," the Unknown Warrior whispered. "Just before the opening, an off-loading space has been excavated for a siding. Do you want the honor?"

"I want the honor."

When the tunnel widened, they switched positions. Kannon crouched behind the heavy canvas tarp that separated the tunnel from the underground site he'd infiltrated just two-and-a-half weeks ago. Dull light fringed around the tarp's edges like an eclipse. He peeled aside one corner of the partition and peered into the lantern-lit chamber. The file cabinet used to block the passageway had been pushed aside.

Kannon drew from his waistband the Chinese Type 59 pistol, an adequate weapon for close quarter combat. He moved the safety to the firing position, lifted the canvas, and slipped into the main chamber. Thanh followed.

A tiger cage lay in the middle of the room. Its door was open. Inside it, a crumpled figure lay still.

"Cô Lan, I detect another's presence." The shrill voice wailed through the gloom as if a corpse had spoken. "I believe we have a second visitor, yes? I wonder if it is your Kannon Ballard. I was not sure he would attempt a rescue."

"Of course, your mind works that way, Hai," Lan said, her voice sounding strong despite her circumstances. "You will never understand honor and loyalty."

Hearing her soulful, resonance tone made Kannon want to shout—there is a God!

"Cover me," he whispered to Thanh, before starting forward.

From behind the cage, Hai sprang to his feet. Naked, his body glistened in the lantern light. An ugly smile on his face, he brandished a pistol at Kannon. "Welcome, *Trung-Úy* Ballard. Our Mr. Ling showed you the back way, yes?"

The action caught Kannon off guard. He recovered in an

instant and started to squeeze the trigger.

"He is holding a Cobra," Lan gasped.

Hai raised his other arm. He held the Cobra at the base of its head, the snake's body writhing. Hai's vacant, black eyes drilled into Kannon's, and he felt his core soul being reamed by the devil.

"You will place your weapon on the ground, yes?" Hai repositioned the snake above the cage. All he had to do was drop it through the wire. "Like all Americans who died in the war, your death, too, will be in vain, Mr. Ballard."

Thanh tugged on Kannon's belt.

Kannon knelt to the dirt floor and dropped the Chicom pistol. He remained in the kneeling position.

Thanh propped the black barrel of his AK on Kannon's shoulder. A shot exploded. The muzzle flash almost blinded Kannon, but he saw the snake ripped from Hai's hand.

Hai snarled, rolled to the ground, and fired two rounds. One ripped Kannon's shirt and scorched his flesh.

Hai maneuvered behind the cage, using Lan as a shield.

"Your time has come," Kannon said.

"*Trung-Úy* Ballard, you have a friend behind you, yes? Is it Major Farber? Do you know this coward conspired to kill you?"

"I do. You are two of a kind. But it's not Farber."

"Then who—"

"*Chiến sĩ vô Danh.*" Thanh appeared on Kannon's right.

Hai stood and stared in disbelief. "You? The Unknown Warrior?"

"*Chào*, number two," Thanh said.

Kannon watched them square off. Even in subdued light, he'd never witnessed two pairs of eyes more intense. He stole a quick glance toward Lan. "Are you all right?"

"Better now." As she crawled from the cage, Kannon noticed she too was nude. She staggered behind him and placed her hands on his shoulders.

"Stand back." Kannon found himself transfixed by the butcher and the Warrior.

"You call yourself a patriot?" Hai asked Thanh.

"The war ended long ago, comrade. You failed the

movement. You exploited our people. Worst of all, you butchered my mother and father. And now, you molest my cousin."

"Your cousin? She is nothing but a whore."

Kannon stepped two paces farther away from Thanh for a better angle at Hai.

"You destroy my family no more." Thanh fired.

Hai anticipated and leaped aside. Kannon crouched, pulled the Type 59's trigger and drilled Hai in the right shoulder. Hai reacted to the shoulder wound by firing high, and his rounds thudded into the earthen ceiling.

Quick as a tiger, Hai dove to the floor, rolled toward a storage shelf, and came upright with an AK. He sprayed the cavern with more wild shots.

Kannon and Thanh dropped to a low-crawl and edged forward. Hai released the spent magazine. Unable to get a clear shot, Kannon sprinted the short distance, jumped Hai, and tried to wrestle away the AK. Despite Kannon's bulk, Hai flung him off.

Inserting a full magazine, Hai aimed at Kannon, but before he could fire, Thanh kicked the rifle from his hands. Kannon again lunged and grabbed Hai in a bear hug. Hai shook loose, but Kannon jabbed a quick left and struck his jaw, which reeled him backward.

Then Thanh whipped the butt of his AK against Hai's head and knocked him into a row of shelving. With his good arm, Hai clutched a support beam and pulled himself upright. Blood spurted from the shoulder wound as if his own heart meted out justice.

Thanh leveled his AK. "How can you do this?" Hai's lips quivered.

"Easy." Thanh cut loose a burst of three 7.62mm rounds, which ripped Hai's abdomen, doubling him over and slamming him against the wall. The sharp, staccato retorts of the AK reverberated through the chamber like monsoon thunderclaps.

The thunder stopped.

"Đăng Đạo . . . Đăng Đạo. Kill . . . Farber," Hai muttered.

Clothed now, Lan approached and knelt in front of Hai. "Đăng Đạo?" She wrapped a shirt around Hai's neck and dragged him to the tiger cage. "Tell me of Đăng Đạo."

Hai sneered, avoided her eyes. "Traitor whore."

She slapped his face, then tied the ends of his shirt to the bars. Hai's eyes rolled in agony as he watched his intestines spill. Lan backed away from Hai and snatched the AK from Thanh's grasp. She gave Kannon a knowing look, then turned to Hai.

"No," Kannon said. He laid his hand over the top of the barrel and forced it downwards. Rounds splattered the hard-packed earth, disgorging clumps of dirt like a pneumatic drill.

"Move aside." Kannon aimed his Chicom at Hai's forehead.

"For Sergeant Malcolm and the rest." But before he could squeeze the trigger, a black shape slithered into view.

The Cobra.

It worked its way between Hai's legs and reached his torn abdomen. Blood dripping from its body, the snake coiled, its head flared—poised to strike.

"No. In Buddha's name. Not the serpent."

Kannon remained motionless, as did the others. Except for the hiss of the Cobra, quiet prevailed. It seemed the cavern demanded a surreal reverence.

"If you have any decency, speak of my nephew," Lan said, breaking the silence.

Hai raised his eyes from the Cobra's and locked on Lan's. The harshness drained from his face. "Đăng Đạo—"

The Cobra struck Hai below his left eye. He screamed as his nerve endings began shutting down.

"Let me die . . . a bullet . . . not the serpent's venom."

Kannon hesitated a moment, then fired a round into the Cobra's head. The shot pierced the snake and tore into Hai's heart.

No longer would that malevolent being work evil.

A smoky haze filled the cavern. As if shocked by his own action, Kannon stepped back. Despite who Hai had been, seeing another man die didn't feel good. It never had. It was like destroying a part of his own soul. Each one of us was in all of us.

Thanh retrieved his weapon from Lan, shouldered the AK, and nudged Hai's body with his foot. "I should have killed him a long time ago."

The gunpowder-charged fog began to drift into the tunnel.

"He's on his way to hell," Kannon said.

Lan shuffled to Kannon. She stood in front of him and, with eyes cast downward, said, "He tried to shame me."

"He didn't?"

"Hai was a eunuch."

It figured, Kannon thought, feeling much relieved no poisonous sperm swam in Lan's body. "Hai's existence shamed mankind."

"Never again," she said.

Kannon took her in his arms and held her close, feeling her quake like a terrified child. They breathed into each other, finding comfort. "Here, you need this." He handed her a bottle of water, then turned to Thanh. "How can I ever thank you?"

A gurgling noise reverberated within the cavern.

"What the hell is that?" Kannon asked. He turned and saw an appalling sight against the back wall. A grotesque form, like someone cramped with diarrhea, sat hunched in a contorted position and appeared to be hovering in space.

"It is Captain Jeffrey," Lan said.

"Jeffrey!" Kannon hadn't expected to find him here.

"We are not free yet," Thanh said. "We must destroy the cache, withdraw, and evade." He looked at Jeffrey. "What of this man?"

Kannon pulled away from Lan and looked at Jeffrey, who had a wide, maniacal grin on his face. "Let's help him."

Gently, Kannon grabbed Jeffrey under his armpits and lifted him off the stake while Thanh cut the ropes which bound his arms to engineer stakes. Jeffrey collapsed on the floor in a heap.

"Can you hear me? This is Kannon Ballard. It's over. We're gonna get you out of here."

Jeffrey blanched, his frozen grin unable to conceal the terrible pain etched in his eyes. His tongue flicked between cracked lips like a serpent's. "Su . . . su . . . sor . . . ry."

Despite what happened, Kannon couldn't hate Jeffrey. "Lan, Hai kept a suitcase buried near the desk. Maybe there are some clothes we can put on him."

Lan rummaged around. "I do not see any suitcase."

"Let me see," Kannon said.

Together, he and Thanh left Jeffrey and went to assist Lan.

"Eh eh eh eh eh eh eh. Ahai ahai ahai." All three turned toward Jeffrey. He sounded like his brain had been fried. Then he shrieked the madman's laugh, a banshee wail that rocked the walls of Hai's tomb.

Kannon shook his head. "I can't leave him here. No matter what he did. He's still an American."

Suddenly, Leonard Jeffrey leaped to his feet and bolted through the tunnel that led to the primary opening.

"Jeffrey. Wait!" How could a half-dead, crazy man move that fast? Kannon started after him.

Thanh grabbed his arm. "No. Remember the traps."

Several seconds passed. "Aieeee . . ."

The blood-curdling scream froze them.

"He found one," Kannon said.

Thanh located the night goggles. "Follow me." He led them into the tunnel and stopped at the spring-operated knife trap. "It activates when approached from the other direction." He disarmed it.

Above ground, the cooling night air washed their skin. Cautiously, Kannon and Lan trailed Thanh along the same booby-trapped trail Kannon had traversed before. They reached the edge of an elongated hole and knelt.

"The goggles," Kannon said. Thanh handed them over. He put 'em on. There the former captain lay, his body impaled on the spindle fulcrum booby trap that had almost taken Kannon's own life.

Jeffrey's lips moved as if trying to speak. Blood trickled from his mouth.

"Farber . . . Farber knew about the attack. He arranged with Hai for the ambush—" A hacking cough interrupted him, then he spoke no more.

"Leave him. There is nothing we can do." Kannon shook his head, then felt a warm hand caress his neck. He rose and faced Lan. She slumped against him, burying her face in his chest.

"It is not over," she said. "I do not understand Hai's words, 'Đăng Đạo, kill Farber.'" Her voice was soft but full of pain.

Fifty-Four

Underground, Kannon kicked the dead Cobra away and searched Hai's pockets. Sticky blood, which had fueled the dead Việt Cộng's malignancy, nauseated him.

"Found his keys. We should take the Citroen instead of loading the motorcycle with three riders."

"You will abandon your motorcycle?" Thanh asked while examining the weapons cache.

"It's served its purpose." Kannon noticed Lan had walked to Hai's body. He commented to Thanh, "In spite of what Lan said, I'm worried what Hai did to her. Is she really all right?"

"Live now," Thanh said. "She is present, and that is all you need to know."

"Buddhism," Kannon said.

"Buddhism," Thanh repeated.

Lan returned.

"Are you ready to get out of here?" Kannon asked.

She raised the water bottle to her mouth and drained it. "I am."

To Kannon, her words sounded strong, but her body spoke otherwise. Still, they needed to act fast. If she could move on her own, great.

Kannon left the main chamber and entered the rail tunnel. After maneuvering two mining cars from the siding onto the primary rail, he linked them. Thanh followed and loaded three Chicom pistols and two AK47s with full magazines into the second car.

"Why the weapons?" Lan asked, trailing behind.

"Precautionary," Thanh said, "until we clear the area."

Kannon offered to assist her in climbing into the forward car, but she waved him aside. "I will manage it." She clambered in on her own.

"Let's destroy the damn place," Kannon said.

"With Hai in it," added Thanh.

"I'm no explosives expert," Kannon said as he headed

toward the ordnance cavity. "What do you suggest? White phosphorus?"

"C-4, detonating cord, non-electric blasting caps, timed fuses, tape, and fuse igniters should do the trick." Thanh began gathering the components.

Kannon remembered the C-4, a soft textured plastic explosive that was malleable. Enterprising soldiers often cut off slices and lit them to heat up C-Rations.

Thanh crimped a blasting cap to one end of the detonating cord, attached a time fuse and igniter to the other end, then bored a hole into two blocks of C-4.

"Hand me two white phosphorus grenades," Thanh said.

Kannon did. Thanh taped the grenades to the blocks of C-4, then plugged the end of the detonating cord with the blasting cap into the hole bored into the C-4. They walked into the opium den and placed the explosive on the second shelf, middle row.

"How long are the time fuses?"

"Two feet. Should give us about two minutes," Thanh said.

"Is that long enough?"

"Rails and the pulley system . . . yes."

I hope so. That's kind of important.

"We need two more charges," Thanh said.

"Roger." Kannon began shaping another charge. When finished, he entered the weapons room and placed the explosive in a strategic location. He exited into the main room, where he encountered Thanh just as he was leaving the inventory room.

"It seems a shame to destroy the cameras and stereos," Kannon said.

Thanh cast a funny look in the yellow light. "You can stay and smuggle them out if you want."

Kannon laughed, a nervous one at that.

They discussed procedures: Thanh to activate the fuse igniters in the opium den and the inventory room while Kannon did the same in the weapons area.

He and Thanh rehearsed three times, including hurrying to the escape tunnel, where Lan waited patiently in the forward rail car.

"The next one's for real," Kannon said. He took a deep

breath to compose himself. "Ready?"

"Ready," Thanh said.

Each walked to his respective room's entrance—Thanh at the opium den first.

"Go!" Thanh said.

His chest heaving hard, Kannon scrambled to his device and activated the fuse igniter, ensured the fuse was burning, then ran like a scared rabbit and jumped into the mining car beside Lan. Thanh followed seconds later.

It was tight, with Lan squeezed into the middle.

"Pull."

Both men grabbed the overhead rope and pumped their arms like pistons. Soon, the mining cars clacked on the rails like manual typewriter keys clacking on a carriage. The pair pulled themselves along the narrow twin rails until reaching the staging chamber.

"Help me with the weapons," Lan said.

They rose out of the ground like specters from a crypt. The air breathed fresh and invigorating, then . . .

Kaboom! Kaboom! Kaboom!

The smell of gunpowder seeped from the underground. Kannon felt as giddy as if he'd blown up Farber as well as obliterated his thirty-two-year link to shame.

Secondary explosions shattered any calm left in Hiệp Hòa District and thundered through hidden tunnel vents like an approaching storm. Sheets of flame penetrated those same vents as if shot from howitzers, and Kannon felt a good chunk of his Việt Nam-connected guilt burn as well.

Kannon cast a hard look at Lan. The color of her skin was as sallow as the moonlight. Her clothes hung like drooping willow leaves. Mud and blood caked her tangled, knotted hair.

"We've got to get some food in you," Kannon said. "Have a doctor check you out."

"I will be fine. The wicked one is gone."

Kannon nodded, but his exhilaration evaporated like a hailstone in hell because Farber's specter remained. Shaking off the distraction, he decided to conceal the Khmer Rouge's body. Except he couldn't find it.

"Where the hell's the dead guard?"

"We have a bigger problem." Thanh unslung his AK.

"What's the matter?"

Thanh pointed to the car.

"Goddamn! The tires are flat . . . the Khmer again," Kannon said.

Thanh nodded.

"How far is the motorcycle?" Lan sat on the ground.

"Two, three kilometers." Kannon considered the idea. "Risky."

"Too dangerous," Thanh said. "The explosions probably attracted the Khmer to the main site. They could be waiting for us."

Kannon shuddered. Being ambushed again held no appeal.

"The river?" Kannon asked.

"The river," Thanh said.

"Perhaps the Cambodians have run away," Lan said. "We should stay and explain to the authorities what happened."

"We wouldn't stand a chance," Kannon said. "Drugs. Weapons. Bodies. The fire won't destroy all the traces. Likely we'd all be accused of murder as well as smuggling. We've got to go."

"No. Kannon, you go to the motorcycle and wait. These are our people. They will listen to us."

"Lan, they won't listen to you. They'll throw you in jail."

"I agree." Thanh turned to Kannon. "She is not thinking well."

"I feel like I died in that pit," Lan said, her lips quivering. "I am ashamed."

Post, combat-high letdown, Kannon realized. Her bravado, elation, and the burst of energy from being freed had died as the wind snuffs out candles.

"Lan, you have nothing to be ashamed of." Kannon dropped to his knees and took her hand. "Maybe this is not the time and place. But . . . I love you. I want us to spend the rest of our lives together. But we've got to leave here. Now!"

She looked into his eyes. "I cannot walk."

"I'll carry you." Kannon lifted her on his shoulder. He pocketed one Chicom and slung an AK over his other shoulder.

Thanh grabbed the remaining two Chicoms and stuffed them in his waistband.

"Lead the way," Kannon said to Thanh.

Unknown no longer, the Warrior started off, carrying his AK at the port arms position. They departed the hedgerow, the smell of gunpowder wafting through the palm and bamboo like a venomous cloud.

Fifty-Five

"If I remember correctly," Kannon said, Lan still draped across his shoulder, "the river's four kilometers west."

"It is an old Việt Cộng staging area," Thanh said. "Fugitive Khmer Rouge guerillas use it now. We must be careful."

"Let's head south and loop around it." All they needed was to run into more conflict.

Thanh shook his head and continued in the same direction. "Sampans."

Kannon was too tired to argue, too tired to travel far on foot. "Okay," he muttered.

Picking their way over dikes, across shallow canals, and through thick hedgerows, they avoided trails and trudged forward. The moon waxed full, which bode good and bad—easier to see but easier to be seen. After one kilometer, Lan no longer felt light. She had become heavy, heavy as if the dead weight of Sergeant Malcolm would forever stake its claim on Kannon.

Lan stirred, squirmed. "Set me down."

Thank God.

"Water," she said, flashing a weak smile.

Kannon accepted another bottle from Thanh. It was their last. He unscrewed the cap and offered the water to Lan, who tipped the spout to her blistered lips and swallowed hard. Then Kannon took several sips. When he finished, Thanh drank as well.

Lan pinched Kannon on the cheek. "A water buffalo is more graceful than you."

"I'll work on my gait."

Thanh uttered a throaty chuckle, then raised a finger to his lips. A cart trundled by not twenty meters to their left. Cackling, high-pitched voices cracked the still air. Secondary explosions still rocked Hai's chamber, and Kannon hoped those sounds occupied the villagers' focus.

Once they had passed, Kannon whispered to Thanh, "What were they saying?"

"A man called police on a cellphone."

"Shit."

"They send a helicopter."

"Helicopter!" A dreaded feeling draped over Kannon. "Lan, can you walk?"

"I can."

"We've come too far to stop now," Kannon said. "Besides, we'll hear the chopper first and can evade it."

As long as it's not equipped with an infrared tracking device and isn't an armed hunter-killer Cobra team.

"'The woods are lovely, dark, and deep, but I have promises to keep,'" Thanh said.

"'And miles to go before I sleep,'" Lan whispered.

Kannon stared at the Warrior. "Where in the hell did you learn Robert Frost?"

"Lan has been teaching me."

"Then let's cover the distance," Kannon said.

The three stalked through the brush like poachers, only they were the hunted. Like all rice country, intermittent hedgerows broke the flow of fields, but it was impossible to reach the river without risking detection in the open.

"Here's what we do," Thanh said. "Creep to a paddy dike, listen for the absence of sound, wait until a cloud covers the moon, then race across the field."

"Thank God for the dry season," Kannon said once they reached cover again. "Lan, how're you holding up?"

"I feel new life," she said. "I feel like I am perspiring away Hai's viciousness."

"Come," Thanh said. "The river is less than three hundred meters away."

Kannon heard it first. "Get down."

A chopper screamed around the bend, flying low enough that Kannon could almost reach up and touch the undercarriage. The staccato chop of thumping rotor blades—whomp, whomp, whomp, whomp—sent goosebumps down his spine. They flattened themselves against the deafening sound and blade backwash.

Kannon gawked at the chopper silhouetted in the night sky.

"Jesus Christ, it looks like an AH-1G Cobra."

A searchlight erratically swept the ground, stabbing and jabbing like a dislodged lighthouse beacon. The angry bird hovered, then darted like a hawk. The pilot brought the gunship to a careening halt like a hockey stop.

A rocket erupted above their heads and thudded in the brush, its hot breath pouring out like a dragon's and toppling a towering palm some distance ahead. Another flurry of 2.75-inch rockets erupted from their pods and screamed through the air, pummeling the ground.

"What are they shooting at?" Lan asked, a look of horror in her eyes.

"I think the Republic of Việt Nam has just lost one wooden buffalo cart," Thanh said.

In the distance, angry shouts in both Khmer and Vietnamese failed to quell the pilot's lust. He raised the bird's nose and directed the Cobra toward the hapless victims.

Then a horde of angry bees masticated the tangled brush not more than twenty meters ahead. Lan hopped on top of Kannon, giggling from fear-induced hysteria. There was no need to ask why. Combat elicited strange reactions for the uninitiated.

"That was a 7.62mm mini-gun," Kannon said. If they continued to sweep the area, he worried, they were done for. Briefly, Kannon considered firing back with the AK but discarded the notion as suicidal. If he brought the chopper down, would that be murder or an act of war? Was there a difference?

"The mini-guns terrified the Việt Cộng," Thanh said. "If the Việt Cộng had had gunships, you Americans would have been driven out of the country long before your people gave up."

Kannon stared at Thanh but didn't respond. What could he say? They lay transfixed, watched in awe as the door gunner sprayed the lethal barrage.

Lan said disgustedly, "Men are idiots."

The firing ceased.

"What were the Vietnamese shouting?" Kannon asked, although he had a good idea.

"Not to fire at them," Thanh said. "Lan is right. We are

idiots. We just killed more of our own people."

A police or military maneuver? Kannon wasn't sure which concerned him more. Whoever it was, they were trigger happy. "I hope they don't deploy ground troops." He watched as the pilot leveled the Cobra gunship's nose, then gain altitude and speed away to the east.

"Probably out of fuel," Thanh said.

"Or ammunition." Somewhat to his embarrassment and shame, Kannon found himself exhilarated by the action. "Ready? Let's hit the river."

Ten minutes passed. Kannon, Thanh, and Lan found themselves at the river's edge. The water, ill-lit because of the shrouded moon, rippled like a black curtain in the breeze.

Lan hugged Kannon's waist. "Ready for a swim?"

"I wish we'd found a posted schedule showing the next pleasure boat due in five minutes," Kannon said.

"It is too dark to search for sampans," Thanh said. "We should camp and get some sleep. Start at first light."

"I'm worried we'll be stopped and searched on the river," Kannon said.

"We will have to abandon weapons and take our chances," Thanh said. "And, you must hide in the boat."

Great, Kannon thought, another steam bath.

"Thanh, hand me your knife," Lan said. "I will cut palm fronds and prepare a shelter."

"Good idea," Thanh said. "Clear space under those bamboo trees."

"Wish we had diesel fuel," Kannon said.

Lan sliced off a palm branch and handed it to Kannon. "What for?"

"Spread it around the perimeter to discourage snakes."

Thirty minutes later, they roosted. They lay on inch-thick palm branches, more than enough cushion for their exhausted physical state, under overhanging bamboo twenty meters from the river.

"I am going to bathe," Lan said.

"Me also," added Thanh.

Fifty-Six

Dawn broke sluggishly as if the sun itself had trouble mustering the will to rise above the eastern horizon, mirroring Kannon's fatigued state. He stood, stretched, and rousted Lan.

"An old fishing trail follows the river," Thanh said.

He must have risen early and scouted the area, Kannon figured. Or else it was an old Việt Cộng route, and Thanh knew about it already.

Kannon remembered how early in the war, farmers had been resettled from their home-based hamlets to isolate and protect them from the Việt Cộng. It backfired. Not only wasn't it home, but communist cadre infiltrated the new settlements and harassed them for rice and taxes anyway.

Lan furrowed her brow. "My brother might have been here."

"Your brother was here," Thanh said. "Come, we must go."

They started off, with Thanh in front, Lan in the middle, and Kannon taking the rear. The narrow trail rounded at its crown, and in isolated patches, river water spilled beyond the bank and created a slick patina. Kannon slipped off the trail just as he had during the war.

Shortly, the sun overcame its lethargic onset and crested above the treetops.

The trail took a sharp bend, and again the river's edge clipped the narrow footpath. Lan tripped on an exposed root and fell into a shoal. Kannon couldn't help himself and chuckled. She sat there, just as if she were waiting to be served on an afternoon picnic, only she wasn't smiling. Her glare penetrated him like shrapnel.

Kannon extended his hands to help her out. She grasped them firmly, and then with a lightning move, pulled him to her while using her bent knees for leverage and threw Kannon over her head into the river.

Only Kannon didn't hit bottom. A poor swimmer, he flailed at the murky water and paddled to the bank. Lan, who hadn't uttered a word, stood on the trail with hands on her hips.

"You two make a great couple," Thanh said.

After hiking another kilometer, they encountered a dense row of bamboo obscuring the trail. Fearful of untended booby traps or unexploded ordinance left from the war, they explored cautiously. Thanh cut through a long stalk of bamboo and sliced off meddlesome branches, then handed the knife to Kannon.

He probed, not only the brush but also his mind. This woman was at least his equal, if not more.

Kannon raked through the brush and discovered a narrow canal emptying into the river. His gaze swept the open area and settled on freshly cut bamboo branches floating in the artery. Startled, he realized what they covered.

"Camouflaged sampans." He pointed them out to Thanh and Lan. Excited, all three eased into the canal and waded to the dugouts.

"Do these remain from the war?" Lan asked.

Kannon considered this a moment. "No. I think Hai and his henchmen used these boats to transport contraband across the river. I bet on the other side there's a trail or road leading straight into Cambodia."

"Thanh?"

"You are correct," he said.

Then Thanh submerged. What the hell was he doing?

"Yaaaaa . . ."

"Jesus Christ!" Kannon found himself looking into the business end of an AK47 protruding from the closest sampan. He whipped out his Chicom, and the two of them faced off, staring each other down.

A Cambodian. Short and stocky, his bull chest heaving like a blacksmith's bellows, the dark, longhaired Cambodian wrapped his finger on the deadly trigger. In horror, Kannon saw the finger contract as it exerted trigger pressure. His life was over, Kannon thought, but the weapon didn't fire. Apparently, they had surprised a sleeping guard who didn't have the presence of mind to flip off the safety.

Not wanting to kill again, Kannon flung his pistol aside. He leaped forward and wrestled with the Cambodian, trying to dislodge the weapon. As they thrashed in the water, Kannon was pulled under. The Cambodian mustered the strength to land a blow in Kannon's mid-section with the butt of the AK. As his breath went out of him, foul river water flooded Kannon's lungs.

Desperate, he grabbed onto the Cambodian's legs, who now stood upright in the canal. As Kannon pulled himself up, he heard a shot and looked at his body to see where he had been hit. He felt no pain, saw no holes.

Not a bad way to die.

The Cambodian stood like a statue, his hands reaching skyward. Kannon turned to see Lan standing in chest-deep water, her Chicom leveled at the Cambodian's heart. She spoke in a language Kannon didn't recognize, but the warning shot had served its purpose. Before either Lan or Kannon could react, the Cambodian dove into the river and never resurfaced.

As Kannon stood, gasping for breath, he rasped out a muddy thank you.

"Are you all right?" Lan asked.

"Yeah, I'm okay," he said, feeling humbled, as he marveled at Lan's transformation. "Let's pick a sampan and get out of here."

Just then, Thanh surfaced.

"Where'd you go?"

"Searching for underwater mines," he said.

"Christ. How long can you hold your breath? You missed the action."

Thanh looked at both of them in puzzlement. After hearing the story, he smiled. "All warriors," he said.

Five sampans floated in the lapping water, all tethered to a single stout palm. The dugouts were each equipped with a single-cylinder motor attached to one end of a steel rod, longer than a car axle, so boatmen could navigate shallow water and leverage the propeller above suffocating weeds floating near the surface.

Lan clambered aboard the first one and yanked the starter. Nothing. More pulls—same result. Kannon checked the fuel tanks. Empty.

She frowned. "No petrol?"

Kannon shook his head.

"There must be some nearby," Thanh said. "It is probably well hidden."

"Let's find it," Kannon said.

They scrambled from the canal and fanned out.

"Here it is," Thanh announced a few minutes later.

Kannon and Lan joined him.

"Where?" There was nothing but undisturbed brush in Kannon's line of sight.

"Right there." They watched while Thanh spread the brush and uncovered a wooden plank. He ran his fingers around the edges and then lifted the cover. Three Jerry Cans, five-gallon containers with donkey-dick spouts intact, were stacked side by side.

Thanh asked Kannon and Lan wryly, "Ready for a boat cruise?"

"What about the guns?" Lan said.

"Throw them in the river," Thanh said.

They boarded. Thanh piloted the wooden craft south on the Vàm Cỏ Đông. Kannon, still dressed in black, with a cone-shaped hat pulled down on his forehead, sat hunched in the middle between two Jerry Cans. Lan perched in front, holding a fishing pole, its line rippling the water like a zipper.

Kannon surveyed the surroundings. The river flowed broad and remote, their sampan the only intruder. "Thanh, you know this country best. How long will we have to be on the river?"

"Bến Lức is south of Sài Gòn. If the eagle flew true, it is perhaps fifty kilometers. Because of bends in the river, we should add twenty percent."

Sixty kilometers. Thirty-six miles. Like most coastal rivers, the Vàm Cỏ Đông had a tide. Considering its ebb and flow, he estimated an average speed of three knots per hour—roughly twelve hours.

"Once we lose ourselves in river traffic, we will not have to worry as much about detection," Lan said.

"Seems reasonable," Kannon said.

Soon they passed the ancient village of Hiêp Hòa, which looked much the same from his vantage point. In contrast, the adjacent sugar mill appeared modernized. Signs of current construction activity littered the grounds. One thing he'd take to the bank, the French weren't involved this time around.

The steady pitch of the engine had a hypnotic effect, much like the drone of an aircraft prop. The water turned from pearl gray to chalky green in the rising sunlight.

More river traffic skimmed the surface now. Lan withdrew the fishing pole from the water and laid it in the sampan, trickling water on Kannon's shirt as if from a rain shower.

"Are you feeling remorse?" she said, turning to him.

"About what?"

"The deaths."

Kannon shifted his legs. The hot, vaporizing breeze riffled the tangled palm and bamboo and laid tracks on the water.

Jeffrey probably was once a good man who'd gone wrong. And despite who Hai had been, even for the ineluctable encounter with the ill-fated Cambodian, he felt sadness. "The consequences linger forever, no matter how justified the actions may seem."

She gripped his hand.

"How're you feeling?" he asked.

"Hungry."

"We'll eat soon. Thanh, you okay?"

Thanh leveraged the propeller out of the water to clear debris. The engine whined like an out of pitch soprano until he dipped the rotor once more.

"All warriors," Thanh said again, but the frown on his face intimated darker emotions. He pointed downriver. "Look."

Kannon and Lan peered forward. A chopper scorched above the waterline like a hornet searching for prey. Kannon hunkered down, drew a tarpaulin up to his waist, and lowered his head. The chopper buzzed their position as it did other craft on the river, creating mini cyclones every time it hovered. After almost capsizing several crafts, the pilot headed north.

A larger boat came into view. The chopper's stinger? Kannon wondered. The boat close fast. Then its commander slowed the craft and pulled alongside a large sampan fifty meters distant. Random checks were being made.

"Let's get . . ." Kannon left the sentence unfinished as the

353

river patrol boat nosed its bow in their direction.

It was too late to slip over the side. "Cover your face," Lan said. "I will tell them you are my ill father, and we are taking you to a hospital."

But the patrol boat veered off at the last instant and left them rocking in its wake.

"Look, a road," Lan said.

Kannon chucked the tarp and locked in on the smell of nước mắm wafting from the riverbank. Then his eyes settled on a road splitting the mangroves before losing itself among the fields.

"Leads to Đức Hòa village," Thanh said, "but I fear the path will be watched."

"Food," Lan said.

"Okay, cousin."

Ten minutes past the wafer-thin road, Thanh poled into the east bank. A sharp, sweet fragrance impregnated the refuge.

They beached the sampan and camped beneath the tropical foliage. Thanh started a fire while Lan cooked the dried rice supply pilfered from the dead Cambodian. She dished out equal portions of boiled rice. Kannon watched the two work their chopsticks like master weavers while he fumbled as if he were wearing gloves.

It would be dark soon. Kannon stood and stretched. "Is it safer to travel the river by night?"

Thanh finished his meal and wiped his mouth. "I believe so. I am for getting far away as fast as possible." He rose. "You will excuse me?" He vanished into the brush.

"Lan, okay with you?"

She cupped Kannon's hand with both of hers. "I am in favor of it. And once we reach Sài Gòn, we will talk."

His neck muscles cramped up as if an implanted vise grip had squeezed shut. His crafted, self-delusional control fractured, its pieces recoiling like compressed springs in an old watch wound too tight.

"I have an urgent matter in the States to attend to."

She stiffened. "It is true then, the words Hai spoke."

"What'd he say?"

"You have a woman in America."

Kannon was flustered. How had that come about? Crandle or Jeffrey must have told Hai about Meghan. But why? All the trials he'd been through, including facing the amoral Hai, seemed secondary now when compared to what lay ahead. He told Lan about Meghan and why Farber had kidnapped her—why he must return and not only confront Farber but dismantle him.

As he spoke, Lan removed her hands from his. With each admission, she retreated further. Gloom clouded her face. Another monsoon had struck.

"Perhaps it is not a good idea to come to America."

His chest heaved like chaffing tectonic plates.

"Please come. I'll take care of Farber. Together, we'll build a life, search for Đăng Đạo."

Lan narrowed her shoulders as if to concentrate on what she was about to say. "With Hai gone, there is no longer a need to flee the country. It is, after all, my home."

"Are you saying you don't love me?"

"As I have said, I am not sure. We made love, and you saved my life. I am eternally grateful. But I need time . . . to heal."

"We can heal together."

"Is that possible? My sense is one must heal separately before joining with another."

The moon laid a channel down the river, golden but choppy, reached into infinity, went everywhere, went nowhere.

His post-Việt Nam life—a pasting together of erratic, disconnected selves that lacked meaning because each stood alone, waiting to be infused with a magical component to mold the disparate selves into a substantive core—he realized, had been false. He had but to decide whether to face life and live.

And now that he had made the decision to live, Lan was choosing, perhaps, not to be part of it.

"Lan, just as your brother Chấn meant no harm when he asked to see me, consequences occurred. Fallout. The same is true for Meghan and me. When I was involved with Meghan, I was lost. And in finding my way, I jeopardized her being. I have a responsibility to her, as well as myself, but it is you I love."

A lonesome cloud scudded between earth and moon. The

river went placid, and across it, the Plain of Reeds beckoned like a sphinx.

"Fallout," she repeated.

The Tiger

Fifty-Seven

Inside a dilapidated shack northeast of Taos, Đăng Đạo gripped a bottle of Coke and sighed. He stared at his five cigar-smoking men clustered around a rickety table. The wobbly platform supported two lit kerosene lanterns, a street map of Santa Fe, and contiguous U.S. National Forest Service topographical maps encompassing Trampas Peak and Bear Mountain, two crags five kilometers apart, both rising above three thousand meters.

After locating the hooch where the woman Meghan O'Brien was being kept—thanks to Quán's surveillance of the man called Hippo—the team had set about determining the best way to neutralize Farber and make money in the process. To get a feel for the terrain surrounding the hooch, they reconnoitered the route twice, once in his Jeep, and the second time on horseback, using *borrowed* horses. The trail that led to the abandoned hunter's cabin, two kilometers ascending a steep, rocky slope, fed off a remote, four-wheel-drive road. A scraggly creek ran parallel to the trail.

"What is your opinion?" After listening again to the tapes and examining the photographs received from his father late last week, Đăng Đạo wanted his team's feedback.

"This man, Christian Farber, actually helped our fathers during the war," Quán said.

"A traitor to America," Kim added.

But not reason enough to let him live, Đăng Đạo thought, even though national loyalties no longer held the allure they once had. He sipped from his coke, then guided a yellow marker over the U.S. National Forest Service Roads that wove near the two peaks, pausing to see whether five pairs of eyes were focused on the mission. One pair wasn't. The new guy was fumbling with his pistol belt. "Goddamnit, Serentino, pay attention."

"Ah, get off it," Serentino said. "Stop riding my ass."

Đăng Đạo jumped up and sent his chair tumbling. He reached across the table and gripped the lapels of Serentino's jacket. "I will not tolerate defiance."

Quán intervened and took the recruit aside. "Are you on board or not?"

"Yeah. Yeah," the recruit said, bristling.

Glaring at Serentino, Đăng Đạo deemed it imperative to maintain absolute control and discipline over the team, especially Serentino, a disgruntled high school dropout who was not only reckless but recalcitrant, and of different lineage. But his raw intellect, physical prowess, and smoldering rage attracted Đăng Đạo. He thought the youngster trainable, perhaps even to Ninjitsu master.

"We must pay attention to detail," Đăng Đạo said, "and follow my orders." He capped the yellow marker, then shuffled the tapes and photographs into a waterproof pouch.

"Did Mr. Hai ever call back?" Kim asked.

"No." Handling the mission did not concern him. What worried Đăng Đạo was that from an earlier conversation Hai demanded he return to Việt Nam. That was what the second call to his father had been about, and it was not like Hai to ignore him. Regardless, Đăng Đạo did not want to return to his native country. He cast another warning glance at Serentino, then returned his attention to the others. "Regarding Farber, he is not to be trusted under any circumstance."

Đăng Đạo rose and walked to the pot-bellied stove. Opening the miniature iron door, he stoked the fire. Wood smoke escaped through fissures in a corroded pipe venting through the roof. Despite the leak in the pipe, the smell from the pungent Cohiba Lanceros overpowered the aroma of crackling pine.

Dead or alive, it was time to break from Hai. It was, as American officers liked to say, a command decision. Instead of using the thirty-two-year-old tapes and photographs as leverage for a continuing line of revenue from Farber, he would get the funds up front.

"This is my show now," Đăng Đạo said. "Everything takes place here." He jabbed at the highlighted coordinates.

Briefing session over, they moved outside. Beneath boiling clouds, the men drew on their cigars, looking like giant fireflies in a fog. Đăng Đạo reached for his satellite phone. It was time to call Christian Farber.

Fifty-Eight

Monday, 17 February—Kannon attempted to lose himself in the mesmerizing swells of the Pacific Ocean as the commercial aircraft winged its way stateside. Stiff and sore from his physical exploits in Việt Nam, self-hypnosis eluded him. Yet, time and body were of small consequence. His heart ached from gaping holes, Lan's uncertain feelings about him, along with Meghan's disappearance.

New Mexico seemed lifetimes ago, but as the flight time passed, he found himself thinking more of the gentle, trusting woman he'd yanked from her safety nest in Silverton. She was real, genuine, and, most probably, genuinely through with him.

Could he find Meghan? Would Farber deal? If only there were a simple out. But every scenario Kannon developed led to self-recrimination and ridicule, particularly the one in which he envisaged filing charges. He could see Farber laughing so hard he could hardly speak as the judge gestured for armed guards to take Kannon away.

Farber, the man who espoused support and feigned loyalty to all that was right about America, yet, one who flagrantly perverted those ideals to accomplish his own ends to the extent of sacrificing soldiers' lives, epitomized all that was wrong.

The scenario played on Kannon's mind as his father and the bear and Farber all rolled into one.

* * *

The plane settled on the Albuquerque tarmac before noon. Kannon hailed a cab and directed the driver to the BMW motorcycle dealer. There, he reclaimed the R1150GS and repacked his riding gear, digital camera, GPS, and the Nighthawks, for which U.S. Customs gave him more flack than the Vietnamese did.

At 1300 hours, he departed the city east on Interstate 40. Fifteen minutes later, at Tijeras, he turned north on State Highway 14 and twisted the throttle near max until he reached Cerrillos. North of town, he found a secluded spot and dry fired the Sig Sauer

.40-caliber he'd left locked in the saddlebags.

When he rode into Santa Fe, the temperature hovered at forty degrees. A thick, palpable mist hung in the air. Exiting the freeway at Cordova Road, he rode to Old Santa Fe Trail, then wound his way up Canyon Road until he reached the side street flanking The Farber Collection.

Kannon parked the motorcycle beside a scaly juniper bordered by purple sage. He cut off part of a dark t-shirt and taped it over the headlight module, then fitted and taped a black sock over each running light. He crossed the street and entered the coffee house, packing the bulging .40-caliber in a quick release holster fastened to the rear of his belt, hidden by a loose-fitting sweater. His camera hung from his shoulder.

He took a corner table and sat, ordered a coffee, and settled in to wait. Clouds shaded from smoky gray to charcoal and finally lost definition as the western hemisphere rotated beyond the sun's reach. Along the narrow street, gallery lights bled chilled metallic.

Five minutes later, Kannon raised his camera and peered through the zoom lens. Two women exited the gallery, which now seemed empty. Suddenly, Farber, dressed in chinos, powder blue sport shirt, and safari-style jacket, appeared in the showroom. Another man, who stood a foot shorter but twice as wide, joined him. The second man gestured like a flailing orangutan, then exited the front door.

Pungent juniper wafted through the heavy air. Kannon sipped his coffee and stroked his mustache. As far as he knew, Farber had no way of knowing what had transpired in the last few days. The element of surprise weighed in Kannon's favor, except Farber must be wondering why Jeffrey hadn't contacted him.

At 1800 hours, Farber extinguished the gallery lights. Kannon slapped ten bucks on the table and hurdled the ornamental balustrade that separated the coffee house from the street. Within seconds he mounted the GS and fired the electric starter. A minute later, Farber, in his disjointed mountain goat gait, walked around the corner and slipped his large frame into a late model GMC Yukon. Kannon shifted into first gear.

Lead me to Meghan, you son of a bitch.

361

The Yukon's engine roared to life. The SUV lurched forward and scattered gravel in an angry wake as if emulating a thunderous rage swirling within the cockpit. Kannon goosed the throttle to maintain pace. Farber charged east on Canyon Road before hooking a sharp left and crossing a bridge over the Santa Fe River. The two vehicles cruised northwest on Palace Avenue and turned right onto Paseo De Peralta. Kannon's speedometer shot to twenty miles per hour above the posted limit.

Farber turned north on U.S. 285. Kannon pursued at a discreet distance, hopeful Farber wouldn't notice his silhouette. The traffic thinned as he clipped off the miles. Impersonal strip malls gave way to neon-lit gambling casinos and clapboard shacks.

Adrenaline pumped through his body. What if a cop spotted him? Kannon questioned his decision to black out the headlamp and running lights.

At Rural 503, Farber veered east and drove fifteen miles until it merged with State 76. From there, they passed through the villages of Cordova and Trampas. A few minutes later, Farber swerved onto an unpaved road. Kannon followed the SUV's flickering taillights as the road wove through the national forest and filtered from gravel to dirt.

Abruptly, brake lights shimmered through the misty veil. Kannon geared down and steered off the road behind an outcrop. He hit the kill switch. Farber squelched the Yukon's lights.

Kannon stripped off his helmet and reached into the tankbag for the night goggles. Putting them on, he barely caught Farber's image before aspen and fir blocked his line of sight. He dismounted, stuffed an extra loaded magazine into his pocket, and crept up the road until he reached Farber's Yukon.

A rocky trail opened just beyond the SUV's front bumper. Despite the dropping temperature, Kannon perspired. He withdrew his pistol, pulled the slide back to chamber a round, and rode the slide forward to muffle the sound. Then he pressed the decocking lever and set upon the trail, which corkscrewed along a narrow, twisting ridgeline. A stream ran alongside.

In the higher altitude, the mist vanished, and a broad swath of sky opened. Stars blazed like etched crystal. A three-quarter moon crowned a distant mountain peak like a candle before the clouds crowded in again. The terrain appeared spectral-green through the night vision goggles.

The last time he'd traveled a path connected with Farber, an ambush had occurred. Sidestepping a few paces from the trail, Kannon watched and waited. Ten minutes passed, another five, then he plotted a path corresponding to the primary trail. He headed upslope. Every ten paces, he stopped to listen and to catch his breath in the thin air.

On the fifth pause, he heard faint footsteps scuffing among the rocks, but saw no one and couldn't gauge how far away the sound. Kannon waited a few more minutes, then returned to the trail and continued his ascent. He'd find Meghan, free her, and be done with the whole mess.

Around a bend and left of the trail stood an old hunting cabin nestled in a clump of fir near the edge of a cliff. The cabin provided a great place to stash a kidnap victim, while the cliff bottom offered an excellent dump site for a body.

An untold number of abandoned cabins probably dotted the area. No light or sound poured from this one. No outside guard was posted.

Kannon crept to the door and groped for a handle. There was none, a bad sign. He burst in. Except for a worn mattress lying on a wood frame and an old cupboard in a corner, an empty room greeted him. Kannon did a quick search and found rope strips affixed to the bed frame's corner posts. The ropes looked new, yet were frayed as if cut by a dull knife.

Outside, several narrow game trails splintered into dense stands of spruce and fir. Meghan could have been transported along any one of them. Had he just missed her? The find fueled both hope and fear.

Frustrated, Kannon descended the mountain. At one bend in the trail, he saw that his GS was exposed. If Farber had been wearing night goggles, he might've noticed the motorcycle. Well, there was nothing he could do about it now.

Further down, he heard the SUV's engine turn over. The tires plowed through the dirt, then nothing but silence filled the mountain air. Kannon pushed on, but the rugged trail impeded his pace. By the time he reached his cycle, Farber's Yukon was well beyond sight and sound. Worse, along the rutted road, he couldn't tell which tire tracks were fresh.

Kannon removed his night vision goggles and caught his breath. Despite his agitation, he brought out his GPS and keyed in the fixed position, storing it in memory under M1 for Meghan. As a last resort, he'd disclose the location to the authorities, while hoping he hadn't trampled any clues.

Why had Farber driven out here? To move Meghan? It didn't seem to be enough time. For a meeting? If so, the other party was a no-show. To set up Kannon? Hell, the Major didn't know he was back in the States.

Clouds obscured the silver moon, so he unsheathed the motorcycle lights. He grabbed his helmet and fired the cycle to life. Skittish of retracing the entry route, he headed the opposite direction, having no idea where the dirt road led. The sinuous track ascended three miles through a blend of aspens and mixed conifers, and the GS's muffled engine riffled through the night air. The wind washed over his head like water. On any other occasion, this would have been a magical ride.

The dirt grew deeper. He stood on the footpegs for stability. After another couple of miles, the road returned to gravel. Then he heard it, the unmistakable, throaty sound of a powerful twin. And it was closing fast. Only a Harley made that sound, or a Buell.

Either he was being paranoid, or someone was chasing him.

The route now trimmed a ridgeline. There was nowhere to pull over. Kannon accelerated to forty miles an hour, then fifty, the road surface like a washboard. His GS clattered around corners as if it were mounted on studded tires trekking over black ice. A halogen headlight behind him sent its beam angling into the sky like a searchlight, followed by the screech of a piercing air horn. The powerful twin continued to close distance. Whoever it was must be an exceptionally good rider.

The road descended. Kannon rounded a tight curve and nearly caromed off the trunk of a large fir. He wasn't going to outrun this guy. He had to outmaneuver.

Before the next tight bend, he downshifted into second and hugged the outside corner. In a few seconds, the powerful twin thundered behind him. Just before the motorcycle came abreast, Kannon executed a strong countersteer to the left and goosed the throttle, cutting off his challenger. The pursuer's front wheel clipped Kannon's rear one, causing the rider to flip over his motorcycle on the high side.

The riderless motorcycle snaked out of control and crashed against a rock pile. Kannon's bike wobbled, but he was able to maintain balance and bring his cycle to a skidding stop. He whipped the kickstand down, leaped off, and approached with pistol drawn, hammer drawn back.

Helmetless, the thrown rider appeared dazed. Racing clouds allowed the three-quarter moon to squint through. In the pale light, Kannon recognized the guy as the one he'd observed earlier in the gallery. Blood trickled down the fallen man's mangled face. Yet, the guy stirred. He rolled onto his stomach, where he rocked back and forth like a beached whale.

"What's your connection with Farber?" Kannon said.

"Fuck you and the horse you rode in on."

"Get up!"

The man got to his knees, then rose to his feet.

"Where's Meghan O'Brien?"

"In case you don't get my drift, asshole, fuck you."

Kannon fired a round into the dirt. The shot rocked the still night, sending echoes reverberating between the cliffs.

"I know nothin' about no woman. I'm just out for a night ride."

"The next round's going to shatter your thick skull. Back up to that tree," Kannon said, pointing with his Sig to a thick spruce by the side of the road. "Place your arms behind you, around the trunk, and grip your wrists."

The fallen rider limped backward to the tree and wrapped his pudgy but stout arms around its scaly trunk. With the muzzle of his semiautomatic pointed at the man's temple, Kannon patted him down and found a military issue .45-caliber in an inside jacket pocket. He ensured the weapon was on safe before stuffing it in his waistband. The guy carried no wallet, just a lighter and a pack of Camels.

Keeping his eye on him, Kannon hustled to his saddlebags. He fumbled through the contents until finding the duct tape he carried for emergency repairs. After returning to the tree and holstering his Sig, he wrapped tight coils of tape around the man's wrists.

"I'm asking you again," Kannon said, now facing his captive. "Where's the woman?"

The man answered with a smirk and a stony silence. Kannon drew his Sig and fingered the trigger. To kill Hai was one thing, but to pull the trigger now would be cold-blooded murder.

"I ought to strip your ass and smear a Snicker's bar all over your body. A wolf pack might like that."

"There're no wolves around here, dumb ass."

"Want to find out?"

With that, Kannon walked to the fallen man's motorcycle and fired three rounds, one each into the tires and one into the gas tank.

"Hey, man. I could freeze out here."

Kannon flicked the man's lighter and lit a Camel. He puffed once before tossing the cigarette into the pooling gasoline, setting the burly twin-engine cycle on fire. "I'll tell your boss you're MIA," he said over his shoulder as he mounted the GS.

A stream of curse words trailed Kannon's departure.

The sky clouded over. When he reached the outskirts of Santa Fe, billowing thunderheads roiled over the Sangre de Cristo Mountains north and east of the city. He rode into a waterfall pouring from the sky.

Soaked to the skin, Kannon navigated through the slick streets of Santa Fe. A chill gripped the city, wrapped it in a brooding bundle of a metallic sky and a blustery wind. The normal, bustling foot traffic in this touristy town slept. Steel security shutters were drawn across storefronts. Streetlamps cast a gloomy glow over a deserted Plaza that resembled a ghost town. St. Francis Cathedral appeared as a dungeon in medieval times.

A temperature sign read forty-five degrees, but Kannon

figured the wind chill factor dropped it by at least twenty. Body heat gone, he shivered as he threaded his way through the inner-city maze en route to Paseo de Peralta and, ultimately, to the amalgam of galleries and craft shops on Canyon Road.

Kannon pulled up on the same side street as he had done two months before and killed the GS's engine. He dismounted and walked the short distance to The Farber Collection. The door was locked. He kicked in the glass, which signaled an alarm. He stepped into the interior, leaving wet, muddy footprints as evidence of his intrusion.

A quick search of the gallery yielded no Farber, no clues to Meghan's location. Computer access was protected by a password. Frustrated, he caved in the screen with the butt of his pistol.

The wailing police siren sounded above the howling winds as Kannon stepped outside. Wind and rain peppered his face. He jogged to his motorcycle, started it, and shifted into first gear. The GS trailed a wake through pooling waters as he rounded the corner just as a police cruiser turned onto Canyon Road.

It was time to make a house call.

Fifty-Nine

"There's no answer, sir," the overseas operator said.

Farber slapped his cellphone down on the kitchen counter. Goddamnit! Where the hell was Jeffrey? Nothing was going right. Even his trump card, Meghan O'Brien, seemed worthless.

"What's the matter?" Buck naked, Jasmine was feeding crushed ice and margarita mix into the blender. She turned it on.

He was in no mood.

The landline rang.

"Check the caller ID," Farber said.

Jasmine answered anyway. "It's for you."

He snatched the cordless from her hands. "Yeah?"

"Where's my husband?"

"Bertha, I told you before, I haven't heard from Jeffrey. I don't know where he is."

"You better find out because—"

He hung up. "Jasmine, how many times have I told you to look at the caller ID before answering the damn phone? And turn off the fucking blender."

"Drink this," she said.

He accepted the cocktail with a scowl. "Jeffrey's missing."

"Oh, my," Jasmine said. "AWOL."

"What?"

"Nothing."

Jeffrey might be dead. Not a bad thing, except Farber had no way of knowing the status of Hai or Kannon, either of whom could cause a lot of grief. Yet, it was possible that Hai and Kannon were no longer among the living. If not, the blackmail threat vacated, and he wouldn't need Meghan O'Brien. He'd be in the clear.

The landline rang again. *Blocked.* This time, though, Farber answered. "Hello?"

"Christian Farber, please."

The unfamiliar but obvious Vietnamese accent rattled his nerves. "Who is this?"

"I am Đăng Đạo, Hai's son. I have in my possession copies of certain photographs and tapes that might be of interest."

"I only negotiate with Hai." Farber gulped down the rest of the margarita. Jasmine refilled his glass.

"I am your American connection," Đăng Đạo said.

"That's not the agreement," Farber yelled.

"No need to get excited, Mr. Farber. We are partners. Partners need to get along. There is profit in this for both sides, money for us, peace of mind for you. Just consider that you have a non-cancelable contract, one that lets you live as long as you comply."

"Don't fucking threaten me." How did this Đăng Đạo fucker learn to speak such good English? "Where the hell are you?"

"Close."

"I want those photographs and tapes."

"You shall have them once you consummate your end of the deal."

"Wait one," Farber said.

He set his drink on the coffee table and walked outside. Thunder rumbled like an artillery barrage, and lightning flashed like angry tracer rounds.

Everyone was conspiring against him. "What are your terms?" Farber hoped for leniency compared to Hai's previous demands referenced by Jeffrey.

"Five million American dollars," Đăng Đạo said.

Farber's heart rate accelerated. "I don't have that kind of money." Besides, he'd already committed a hundred grand to Hippo, with another hundred due.

"You will wire five million to my Isle of Man account," the caller said.

"Hai offered terms—"

"There will be no *earn-out*."

"Are you deaf? I can't access that amount of funds."

"Your last chance, Mr. Farber."

"How can I be assured you'll give me what I need . . . that no other copies exist?"

"You have my word."

"Are you shittin' me? A gook's fucking word means nothing."

"You are pissing me off, Mr. Farber. I know where you live, the location of your office, and the coordinates of the hooch where you're keeping the lady. I will be seeing you."

"No. Wait." Farber felt the vice tighten. "When and where?"

"It is zero-three-hundred hours now," Đăng Đạo said. "We will meet at the hooch in twenty-four hours."

"In the mountains?" Farber was incredulous. "Just how am I to wire funds in the middle of the night? There's no Internet or cell service up there."

"You have ample time to prearrange the wire. At the hooch, once you are satisfied with your *merchandise*, you will call by satellite phone to have the funds released."

Farber listened to his final *instructions*.

"I suppose," Farber said, "after you receive confirmation, I'm free to go."

"Correct."

Sixty

If she lived through this, she was going to sue Kannon Ballard's butt for all it was worth. It was the fifth day since Meghan had been moved from her first confinement. "For better accommodations," they'd said. Bullshit. It was to keep anyone from finding her. Upon realizing she'd not mentioned to her friend Elizabeth either Jeffrey's name or the name of the gallery, she began to lose hope. Other than Jeffrey's description, Santa Fe was the only connection Elizabeth could give police—too many galleries, too much territory to search.

She pounded herself with a persistent worry. What if they had taken Elizabeth, or worse, killed her?

Feeling like her heart was shriveling, Meghan flopped on the mattress. Left alone the first three days, she learned a new meaning to the words "cabin fever." Her windowless room, which contained a basin and toilet bowl in one corner and a skimpy mattress on a boarded platform in another, offered security—its one door secured by two deadbolt locks—but no solace.

The nights were cold. She was still barefooted. There was no electricity, and her meals consisted of leftover C-rations. These she opened with a tool the size of a fingernail file. Meghan blanched while suffering their stale taste and metallic smell.

At dawn on the third day, she'd heard the pounding of horses' hooves and became excited. She yelled until hoarse, but the solid walls muffled her screams, and she got no response. And when murmuring voices reached her, the language oozed tangled and foreign, as if spoken in tongues, and she wondered whether she'd been dreaming.

On the fourth day, Sadie had returned, gagged and tied Meghan, then forced her to listen to squeaking bedsprings and grunts of lovemaking coming from the other room. It wasn't until the next morning, after the front door had been slammed shut and silence ensued, that Sadie had come in and untied her.

She prayed for the return of the horsemen.

The clicking sound from an inserted key redirected Meghan's thoughts. She turned toward the door. As it opened, the aroma of chopped beef made her glands salivate.

Sadie entered, leering. "Real food," she said, brandishing a pistol in one hand and a plastic tray in the other.

"About time."

Sadie knelt and set the tray on the floor, slipped a pair of handcuffs from her pocket and tossed them on the bed.

"Secure your left hand to the corner post," Sadie said.

Meghan grabbed the bedpost as she was told and imprisoned herself. Sadie placed the tray on Meghan's lap, touching her breasts as she did so.

Meghan bristled. "Why are you touching me? You got a man, right?"

"Honey, you got no call to be ugly," Sadie said. "I like both."

"Why try to seduce a woman who has no interest in you, or any other woman?"

"I love women who don't want it."

"Then what are you waiting for?" Meghan taunted. If she could distract Sadie, get free, then—

"Hippo told me to wait. Says if I touch you without him, he'll cut me up. But after our contract terminates, you're ours."

Meghan grew nauseous, couldn't stand the idea of being violated by either one. "Farber won't turn me over to you. I know too much. He can't let me live."

"Hippo promised."

"Sadie, get real. Hippo has no power. Farber's going to kill me, you, and Hippo."

"No, he won't. He won't kill my man Hippo."

"Farber is ruthless. He sent his own men to be ambushed and killed in Việt Nam."

"I don't know nothing 'bout 'Nam business."

"Farber's all about control. He wants to eliminate anything that threatens his world. What makes you think he'll be any different this time? Why should he, why would he, keep you alive?"

Meghan knew she had struck a nerve. Sadie's thin,

masculine mouth tightened, her limbs flinched. Perhaps Sadie wasn't too smart, hadn't ever considered that she might be *expendable*.

"You don't know what you're talking about," Sadie said. She handed Meghan the handcuff key, left the room, and clicked in place the two deadbolt door locks. Unfortunately, the thumbturns were on the outside of the door.

* * *

The next morning, Sadie burst into the holding room. Wielding her pistol, she motioned for Meghan to remain seated. No cuffs this time.

"Been reasoning on what you said last night. Maybe you're right about Farber and Hippo. I have a proposition for you."

"Proposition?" Meghan asked, imagining she already knew the answer.

"Go down on me, and I'll set you loose. If not, well, there's Farber and Hippo. But I'll be long gone." Sadie backed toward the door. "You've got a decision to make. I'll be back."

Meghan watched the door close, heard the thumbturns click. Now what? Sacrifice her morals and principles in order to live? If so, could she live with herself afterward? Even if she did *service* Sadie, would the woman turn her loose? Or kill her? She didn't think Sadie was capable of murder, but—

A muffled sound reached her ears. Was someone else there? Pressing her ear to the door, Meghan heard nothing but acknowledging uh-huhs and yes-sirs. Her captor bitch must be talking on a phone or by radio.

"You've lost your reason for being, sweetheart," Sadie said upon reentering the room. "Seems your man Kannon disappeared in Việt Nam."

Meghan cringed. "Is that true?"

Sadie nodded.

A man she'd once cared for and wanted to help heal, but the man who'd gotten her into this mess was gone? She was too numb to feel.

"As I've told you time and again, he's not my man. We broke up, you idiot. What do I have to do to get you to believe me?"

"That doesn't matter. Farber and Hippo are on their way. Be here by nightfall."

Sadie vanished. The day wore on. As Sadie's absence grew longer, Meghan wondered if she'd already been abandoned. Her thoughts ran wild. Kannon's alleged death did little to mitigate her intense anger toward him. Now she was in danger of being raped and losing her life. What had started out as innocuous surveillance of Farber and his gallery had degenerated into something beyond her control.

Footsteps sounded outside her wooden cell. A thin beam of light crawled beneath the door.

"Honey, I'm home," Sadie said.

Her captor entered and immediately started taking off her clothes. One thing rang clear. There was only one person who could save herself. It was Meghan O'Brien.

Sixty-One

Exhausted from the overseas flight and last night's false run, Kannon had slept all day. Now, he felt replenished. As he walked back to his motel after eating, darkness draped over the Sangre de Cristos. Cultivated sage released an intoxicating, aromatic mint beneath a fading full moon.

Inside his room, he retrieved and holstered his semiautomatic. Stuffed the fat man's .45 inside his waistband. A moment later, he was back outside and noticed the absence of the mint smell. Instead, pungent ozone intimated another storm brewing. He looked for the foretelling clouds and saw that they brewed in the west. Mounting his motorcycle, he started it, then cruised toward Farber's residence. Once he reached the sequestered home, Kannon positioned the bike behind a copse of juniper and tossed his helmet and jacket on the ground.

Farber's gate connected to a massive adobe wall, which stood tall and slick and precluded his gaining a foothold. The gate would be easy to climb, providing no electrical charge surged through it. At a minimum, it was likely monitored by a silent alarm. He hesitated a moment. To hell with it. With a gloved hand, he jostled the gate. No sparks flew. He scaled it.

A tree-lined canopy bordered a winding drive, which led to a broad view of Farber's large, well-lit adobe house dominating a hilltop, approximately thirty yards from Kannon's position. The vegetation had been trimmed in a circular pattern like cleared fields of fire in a defensive, military position.

He retreated into the brush and circled to his left. Like a probing advance guard, a gust of wind struck and made dance slender fingers of juniper and piñon pine, then slackened as if to prepare its main force elements for an assault. In the lull, Kannon halted, sensed movement, and knelt to the ground.

The sound of padding feet across gravelly loam, then vicious snarling, broke nature's grip. The howling sounded closer. Kannon spread the foliage, peered through, and saw two Rottweilers charged from either side of the fortress.

"Fang. Snarl. Come back, you fucking idiots." It was Farber. And he sounded exasperated.

The hounds, howling as if someone had stuck hot coals down their throats, ignored their master's call. They closed the gap, saliva drooling from the corners of their mouths as they anticipated a kill.

What the dogs didn't anticipate was Kannon's semiautomatic. He took a shooter's stance, leveled the pistol, and popped off two quick rounds. The dog on the left went down without a whimper. The second, aware he was absent his snarling mate, turned and high-tailed it out of sight.

"Hippo! Is that you?" Farber yelled.

Kannon trotted forward and closed the distance. Surprisingly, Farber stood exposed beneath a flood lamp on the front alcove. He was dressed in jeans and a knit shirt black as coal and didn't appear armed.

"Guess again," Kannon said, slowing his pace. He stopped several feet short of the major.

"You!" Farber swore.

"Good to see you again, too." Kannon held his Sig at waist level. "Step away from the door."

Lips clamped tight, Farber shuffled from the protective alcove.

"Jeffrey and Hai are dead, Farber."

"Too bad you're not. What happened to Jeffrey?"

"You mean after Hai had crammed an entrenching tool handle up Jeffrey's ass? I set him free. But your gofer bolted right into a booby trap pit. You know the kind, body length, and deep. It was ugly."

Farber winced.

"Should've been you," Kannon added.

"So you say."

"You have no remorse, do you?"

"Did nothing wrong," Farber said, scratching his neck.

"Right!" Kannon said. "Aren't you wondering about the fat man?"

Farber shrugged.

"He blew it. I left him hugging a tree."

Lightning flashed. Thunder followed. A light rain began. Despite the coming storm, Kannon felt calm, as if he were the eye in a hurricane.

"Get to the point, Ballard."

"The only leverage you've got left is Meghan. It's time to settle up."

The front door flung open. Kannon glanced at a long-legged, sensuous woman clad in a pink camisole, her mouth agape at the pistol pointed at her husband's heart. She hurried toward them.

Kannon stuck out his left palm. She stopped.

"Christian. What's going on?" the woman asked.

"Get back inside, Jasmine." Farber's eyes never left Kannon.

Raindrops soaked the woman's camisole. Shivering, she folded her arms and stared at Kannon before backing away. "I'm calling the police," she said.

"No! It's a personal matter," Farber said.

She went back inside. Kannon figured her to be an enabler.

"Come in and have a drink," Farber said. "Get out of the rain. Discuss this like gentlemen."

"I think not." Careful not to get boxed in, Kannon moved just beneath the top canopy extending beyond the alcove. He motioned Farber likewise, yet maintained a safe distance.

"You're a fool, Ballard. The moment you hit Việt Nam soil, I knew you were one of those who played by the rules. I'm a born leader. I know how to create power. You're nothing but a pawn."

"Was a pawn," Kannon corrected. "I'm in control now. You're finished."

"Am I?"

"Yeah." Farber was stalling. Why? He had nothing to gain. "You don't give a shit about anybody but yourself."

"Is that right?" Farber steepled his fingers. "If you hadn't stirred up all this shit, Jeffrey would be alive. The Meghan broad would be safe. It seems we operate under a similar code of ethics."

"My code involves eradicating the poison you released thirty-two years ago."

"Bullshit!" Farber said through clenched teeth. "You were

the team leader. It was your responsibility to avoid detection. I should've followed through on the court-martial."

"You didn't because you were afraid the truth would come out. Your biggest mistake was letting Chấn live." If not for his former interpreter—

"An oversight, yes, one that should have been taken care of by Hai."

"You admit it."

"I admit nothing."

"Your lies can't hurt me anymore, Farber. Just because you weren't caught doesn't exonerate you from murder, smuggling, and treason."

"No jury would convict me."

"I convict you." Kannon visualized bringing Lan's cousin, Thanh, the Unknown Warrior, to America to nail the former major from the witness chair. Whether a jury would believe an ex-Việt Cộng was another matter.

"No proof," Farber said.

"Maybe not. But kidnapping Meghan O'Brien was a huge mistake. I've got the fat man. He'll turn on you."

"Assuming I know what you're referring to, which I don't, based upon what you said you did to the guy, I doubt he'll be happy with you."

Kannon rubbed the nape of his neck. An unknown lurked, but he couldn't identify it. Farber looked like a smug poker player who knew he held an ace underneath his sleeve, or worse, acted as if he had nothing to lose.

"Enough chatter," Kannon said. "It's time—"

"What kidnapping? Who's Meghan?" asked an anxious voice emitted through a speaker mounted in the alcove. Apparently, Farber's wife had been listening via the intercom.

"Jasmine, it's none of your damn business," Farber said. He turned to Kannon. "We have a war to fight in the Sangre de Cristo Mountains."

"War?"

"You want the Meghan broad. I want Đăng Đạo, Hai's son."

Kannon pursed his lips. *Đăng Đạo! Chấn's boy.* Were Chấn

alive, he'd be sick to know what had become of his son.

A sickening feeling welled in his gut—Farber intended for all of them to die—him, Meghan, Jasmine, maybe even Farber himself.

"Jasmine! You still there?" Farber smiled at Kannon.

"Yes, dear."

"Let's give our boy here a blow job."

What the fuck?

Rapid splashes over wet ground sounded behind him. Kannon turned just as the surviving Rottweiler lunged, clamping its jagged jaws on Kannon's wrist. The gun went clattering across the concrete in the alcove.

"Snarl. Sit. Good girl." Laughing, Farber picked up Kannon's weapon and also yanked the fat man's .45 from his waistband. "Blow job is Jasmine's cue to blow a dog whistle, you fucking retard."

Blood oozed from Kannon's right wrist. But it was facing the muzzle of his own .40-cal that really bothered him.

"Kindly turn around and put your arms behind you."

Dazzling images flashed as his head absorbed the blow.

"That's for killing my fucking dog."

Sixty-Two

The thunderstorm renewed its assault on Bear Mountain. Harsh as the storm was, Đăng Đạo considered it appropriate nature chose this day to deliver it, perfect weather conditions for his own assault.

At 0200 hours, he gathered his squad together for a final briefing. They had slipped and slid their way over the muddy road and parked their Jeep a kilometer away. From there, they hustled to the creek and huddled a hundred yards from the cabin, where light seeped through a front window.

"Weapons check," Đăng Đạo said. The team stood at attention while he inspected his troops: white phosphorus and colored smoke grenades secured to web gear, tonfas slung over their shoulders, throwing stars tucked in accessible pouches. All carried sidearms, plastic-framed Glock 20s, which fired 10mm rounds.

Due to the weather and adverse terrain, he had decided to leave the two lightweight but short-range PRC-126 radios in the Jeep. They would use whistles instead.

A satphone wrapped in protective plastic was nested inside his jacket pocket. Quán carried the waterproof pouch containing the tapes and photographs.

"Listen up," he said. "You four will assume the nine, eleven, one, and three o'clock positions, respectively, at twenty-five meters, leaving the six o'clock position open for Farber to approach the cabin. He is due to rendezvous in one hour."

"Is the large man inside?" one of the team asked.

"He spends his nights elsewhere," Đăng Đạo said.

"The hot white woman," Serentino grabbed his crotch, "I want her."

"That will not happen." Đăng Đạo decided this would be Serentino's final mission. "Such an act destroys unit discipline and integrity."

Quán, his second-in-command, grasped Serentino's collar and yanked him aside. "Do not fuck this up."

The recalcitrant gang member glowered as he wrested free.

"I will man the trailhead to wait on Farber," Đăng Đạo said, with an eye on Serentino, "and will guide him to the cabin."

"It is there we will make the exchange," Đăng Đạo added. "Questions?"

"What if this Farber shit doesn't have the money?" Kim asked.

"We will feast on grilled Christian Farber," Đăng Đạo said.

"If Farber is accompanied by others?" another team member asked.

"I will assess the situation and use our standard whistle drill to move you into the proper formation."

"What if the man does not come at all?"

"He will come," Đăng Đạo said. "As a last resort, we will use the following call signs."

"Lửa." (Fire.)

"Nước." (Water.)

"Everyone got that?" Quán asked.

* * *

Serentino slipped away to relieve himself. While emptying his piss, he stared at the cabin. The window light went out.

Who the fuck did Đăng Đạo and those other dinks think he was? It wasn't fair for them to deny him this woman prize.

The black sky covered his approach as he covered the remaining distance to the cabin. He'd get inside, have his way with the woman, and then disappear.

* * *

"We have to leave," Sadie said. "Farber and Hippo will be here at any moment."

Meghan nodded. Untied but not yet free, she eyed the doorway to freedom from this, her third cell of imprisonment, this one with electricity. She placed her hand on the doorknob. It turned, but not of her doing. She put a finger to her lips. "Someone's outside," she whispered.

"Hippo?" Sadie looked alarmed.

Meghan shrugged.

She and Sadie slunk away. In so doing, Meghan displaced a

ragged Native American rug covering the center of the room. "What's this?"

"Looks like a trap door," Sadie said.

"Come on, help me lift it," Meghan said.

Sadie didn't. Just stood there, holding her pistol.

"Sadie."

But Sadie ignored her. Meghan watched in disbelief as she fired a round through the door.

"Goddamned bitches." The handle shattered as several rounds ripped it from outside. The door burst open. A dark figure holding his arm in obvious pain blocked their exit.

"Move, and you die," Sadie said, exerting trigger pressure for another shot.

Loud retorts sounded from outside. The window glass shattered, distracting Sadie. The intruder kicked the gun from Sadie's hand.

Meghan clawed at the trap door. Blood flowed from torn nails and splintered fingers.

Sadie pounced on the man and wrenched him to the floor. They rolled on the floor like alligators flipping and disorienting their victims.

Meghan edged forward on her butt toward the front door and tried to stand, but the intruder kicked her left ankle and cut her feet from under her. She crawled to Sadie's bunk. Using it for support, she gained her footing and switched on the light.

"Where's the pistol?" she yelled, as Sadie and the man continued grappling on the floor. The man cursed when Sadie clamped one hand on his wounded arm.

An egg-shaped missile crashed through the window. Meghan froze. The lethal canister spun on the floor like a whirling top, then wobbled to a stop. She covered her face and anticipated the explosion that would end her life. Instead, it popped, and purple smoke poured forth.

But now the man stood over Sadie, wielding a club and preparing to strike. Then an explosion sounded from outside the front door and knocked him off his feet.

Sadie blew past him and charged into the forest. Meghan

struggled to catch up. When she did, she found Sadie bearing a haunted expression and huddling beneath a cluster of fallen pine bough.

Obviously, several men were involved. From her vantage point, Meghan witnessed the wood shack being pummeled by incendiary grenades.

Fire dragons.

The rain turned into hail. Meghan, dressed in jeans and a thin cotton pullover, her bare feet again bloodied by rocks, shivered in the cold. Icy pellets streaked through the tree cover and smacked her body.

Sadie, wearing only a long-sleeved shirt, panties, and a pair of tennis shoes, stood. "This pisses me off."

"Get down," Meghan said. "They don't know where we are."

Sadie ignored her. "Who the fuck are they? It can't be Farber and Hippo."

"Yes, it could." Meghan stared at the shrouded figures encircling her former cell. The cabin, impervious to the deluge, was now engulfed in a blazing inferno.

"In the lightning, they look like disco dancers," Sadie said. "I'm going to join the party."

Meghan stared at Sadie, who seemed to have lost her world. "Come on. We've got to leave."

"No." Sadie stood.

"What are you doing?"

Sadie didn't answer but instead burst into tears. She took off her shirt and underwear, then spread her arms wide. "I'm a worthless piece of shit. I'll distract 'em. You run like hell."

Meghan grabbed Sadie's shoulders. "Don't do it. It's never too late to change. I'll tell the police you helped me escape."

"Forget it."

Shaking loose, Sadie turned toward the clearing. Meghan lurched at her former captor but slipped on the muddy ground and could only watch Sadie waddle toward the burning cabin. An absurd image crossed her mind that Sadie's ample rear end swayed like a baboon's.

Intermittent flashes of light silhouetted five men forming a line. Thunder drowned out voices. One of the men raised his arm like a baseball pitcher. The others did the same. Sadie faced them, hands on her hips. In perfect unison, the five arms propelled forward. The five-pointed stars struck center mass. Sadie slumped to the ground.

Her ankle aching, Meghan turned and ran. Low-hanging tree branches transformed into a gauntlet of persecutors that flogged her upper body like wet rawhide. She raked her numbed, bare feet over jagged rocks, cursing from frustration and pain. She burst into a clearing, her tattered, bloody shirt hanging from her shoulders like scarlet streamers. Vapor escaped her heaving chest like smoke as she charged forward again, then halted in disbelief.

Not ten yards in front of her, a figure loomed.

* * *

"Anybody seen Serentino?" Đăng Đạo asked.

The team members shook their heads.

"Probably burned in the cabin," one said.

"The other woman?"

"Don't know."

Đăng Đạo fumed. "I never should have trusted the son of a bitch." Once realizing what had happened, he aborted his trek to the trailhead below and ordered the assault. "It is my fault."

Still, all was not lost. Fifteen minutes remained before rendezvous time.

"Fan out. Search for Serentino and the other woman," Đăng Đạo said. "Reconvene at the trailhead in fifteen minutes."

Amid the rumbling thunder and crackling lightning, his team spread out. Đăng Đạo was ashamed. Attacking women was not his thing. Further, in his anxiety about Serentino's performance, he wondered whether he had created a self-fulfilling prophecy.

Đăng Đạo headed for the trailhead. He wanted his one million dollars and hoped the fire would not scare off Farber.

* * *

Serentino tightened the bandana around his wound, a superficial graze, yet deep enough to draw blood. It increased his fury, a wolf circling for the kill.

He emerged from behind the tree. "Ahuoo! Ahuoo!" The

384

horror written on the woman's face excited him.

"Leave me alone!"

She spun around to escape, but he tripped the woman and sent her sprawling.

Serentino stood over his victim as she lay there, curved breasts rising and falling like supple globes, nipples plastered against her shirt.

"Go away."

"You will die, white woman, but not before I come inside you. Courtesy of Serentino." He visualized her flat stomach and the dark patch between her thighs.

"Go to hell."

Then came the blow to his groin, catching him off guard. Serentino clutched his balls and fell to his knees, gasping for breath, while she jumped up and fled.

He scrambled to his feet and loped after her. "Fucking bitch." He yelled into the wind.

The woman stumbled onto the road and ran crazy like a witch about to be burned. Serentino overcame his pain and again moved like the wolf.

"Hey, woman, we run together, huh?"

She flailed at him.

"Is that the best you can do?" He brought her down in a crumpling tackle.

Serentino turned the woman over, withdrew the tonfa, and whacked her forehead just enough to render her immobile but not unconscious. Then, in the driving rain, Serentino slipped off his gear and camouflage fatigues. He stood naked above her, his member extended and taunting. "You will move your hips beneath me."

Eyes glazing, the woman whimpered, "No."

"Ahuoo! Ahuoo!" he howled again. A lone wolf separated from its pack, Serentino squatted, unbuttoned the woman's jeans, and jerked them off. "Now, I spread your thighs." Just as he planted a knee between her legs, a flare of light stung his eyes. He looked up. Headlights. The beams reflected off the wet granite wall like bouncing silver balls.

Not a good time.

Sixty-Three

Kannon regained consciousness. It was like awakening from a troubled dream. Except all this was real. The back of his head ached from Farber's blow. He was tired. And his hands and ankles were numbed from the nylon ropes binding them. At least he wasn't blindfolded.

He sat slumped in the back seat of an SUV, a Yukon, and Farber was driving. Jasmine, whose adult body held the look of arrested development, sat beside him in the back seat. Snarl, the surviving Rottweiler, occupied the front passenger seat. The hound's intensity mirrored that of a soldier dog hunting drugs.

The clock on the dash read 0200 hours, an inappropriate time for a picnic. *Blow job. Dog Whistle. Stupid! Stupid! Stupid!*

The hound barked, and Farber lowered the passenger window so Snarl could stick his head out. A cold wind swirled inside the vehicle and slanting rainfall soddened the headrest.

"Christian, raise the window. I'm getting soaked."

"It's fogging up in here, Jasmine. Can't you see that!"

"You stopped seeing long ago, Farber," Kannon said, his mouth as dry as talc.

"Shut up, Ballard."

The Yukon jostled along a treacherous, slushy road. Kannon, having trouble maintaining balance, scooted forward for better control and a clearer view. Affixed to the forward antenna were three pocket-sized flags.

Signals. For damn sure this isn't a diplomatic vehicle.

"What the fuck is that?" Farber brought the Yukon to a stop.

Kannon strained his eyes peering through the windshield, but the pounding storm rendered the windshield wipers impotent. All he could see were random flashes of lightning that reminded him of an airburst of magnesium illumination flares.

Jasmine lowered her window and looked out. "Someone's tied to a tree."

Shit, it's the fat man. They were on the same damn road.

Kannon studied the huddled form, watching for movement, hoping the bastard was dead.

Farber killed the engine, opened the door, and approached the tree. Snarl leaped from the front seat and followed. Yelping like his balls had been cut off, the dog circled the spruce while Farber cut away the tape.

The son of a bitch was quite alive, thank you.

"Greet Hippo," Farber said, opening the front passenger door.

The fat man peered inside and spotted Kannon. Hippo flashed a crooked but satisfied smile. "You're dead, motherfucker." Then he turned to Farber. "The bastard burned my motorcycle. Stole my .45."

"Drive," Farber said.

"What?" Hippo's eyes widened when he found himself facing the muzzle of a large-bore pistol.

What's coming down? Kannon wondered. But then Faber tossed the weapon to the fat man. "Found it on Ballard."

"There's no magazine," Hippo said, seemingly nonplussed.

"I don't want you handling a loaded weapon just now."

Neither did Kannon.

"Get behind the wheel." Farber, brandishing his own weapon now, and which was presumably loaded, nodded at Hippo.

"The motorcycle chase didn't happen by accident," Kannon said. "What tipped you off?"

Hippo put the SUV in gear.

"You might've gotten away with it, Ballard." Farber twisted in his seat and smirked. "I didn't know that you'd survived 'Nam the second time around, much less knew that you were back in the States."

"You spotted me following you."

"Nope. I came across the motorcycle on the trail the other night. Thought it belonged to my man here. But since Hippo wasn't around, I called him."

"And Hippo came running."

"Affirmative," Farber said. "I didn't know for sure it was you until you came calling."

"Cut me loose," Kannon said, wriggling his wrists, "and I'll give Hippo riding lessons."

"The only *thing* that's gonna be cut is you," Hippo growled over his shoulder. "You'll suffer a long and hard death, fuckin' smartass."

"Watch the goddamn road," Farber said. "I have other plans for Ballard."

"What would that be?" Kannon said.

"You'll see." Farber turned to the fat man. "I figured you could take care of yourself. Obviously, you can't."

"Thanks for the vote of confidence."

"You fucked up the deal."

"I got the broad moved. Sadie's watching the bitch."

"Fine. I'll pay Sadie the second hundred grand."

"No fucking way."

"So, Meghan's alive." Kannon glanced at Jasmine, who sat with folded arms.

"Don't matter none to you," Hippo said, looking at Kannon via the rearview mirror.

"I'll pay for her," Kannon said, scrambling for leverage.

"No deal, Ballard," Farber answered instead of Hippo. But the fat man took notice.

"Why bring your wife, Farber? Are you going to kill her too?" Jasmine stiffened at Kannon's remark.

"Shut the fuck up." Farber sounded pissed.

"Why do ya want to keep the fucker alive?" Hippo said in a pleading voice. "I ran recon in 'Nam. Any dumb fuck lieutenant who'd lead his men into ambush deserves to die."

"Farber didn't tell you the rest of the story?" Kannon was tired, very tired. His head hurt like hell, and his strength was ebbing. So was his resolve.

Hail clattered on the SUV's roof, then ceased. Sheets of rain followed. He wished they'd run off the road in this worsening weather, a distraction so he could work on loosening his bonds.

"Hey, Hippo, slow down," Jasmine protested. "You're bouncing me all over the place."

Farber backslapped her. She didn't blink, just stared straight ahead. Did this woman have no substance? "Shit, Farber. What'd you do, give your woman a lobotomy?"

"Shut your goddamned mouth," she mouthed.

Kannon felt a sharp jab as Jasmine crammed a pistol in his ribs. His pistol. How'd she get his weapon? He doubted Farber would've given it to her, but it didn't matter. "Sorry," he mouthed back.

She didn't seem mollified.

Could he rattle the fat man?

"Hippo," Kannon said, "you're not going to live through this. You know that, right?" He waited for a reaction. If an alarm registered in the fat man's thick skull, it didn't show.

"You've played your final hand, Ballard," Farber said.

The venomous tone infected Kannon's brain like the stench of death and brought close the coming reality of his own. Perched on the precipice of failure once again, his living or dying depended on a man he defined in one word—amoral. He'd confronted Christian Farber and lost, uncovered the truth, only to witness its burial, found love, yet would never mend the rift in his heart concerning Lan and Meghan. And one or both women might die.

Stefan would forever view his father as a hapless veteran who wouldn't let go of the war, who failed to value family—treating it as a nuisance and intrusion, and who sullied his universe with alcohol. His son would conclude it had not been the war that killed his father, but that his father killed himself.

Should've let things be, he thought. Should've shredded Chấn's letter. Should've never connected with Meghan, much less returned to 'Nam.

Feeling his scrambled options sinking, he wanted to make things right with God. First, he'd pray for forgiveness, from Meghan, Lan, and Stefan, even his ex-wife, and hoped the universe would carry the message. Second, he'd pray for his lost men and the absence of war.

Kannon stared out the SUV rear window. The crappy weather in the Sangre de Cristos reminded him of his motorcycle trip last fall in the San Juans. None of this would have happened if he hadn't wrecked his motorcycle. The injured ankle, the cold, the rock, the sapling, ah, the sapling, the one he'd flicked, the one that had snapped back to life.

"Untie me."

Jasmine shook her head.

"He's not going to let you live."

She shot Kannon the finger.

"Look, there." Hippo's hoarse voice broke the silence as they rounded a curve.

"Goddamn! Better not be who I think it is."

Hippo slowed the Yukon and lowered his window. A shapeless mass lay in the road.

"Stop!" Farber said.

The SUV braked to a halt. Hippo opened the driver's door and hopped out.

"It's the package," Hippo said. "Looks like she's been through a threshing machine."

Package meant Meghan.

"Alive?" Farber asked.

"Shit! I ain't no medic." Hippo scratched his head.

Farber scrambled out of the Yukon. He sloshed through the mud and shoved the fat man aside.

"Some dude's running down the road," Hippo said.

"What?" Farber gaped.

Indeed, a guy was running hell-bent-for-leather in the opposite direction. And he was naked.

"Snarl," Farber hollered.

Snarl bolted from the Yukon and took after the runner.

"That fucker won't get far," Farber said. He knelt beside Meghan and placed two fingers on her neck, then rose and faced the SUV.

"Let me see her!" Kannon attempted to slither from the SUV. Jasmine restrained him. Next thing he knew, she was tugging at the knotted rope binding his hands and wrists. Her fingers were strong yet lithe. When done, she placed Kannon's service weapon beside him. The treatment of Meghan must've turned her. Or maybe Jasmine was smarter than she let on and intended all along to betray the major.

"She has a pulse," Farber said.

Thank God!

Jasmine joined the two men outside the vehicle, but took a position opposite them, forcing their attention away from Kannon. "Assholes!" she yelled.

Kannon bent forward and untied the ropes binding his feet. He looked up in time to see Farber brush his wife aside and stare down the road.

"Snarl's ripping the bastard apart," Farber said.

"Was the naked guy Đăng Đạo?" Hippo asked.

"How the fuck would I know!"

Kannon could just make out the fallen man trying to fend off the attack dog, roughly forty yards away.

Ignoring the commotion, Jasmine assisted Meghan to her feet and draped a blanket around her. "Come. Get inside the car," she said.

A camera light flashed from near the attack site. That was weird. No, wait, the flash didn't come from a camera. It came from an electronic strobe. A signal, and Farber and Hippo had seen it. This was the opportune time to take them down.

Yet there was no clear shot from the back seat, and he'd be seen exiting the SUV by the door closest to Farber. Kannon started to slip out the other side, but by then, Jasmine and Meghan blocked his path. No way would he risk putting the women in the middle of a crossfire. Also, the unknown of what lay ahead worried him. *Better to wait.* He slid the pistol under his legs, then clasped his palms together as if they were still tied.

Farber and Hippo hustled to the Yukon as Meghan shuffled into the back seat. She didn't seem to realize Kannon was there. He wanted to touch and comfort her, but doing so would announce the freedom of his limbs.

"Meghan . . ."

She turned. Kannon didn't know eyes could open that wide. Meghan grabbed hold of his hair and yanked. "You son of a bitch. I am going to rip your heart out."

"I'm sorry. I—"

Meghan slapped the crap out of him. And again. And again.

She pounded on his chest. He sat and took it. Finally, Meghan exhausted her energy, and Jasmine put her arm around her.

His face stung, but he didn't care. Despite Meghan's anger, Kannon was relieved. The woman he'd mislead into a web of deceit and treachery was alive. He chanced another looked at her. She glared, then closed her eyes and went silent. Kannon wondered if hell might be cold instead of hot.

The electronic strobe pulsed again.

Farber jumped behind the wheel. He started the Yukon and flicked the headlights several times.

"Appears like you're the one rushing into an ambush, Farber," Kannon said through gritted teeth.

"Hell, Ballard, if you hadn't told me about Hai's death, I would've never come up with this idea. You're trade bait."

Right! Trade me for evidence of Farber's treachery.

"Hell, Farber. Đăng Đạo wants money, doesn't he? And you don't have it."

Jasmine reached over and touched Kannon's arm, her switch of allegiance confirmed.

"Thank you," he whispered.

In the Sangre de Cristos, gale force winds lashed at the ponderosa pine, driving the needles with such force it appeared as if they alone screamed like banshees. Lightning ripped through the sky like distended tracer rounds. The flashes refracted off the short-nosed blue spruce, creating a specter of razor-thin, glistening daggers.

The Yukon edged forward.

A gunshot cracked through the night. Snarl buckled to the ground. In the headlight's glare, Kannon got a good look at the man who shot the dog.

Chấn's clone stood ahead.

Sixty-Four

Thinking about the large woman, Đăng Đạo approached the trail intersection at the road sooner than expected. He screened himself behind an earth-hugging stand of fir and waited.

The mission was not going well. Worried, Đăng Đạo feared hearing the hoot of an owl, a Vietnamese harbinger of doom as passed along by Hai. If there was an owl nearby, perhaps the storm would drown any sound. Đăng Đạo wondered whether a terrible fate had befallen his father. He recalled the long-ago story told by a man named Thanh that Hai was not his birth father, that—

A beam of light crawled through the rain and fog. It was an SUV. The vehicle stopped. Đăng Đạo saw the three luminescent banners streaming from the SUV's antenna. It was Farber.

"Lửa." (Fire). The voice belonged to Quán.

Focused on the approaching vehicle, Đăng Đạo was startled by the password. *"Nước,"* he answered. (Water.)

Quán stepped into the open.

"Did you find anything?" Đăng Đạo asked, turning to see Kim and his remaining two men fall in behind Quán.

"No."

"Okay." Đăng Đạo sighed and activated his electronic strobe. There was no response. Then he noticed the figure lying on the road. One, then two men huddled above the form. The other woman, he reasoned.

"What the fuck is that?" Kim asked.

A naked man ran toward them. A growling dog tracked the man and was closing fast.

"It's Serentino," Quán said.

"Let the dog have him." It did not take a genius to discern what was going on.

Đăng Đạo crouched in a shallow depression and watched his defiant team member.

Losing ground, Serentino stopped, grabbed his balls, and braced himself. The dog thudded into him and knocked him sprawling. Like an attacking tiger, the hound clamped his jaws on Serentino's neck.

The headlights from the SUV blinked three times, then, after a ten-second pause, twice more. "The vehicle wears proper identification." He tossed his strobe to Kim and told him to confirm.

Đăng Đạo remained still for a moment, then stood, and walked onto the road. He drew his Glock 20 and shot the dog.

"Goddamnit, Serentino, you have fucked up the whole operation."

Blood spurting from his neck, the rebellious team member, full of promise but short on delivery, rose to his feet. "It was a stupid plan."

"You abandoned discipline and team integrity."

"I answer to no one," Serentino said as he charged.

Đăng Đạo cut Serentino down in mid-stride, ripping his abdomen open with a burst of three from the semiautomatic pistol.

He raised his whistle to his mouth, blew two short blasts, then one long one. Kim and the other three men disappeared alongside the road boundary.

Sixty-Five

"Hey, Farber, your number two dog is dead." Kannon wanted to rattle the major.

Farber slammed on the brakes and leaned on the horn. "Fucking gook! I'm going to kill the son of a bitch."

"And look at those flames on the mountain," Kannon added. "Think the fire won't draw attention."

"Keep mouthing off, Ballard. You're gonna wind up like Jeffrey."

"Hell, Major, what've you gotten us into?" Hippo said. "No telling how many men that Đăng Đạo fucker has got roaming the woods."

"Not to mention the sheriffs, firemen, and rangers on their way," Kannon said.

"I'll make the trade and get the hell out." Farber's tone lacked confidence.

Between blasts of thunder, a second, distinct staccato report of gunfire rocked the night. An unlucky victim grabbed his stomach and tumbled to the ground.

Jesus. This is getting ugly.

The sight of the man just shot and the notion of being handed over to Đăng Đạo, perhaps to suffer a fate similar to Jeffrey's, ratcheted Kannon's heartbeat into overdrive.

Farber lowered his window and stomped on the accelerator. The Yukon's wheels spun, found traction, and skittered to within fifteen yards of the man who had just been shot.

With Farber and Hippo riveted on what lay ahead, Kannon secured his pistol. He motioned for Meghan and Jasmine to stay hunkered down on the floorboard.

Facing the Yukon was the man Kannon now knew to be Đăng Đạo, a semiautomatic hanging loosely at his side. Đăng Đạo held a whistle in his other hand. He placed it between his lips and blew. The shrill blast commanded four men to emerge from the tree line on the other side of the road and stand alongside Đăng Đạo.

395

Kannon rolled onto his back in the rear seat. He could both hear and see out. Since the windows were coated, he latched onto the hope outsiders couldn't see in.

"Đăng Đạo?" Farber said, his voice exuding tension.

"I am," Chẩn's son said. "Exit the SUV and advance with palms exposed. Hurry, we must exchange quickly."

Farber opened the driver's door but left the engine running.

"Major, I need the clip for my weapon," Hippo said.

Reaching into his pocket, Farber withdrew a magazine and tossed it to the fat man, who rammed it into the magazine well.

Farber then exited the vehicle. Kannon couldn't tell whether the major was carrying his .45.

Hippo crawled from the passenger side and joined the major. Both doors were slammed shut.

"You got the tapes, the photographs?" Farber asked.

"Yes. They are most interesting," Đăng Đạo said. "It is no wonder you want them."

"Show me," Farber said.

"I need confirmation the wire has been arranged."

"I've something for you more important than money."

Đăng Đạo extended his gun-holding arm and steadied his aim at Farber's forehead. "We made a deal. It will not change."

Kannon cracked open the door opposite the confrontation taking place on the road.

"Be careful," Jasmine whispered.

Lips pressed together, Meghan averted her eyes.

Kannon pulled the slide back and chambered a round. He crab-walked to the rear of the Yukon on the driver's side. Leaning forward, he obtained a side view of Đăng Đạo facing Farber and Hippo, who stood together.

"How about instead I give you the man who murdered your father?" Farber said.

"Hai is dead?" Đăng Đạo sounded unfazed. "I thought as much. I will have his killer and the money."

"I'll give you his murderer. He's tied up and is in the back seat."

"You are in no position to bargain."

A shot! Kannon flinched. The spent bullet splattered the mud at Farber's feet. The major and Hippo jumped like jackrabbits.

Shit. We're all going to be wiped out.

"Okay, okay," Farber said. "I'll call my contact and release the funds."

Farber had placed himself in a no-win situation and was stalling.

"Make the call," Đăng Đạo said.

Farber did . . . or at least faked it. Đăng Đạo followed with a call to his own source.

"Confirmation must occur within two minutes," Đăng Đạo said. "If not, you will die."

"It'll come," Farber said. "The tapes—"

"Quán!"

The gang member came forward and handed his leader a pouch. "It is all here," Đăng Đạo said to the major. "Where is my father's killer?"

"Hippo, get Ballard," Farber said.

This is it.

The fat man opened the rear door on the driver's side. He rejoined the group, his mouth agape. "He ain't there."

"What?"

"You're looking in the wrong place." Kannon sidestepped into the open and leveled his .40-caliber Sig at Farber. "I suggest you not move."

"Goddamnit! How'd you get loose?" Farber glared toward the Yukon.

Appearing as startled as Farber, Đăng Đạo kept his semiautomatic aimed at the major. The other Vietnamese men gathered around their leader, seemingly unsure of what to do.

"Holster your weapons," Đăng Đạo said to his men. "I will handle this."

Roughly five yards separated each party from the other two, forming a potentially deadly triangle. Farber's and the fat man's pistols weren't visible, but Kannon figured they were easily within their reach.

"Đăng Đạo, my name is Kannon Ballard. It's true. I killed

Hai, but he was not your real father."

"He's lying," Farber said.

Another shot that could have been dismissed as a sharp crack of thunder rang through the night.

"A sign of my impatience," Đăng Đạo said.

"I'm lying?" Kannon shook his head. "Where's that wire confirmation for Đăng Đạo? Your two minutes is up, Major."

Farber recoiled but didn't go for a weapon. "What're you gonna do Ballard, take us all out by yourself?"

"I'm not part of this," Hippo said, seemingly impotent.

"Silence. All of you." Đăng Đạo turned to Kannon. "Put away your weapon."

"Can't do that," Kannon said. His face grew more taut as he held onto the semiautomatic. "I have no beef with you. It's Farber I want. Hear the truth first. If you don't buy it, kill us all."

"You have little time," Đăng Đạo said. "How do you know the name Hai?"

"Hai was a rogue Việt Cộng who betrayed your real father. He took you when the communists overran the country. Your birth father's name was Chấn. We served together during the war."

"What happened to this man Chấn?" Đăng Đạo asked.

"Sent to the reeducation camps. He died months ago from hepatitis. Before dying, he wrote, wanting me to return to Việt Nam, which I did. He told me the whole story . . . the cell, your kidnapping, the ambush."

"Bullshit," Farber said. "Ballard was an incompetent officer who got his men killed."

"Quiet, big man. Who listens to a traitor to his country," Đăng Đạo said. Then he stared at Kannon. "What was the name of Hai's cell?"

"The Monsoon Killed the Tiger."

"What Kannon says is true," Meghan said, emerging from the other side of the vehicle and exposing herself to the headlight's side glare. All eyes turned to her. Matted hair, slashed shirt plastered to her chest, and blood trickling down her arms failed to cloak her vehement expression that looked as lethal as a well-aimed pistol shot.

"This is a cluster fuck." Hippo started to sit down. After Đăng Đạo raked the ground with three rounds, Hippo remained standing.

"Meghan, get behind the Yukon," Kannon said.

"Don't tell me what to do!" She stepped closer to Kannon and whispered, "Ever."

Kannon kept his semiautomatic pointed at Farber but cast a side-glance toward Meghan. "I had no idea it would come to this. I never intended to put you in danger."

"He's placed people in danger his whole life," Farber said.

Meghan placed her hands on her hips, stood resolute. "How many more must die before you idiots let the war go?"

Kannon didn't have an answer.

"Tell me how you know Kannon Ballard's words about Hai to be true," Đăng Đạo said to Meghan.

Jasmine approached Meghan and draped the same blanket around her. "Come on, we've got to—"

"Wait," Meghan said. She turned to Kannon. "Did you ever get those computer-aged photographs?"

Kannon patted his rear pocket. Meghan had beat him to the draw. That was the next card he was going to play.

"He has proof," she said.

"What the fuck difference does it make?" Farber said. "Anybody can doctor photographs. Besides," he gestured toward the fire, "there's no time. That blaze can be seen for miles. Let's do the exchange."

"The wire transfer confirmation call has not come," Đăng Đạo said. "No money, no tapes."

"He's got no money," Kannon said, shifting his weight. "Let me have this bastard. I'll see he gets his due in court."

"Never happen," Farber said.

"I'll pay for the tapes," Kannon said.

"Farber has violated a contract. He will be punished my way," Đăng Đạo said. He shifted his gaze to Kannon. "I need no proof of my father. I have known but one."

"At least look at the photographs." Meghan refused to back down. Kannon couldn't believe she supported him now.

Đăng Đạo's lips curled into a tight smile. "You impress me, woman." To Kannon, "You have thirty seconds."

"Your father's sister, Lan, lives," Kannon said. "She's been trying to find you. I have pictures of your birth father, you as a two-year-old, and me, together. I also have a computer-enhanced image of your age-two-photograph that projects your appearance now. You look like Chấn."

"Twenty seconds."

Kannon held his pistol steady and used his other hand to retrieve his wallet. He opened it, gripped the plastic-coated photos, then held them out in his palm. Captions were imprinted on the images.

"Bring them to me." Đăng Đạo motioned to Meghan.

Meghan took the photos from Kannon and handed them over.

Đăng Đạo shifted his gaze between Farber and Hippo and the scanned photographs displayed before him. Then he glanced at Kannon. "Chấn was the Deer Walker?"

"Yes. I gave Chấn this second name because he ran gracefully like the deer." Kannon's weapon was growing heavy. "Also, there is a cousin named Thanh. He helped your Aunt Lan and me."

"I know these names—Chấn and Thanh. I once heard the birth father story long ago but did not believe it." A slight smile etched onto Đăng Đạo's face. "This man Chấn does resemble me."

"Hold on, damn it," Farber said. "I'm Hai's partner. We have a contract."

"Your contract has been canceled." Đăng Đạo's smile was gone.

Kannon tightened his grip on the trigger.

"Christian Farber, you and your partner's jacket pockets are bulging. Each of you grab your pistol's handgrip with two fingers and place your weapons on the ground," Đăng Đạo said. He glanced at Kannon and frowned.

The wind rustled the thin line of conifers bordering the road.

"Fuckin' slopehead." Assuming a shooter's stance, Farber reached inside his jacket and produced his .45 with two fingers on the handgrip.

"*Đứng lại!*" Đăng Đạo yelled. (Stop!)

With amazing quickness, Farber flipped his weapon into his palm and fired at Đăng Đạo, catching him by surprise. He missed but loosed a shot at Kannon. The round struck his left shoulder, above his heart. Instinctively, Kannon fired at Farber before the searing pain drove him to his knees. Two more rounds sizzled over his head.

Đăng Đạo flopped to the prone position.

Screaming, Meghan and Jasmine disappeared behind the Yukon. Farber whirled and leaped for the side of the road opposite Đăng Đạo and his men.

Hippo, his reactions perhaps dulled from overnight exposure to the elements, drew his own .45 but apparently had forgotten to chamber a round. Rounds popped. Clean, round punctures, as smooth as carpenter bee holes, marked Hippo's forehead. Exit wounds were another matter. The rear of his skull was missing. He slumped to his knees beside Snarl's carcass.

Kannon hugged the mud. His energy was fading. The bullet-driven incision above his heart was hot, hot, hot.

Breathe into the pain.

Farber kept firing from a shallow depression on the roadside. How many magazines was his former commander carrying?

Lightning burned the sky. The rain turned torrential. Wind-driven drops stung like flechette rounds fired from a distant M-79 grenade launcher. His vision blurred, Kannon aimed his .40-caliber at Farber and fired three rounds. Then he lowered his head and laid his gun hand over his left.

"Stop shooting. Stop shooting. Keep the fucking tapes," Farber screamed.

"Toss your weapon in the road and come forward!" Đăng Đạo said.

A .45 was plopped into the muck. Farber, hands clasped behind his neck, stood and limped forward.

"Chấn, see if the two women are armed," Đăng Đạo said, changing magazines, "and if anyone else is back there." He nodded toward the Yukon's rear.

A mistake, and Farber took advantage. "Bastards! You've ruined everything." He pulled a carry weapon from his coat sleeve and, ranting like a demon, charged Kannon, firing wildly.

Kannon raised his Sig and emptied the magazine. A sea of red squirted from holes in Farber's chest. Then he felt a cold muzzle pressed against his temple.

"It is over," Đăng Đạo said, standing over Kannon.

Meghan and Jasmine rushed to his side.

"Back away," Đăng Đạo said to both. He leaned down and put his hand on Kannon's chest, his lips close to Kannon's ear. "Live if you will. But we must never meet again. I will not spare you the next time."

"Your aunt . . ." Kannon's words slipped from his mouth like muddy gravel.

"She is better off without me." The gang leader rose. "Morphine!"

One of the men came forward and handed Đăng Đạo a kit. To another, the gang leader said, "Pick up Serentino's body and dump it in our four-wheel. Leave Farber's and his comrade's bodies for the coyotes."

Đăng Đạo thrust a needle into Kannon's thigh. One woman cradled him. Another pressed a wet compress to his forehead. His eyelids grew heavy as enveloping warmth flooded his body.

Sixty-Six

A sea of Colorado Columbine and Indian Paintbrush sailed on gossamer clouds and settled in a bowl-shaped meadow encapsulated by the San Juan mountains. From out of the ethereal mist, a Phoenix soared and showered the wildflowers with powdered crystals, transforming them into verdant rice fields that beckoned in a collective wave.

Kannon opened his eyes. "I've seen and heard the strangest things."

"Shhh." Meghan rose from a chair, walked to him, and pressed a finger to his lips. "Don't talk."

At first, her face appeared blurry, then slowly came into focus. Using his right hand, Kannon encircled her finger and gently pushed it aside. "Where am I?"

"Hospital. In Albuquerque." She spoke through trembling lips. "You're going to be all right."

Even though she looked disheveled and thin, her presence was angelic.

"Shoulder hurt much?"

"A lot," he said. Every movement hurt. "How'd we get off the mountain?"

"The storm broke. Đăng Đạo let me use his satellite phone. I contacted a ranger station, and they arranged for a helicopter to pick us up."

"Reminds me of the medevacs in Việt Nam."

Meghan gave Kannon a measured look. "Can you finally let it go?"

"Yes."

"What a bunch of crap!" Meghan sat at the edge of his bed and took his hand. "Your subconscious speaks no lies. You have to find her."

A lump formed in his throat, and he had to wait before he could speak. "Lan?"

"Yeah."

"She may not want to be found." He stared through the hospital window and observed a brilliant sky, then returned his stare to Meghan. "Do you forgive me?"

"I prayed you would live so I could kill you."

His lips parted, and his eyes widened.

Meghan laughed. "I've been waiting for that one." Her laughter faded, and her face grew solemn. "I was quite angry. It kept my hope alive. But when I saw you shot, well, I forgive you."

"I'd have never made it without you."

"I know."

Kannon attempted to squeeze her hand, but his strength failed him.

"The authorities?"

"They're waiting in the hall."

"What'd you tell them?"

"What I knew."

Kannon would have some explaining to do.

She gave him a sip of water, and he managed a feeble smile. "What about Đăng Đạo and his men?"

Meghan took a deep breath and let it out. "They took off. Under different conditions, I think I'd like him."

"No, I mean, what did you say about them to the police?"

"I couldn't give them any description. It was too dark."

"Good. And Jasmine?"

"Same," Meghan said. "Đăng Đạo kept the photographs of you and Chấn."

"That's best."

"You don't want Đăng Đạo found, do you?"

"No."

Kannon shifted position. Pain shot through him as if he'd been struck by another bullet.

Redemption! It hadn't ended clean as he'd hoped. Farber was dead, by Kannon's own hand. He would've preferred Farber lived to face a civil trial for sure, a criminal trial possibly. Yet either one or both could've dragged on with no settlement or conviction, a risk that might've worn Kannon down.

His mind seemed mired in a fog. After a few deep breaths,

he approached the evidence issue. "Do you know if those tapes and photographs of Farber with the Việt Cộng are still available?"

"Đăng Đạo left them for you."

"That's a relief."

"He also said to tell you something."

Kannon waited. She seemed pleased with his anticipation.

"He said, 'I am my father's son. And you, Kannon Ballard, are a good man, a warrior.'"

Epilogue

Three months later . . .

They were sitting on Kannon's patio. A taste of late spring filtered through Texas live oak and scrub cedar. The humidity was low, the air fresh and crisp.

"In spite of everything, I feel responsible for walking into the ambush and the death of those fifteen men." Kannon stopped rocking in his cedar chair and grimaced. "The consequences never go away."

"Some story, bro'." His brother Roger and his sister-in-law Karen wiped misty eyes. "Why didn't you ever tell anyone?"

"Who would have believed me? I couldn't comprehend it myself for a long time."

"Kannon, we haven't always gotten along," Karen said. "But I care. I'm happy for you it's over." She gathered her breath as if she were preparing to say something difficult. "I wish . . . I wish you'd try to reconcile with Stefan."

"I've begun the process. Stefan's been traveling, researching for an upcoming trial. We're getting together soon."

"Good," Roger said. "Meghan return to Silverton?"

"Yep. Dating a guy named Darien from Durango."

"And Lan?"

Kannon had little else on his mind. "I'm still stiff and sore. As soon as I can ride the motorcycle, I'll know I'm ready."

"For what?"

"Return to 'Nam. Find Lan."

Roger squeezed Kannon's good arm. "This time, I'm going with you."

The doorbell rang.

"I'll answer it," Karen said, staring at her husband as if he'd gone crazy.

Kannon felt hopeful. "Maybe it's Stefan."

"Roger, how about freshening my scotch? Care for a Cuban Cohiba?"

"Where in the hell did you get those?"

"Some guy delivered them to my hospital room."

Roger clipped two cigars and lit both. "What's taking Karen so long?"

Kannon turned. "Here she comes." A wide grin brightened his sister-in-law's face.

"UPS," she said.

"Let's see what I got." Kannon thumbed open the envelope and became nonplussed at what he saw. He looked at Karen, then at Roger.

"What is it?" Roger asked.

"Hell, I don't know. It looks like a picture of a hurricane. Why would somebody send me a picture of a hurricane?"

"There's writing on it."

Kannon examined the inscription. "Derrick Walker. When did they start giving hurricanes two names?"

Karen burst out laughing.

Kannon exhaled, feeling miffed at her behavior. "What's going on? Obviously, there's a joke here I don't get."

"It's a hurricane, all right," she said.

Kannon wondered if she was high on something. "What are you talking about?"

She took Roger aside and whispered in his ear.

"No shit!" Then his brother extended his hand. "Congratulations."

"I think you've both gone nuts."

"It's not a picture of a hurricane. It's a sonogram. And you're looking at a picture of your son, Derrick Walker. You know . . . Deer Walker, Jr."

"What?"

Roger and Karen stepped aside.

Standing near the study door, Lan, dressed in a flowing purple áo dài, her auburn hair framing copper-colored skin, beamed like the bright sun washing a fresh sky.

www.ingramcontent.com/pod-product-compliance
Lightning Source LLC
Chambersburg PA
CBHW051545250626
47157CB00001B/189